carol

carol

Patricia Highsmith

BLOOMSBURY

First published in the U.S.A under the title The Price Of Salt, 1952
Revised edition with an Afterword by the Author, 1984
First published in Great Britain 1990
This paperback edition published 2003

The lyrics quoted on pages 116 and 118 are from the song
'Easy Living' by Leo Robin and Ralph Ranger, copyright ©1937
by Famous Music Corporation and are reprinted with their
permission. The author and the publishers would also like to thank
Faber and Faber Ltd for permission to quote from
'The Lovesong of J. Alfred Prufrock' by T.S. Eliot,
from Collected Poems 1909-1962

Bloomsbury Publishing Plc, 38 Soho Square, London W1D 3HB

A CIP catalogue is available from the British Library

ISBN 0 7475 5400 6

10 9 8 7 6 5 4 3 2

All papers used by Bloomsbury Publishing are natural, recyclable
products made from wood grown in well-managed forests.
The manufacturing processes conform to the
environmental regulations of the country of origin.

Printed in Great Britain by Clays Ltd, St Ives plc

TO EDNA, JORDY AND JEFF

I

CHAPTER ONE

T he lunch hour in the co-workers' cafeteria at Frankenberg's had reached its peak.

There was no room left at any of the long tables, and more and more people were arriving to wait back of the wooden barricades by the cash register. People who had already got their trays of food wandered about between the tables in search of a spot they could squeeze into, or a place that somebody was about to leave, but there was no place. The roar of dishes, chairs, voices, shuffling feet, and the *bra-a-ack* of the turnstiles in the bare-walled room was like the din of a single huge machine.

Therese ate nervously, with the 'Welcome to Frankenberg' booklet propped up in front of her against a sugar container. She had read the thick booklet through last week, in the first day of training class, but she had nothing else with her to read, and in the co-workers' cafeteria, she felt it necessary to concentrate on something. So she read again about vacation benefits, the three weeks' vacation given to people who had worked fifteen years at Frankenberg's, and she ate the hot plate special of the day – a greyish slice of roast beef with a ball of mashed potatoes covered with brown gravy, a heap of peas, and a tiny paper cup of horse-radish. She tried to imagine what it would be like to have worked fifteen years in Frankenberg's department store, and she found she was unable to. 'Twenty-five Yearers' got four weeks' vacation, the booklet said. Frankenberg's also provided a camp for summer and winter vacationers. They should have a church, too, she thought, and a hospital for the birth of babies. The store was organized so much like a prison, it frightened her now and then to realize she was a part of it.

She turned the pages quickly, and saw in big black script across two pages: 'Are *You* Frankenberg Material?'

She glanced across the room at the windows and tried to think of something else. Of the beautiful black and red Norwegian sweater she had seen at Saks and might buy for Richard for Christmas, if she couldn't find a better-looking wallet than the ones she had seen for twenty dollars. Of the possibility of driving with the Kellys next Sunday up to West Point to see a hockey game. The great square window across the room looked like a painting by – who was it? Mondrian. The little square section of window in the corner open to a white sky. And no bird to fly in or out. What kind of a set would one make for a play that took place in a department store? She was back again.

But it's so different with you, Terry, Richard had said to her. You've got an absolute conviction you'll be out of it in a few weeks and the others haven't. Richard said she could be in France next summer. Would be. Richard wanted her to go with him, and there was really nothing that stood in the way of her going with him. And Richard's friend Phil McElroy had written him that he might be able to get her a job with a theatre group next month. Therese had not met Phil yet, but she had very little faith that he could get her a job. She had combed New York since September, gone back and combed it a few times more, and she hadn't found anything. Who gave a job in the middle of the winter to a stage-designer apprentice just beginning to be an apprentice? It didn't seem real either that she might be in Europe with Richard next summer, sitting with him in sidewalk cafés, walking with him in Arles, finding the places Van Gogh had painted, she and Richard choosing towns to stop in for a while and paint. It seemed less real these last few days since she had been working at the store.

She knew what bothered her at the store. It was the sort of thing she wouldn't try to tell Richard. It was that the store intensified things that had always bothered her, as long as she could remember. It was the pointless actions, the meaningless chores that seemed to keep her from doing what she wanted to do, might have done – and

4

here it was the complicated procedures with moneybags, coat checkings, and time clocks that kept people even from serving the store as efficiently as they might – the sense that everyone was incommunicado with everyone else and living on an entirely wrong plane, so that the meaning, the message, the love, or whatever it was that each life contained, never could find its expression. It reminded her of conversations at tables, on sofas, with people whose words seemed to hover over dead, unstirrable things, who never touched a string that played. And when one tried to touch a live string, looked at one with faces as masked as ever, making a remark so perfect in its banality that one could not even believe it might be subterfuge. And the loneliness, augmented by the fact one saw within the store the same faces day after day, the few faces one might have spoken to and never did, or never could. Not like the face on the passing bus that seems to speak, that is seen once and at least is gone for ever.

She would wonder, standing in the time-clock queue in the basement every morning, her eyes sorting out unconsciously the regular employees from the temporary ones, just how she had happened to land here – she had answered an ad, of course, but that didn't explain fate – and what was coming next instead of a stage-designing job. Her life was a series of zigzags. At nineteen, she was anxious.

'You must learn to trust people, Therese. Remember that,' Sister Alicia had often told her. And often, quite often, Therese tried to apply it.

'Sister Alicia,' Therese whispered carefully, the sibilant syllables comforting her.

Therese sat up again and picked up her fork, because the clean-up boy was working in her direction.

She could see Sister Alicia's face, bony and reddish like pink stone when the sunlight was on it, and the starched blue billow of her bosom. Sister Alicia's big bony figure coming around a corner in a hall, between the white enamel tables in the refectory. Sister Alicia in a thousand places, her small blue eyes always finding her out among the other girls, seeing her differently, Therese knew, from all the other girls, yet the thin pink lips always set in the same straight line. She could see Sister Alicia handing her the knitted green gloves wrapped in tissue, not smiling, only presenting them to her directly, with hardly a word, on her eighth birthday. Sister

Alicia telling her with the same straight mouth that she must pass her arithmetic. Who else had cared if she passed her arithmetic? Therese had kept the green gloves at the bottom of her tin locker at school, for years after Sister Alicia had gone away to California. The white tissue had become limp and crackleless like ancient cloth, and still she had not worn the gloves. Finally, they were too small to wear.

Someone moved the sugar container, and the propped booklet fell flat.

Therese looked at the pair of hands across from her, a woman's plump, ageing hands, stirring her coffee, breaking a roll now with a trembling eagerness, daubing half the roll greedily into the brown gravy of the plate that was identical with Therese's. The hands were chapped, there was dirt in the parallel creases of the knuckles, but the right hand bore a conspicuous silver filigree ring set with a clear green stone, the left a gold wedding ring, and there were traces of red polish in the corners of the nails. Therese watched the hand carry a forkful of peas upward, and she did not have to look at the face to know what it would be like. It would be like all the fifty-year-old faces of women who worked at Frankenberg's, stricken with an everlasting exhaustion and terror, the eyes distorted behind glasses that enlarged or made smaller, the cheeks splotched with rouge that did not brighten the greyness underneath. Therese could not look.

'You're a new girl, aren't you?' The voice was shrill and clear in the din, almost a sweet voice.

'Yes,' Therese said, and looked up. She remembered the face. It was the face whose exhaustion had made her see all the other faces. It was the woman Therese had seen creeping down the marble stairs from the mezzanine at about six-thirty one evening when the store was empty, sliding her hands down the broad marble banister to take some of the weight from her bunioned feet. Therese had thought: she is not ill, she is not a beggar, she simply works here.

'Are you getting along all right?'

And here was the woman smiling at her, with the same terrible creases under her eyes and around her mouth. Her eyes were actually alive now, and rather affectionate.

'Are you getting along all right?' the woman repeated, for there was a great clatter of voices and dishes all around them.

Therese moistened her lips. 'Yes, thank you.'

'Do you like it here?'

Therese nodded.

'Finished?' A young man in a white apron gripped the woman's plate with an imperative thumb.

The woman made a tremulous, dismissing gesture. She pulled her saucer of canned sliced peaches towards her. The peaches, like slimy little orange fishes, slithered over the edge of the spoon each time the spoon lifted, all except one which the woman would eat.

'I'm on the third floor in the sweater department. If you want to ask me anything' – the woman said with nervous uncertainty, as if she were trying to deliver a message before they would be cut off or separated – 'come up and talk to me some time. My name is Mrs Robichek, Mrs Ruby Robichek, five forty-four.'

'Thank you very much,' Therese said. And suddenly the woman's ugliness disappeared, because her reddish-brown eyes behind the glasses were gentle, and interested in her. Therese could feel her heart beating, as if it had come to life. She watched the woman get up from the table, and watched her short, thick figure move away until it was lost in the crowd that waited behind the barricade.

Therese did not visit Mrs Robichek, but she looked for her every morning when the employees trickled into the building around a quarter to nine, and she looked for her in the elevators and in the cafeteria. She never saw her, but it was pleasant to have someone to look for in the store. It made all the difference in the world.

Nearly every morning when she came to work on the seventh floor, Therese would stop for a moment to watch a certain toy train. The train was on a table by itself near the elevators. It was not a big fine train like the one that ran on the floor at the back of the toy department, but there was a fury in its tiny pumping pistons that the bigger trains did not possess. Its wrath and frustration on the closed oval track held Therese spellbound.

Awrr rr rr rrgh! it said as it hurled itself blindly into the papier-mâché tunnel. And *Urr rr rr rrgh!* as it emerged.

The little train was always running when she stepped out of the elevator in the morning, and when she finished work in the evening. She felt it cursed the hand that threw its switch each day. In the jerk of its nose around the curves, in its wild dashes down the straight lengths of track, she could see a frenzied and futile pursuit of a tyrannnical master. It drew three Pullman cars in which minuscule human figures showed flinty profiles at the windows, behind these an open boxcar of real miniature lumber, a boxcar of coal that was not real, and a caboose that snapped round the curves and clung to the fleeing train like a child to its mother's skirts. It was like something gone mad in imprisonment, something already dead that would never wear out, like the dainty, springy-footed foxes in the Central Park Zoo, whose complex footwork repeated and repeated as they circled their cages.

This morning, Therese turned away quickly from the train, and went on towards the doll department, where she worked.

At five past nine, the great block-square toy department was coming to life. Green cloths were being pulled back from the long tables. Mechanical toys began to toss balls into the air and catch them, shooting galleries popped and their targets rotated. The table of barnyard animals squawked, cackled and brayed. Behind Therese, a weary *rat-tat-tat—tat-tat* had started up, the drumbeats of the giant tin soldier who militantly faced the elevators and drummed all day. The arts and handicrafts table gave out a smell of fresh modelling clay, reminiscent of the art room at school when she was very small, and also of a kind of vault on the school grounds, rumoured to be the real tomb of someone, which she had used to stick her nose into through iron bars.

Mrs Hendrickson, section manager of the doll department, was dragging dolls from the stock shelves and seating them, splay-legged, on the glass counters.

Therese said hello to Miss Martucci, who stood at the counter counting the bills and coins from her moneybag with such concentration she could give Therese only a deeper nod of her rhythmically nodding head. Therese counted twenty-eight fifty from her own moneybag, recorded it on a slip of white paper for the sales receipts envelope, and transferred the money by denominations into her drawer in the cash register.

By now, the first customers were emerging from the elevators, hesitating a moment with the bewildered, somewhat startled expressions that people always had on finding themselves in the toy department, then starting off on weaving courses.

'Do you have the dolls that wet?' a woman asked her.

'I'd like this doll, but with a yellow dress,' a woman said, pushing a doll towards her, and Therese turned and got the doll she wanted out of a stock shelf.

The woman had a mouth and cheeks like her mother's, Therese noticed, slightly pocked cheeks under dark pink rouge, separated by a thin red mouth full of vertical lines.

'Are the Drinksy-Wetsy dolls all this size?'

There was no need of salesmanship. People wanted a doll, any doll, to give for Christmas. It was a matter of stooping, pulling out boxes in search of a doll with brown eyes instead of blue, calling Mrs Hendrickson to open a showcase window with her key, which she did grudgingly if she were convinced the particular doll could not be found in stock, a matter of sidling down the aisle behind the counter to deposit a purchased doll on the mountain of boxes on the wrapping counter that was always growing, always toppling, no matter how often the stock boys came to take the packages away. Almost no children came to the counter. Santa Claus was supposed to bring the dolls, Santa Claus represented by the frantic faces and the clawing hands. Yet there must be a certain good will in all of them, Therese thought, even behind the cool, powdered faces of the women in mink and sable, who were generally the most arrogant, who hastily bought the biggest and most expensive dolls, the dolls with real hair and changes of clothing. There was surely love in the poor people, who waited their turn and asked quietly how much a certain doll cost, and shook their heads regretfully and turned away. Thirteen dollars and fifty cents for a doll only ten inches high.

'Take it,' Therese wanted to say to them. 'It really is too expensive, but I'll give it to you. Frankenberg's won't miss it.'

But the women in the cheap cloth coats, the timid men huddled inside shabby mufflers would be gone, wistfully glancing at other counters as they made their way back to the elevators. If people came for a doll, they didn't want anything else. A doll was a special kind of Christmas gift, practically alive, the next thing to a baby.

There were almost never any children, but now and again one would come up, generally a little girl, very rarely a little boy, her hand held firmly by a parent. Therese would show her the dolls she thought the child might like. She would be patient, and finally a certain doll would bring that metamorphosis in the child's face, that response to make-believe that was the purpose of all of it, and usually that was the doll the child went away with.

Then one evening after work, Therese saw Mrs Robichek in the coffee and doughnut shop across the street. Therese often stopped in the doughnut shop to get a cup of coffee before going home. Mrs Robichek was at the back of the shop, at the end of the long curving counter, dabbling a doughnut into her mug of coffee.

Therese pushed and thrust herself towards her, through the press of girls and coffee mugs and doughnuts. Arriving at Mrs Robichek's elbow, she gasped, 'Hello,' and turned to the counter, as if a cup of coffee had been her only objective.

'Hello,' said Mrs Robichek, so indifferently that Therese was crushed.

Therese did not dare look at Mrs Robichek again. And yet their shoulders were actually pressed together! Therese was half finished with her coffee when Mrs Robichek said dully, 'I'm going to take the Independent subway. I wonder if we'll ever get out of here.' Her voice was dreary, not as it had been that day in the cafeteria. Now she was like the hunched old woman Therese had seen creeping down the stairs.

'We'll get out,' Therese said reassuringly.

Therese forced a path for both of them to the door. Therese was taking the Independent subway, too. She and Mrs Robichek edged into the sluggish mob at the entrance of the subway, and were sucked gradually and inevitably down the stairs, like bits of floating waste down a drain. They found they both got off at the Lexington Avenue stop, too, though Mrs Robichek lived on Fifty-fifth Street, just east of Third Avenue. Therese went with Mrs Robichek into the delicatessen where she was going to buy something for her dinner. Therese might have bought something for her own dinner, but somehow she couldn't in Mrs Robichek's presence.

'Do you have food at home?'

'No, I'm going to buy something later.'

'Why don't you come and eat with me? I'm all alone. Come on.' Mrs Robichek finished with a shrug, as if that were less effort than a smile.

Therese's impulse to protest politely lasted only a moment. 'Thank you. I'd like to come.' Then she saw a cellophane-wrapped cake on the counter, a fruit cake like a big brown brick topped with red cherries, and she bought it to give to Mrs Robichek.

It was a house like the one Therese lived in, only brownstone and much darker and gloomier. There were no lights at all in the halls, and when Mrs Robichek put on the light in the third-floor hall, Therese saw that the house was not very clean. Mrs Robichek's room was not very clean either, and the bed was unmade. Did she get up as tired as she went to bed, Therese wondered. Therese was left standing in the middle of the room while Mrs Robichek moved on dragging feet towards the kitchenette, carrying the bag of groceries she had taken from Therese's hands. Now that she was home, Therese felt, where no one could see her, she allowed herself to look as tired as she really was.

Therese could never remember how it began. She could not remember the conversation just before and the conversation didn't matter, of course. What happened was that Mrs Robichek edged away from her, strangely, as if she were in a trance, suddenly murmuring instead of talking, and lay down flat on her back on the unmade bed. It was because of the continued murmuring, the faint smile of apology, and the terrible, shocking ugliness of the short, heavy body with the bulging abdomen, and the apologetically tilted head still so politely looking at her, that she could not make herself listen.

'I used to have my own dress shop in Queens. Oh, a fine big one,' Mrs Robichek said, and Therese caught the note of boasting and began to listen despite herself, hating it. 'You know, the dresses with the V at the waist and the little buttons running up. You know, three, five years ago – ' Mrs Robichek spread her stiff hands inarticulately across her waist. The short hands did not nearly span the front half of herself. She looked very old in the dim lamplight that made the shadows under her eyes black. 'They called them Caterina dresses. You remember? I designed them. They come out of my shop in Queens. They famous, all right!'

Mrs Robichek left the table and went to a small trunk that stood against the wall. She opened it, talking all the while, and began to drag out dresses of dark, heavy-looking material, which she let fall on the floor. Mrs Robichek held up a garnet-red velvet dress with a white collar and tiny white buttons that came to a V down the front of the narrow bodice.

'See, I got lots of them. I made them. Other stores copied.' Above the white collar of the dress, which she gripped with her chin, Mrs Robichek's ugly head was tilted grotesquely. 'You like this? I give you one. Come here. Come here, try one on.'

Therese was repelled by the thought of trying one on. She wished Mrs Robichek would lie down and rest again, but obediently Therese got up, as if she had no will of her own, and came towards her.

Mrs Robichek pressed a black velvet dress upon Therese with trembling and importunate hands, and Therese suddenly knew how she would wait on people in the store, thrusting sweaters upon them helter-skelter, for she could not have performed the same action in any other way. For four years, Therese remembered, Mrs Robichek had said she had worked at Frankenberg's.

'You like the green one better? Try it on.' And in the instant Therese hesitated, she dropped it and picked up another, the dark red one. 'I sell five of them to girls at the store, but you I give one. Left over, but they still in style. You like this one better?'

Therese liked the red better. She liked red, especially garnet red, and she loved red velvet. Mrs Robichek pressed her towards a corner, where she could take off her clothing and lay it on an armchair. But she did not want the dress, did not want to be given it. It reminded her of being given clothing at the Home, hand-me-downs, because she was considered practically as one of the orphan girls, who made up half the school, who never got packages from outside. Therese pulled off her sweater and felt completely naked. She gripped her arms above the elbow, and her flesh there felt cold and sensationless.

'I sewed,' Mrs Robichek was saying ecstatically to herself, 'how I sewed, morning to night! I managed four girls. But my eyes got bad. One blind, this one. Put the dress on.' She told Therese about the operation on the eye. It was not blind, only partially blind. But it was very painful. Glaucoma. It still gave her pain. That and her back. And her feet. Bunions.

Therese realized she was relating all her troubles and her bad luck so that she, Therese, would understand why she had sunk so low as to work in a department store.

'It fits?' Mrs Robichek asked confidently.

Therese looked in the mirror in the wardrobe door. It showed a long thin figure with a narrowish head that seemed ablaze at the outline, bright yellow fire running down to the bright red bar on either shoulder. The dress hung in straight draped folds down almost to her ankles. It was the dress of queens in fairy tales, of a red deeper than blood. She stepped back, and pulled in the looseness of the dress behind her, so it fitted her ribs and her waist, and she looked back at her own dark hazel eyes in the mirror. Herself meeting herself. This was she, not the girl in the dull plaid skirt and the beige sweater, not the girl who worked in the doll department at Frankenberg's.

'Do you like it?' Mrs Robichek asked.

Therese studied the surprisingly tranquil mouth, whose modelling she could see distinctly, though she wore no more lipstick than she might if someone had kissed her. She wished she could kiss the person in the mirror and make her come to life, yet she stood perfectly still, like a painted portrait.

'If you like it, take it,' Mrs Robichek urged impatiently, watching from a distance, lurking against the wardrobe as saleswomen lurk while women try on coats and dresses in front of mirrors in department stores.

But it wouldn't last, Therese knew. She would move, and it would be gone. Even if she kept the dress, it would be gone, because it was a thing of a minute, this minute. She didn't want the dress. She tried to imagine the dress in her closet at home, among her other clothing, and she couldn't. She began to unbutton the buttons, to unfasten the collar.

'You like it, yes?' Mrs Robichek asked as confidently as ever.

'Yes,' Therese said firmly, admitting it.

She couldn't get the hook and eye unfastened at the back of the collar. Mrs Robichek had to help her, and she could hardly wait. She felt as if she were being strangled. What was she doing here? How did she happen to have put on a dress like this? Suddenly Mrs Robichek and her apartment were like a horrible dream that she had just realized she was dreaming. Mrs Robichek was the hunchbacked keeper of the dungeon. And she had been brought here to be tantalized.

'What's the matter? A pin stick you?'

Therese's lips opened to speak, but her mind was too far away. Her mind was at a distant point, at a distant vortex that opened on the scene in the dimly lighted, terrifying room where the two of them seemed to stand in desperate combat. And at the point of the vortex where her mind was, she knew it was the hopelessness that terrified her and nothing else. It was the hopelessness of Mrs Robichek's ailing body and her job at the store, of her stack of dresses in the trunk, of her ugliness, the hopelessness of which the end of her life was entirely composed. And the hopelessness of herself, of ever being the person she wanted to be and of doing the things that person would do. Had all her life been nothing but a dream, and was *this* real? It was the terror of this hopelessness that made her want to shed the dress and flee before it was too late, before the chains fell around her and locked.

It might already be too late. As in a nightmare, Therese stood in the room in her white slip, shivering, unable to move.

'What's the matter? You cold? It's hot.'

It was hot. The radiator hissed. The room smelled of garlic and the fustiness of old age, of medicines, and of the peculiar metallic smell that was Mrs Robichek's own. Therese wanted to collapse in the chair where her skirt and sweater lay. Perhaps if she lay on her own clothing, she thought, it wouldn't matter. But she shouldn't lie down at all. If she did, she was lost. The chains would lock, and she would be one with the hunchback.

Therese trembled violently. She was suddenly out of control. It was a chill, not merely fright or tiredness.

'Sit down,' Mrs Robichek's voice said from a distance, and with shocking unconcern and boredom, as if she were quite used to girls feeling faint in her room, and from a distance, too, her dry, rough-tipped fingers pressed against Therese's arms.

Therese struggled against the chair, knowing she was going to succumb to it, and even aware that she was attracted to it for that reason. She dropped into the chair, felt Mrs Robichek tugging at her skirt to pull it from under her, but she couldn't make herself move. She was still at the same point of consciousness, however, still had the same freedom to think, even though the dark arms of the chair rose about her.

Mrs Robichek was saying, 'You stand up too much at the store. It's hard these Christmases. I seen four of them. You got to learn how to save yourself a little.'

Creeping down the stairs clinging to the banister. Save herself by eating lunch in the cafeteria. Taking shoes off bunioned feet like the row of women perched on the radiator in the women's room, fighting for a bit of the radiator to put a newspaper on and sit for five minutes.

Therese's mind worked very clearly. It was astonishing how clearly it worked, though she knew she was simply staring into space in front of her, and that she could not have moved if she had wanted to.

'You just tired, you baby,' Mrs Robichek said, tucking a woollen blanket about her shoulders in the chair. 'You need to rest, standing up all day and standing up tonight, too.'

A line from Richard's Eliot came to Therese. *That is not what I meant at all. That is not it, at all.* She wanted to say it, but she could not make her lips move. Something sweet and burning was in her mouth. Mrs Robichek was standing in front of her, spooning something from a bottle, and pushing the spoon between her lips. Therese swallowed it obediently, not caring if it were poison. She could have moved her lips now, could have gotten up from the chair, but she didn't want to move. Finally, she lay back in the chair, and let Mrs Robichek cover her with the blanket, and she pretended to go to sleep. But all the while she watched the humpbacked figure moving about the room, putting away the things from the table, undressing for bed. She watched Mrs Robichek remove a big laced corset and then a strap device that passed around her shoulders and partially down her back. Therese closed her eyes then in horror, pressed them tight shut, until the creaking of a spring and a long groaning sigh told her that Mrs Robichek had gone to bed. But that was not all. Mrs Robichek reached for the alarm clock and wound it, and, without lifting her head from the pillow, groped with the clock for the straight chair beside the bed. In the dark, Therese could barely see her arm rise and fall four times before the clock found the chair.

I shall wait fifteen minutes until she is asleep and then go, Therese thought.

And because she was tired, she tensed herself to hold back that spasm, that sudden seizure that was like falling, that came every night long before sleep, yet heralded sleep. It did not come. So after what she thought was fifteen minutes, Therese dressed herself and went silently out the door. It was easy, after all, simply to open the door and escape. It was easy, she thought, because she was not really escaping at all.

15

CHAPTER TWO

'Terry, remember that fellow Phil McElroy I told you about? The one with the stock company? Well, he's in town, and he says you've got a job in a couple of weeks.'

'A real job? Where?'

'A show in the Village. Phil wants to see us tonight. I'll tell you about it when I see you. I'll be over in about twenty minutes. I'm just leaving school now.'

Therese ran up the three flights of stairs to her room. She was in the middle of washing up, and the soap had dried on her face. She stared down at the orange washcloth in the basin.

'A job!' she whispered to herself. The magic word.

She changed into a dress, and hung a short silver chain with a St Christopher medallion, a birthday present from Richard, around her neck, and combed her hair with a little water so it would look neater. Then she set some loose sketches and cardboard models just inside the closet where she could reach them easily when Phil McElroy asked to see them. No, I haven't had much actual experience, she would have to say, and she felt a sink of failure. She hadn't even an apprentice's job behind her, except that two-day job in Montclair, making the cardboard model that the amateur group had finally used, if that could be called a job. She had taken two courses in scenic design in New York, and she had read a lot of books. She could hear Phil McElroy – an intense and very busy young man, probably, a little annoyed at having come to see her for nothing – saying regretfully that she wouldn't do after all. But with Richard present,

Therese thought, it wouldn't be quite as crushing as if she were alone. Richard had quit or been fired from about five jobs since she had known him. Nothing bothered Richard less than losing and finding jobs. Therese remembered being fired from the Pelican Press a month ago, and she winced. They hadn't even given her notice, and the only reason she had been fired, she supposed, was that her particular research assignment had been finished. When she had gone in to speak to Mr Nussbaum, the president, about not being given notice, he had not known, or had pretended not to know, what the term meant. 'Notiz? – Wuss?' he had said indifferently, and she had turned and fled, afraid of bursting into tears in his office. It was easy for Richard, living at home with a family to keep him cheerful. It was easier for him to save money. He had saved about two thousand in a two-year hitch in the Navy, and a thousand more in the year since. And how long would it take her to save the fifteen hundred dollars that a junior membership in the stage designers' union cost? After nearly two years in New York, she had only about five hundred dollars of it.

'Pray for me,' she said to the wooden Madonna on the bookshelf. It was the one beautiful thing in her apartment, the wooden Madonna she had bought the first month she had been in New York. She wished there were a better place for it in the room than on the ugly bookshelf. The bookshelf was like a lot of fruit crates stacked up and painted red. She longed for a bookshelf of natural-coloured wood, smooth to the touch and sleek with wax.

She went down to the delicatessen and bought six cans of beer and some blue cheese. Then, when she came upstairs, she remembered the original purpose of her going to the store, to buy some meat for dinner. She and Richard had planned to have dinner in tonight. That might be changed now, but she didn't like to take it on her own initiative to alter plans where Richard was concerned, and she was about to run down again for the meat when Richard's long ring sounded. She pressed the release button.

Richard came up the steps at a run, smiling. 'Did Phil call?'

'No,' she said.

'Good. That means he's coming.'

'When?'

'In a few minutes, I guess. He probably won't stay long.'

'Does it really sound like a definite job?'

17

'Phil says so.'

'Do you know what kind of play it is?'

'I don't know anything except they need somebody for sets, and why not you?' Richard looked her over critically, smiling. 'You look swell tonight. Don't be nervous, will you? It's just a little company in the Village, and you've probably got more talent than all the rest of them put together.'

She took the overcoat he had dropped on a chair and hung it in the closet. Under the overcoat was a roll of charcoal paper he had brought from art school. 'Did you do something good today?' she asked.

'So-so. That's something I want to work on at home,' he said carelessly. 'We had that red-headed model today, the one I like.'

Therese wanted to see his sketch, but she knew Richard probably didn't think it good enough. Some of his first paintings were good, like the lighthouse in blues and blacks that hung over her bed, that he had done when he was in the Navy and just starting to paint. But his life drawing was not good yet, and Therese doubted that it ever would be. There was a new charcoal smudge all over one knee of his tan cotton trousers. He wore a shirt inside the red and black checked shirt, and buckskin moccasins that made his big feet look like shapeless bear paws. He was more like a lumberjack or a professional athlete of some sort, Therese thought, than anything else. She could more easily imagine him with an axe in his hand than a paintbrush. She had seen him with an axe once, cutting wood in the yard back of his house in Brooklyn. If he didn't prove to his family that he was making some progress in his painting, he would probably have to go into his father's bottled-gas business this summer, and open the branch in Long Island that his father wanted him to.

'Will you have to work this Saturday?' she asked, still afraid to talk about the job.

'Hope not. Are you free?'

She remembered now, she was not. 'I'm free Friday,' she said resignedly. 'Saturday's a late day.'

Richard smiled. 'It's a conspiracy.' He took her hands and drew her arms around his waist, his restless prowling of the room at an end. 'Maybe Sunday? The family asked if you could come out for dinner, but we don't have to stay long. I could borrow a truck and we could drive somewhere in the afternoon.'

'All right.' She liked that and so did Richard, sitting up in front of the big empty gas-tank, and driving anywhere, as free as if they rode a butterfly. She took her arms from around Richard. It made her feel self-conscious and foolish, as if she stood embracing the stem of a tree, to have her arms around Richard. 'I did buy a steak for tonight, but they stole it at the store.'

'Stole it? From where?'

'Off the shelf where we keep our handbags. The people they hire for Christmas don't get any regular lockers.' She smiled at it now, but this afternoon she had almost wept. Wolves, she had thought, a pack of wolves, stealing a bloody bag of meat just because it was food, a free meal. She had asked all the salesgirls if they had seen it, and they had all denied it. Bringing meat into the store wasn't allowed, Mrs Hendrickson had said indignantly. But what was one to do, if all the meat stores closed at six o'clock?

Richard lay back on the studio couch. His mouth was thin and its line uneven, half of it downward slanting, giving an ambiguity to his expression, a look sometimes of humour, sometimes of bitterness, a contradiction that his rather blank and frank blue eyes did nothing to clarify. He said slowly and mockingly, 'Did you go down to the lost and found? Lost, one pound of beefsteak. Answers to the name Meatball.'

Therese smiled, looking over the shelves in her kitchenette. 'Do you think you're joking? Mrs Hendrickson did tell me to go down to the lost and found.'

Richard gave a hooting laugh and stood up.

'There's a can of corn here and I've got lettuce for a salad. And there's bread and butter. Shall I go get some frozen pork chops?'

Richard reached a long arm over her shoulder and took the square of pumpernickel bread from the shelf. 'You call that bread? It's fungus. Look at it, blue as a mandrill's behind. Why don't you eat bread once you buy it?'

'I use that to see in the dark with. But since you don't like it – ' She took it from him and dropped it into the garbage bag. 'That wasn't the bread I meant anyway.'

'Show me the bread you meant.'

The doorbell shrieked right beside the refrigerator, and she jumped for the button.

'That's them,' Richard said.

There were two young men. Richard introduced them as Phil McElroy and his brother, Dannie. Phil was not at all what Therese had expected. He did not look intense or serious, or even particularly intelligent. And he scarcely glanced at her when they were introduced.

Dannie stood with his coat over his arm until Therese took it from him. She could not find an extra hanger for Phil's coat, and Phil took it back and tossed it on to a chair, half on the floor. It was an old dirty polo coat. Therese served the beer and cheese and crackers, listening all the while for Phil and Richard's conversation to turn to the job. But they were talking about things that had happened since they had seen each other last in Kingston, New York. Richard had worked for two weeks last summer on some murals in a roadhouse there, where Phil had had a job as a waiter.

'Are you in the theatre, too?' she asked Dannie.

'No, I'm not,' Dannie said. He seemed shy, or perhaps bored and impatient to leave. He was older than Phil and a little more heavily built. His dark brown eyes moved thoughtfully from object to object in the room.

'They haven't got anything yet but a director and three actors,' Phil said to Richard, leaning back on the couch. 'A fellow I worked with in Philly once is directing. Raymond Cortes. If I recommend you, it's a cinch you'll get in,' he said with a glance at Therese. 'He promised me the part of the second brother in the play. It's called *Small Rain*.'

'A comedy?' Therese asked.

'Comedy. Three acts. Have you done any sets so far by yourself?'

'How many sets will it take?' Richard asked, just as she was about to answer.

'Two at the most, and they'll probably get by on one. Georgia Halloran has the lead. Did you happen to see that Sartre thing they did in the fall down there? She was in that.'

'Georgia?' Richard smiled. 'Whatever happened with her and Rudy?'

Disappointedly, Therese heard their conversation settling down on Georgia and Rudy and other people she didn't know. Georgia might have been one of the girls Richard had had an affair with, Therese supposed. He had once mentioned about five. She couldn't remember any of their names except Celia.

'Is this one of your sets?' Dannie asked her, looking at the cardboard model that hung on the wall, and when she nodded he got up to see it.

And now Richard and Phil were talking about a man who owed Richard money from somewhere. Phil said he had seen the man last night in the San Remo bar. Phil's elongated face and his clipped hair was like an El Greco, Therese thought, yet the same features in his brother looked like an American Indian. And the way Phil talked completely destroyed the illusion of El Greco. He talked like any of the people one saw in Village bars, young people who were supposed to be writers or actors, and who usually did nothing.

'It's very attractive,' Dannie said, peering behind one of the little suspended figures.

'It's a model for *Petrushka*. The fair scene,' she said, wondering if he would know the ballet. He might be a lawyer, she thought, or even a doctor. There were yellowish stains on his fingers, not the stains of cigarettes.

Richard said something about being hungry, and Phil said he was starving, but neither of them ate any of the cheese that was in front of them.

'We're due in half an hour, Phil,' Dannie repeated.

Then, a moment later, they were all standing up, putting on their coats.

'Let's eat out somewhere, Terry,' Richard said. 'How about the Czech place up on Second?'

'All right,' she said, trying to sound agreeable. This was the end of it, she supposed, and nothing was definite. She had an impulse to ask Phil a crucial question, but she didn't.

And on the street, they began to walk downtown instead of up. Richard walked with Phil, and only glanced back once or twice at her, as if to see if she were still there. Dannie held her arm at the kerbs, and across the patches of dirty slippery stuff, neither snow nor ice, that were the remains of a snowfall three weeks ago.

'Are you a doctor?' she asked Dannie.

'Physicist,' Dannie replied. 'I'm taking graduate courses at N.Y.U. now.' He smiled at her, but the conversation stopped there for a while.

Then he said, 'That's a long way from stage designing, isn't it.'

She nodded. 'Quite a long way.' She started to ask him if he intended to do any work pertaining to the atom bomb, but she didn't, because what would it matter if he did or didn't? 'Do you know where we're going?' she asked.

He smiled broadly, showing square white teeth. 'Yes. To the subway. But Phil wants a bite somewhere first.'

They were walking down Third Avenue. And Richard was talking to Phil about their going to Europe next summer. Therese felt a throb of embarrassment as she walked along behind Richard, like a dangling appendage, because Phil and Dannie would naturally think she was Richard's mistress. She wasn't his mistress, and Richard didn't expect her to be in Europe. It was a strange relationship, she supposed, and who would believe it? Because from what she had seen in New York, everybody slept with everybody they had dates with more than once or twice. And the two people she had gone out with before Richard – Angelo and Harry – had certainly dropped her when they discovered she didn't care for an affair with them. She had tried to have an affair with Richard three or four times in the year she had known him, though with negative results; Richard said he preferred to wait. He meant wait until she cared more for him. Richard wanted to marry her, and she was the first girl he had ever proposed to, he said. She knew he would ask her again before they left for Europe, but she didn't love him enough to marry him. And yet she would be accepting most of the money for the trip from him, she thought with a familiar sense of guilt. Then the image of Mrs Semco, Richard's mother, came before her, smiling approval on them, on their marrying, and Therese involuntarily shook her head.

'What's the matter?' Dannie asked.

'Nothing.'

'Are you cold?'

'No. Not at all.'

But he tucked her arm closer anyway. She was cold, and felt rather miserable in general. It was the half dangling, half cemented relationship with Richard, she knew. They saw more and more of each other, without actually growing closer. She still wasn't in love with him, not after ten months, and maybe she never could be, though the fact remained that she liked him better than any one person she had ever known, certainly any man. Sometimes she

22

thought she was in love with him, waking up in the morning and looking blankly at the ceiling, remembering suddenly that she knew him, remembering suddenly his face shining with affection for her because of some gesture of affection on her part, before her sleepy emptiness had time to fill up with the realization of what time it was, what day, what she had to do, the solider substance that made up one's life. But the feeling bore no resemblance to what she had read about love. Love was supposed to be a kind of blissful insanity. Richard didn't act blissfully insane either, in fact.

'Oh, everything's called St Germain-des-Près!' Phil shouted with a wave of his hand. 'I'll give you some addresses before you go. How long do you think you'll be there?'

A truck with rattling, slapping chains turned in front of them, and Therese couldn't hear Richard's answer. Phil went into the Riker's shop on the corner of Fifty-third Street.

'We don't have to eat here. Phil just wants to stop a minute.' Richard squeezed her shoulder as they went in the door. 'It's a great day, isn't it, Terry? Don't you feel it? It's your first real job!'

Richard was convinced, and Therese tried hard to realize it might be a great moment. But she couldn't recapture even the certainty she remembered when she had looked at the orange washcloth in the basin after Richard's telephone call. She leaned against the stool next to Phil's, and Richard stood beside her, still talking to him. The glaring white light on the white tile walls and the floor seemed brighter than sunlight, for here there were no shadows. She could see every shiny black hair in Phil's eyebrows, and the rough and smooth spots on the pipe Dannie held in his hand, unlighted. She could see the details of Richard's hand, which hung limply out of his overcoat sleeve, and she was conscious again of their incongruity with his limber, long-boned body. They were thick, even plump-looking hands, and they moved in the same inarticulate, blind way if they picked up a salt shaker or the handle of a suitcase. Or stroked her hair, she thought. The insides of his hands were extremely soft, like a girl's, and a little moist. Worst of all, he generally forgot to clean his nails, even when he took the trouble to dress up. Therese had said something about it a couple of times to him, but she felt now that she couldn't say anything more without irritating him.

Dannie was watching her. She was held by his thoughtful eyes for a moment, then she looked down. Suddenly she knew why she couldn't recapture the feeling she had had before: she simply didn't believe Phil McElroy could get her a job on his recommendation.

'Are you worried about that job?' Dannie was standing beside her.

'No.'

'Don't be. Phil can give you some tips.' He poked his pipe stem between his lips, and seemed to be about to say something else, but he turned away.

She half listened to Phil's conversation with Richard. They were talking about boat reservations.

Dannie said, 'By the way, the Black Cat Theatre's only a couple of blocks from Morton Street where I live. Phil's staying with me, too. Come and have lunch some time with us, will you?'

'Thanks very much. I'd like to.' It probably wouldn't be, she thought, but it was nice of him to ask her.

'What do you think, Terry?' Richard asked. 'Is March too soon to go to Europe? It's better to go early than wait till everything's so crowded over there.'

'March sounds all right,' she said.

'There's nothing to stop us, is there? I don't care if I don't finish the winter term at school.'

'No, there's nothing to stop us.' It was easy to say. It was easy to believe all of it, and just as easy not to believe any of it. But if it were all true, if the job were real, the play a success, and she could go to France with at least a single achievement behind her –

Suddenly, Therese reached out for Richard's arm, slid her hand down it to his fingers. Richard was so surprised, he stopped in the middle of a sentence.

The next afternoon, Therese called the Watkins number that Phil had given her. A very efficient sounding girl answered. Mr Cortes was not there, but they had heard about her through Phil McElroy. The job was hers, and she would start work December twenty-eighth at fifty dollars a week. She could come in beforehand and show Mr Cortes some of her work, if she wanted to, but it wasn't necessary, not if Mr McElroy had recommended her so highly.

Therese called up Phil to thank him, but nobody answered the telephone. She wrote him a note, care of the Black Cat Theatre.

CHAPTER THREE

Roberta Walls, the youngest supervisor in the toy department, paused just long enough in her mid-morning flurry to whisper to Therese, 'If we don't sell this twenty-four ninety-five suitcase today, it'll be marked down Monday and the department'll take a two-dollar loss!' Roberta nodded at the brown pasteboard suitcase on the counter, thrust her load of grey boxes into Miss Martucci's hands, and hurried on.

Down the long aisle, Therese watched the salesgirls make way for Roberta. Roberta flew up and down counters and from one corner of the floor to the other, from nine in the morning until six at night. Therese had heard that Roberta was trying for another promotion. She wore red harlequin glasses, and unlike the other girls always pushed the sleeves of her green smock up above her elbows. Therese saw her flit across an aisle and stop Mrs Hendrickson with an excited message delivered with gestures. Mrs Hendrickson nodded agreement, Roberta touched her shoulder familiarly, and Therese felt a small start of jealousy. Jealousy, though she didn't care in the least for Mrs Hendrickson, even disliked her.

'Do you have a doll made of cloth that cries?'

Therese didn't know of such a doll in stock, but the woman was positive Frankenberg's had it, because she had seen it advertised. Therese pulled out another box, from the last spot it might possibly be, and it wasn't.

'Wotcha lookin' fuh?' Miss Santini asked her. Miss Santini had a cold.

'A doll made of cloth that cries,' Therese said. Miss Santini had been especially courteous to her lately. Therese remembered the stolen meat. But now Miss Santini only lifted her eyebrows, stuck out her bright red underlip with a shrug, and went on.

'Made of cloth? With pigtails?' Miss Martucci, a lean, straggly-haired Italian girl with a long nose like a wolf's, looked at Therese. 'Don't let Roberta hear you,' Miss Martucci said with a glance around her. 'Don't let anybody hear you, but those dolls are in the basement.'

'Oh.' The upstairs toy department was at war with the basement toy department. The tactics were to force the customer into buying on the seventh floor, where everything was more expensive. Therese told the woman the dolls were in the basement.

'Try and sell this today,' Miss Davis said to her as she sidled past, slapping the battered imitation alligator suitcase with her red-nailed hand.

Therese nodded.

'Do you have any stiff-legged dolls? One that stands up?'

Therese looked at the middle-aged woman with the crutches that thrust her shoulders high. Her face was different from all the other faces across the counter, gentle, with a certain cognizance in the eyes, as if they actually saw what they looked at.

'That's a little bigger than I wanted,' the woman said when Therese showed her a doll. 'I'm sorry. Do you have a smaller one?'

'I think so.' Therese went further down the aisle, and was aware that the woman followed her on her crutches, circling the press of people at the counter, so as to save Therese walking back with the doll. Suddenly Therese wanted to take infinite pains, wanted to find exactly the doll the woman was looking for. But the next doll wasn't quite right, either. The doll didn't have real hair. Therese tried in another place and found the same doll with real hair. It even cried when it bent over. It was exactly what the woman wanted. Therese laid the doll down carefully in fresh tissue in a new box.

'That's just perfect,' the woman repeated. 'I'm sending this to a friend in Australia who's a nurse. She graduated from nursing school with me, so I made a little uniform like ours to dress a doll in. Thank you so much. And I wish you a merry Christmas!'

'Merry Christmas to you!' Therese said, smiling. It was the first Merry Christmas she had heard from a customer.

'Have you had your relief yet, Miss Belivet?' Mrs Hendrickson asked her, as sharply as if she reproached her.

Therese hadn't. She got her pocketbook and the novel she was reading from the shelf under the wrapping counter. The novel was Joyce's *Portrait of the Artist as a Young Man*, which Richard was anxious for her to read. How anyone could have read Gertrude Stein without reading any Joyce, Richard said, he didn't know. She felt a bit inferior when Richard talked with her about books. She had browsed all over the bookshelves at school, but the library assembled by the Order of St Margaret had been far from catholic, she realized now, though it had included such unexpected writers as Gertrude Stein.

The hall to the employees' rest rooms was blocked by big shipping carts piled high with boxes. Therese waited to get through.

'Pixie!' one of the shipping-cart boys shouted to her.

Therese smiled a little because it was silly. Even down in the cloakroom in the basement, they yelled 'Pixie!' at her morning and night.

'Pixie, waiting for me?' the raw-edged voice roared again, over the crash and bump of the stock carts.

She got through, and dodged a shipping cart that hurtled towards her with a clerk aboard.

'No smoking here!' shouted a man's voice, the very growly voice of an executive, and the girls ahead of Therese who had lighted cigarettes blew their smoke into the air and said loudly in chorus just before they reached the refuge of the women's room, 'Who does he think *he* is, Mr Frankenberg?'

'Yoo-hoo! Pixie!'

'Ah'm juss bahdin mah tahm, Pixie!'

A shipping cart skidded in front of her, and she struck her leg against its metal corner. She went on without looking down at her leg, though pain began to blossom there, like a slow explosion. She went on into the different chaos of women's voices, women's figures, and the smell of disinfectant. Blood was running to her shoe, and her stocking was torn in a jagged hole. She pushed some skin back into place and, feeling sickened, leaned against the wall and held on to a water-pipe. She stayed there a few seconds, listening to the confusion of voices among the girls at the mirror. Then she wet toilet paper and daubed until the red was gone from her stocking, but the red kept coming.

'It's all right, thanks,' she said to a girl who bent over her for a moment, and the girl went away.

Finally, there was nothing to do but buy a sanitary napkin from the slot machine. She used a little of the cotton from inside it, and tied it on her leg with the gauze. And then it was time to go back to the counter.

Their eyes met at the same instant, Therese glancing up from a box she was opening, and the woman just turning her head so she looked directly at Therese. She was tall and fair, her long figure graceful in the loose fur coat that she held open with a hand on her waist. Her eyes were grey, colourless, yet dominant as light or fire, and, caught by them, Therese could not look away. She heard the customer in front of her repeat a question, and Therese stood there, mute. The woman was looking at Therese, too, with a preoccupied expression, as if half her mind were on whatever it was she meant to buy here, and though there were a number of salesgirls between them, Therese felt sure the woman would come to her. Then Therese saw her walk slowly towards the counter, heard her heart stumble to catch up with the moment it had let pass, and felt her face grow hot as the woman came nearer and nearer.

'May I see one of those valises?' the woman asked, and leaned on the counter, looking down through the glass top.

The damaged valise lay only a yard away. Therese turned around and got a box from the bottom of a stack, a box that had never been opened. When she stood up, the woman was looking at her with the calm grey eyes that Therese could neither quite face nor look away from.

'That's the one I like, but I don't suppose I can have it, can I?' she said, nodding towards the brown valise in the show window behind Therese.

Her eyebrows were blonde, curving around the bend of her forehead. Her mouth was as wise as her eyes, Therese thought, and her voice was like her coat, rich and supple, and somehow full of secrets.

'Yes,' Therese said.

Therese went back to the stockroom for the key. The key hung just inside the door on a nail, and no one was allowed to touch it but Mrs Hendrickson.

Miss Davis saw her and gasped, but Therese said, 'I need it,' and went out.

She opened the show window, took the suitcase down and laid it on the counter.

'You're giving me the one on display?' She smiled as if she understood. She said casually, leaning both forearms on the counter, studying the contents of the valise, 'They'll have a fit, won't they?'

'It doesn't matter,' Therese said.

'All right. I'd like this. That's C.O.D. And what about clothes? Do these come with it?'

There were cellophane-wrapped clothes in the lid of the suitcase, with a price tag on them. Therese said, 'No, they're separate. If you want dolls' clothes – these aren't as good as the clothes in the dolls'-clothing department across the aisle.'

'Oh! Will this get to New Jersey before Christmas?'

'Yes, it'll arrive Monday.' If it didn't, Therese thought, she would deliver it herself.

'Mrs H. F. Aird,' the woman's soft, distinct voice said, and Therese began to print it on the green C.O.D. slip.

The name, the address, the town appeared beneath the pencil point like a secret Therese would never forget, like something stamping itself in her memory for ever.

'You won't make any mistakes, will you?' the woman's voice asked.

Therese noticed the woman's perfume for the first time, and instead of replying could only shake her head. She looked down at the slip to which she was laboriously adding the necessary figures, and wished with all her power to wish anything that the woman would simply continue her last words and say, 'Are you really so glad to have met me? Then why can't we see each other again? Why can't we even have lunch together today?' Her voice was so casual, and she might have said it so easily. But nothing came after the 'will you?' – nothing to relieve the shame of having been recognized as a new salesgirl, hired for the Christmas rush, inexperienced and liable to make mistakes. Therese slid the book towards her for her signature.

Then the woman picked up her gloves from the counter, and turned, and slowly went away, and Therese watched the distance widen and widen. Her ankles below the fur of the coat were pale and thin. She wore plain black suede shoes with high heels.

'That's a C.O.D. order?'

Therese looked into Mrs Hendrickson's ugly meaningless face. 'Yes, Mrs Hendrickson.'

'Don't you know you're supposed to give the customer the strip at the top? How do you expect them to claim the purchase when it comes? Where's the customer? Can you catch her?'

'Yes.' She was only ten feet away, across the aisle at the dolls'-clothing counter. And with the green slip in her hand, she hesitated a moment, then carried it around the counter, forcing herself to advance, because she was suddenly abashed by her appearance, the old blue skirt, the cotton blouse – whoever assigned the green smocks had missed her – and the humiliating flat shoes. And the horrible bandage through which the blood was probably showing again.

'I'm supposed to give you this,' she said, laying the miserable little scrap beside the hand on the edge of the counter, and turning away.

Behind the counter again, Therese faced the stock boxes, sliding them thoughtfully out and back, as if she were looking for something. Therese waited until the woman must have finished at the counter and gone away. She was conscious of the moments passing like irrevocable time, irrevocable happiness, for in these last seconds she might turn and see the face she would never see again. She was conscious, too, dimly now and with a different horror, of the old, unceasing voices of customers at the counter calling for assistance, calling to her, and of the low, humming *rrrrrrr* of the little train, part of the storm that was closing in and separating her from the woman.

But when she turned finally, she looked directly into the grey eyes again. The woman was walking towards her, and as if time had turned back, she leaned gently on the counter again and gestured to a doll and asked to see it.

Therese got the doll and dropped it with a clatter on the glass counter, and the woman glanced at her.

'Sounds unbreakable,' the woman said.

Therese smiled.

'Yes, I'll get this, too,' she said in the quiet slow voice that made a pool of silence in the tumult around them. She gave her name and address again, and Therese took it slowly from her lips, as if she did not already know it by heart. 'That really will arrive before Christmas?'

'It'll come Monday at the latest. That's two days before Christmas.'

'Good. I don't mean to make you nervous.'

Therese tightened the knot in the string she had put around the doll box, and the knot mysteriously came open. 'No,' she said. In an embarrassment so profound there was nothing left to defend, she got the knot tied under the woman's eyes.

'It's a rotten job, isn't it?'

'Yes.' Therese folded the C.O.D. slips around the white string, and fastened them with a pin.

'So forgive me for complaining.'

Therese glanced at her, and the sensation returned that she knew her from somewhere, that the woman was about to reveal herself, and they would both laugh then, and understand. 'You're not complaining. But I know it'll get there.' Therese looked across the aisle, where the woman had stood before, and saw the tiny slip of green paper still on the counter. 'You really are supposed to keep that C.O.D. slip.'

Her eyes changed with her smile now, brightened with a grey, colourless fire that Therese almost knew, almost could place. 'I've gotten things before without them. I always lose them.' She bent to sign the second C.O.D. slip.

Therese watched her go away with a step as slow as when she had come, saw her look at another counter as she passed it, and slap her black gloves across her palm twice, three times. Then she disappeared into an elevator.

And Therese turned to the next customer. She worked with an indefatigable patience, but her figures on the sales slips bore faint tails where the pencil jerked convulsively. She went to Mr Logan's office, which seemed to take hours, but when she looked at the clock only fifteen minutes had passed, and now it was time to wash up for lunch. She stood stiffly in front of the rotating towel, drying her hands, feeling unattached to anything or anyone, isolated. Mr Logan had asked her if she wanted to stay on after Christmas. She could have a job downstairs in the cosmetic department. Therese had said no.

In the middle of the afternoon, she went down to the first floor and bought a card in the greetings-card department. It was not a very interesting card, but at least it was simple, in plain blue and gold. She stood with the pen poised over the card, thinking of what she might have written – 'You are magnificent' or even 'I love you' – finally writing quickly the excruciatingly dull and impersonal: 'Special salutations from Frankenberg's'. She added her number, 645-A, in lieu of a signature. Then she went down to the post office in the basement, hesitated at the letter drop, losing her nerve suddenly at the sight of her hand holding the letter half in the slot. What would happen? She was going to leave the store in a few days, anyway. What would Mrs H. F. Aird care? The blonde eyebrows would perhaps lift a little, she would look at the card a moment, then forget it. Therese dropped it.

On the way home, an idea came to her for a stage set, a house interior with more depth than breadth, with a kind of vortex down the centre, from which rooms would go off on either side. She wanted to begin the cardboard model that night, but at last she only elaborated on her pencil sketch of it. She wanted to see someone – not Richard, not Jack or Alice Kelly downstairs, maybe Stella, Stella Overton, the stage designer she had met during her first weeks in New York. Therese had not seen her, she realized, since she had come to the cocktail party Therese had given before she left her other apartment. Stella was one of the people who didn't know where she lived now. Therese was on her way down to the telephone in the hall when she heard the short, quick rings of her doorbell that meant there was a call for her.

'Thank you,' Therese called down to Mrs Osborne.

It was Richard's usual call around nine o'clock. Richard wanted to know if she felt like seeing a movie tomorrow night. It was the movie at the Sutton they still hadn't seen. Therese said she wasn't doing anything, but she wanted to finish a pillow cover. Alice Kelly had said she could come down and use her sewing machine tomorrow night. And besides, she had to wash her hair.

'Wash it tonight and see me tomorrow night,' Richard said.

'It's too late. I can't sleep if my head's wet.'

'I'll wash it tomorrow night. We won't use the tub, just a couple of buckets.'

She smiled. 'I think we'd better not.' She had fallen into the tub the time Richard had washed her hair. Richard had been imitating the tub drain with writhings and gluggings, and she had laughed so hard her feet slipped on the floor.

'Well, what about that art show Saturday? It's open Saturday afternoon.'

'But Saturday's the day I have to work to nine. I can't get away till nine-thirty.'

'Oh. Well, I'll stay around school and meet you on the corner about nine-thirty. Forty-fourth and Fifth. All right?'

'All right.'

'Anything new today?'

'No. With you?'

'No. I'm going to see about boat reservations tomorrow. I'll call you tomorrow night.'

Therese did not telephone Stella after all.

The next day was Friday, the last Friday before Christmas, and the busiest day Therese had known since she had been working at Frankenberg's, though everyone said tomorrow would be worse. People were pressed alarmingly hard against the glass counters. Customers she started to wait on got swept away and lost in the gluey current that filled the aisle. It was impossible to imagine any more people crowding on to the floor, but the elevators kept emptying people out.

'I don't see why they don't close the doors downstairs!' Therese remarked to Miss Martucci, when they were both stooping by a stock shelf.

'What?' Miss Martucci answered, unable to hear.

'Miss Belivet!' somebody yelled, and a whistle blew.

It was Mrs Hendrickson. She had been using a whistle to get

attention today. Therese made her way towards her past salesgirls and through empty boxes on the floor.

'You're wanted on the telephone,' Mrs Hendrickson told her, pointing to the telephone by the wrapping table.

Therese made a helpless gesture that Mrs Hendrickson had no time to see. It was impossible to hear anything on a telephone now. And she knew it was probably Richard being funny. He had called her once before.

'Hello?' she said.

'Hello, is this co-worker six forty-five A, Therese Belivet?' the operator's voice said over clickings and buzzings. 'Go ahead.'

'Hello?' she repeated, and barely heard an answer. She dragged the telephone off the table and into the stockroom a few feet away. The wire did not quite reach, and she had to stoop on the floor. 'Hello?'

'Hello,' the voice said. 'Well – I wanted to thank you for the Christmas card.'

'Oh. Oh, you're – '

'This is Mrs Aird,' she said. 'Are you the one who sent it? Or not?'

'Yes,' Therese said, rigid with guilt suddenly, as if she had been caught in a crime. She closed her eyes and wrung the telephone, seeing the intelligent, smiling eyes again as she had seen them yesterday. 'I'm very sorry if it annoyed you,' Therese said mechanically, in the voice with which she spoke to customers.

The woman laughed. 'This is very funny,' she said casually, and Therese caught the same easy slur in her voice that she had heard yesterday, loved yesterday, and she smiled herself.

'Is it? Why?'

'You must be the girl in the toy department.'

'Yes.'

'It was extremely nice of you to send me the card,' the woman said politely.

Then Therese understood. She had thought it was from a man, some other clerk who had waited on her. 'It was very nice waiting on you,' Therese said.

'Was it? Why?' She might have been mocking Therese. 'Well –

34

since it's Christmas, why don't we meet for a cup of coffee, at least? Or a drink.'

Therese flinched as the door burst open and a girl came into the room, stood right in front of her. 'Yes – I'd like that.'

'When?' the woman asked. 'I'm coming in to New York tomorrow in the morning. Why don't we make it for lunch? Do you have any time tomorrow?'

'Of course. I have an hour, from twelve to one,' Therese said, staring at the girl's feet in front of her in splayed flat moccasins, the back of her heavy ankles and calves in lisle stockings, shifting like an elephant's legs.

'Shall I meet you downstairs at the Thirty-fourth Street entrance at about twelve?'

'All right. I – ' Therese remembered now she went to work at one sharp tomorrow. She had the morning off. She put her arm up to ward off the avalanche of boxes the girl in front of her had pulled down from the shelf. The girl herself teetered back on to her. 'Hello?' she shouted over the noise of tumbling boxes.

'I'm sow-ry,' Mrs Zabriskie said irritatedly, ploughing out the door again.

'Hello?' Therese repeated.

The line was dead.

CHAPTER FOUR

'Hello,' the woman said, smiling.

'Hello.'

'What's the matter?'

'Nothing.' At least the woman had recognized her, Therese thought.

'Do you have any preference as to restaurants?' the woman asked on the sidewalk.

'No. It'd be nice to find a quiet one, but there aren't any in this neighbourhood.'

'You haven't time for the East Side? No, you haven't, if you've only got an hour. I think I know a place a couple of blocks west on this street. Do you think you have time?'

'Yes, certainly.' It was twelve-fifteen already. Therese knew she would be terribly late, and it didn't matter at all.

They did not bother to talk on the way. Now and then the crowds made them separate, and once the woman glanced at Therese, across a pushcart full of dresses, smiling. They went into a restaurant with wooden rafters and white tablecloths, that miraculously was quiet, and not half filled. They sat down in a large wooden booth, and the woman ordered an old-fashioned without sugar, and invited Therese to have one, or a sherry, and when Therese hesitated, sent the waiter away with the order.

She took off her hat and ran her fingers through her blonde hair, once on either side, and looked at Therese. 'And where did you get the nice idea of sending me a Christmas card?'

'I remembered you,' Therese said. She looked at the small pearl earrings, that were somehow no lighter than her hair itself, or her eyes. Therese thought her beautiful, though her face was a blur now because she could not bear to look at it directly. She got something out of her handbag, a lipstick and compact, and Therese looked at her lipstick case — golden like a jewel, and shaped like a sea chest. She wanted to look at the woman's mouth, but the grey eyes so close drove her away, flickering over her like fire.

'You haven't been working there very long, have you?'

'No. Only about two weeks.'

'And you won't be much longer – probably.' She offered Therese a cigarette.

Therese took one. 'No. I'll have another job.' She leaned towards the lighter the woman was holding for her, towards the slim hand with the oval red nails and a sprinkling of freckles on its back.

'And do you often get inspired to send post-cards?'

'Post-cards?'

'Christmas cards?' She smiled at herself.

'Of course not,' Therese said.

'Well, here's to Christmas.' She touched Therese's glass and drank. 'Where do you live? In Manhattan?'

Therese told her. On Sixty-third Street. Her parents were dead, she said. She had lived in New York the past two years, and before that at a school in New Jersey. Therese did not tell her that the school was semi-religious, Episcopalian. She did not mention Sister Alicia whom she adored and thought of so often, with her pale blue eyes and her ugly nose and her loving sternness. Because since yesterday morning, Sister Alicia had been thrust far away, far below the woman who sat opposite her.

'And what do you do in your spare time?' The lamp on the table made her eyes silvery, full of liquid light. Even the pearl at her earlobe looked alive, like a drop of water that a touch might destroy.

'I – ' Should she tell her she usually worked on her stage models? Sketched and painted sometimes, carved things like cats' heads and tiny figures to go in her ballet sets, but that she liked best to take long walks practically anywhere, liked best simply to dream? Therese felt she did not have to tell her. She felt the woman's eyes could not look at anything without understanding completely. Therese took

37

some more of her drink, liking it, though it was like the woman to swallow, she thought, terrifying, and strong.

The woman nodded to the waiter, and two more drinks arrived.

'I like this.'

'What?' Therese asked.

'I like it that someone sent me a card, someone I didn't know. It's the way things should be at Christmas. And this year I like it especially.'

'I'm glad.' Therese smiled, wondering if she were serious.

'You're a very pretty girl,' she said. 'And very sensitive, too, aren't you?'

She might have been speaking of a doll, Therese thought, so casually had she told her she was pretty. 'I think you are magnificent,' Therese said with the courage of the second drink, not caring how it might sound, because she knew the woman knew anyway.

She laughed, putting her head back. It was a sound more beautiful than music. It made a little wrinkle at the corner of her eyes, and it made her purse her red lips as she drew on her cigarette. She gazed past Therese for a moment, her elbows on the table and her chin propped up on the hand that held her cigarette. There was a long line from the waist of her fitted black suit up to the widening shoulder, and then the blonde head with the fine, unruly hair held high. She was about thirty or thirty-two, Therese thought, and her daughter, for whom she had bought the valise and the doll, would be perhaps six or eight. Therese could imagine the child, blonde-haired, the face golden and happy, the body slim and well proportioned, and always playing. But the child's face, unlike the woman's with its short cheeks and rather Nordic compactness, was vague and nondescript. And the husband? Therese could not see him at all.

Therese said, 'I'm sure you thought it was a man who sent you the Christmas card, didn't you?'

'I did,' she said through a smile. 'I thought it just might be a man in the ski department who'd sent it.'

'I'm sorry.'

'No, I'm delighted.' She leaned back in the booth. 'I doubt very much if I'd have gone to lunch with him. No, I'm delighted.'

The dusky and faintly sweet smell of her perfume came to Therese again, a smell suggestive of dark green silk, that was hers alone, like the smell of a special flower. Therese leaned closer towards it, looking down at her glass. She wanted to thrust the table aside and spring into her arms, to bury her nose in the green and gold scarf that was tied close about her neck. Once the backs of their hands brushed on the table, and Therese's skin there felt separately alive now, and rather burning. Therese could not understand it, but it was so. Therese glanced at her face that was somewhat turned away, and again she knew that instant of half-recognition. And knew, too, that it was not to be believed. She had never seen the woman before. If she had, could she have forgotten? In the silence, Therese felt they both waited for the other to speak, yet the silence was not an awkward one. Their plates had arrived. They had ordered creamed spinach with an egg on top, steamy and buttery smelling.

'How is it you live alone?' the woman asked, and before Therese knew it, she had told the woman her life story.

But not in tedious detail. In six sentences, as if it all mattered less to her than a story she had read somewhere. And what did the facts matter after all, whether her mother was French or English or Hungarian, or if her father had been an Irish painter, or a Czechoslovakian lawyer, whether he had been successful or not, or whether her mother had presented her to the Order of St Margaret as a troublesome, bawling infant, or as a troublesome, melancholy eight year old? Or whether she had been happy there. Because she was happy now, starting today. She had no need of parents or background.

'What could be duller than past history!' Therese said, smiling.

'Maybe futures that won't have any history.'

Therese did not ponder it. It was right. She was still smiling, as if she had just learned how to smile and did not know how to stop. The woman smiled with her, amusedly, and perhaps she was laughing at her, Therese thought.

'What kind of a name is Belivet?' she asked.

'It's Czech. It's changed,' Therese explained awkwardly. 'Origi-nally – '

'It's very original.'

'What's your name?' Therese asked. 'Your first name?'

'My name? Carol. Please don't ever call me Carole.'

'Please don't ever call me Thereese,' Therese said, pronouncing the 'th'.

'How do you like it pronounced? Therese?'

'Yes. The way you do,' she answered. Carol pronounced her name the French way, Terez. She was used to a dozen variations, and sometimes she herself pronounced it differently. She liked the way Carol pronounced it, and she liked her lips saying it. An indefinite longing, that she had been only vaguely conscious of at times before, became now a recognizable wish. It was so absurd, so embarrassing a desire, that Therese thrust it from her mind.

'What do you do on Sundays?' Carol asked.

'I don't always know. Nothing in particular. What do you do?'

'Nothing — lately. If you'd like to visit me some time, you're welcome to. At least there's some country around where I live. Would you like to come out this Sunday?' The grey eyes regarded her directly now, and for the first time Therese faced them. There was a measure of humour in them, Therese saw. And what else? Curiosity, and a challenge, too.

'Yes,' Therese said.

'What a strange girl you are.'

'Why?'

'Flung out of space,' Carol said.

CHAPTER FIVE

Richard was standing on the street corner, waiting for her, shifting from foot to foot in the cold. She wasn't cold at all tonight, she realized suddenly, even though other people on the streets were hunched in their overcoats. She took Richard's arm and squeezed it affectionately tight.

'Have you been inside?' she asked. She was ten minutes late.

'Of course not. I was waiting.' He pressed his cold lips and nose into her cheek. 'Did you have a rough day?'

'No.'

The night was very black, in spite of the Christmas lights on some of the lampposts. She looked at Richard's face in the flare of his match. The smooth slab of his forehead overhung his narrowed eyes, strong looking as a whale's front, she thought, strong enough to batter something in. His face was like a face sculpted in wood, planed smooth and unadorned. She saw his eyes open like unexpected spots of blue sky in the darkness.

He smiled at her. 'You're in a good mood tonight. Want to walk down the block? You can't smoke in there. Like a cigarette?'

'No, thanks.'

They began to walk. The gallery was just beside them, a row of lighted windows, each with a Christmas wreath, on the second floor of the big building. Tomorrow she would see Carol, Therese thought, tomorrow morning at eleven. She would see her only ten blocks from here, in a little more than twelve hours. She started to take

Richard's arm again, and suddenly felt self-conscious about it. Eastward, down Forty-third Street, she saw Orion exactly spread in the centre of the sky between the buildings. She had used to look at him from windows in school, from the window of her first New York apartment.

'I got our reservations today,' Richard said. 'The *President Taylor* sailing March seventh. I talked with the ticket fellow, and I think he can get us outside rooms, if I keep after him.'

'March seventh?' She heard the start of excitement in her voice, though she did not want to go to Europe now at all.

'About ten weeks off,' Richard said, taking her hand.

'Can you cancel the reservation in case I can't go?' She could as well tell him now that she didn't want to go, she thought, but he would only argue, as he had before when she hesitated.

'Of . . . of course, Terry!' And he laughed.

Richard swung her hand as they walked. As if they were lovers, Therese thought. It would be almost like love, what she felt for Carol, except that Carol was a woman. It was not quite insanity, but it was certainly blissful. A silly word, but how could she possibly be happier than she was now, and had been since Thursday?

'I wish we could share one together,' Richard said.

'Share what?'

'Share a room!' Richard boomed out, laughing, and Therese noticed the two people on the sidewalk who turned to look at them. 'Should we have a drink somewhere just to celebrate? We can go in the Mansfield around the corner.'

'I don't feel like sitting still. Let's have it later.'

They got into the show at half price on Richard's art-school passes. The gallery was a series of high-ceilinged, plush carpeted rooms, a background of financial opulence for the commercial advertisements, the drawings, lithographs, illustrations, or whatever that hung in a crowded row on the walls. Richard pored over some of them for minutes at a time, but Therese found them a little depressing.

'Did you see this?' Richard asked, pointing to a complicated drawing of a lineman repairing a telephone wire that Therese had seen somewhere before, that tonight actually pained her to look at.

'Yes,' she said. She was thinking of something else. If she stopped scrimping to save money for Europe – which had been silly anyway because she wasn't going – she could buy a new coat. There would be sales right after Christmas. The coat she had now was a kind of black polo coat, and she always felt drab in it.

Richard took her arm. 'You haven't enough respect for technique, little girl.'

She gave him a mocking frown, and took his arm again. She felt very close to him suddenly, as warm and happy with him as she had been the first night she met him, at the party down on Christopher Street where Frances Cotter had taken her. Richard had been a little drunk, as he had never been since with her, talking about books and politics and people more positively than she had ever heard him talk since, too. He had talked with her all evening, and she had liked him so very much that night for his enthusiasms, his ambitions, his likes and dislikes, and because it was her first real party and he had made it a success for her.

'You're not looking,' Richard said.

'It's exhausting. I've had enough when you have.'

Near the door, they met some people Richard knew from the League, a young man, a girl, and a young black man. Richard introduced Therese to them. She could tell they were not close friends of Richard's, but he announced to all of them, 'We're going to Europe in March.'

And they all looked envious.

Outside, Fifth Avenue seemed empty and waiting, like a stage set, for some dramatic action. Therese walked along quickly beside Richard, her hands in her pockets. Somewhere today she had lost her gloves. She was thinking of tomorrow, at eleven o'clock. She wondered if she would possibly still be with Carol this time tomorrow night.

'What about tomorrow?' Richard asked.

'Tomorrow?'

'You know. The family asked if you could come out this Sunday and have dinner with us.'

Therese hesitated, remembering. She had visited the Semcos four or five Sunday afternoons. They had a big dinner around two o'clock, and then Mr Semco, a short man with a bald head, would want to dance with her to polkas and Russian folk music on the phonograph.

'Say, you know Mamma wants to make you a dress?' Richard

43

went on. 'She's already got the material. She wants to measure you for it.'

'A dress – that's so much work.' Therese had a vision of Mrs Semco's embroidered blouses, white blouses with rows upon rows of stitches. Mrs Semco was proud of her needlework. Therese did not feel she should accept such a colossal labour.

'She loves it,' Richard said. 'Well, what about tomorrow? Want to come out around noon?'

'I don't think I want to this Sunday. They haven't made any great plans, have they?'

'No,' Richard said, disappointed. 'You just want to work or something tomorrow?'

'Yes. I'd rather.' She didn't want Richard to know about Carol, or even ever meet her.

'Not even take a drive somewhere?'

'I don't think so, thanks.' Therese didn't like his holding her hand now. His hand was moist, which made it icy cold.

'You don't think you'll change your mind?'

Therese shook her head. 'No.' There were some mitigating things she might have said, excuses, but she did not want to lie about tomorrow either, any more than she had already lied. She heard Richard sigh, and they walked along in silence for a while.

'Mamma wants to make you a white dress with lace edging. She's going crazy with frustration with no girls in the family but Esther.'

That was his cousin by marriage, whom Therese had seen only once or twice. 'How is Esther?'

'Just the same.'

Therese extricated her fingers from Richard's. She was hungry suddenly. She had spent her dinner hour writing something, a kind of letter to Carol that she hadn't mailed and didn't intend to. They caught the uptown bus at Third Avenue, then walked east to Therese's house. Therese did not want to invite Richard upstairs, but she did anyway.

'No, thanks, I'll shove on,' Richard said. He put a foot on the first step. 'You're in a funny mood tonight. You're miles away.'

'No, I'm not,' she said, feeling inarticulate and resenting it.

'You are now. I can tell. After all, don't you – '

'What?' she prompted.

'We aren't getting very far, are we?' he said, suddenly earnest. 'If you don't even want to spend Sundays with me, how're we going to spend months together in Europe?'

'Well – if you want to call it all off, Richard.'

'Terry, I love you.' He brushed his palm over his hair, exasperatedly. 'Of course, I don't want to call it all off, but – ' He broke off again.

She knew what he was about to say, that she gave him practically nothing in the way of affection, but he wouldn't say it, because he knew very well that she wasn't in love with him, so why did he really expect her affection? Yet the simple fact that she wasn't in love with him made Therese feel guilty, guilty about accepting anything from him, a birthday present, or an invitation to dinner at his family's, or even his time. Therese pressed her fingertips hard on the stone banister. 'All right – I know. I'm not in love with you,' she said.

'That's not what I mean, Terry.'

'If you ever want to call the whole thing off – I mean, stop seeing me at all, then do it.' It was not the first time she had said that, either.

'Terry, you know I'd rather be with you than anyone else in the world. That's the hell of it.'

'Well, if it's hell – '

'Do you love me at all, Terry? How do you love me?'

Let me count the ways, she thought. 'I don't love you, but I like you. I felt tonight, a few minutes ago,' she said, hammering the words out however they sounded, because they were true, 'that I felt closer to you than I ever have, in fact.'

Richard looked at her, a little incredulously. 'Do you?' He started slowly up the steps, smiling, and stopped just below her. 'Then – why not let me stay with you tonight, Terry? Just let's try, will you?'

She had known from his first step towards her that he was going to ask her that. Now she felt miserable and ashamed, sorry for herself and for him, because it was so impossible, and so embarrassing because she didn't want it. There was always that tremendous block of not even wanting to try it, which reduced it all to a kind of wretched embarrassment and nothing more, each time he asked her.

She remembered the first night she had let him stay, and she writhed again inwardly. It had been anything but pleasant, and she had asked right in the middle of it, 'Is this right?' How could it be right and so unpleasant, she had thought. And Richard had laughed, long and loud and with a heartiness that had made her angry. And the second time had been even worse, probably because Richard had thought all the difficulties had been gotten over. It was painful enough to make her weep, and Richard had been very apologetic and had said she made him feel like a brute. And then she had protested that he wasn't. She knew very well that he wasn't, that he was angelic compared to what Angelo Rossi would have been, for instance, if she had slept with him the night he stood here on the same steps, asking her the same question.

'Terry, darling – '

'No,' Therese said, finding her voice at last. 'I just can't tonight, and I can't go to Europe with you either,' she finished with an abject and hopeless frankness.

Richard's lips parted in a stunned way. Therese could not bear to look at the frown above them. 'Why not?'

'Because. Because I can't,' she said, every word agony. 'Because I don't want to sleep with you.'

'Oh, Terry!' Richard laughed. 'I'm sorry I asked you. Forget about it, honey, will you? And in Europe, too?'

Therese looked away, noticed Orion again, tipped at a slightly different angle, and looked back at Richard. But I can't, she thought. I've got to think about it some time, because you think about it. It seemed to her that she spoke the words and that they were solid as blocks of wood in the air between them, even though she heard nothing. She had said the words before to him, in her room upstairs, once in Prospect Park when she was winding a kite string. But he wouldn't consider them, and what could she do now, repeat them? 'Do you want to come up for a while anyway?' she asked, tortured by herself, by a shame she could not really account for.

'No,' Richard said with a soft laugh that shamed her all the more for its tolerance and its understanding. 'No, I'll go on. Good night, honey. I love you, Terry.' And with a last look at her, he went.

CHAPTER SIX

Therese stepped out into the street and looked, but the streets were empty with a Sunday morning emptiness. The wind flung itself around the tall cement corner of Frankenberg's as if it were furious at finding no human figure there to oppose. No one but her, Therese thought, and grinned suddenly at herself. She might have thought of a more pleasant place to meet than this. The wind was like ice against her teeth. Carol was a quarter of an hour late. If she didn't come, she would probably keep on waiting, all day and into the night. One figure came out of the subway's pit, a splintery thin hurrying figure of a woman in a long black coat under which her feet moved as fast as if four feet were rotating on a wheel.

Then Therese turned around and saw Carol in a car drawn up by the kerb across the street. Therese walked towards her.

'Hi!' Carol called, and leaned over to open the door for her.

'Hello. I thought you weren't coming.'

'Awfully sorry I'm late. Are you freezing?'

'No.' Therese got in and pulled the door shut. The car was warm inside, a long dark green car with dark green leather upholstery. Carol drove slowly west.

'Shall we go out to the house? Where would you like to go?'

'It doesn't matter,' Therese said. She could see freckles along the bridge of Carol's nose. Her short fair hair that made Therese think of perfume held to a light was tied back with the green and gold scarf that circled her head like a band.

'Let's go out to the house. It's pretty out there.'

They drove uptown. It was like riding inside a rolling mountain that could sweep anything before it, yet was absolutely obedient to Carol.

'Do you like driving?' Carol asked without looking at her. She had a cigarette in her mouth. She drove with her hands resting lightly on the wheel, as if it were nothing to her, as if she sat relaxed in a chair somewhere, smoking. 'Why're you so quiet?'

They roared into the Lincoln Tunnel. A wild, inexplicable excitement mounted in Therese as she stared through the windshield. She wished the tunnel might cave in and kill them both, that their bodies might be dragged out together. She felt Carol glancing at her from time to time.

'Have you had breakfast?'

'No, I haven't,' Therese answered. She supposed she was pale. She had started to have breakfast, but she had dropped the milk bottle in the sink, and then given it all up.

'Better have some coffee. It's there in the thermos.'

They were out of the tunnel. Carol stopped by the side of the road.

'There,' Carol said, nodding at the thermos between them on the seat. Then Carol took the thermos herself and poured some into the cup, steaming and light brown.

Therese looked at the coffee gratefully. 'Where'd it come from?'

Carol smiled. 'Do you always want to know where things come from?'

The coffee was very strong and a little sweet. It sent strength through her. When the cup was half empty, Carol started the car. Therese was silent. What was there to talk about? The gold four-leaf clover with Carol's name and address on it that dangled from the key chain on the dashboard? The stand of Christmas trees they passed on the road? The bird that flew by itself across a swampy looking field? No. Only the things she had written to Carol in the unmailed letter were to be talked about, and that was impossible.

'Do you like the country?' Carol asked as they turned into a smaller road.

They had just driven into a little town and out of it. Now on the driveway that made a great semicircular curve, they approached a white two-storey house that had projecting side wings like the paws of a resting lion.

There was a metal door-mat, a big shining brass mailbox, a dog barking hollowly from around the side of the house, where a white garage showed beyond some trees. The house smelled of some spice, Therese thought, mingled with a separate sweetness that was not Carol's perfume either. Behind her, the door closed with a light, firm double report. Therese turned and found Carol looking at her puzzledly, her lips parted a little as if in surprise, and Therese felt that in the next second Carol would ask, 'What are you doing here?' as if she had forgotten, or had not meant to bring her here at all.

'There's no one here but the maid. And she's far away,' Carol said, as if in reply to some question of Therese's.

'It's a lovely house,' Therese said, and saw Carol's little smile that was tinged with impatience.

'Take off your coat.' Carol took the scarf from around her head and ran her fingers through her hair. 'Wouldn't you like a little breakfast? It's almost noon.'

'No, thanks.'

Carol looked around the living room, and the same puzzled dissatisfaction came back to her face. 'Let's go upstairs. It's more comfortable.'

Therese followed Carol up the wide wooden staircase, past an oil painting of a small girl with yellow hair and a square chin like Carol's, past a window where a garden with an S-shaped path, a fountain with a blue-green statue appeared for an instant and vanished. Upstairs, there was a short hall with four or five rooms around it. Carol went into a room with green carpet and walls, and took a cigarette from a box on a table. She glanced at Therese as she lighted it. Therese didn't know what to do or say, and she felt Carol expected her to do or say something, anything. Therese studied the simple room with its dark green carpet and the long green pillowed bench along one wall. There was a plain table of pale wood in the centre. A game room, Therese thought, though it looked more like a study with its books and music albums and its lack of pictures.

'My favourite room,' Carol said, walking out of it. 'But that's my room over there.'

Therese looked into the room opposite. It had flowered cotton upholstery and plain blonde woodwork like the table in the other room. There was a long plain mirror over the dressing table, and throughout a look of sunlight, though no sunlight was in the room. The bed was a double bed. And there were military brushes on the dark bureau across the room. Therese glanced in vain for a picture of him. There was a picture of Carol on the dressing table, holding up a small girl with blonde hair. And a picture of a woman with dark curly hair, smiling broadly, in a silver frame.

'You have a little girl, haven't you?' Therese asked.

Carol opened a wall panel in the hall. 'Yes,' she said. 'Would you like a Coke?'

The hum of the refrigerator came louder now. Through all the house, there was no sound but those they made. Therese did not want the cold drink, but she took the bottle and carried it downstairs after Carol, through the kitchen and into the back garden she had seen from the window. Beyond the fountain were a lot of plants some three feet high and wrapped in burlap bags that looked like something, standing there in a group, Therese thought, but she didn't know what. Carol tightened a string that the wind had loosened. Stooped in the heavy wool skirt and the blue cardigan sweater, her figure looked solid and strong, like her face, but not like her slender ankles. Carol seemed oblivious of her for several minutes, walking about slowly, planting her moccasined feet firmly, as if in the cold flowerless garden she was at last comfortable. It was bitterly cold without a coat, but because Carol seemed oblivious of that, too, Therese tried to imitate her.

'What would you like to do?' Carol asked. 'Take a walk? Play some records?'

'I'm very content,' Therese told her.

She was preoccupied with something, and regretted after all inviting her out to the house, Therese felt. They walked back to the door at the end of the garden path.

'And how do you like your job?' Carol asked in the kitchen, still with her air of remoteness. She was looking into the big refrigerator. She lifted out two plates covered with wax paper. 'I wouldn't mind some lunch, would you?'

Therese had intended to tell her about the job at the Black Cat

Theatre. That would count for something, she thought, that would be the single important thing she could tell about herself. But this was not the time. Now she replied slowly, trying to sound as detached as Carol, though she heard her shyness predominating, 'I suppose it's educational. I learn how to be a thief, a liar, and a poet all at once.' Therese leaned back in the straight chair so her head would be in the warm square of sunlight. She wanted to say, and how to love. She had never loved anyone before Carol, not even Sister Alicia.

Carol looked at her. 'How do you become a poet?'

'By feeling things – too much, I suppose,' Therese answered conscientiously.

'And how do you become a thief?' Carol licked something off her thumb and frowned. 'You don't want any caramel pudding, do you?'

'No, thank you. I haven't stolen yet, but I'm sure it's easy there. There are pocketbooks all around, and one just takes something. They steal the meat you buy for dinner.' Therese laughed. One could laugh at it with Carol. One could laugh at anything, with Carol.

They had sliced cold chicken, cranberry sauce, green olives, and crisp white celery. But Carol left her lunch and went into the living room. She came back carrying a glass with some whisky in it, and added some water to it from the tap. Therese watched her. Then for a long moment, they looked at each other, Carol standing in the doorway and Therese at the table, looking over her shoulder, not eating.

Carol asked quietly, 'Do you meet a lot of people across the counter this way? Don't you have to be careful whom you start talking to?'

'Oh, yes,' Therese smiled.

'Or whom you go out to lunch with?' Carol's eyes sparkled. 'You might run into a kidnapper.' She rolled the drink around in the iceless glass, then drank it off, the thin silver bracelets on her wrist rattling against the glass. 'Well – do you meet many people this way?'

'No,' Therese said.

'Not many? Just three or four?'

'Like you?' Therese met her eyes steadily.

And Carol looked fixedly at her, as if she demanded another word, another phrase from Therese. But then she set the glass down on the stove top and turned away. 'Do you play the piano?'

'Some.'

'Come and play something.' And when Therese started to refuse, she said imperatively, 'Oh, I don't care how you play. Just play something.'

Therese played some Scarlatti she had learned at the Home. In a chair on the other side of the room, Carol sat listening, relaxed and motionless, not even sipping the new glass of whisky and water. Therese played the C major Sonata, which was slowish and rather simple, full of broken octaves, but it struck her as dull, then pretentious in the trill parts, and she stopped. It was suddenly too much, her hands on the keyboard that she knew Carol played, Carol watching her with her eyes half closed, Carol's whole house around her, and the music that made her abandon herself, made her defenceless. With a gasp, she dropped her hands in her lap.

'Are you tired?' Carol asked calmly.

The question seemed not of now but of always. 'Yes.'

Carol came up behind her and set her hands on Therese's shoulders. Therese could see her hands in her memory – flexible and strong, the delicate tendons showing as they pressed her shoulders. It seemed an age as her hands moved towards her neck and under her chin, an age of tumult so intense it blotted out the pleasure of Carol's tipping her head back and kissing her lightly at the edge of her hair. Therese did not feel the kiss at all.

'Come with me,' Carol said.

She went with Carol upstairs again. Therese pulled herself up by the banister and was reminded suddenly of Mrs Robichek.

'I think a nap wouldn't hurt you,' Carol said, turning down the flowered cotton bedspread and the top blanket.

'Thanks, I'm not really – '

'Slip your shoes off,' Carol said softly, but in a tone that commanded obedience.

Therese looked at the bed. She had hardly slept the night before. 'I don't think I shall sleep, but if I do – '

'I'll wake you in half an hour.' Carol pulled the blanket over her when she lay down. Carol sat down on the edge of the bed. 'How old are you, Therese?'

Therese looked up at her, unable to bear her eyes now but bearing them nevertheless, not caring if she died that instant, if Carol strangled her, prostrate and vulnerable in her bed, the intruder. 'Nineteen.' How old it sounded. Older than ninety-one.

Carol's eyebrows frowned, though she smiled a little. Therese felt that she thought of something so intensely, one might have touched the thought in the air between them. Then Carol slipped her hands under her shoulders, and bent her head down to Therese's throat, and Therese felt the tension go out of Carol's body with the sigh that made her neck warm, that carried the perfume that was in Carol's hair.

'You're a child,' Carol said, like a reproach. She lifted her head. 'What would you like?'

Therese remembered what she had thought of in the restaurant, and she set her teeth in shame.

'What would you like?' Carol repeated.

'Nothing, thanks.'

Carol got up and went to her dressing table and lighted a cigarette. Therese watched her through half-closed lids, worried by Carol's restlessness, though she loved the cigarette, loved to see her smoke.

'What would you like, a drink?'

Therese knew she meant water. She knew from the tenderness and the concern in her voice, as if she were a child sick with fever. Then Therese said it: 'I think I'd like some hot milk.'

The corner of Carol's mouth lifted in a smile. 'Some hot milk,' she mocked. Then she left the room.

And Therese lay in a limbo of anxiety and sleepiness all the long while until Carol reappeared with the milk in a straight-sided white cup with a saucer under it, holding the saucer and the cup handle, and closing the door with her foot.

'I let it boil and it's got a scum on it,' Carol said, sounding annoyed. 'I'm sorry.'

But Therese loved it, because she knew this was exactly what Carol would always do, be thinking of something else and let the milk boil.

'Is that the way you like it? Plain like that?'

Therese nodded.

'Ugh,' Carol said, and sat down on the arm of a chair and watched her.

Therese was propped on one elbow. The milk was so hot, she could barely let her lip touch it at first. The tiny sips spread inside her mouth and released a *mélange* of organic flavours. The milk seemed to taste of bone and blood, of warm flesh, or hair, saltless as chalk yet alive as a growing embryo. It was hot through and through to the bottom of the cup, and Therese drank it down, as people in fairy tales drink the potion that will transform, or the unsuspecting warrior the cup that will kill. Then Carol came and took the cup, and Therese was drowsily aware that Carol asked her three questions, one that had to do with happiness, one about the store, and one about the future. Therese heard herself answering. She heard her voice rise suddenly in a babble, like a spring that she had no control over, and she realized she was in tears. She was telling Carol all that she feared and disliked, of her loneliness, of Richard, and of gigantic disappointments. And of her parents. Her mother was not dead. But Therese had not seen her since she was fourteen.

Carol questioned her, and she answered, though she did not want to talk about her mother. Her mother was not that important, not even one of the disappointments. Her father was. Her father was quite different. He had died when she was six – a lawyer of Czechoslovakian descent who all his life had wanted to be a painter. He had been quite different, gentle, sympathetic, never raising his voice in anger against the woman who had nagged at him, because he had been neither a good lawyer nor a good painter. He had never been strong, he had died of pneumonia, but in Therese's mind, her mother had killed him. Carol questioned and questioned her, and Therese told of her mother's bringing her to the school in Montclair when she was eight, of her mother's infrequent visits afterwards, for her mother had travelled a great deal around the country. She had been a pianist – no, not a first-rate one, how could she be, but she had always found work because she was pushing. And when Therese was about ten, her mother had remarried. Therese had visited at her mother's house in Long Island in the Christmas holidays, and they had asked her to stay with them, but not as if they wanted her to stay. And Therese had not liked the husband, Nick, because he was exactly like her mother, big and dark-haired, with a loud voice, and violent and passionate gestures. Therese was sure their marriage would be perfect. Her mother had been pregnant even then, and now there were two children. After a week with them, Therese had returned to the Home. There had been perhaps three or four visits from her mother afterwards, always with some present for her, a blouse, a book, once a cosmetic kit that Therese had loathed simply because it reminded her of her mother's brittle, mascaraed eyelashes, presents handed her self-consciously by her mother, like hypocritical peace offerings. Once her mother had brought the little boy, her half brother, and then Therese had known she was an outsider. Her mother had not loved her father, had chosen to leave her at a school when she was eight, and why did she bother now even to visit her, to claim her at all? Therese would have been happier to have no parents, like half the girls in the school. Finally, Therese had told her mother she did not want her to visit again, and her mother hadn't, and the ashamed, resentful expression, the nervous sidewise glance of the brown eyes, the twitch of a smile and the silence – that was the last she remembered of her mother. Then she had become fifteen. The sisters at the school had known her mother was not writing. They had asked her mother to write, and she had, but Therese had not answered. Then when graduation came, when she was seventeen, the school had asked her mother for two hundred dollars. Therese hadn't wanted any money from her, had half believed her mother wouldn't give her any, but she had, and Therese had taken it.

'I'm sorry I took it. I never told anyone but you. Some day I want to give it back.'

'Nonsense,' Carol said softly. She was sitting on the arm of the chair, resting her chin in her hand, her eyes fixed on Therese, smiling. 'You were still a child. When you forget about paying her back, then you'll be an adult.'

Therese did not answer.

'Don't you think you'll ever want to see her again? Maybe in a few years from now?'

Therese shook her head. She smiled, but the tears still oozed out of her eyes. 'I don't want to talk any more about it.'

'Does Richard know all this?'

'No. Just that she's alive. Does it matter? This isn't what matters.'

She felt if she wept enough, it would all go out of her, the tiredness and the loneliness and the disappointment, as though it were in the tears themselves. And she was glad Carol left her alone to do it now. Carol was standing by the dressing table, her back to her. Therese lay rigid in the bed, propped up on her elbow, racked with the half-suppressed sobs.

'I'll never cry again,' she said.

'Yes, you will.' And a match scraped.

Therese took another cleansing tissue from the bed table and blew her nose.

'Who else is in your life besides Richard?' Carol asked.

She had fled them all. There had been Lily, and Mr and Mrs Anderson in the house where she had first lived in New York. Frances Cotter and Tim at the Pelican Press. Lois Vavrica, a girl who had been at the Home in Montclair, too. Now who was there? The Kellys who lived on the second floor at Mrs Osborne's. And Richard. 'When I was fired from that job last month,' Therese said, 'I was ashamed and I moved – ' She stopped.

'Moved where?'

'I didn't tell anyone where, except Richard. I just disappeared. I suppose it was my idea of starting a new life, but mostly I was ashamed. I didn't want anyone to know where I was.'

Carol smiled. 'Disappeared! I like that. And how lucky you are to be able to do it. You're free. Do you realize that?'

Therese said nothing.

'No,' Carol answered herself.

Beside Carol on the dressing table, a square grey clock ticked faintly, and as Therese had done a thousand times in the store, she read the time and attached a meaning to it. It was four fifteen and a little more, and suddenly she was anxious lest she had lain there too long, lest Carol might be expecting someone to come to the house.

Then the telephone rang, sudden and long like the shriek of an hysterical woman in the hall, and they saw each other start.

Carol stood up, and slapped something twice in her palm, as she had slapped the gloves in her palm in the store. The telephone screamed again, and Therese was sure Carol was going to throw whatever it was she held in her hand, throw it across the room against the wall. But Carol only turned and laid the thing down quietly, and left the room.

Therese could hear Carol's voice in the hall. She did not want to hear what she was saying. She got up and put her skirt and her shoes on. Now she saw what Carol had held in her hand. It was a shoehorn of tan-coloured wood. Anyone else would have thrown it, Therese thought. Then she knew one word for what she felt about Carol: pride. She heard Carol's voice repeating the same tones, and now, opening the door to leave, she heard the words, 'I have a guest,' for the third time calmly presented as a barrier. 'I think it's an excellent reason. What better? . . . What's the matter with tomorrow? If you – '

Then there was no sound until Carol's first step on the stair, and Therese knew whoever had been talking to her had hung up on her. Who dared, Therese wondered.

'Shouldn't I leave?' Therese asked.

Carol looked at her in the same way she had when they first entered the house. 'Not unless you want to. No. We'll take a drive later, if you want to.'

She knew Carol did not want to take another drive. Therese started to straighten the bed.

'Leave the bed.' Carol was watching her from the hall. 'Just close the door.'

'Who is it that's coming?'

Carol turned and went into the green room. 'My husband,' she said. 'Hargess.'

Then the doorbell chimed twice downstairs, and the latch clicked at the same time.

'No end prompt today,' Carol murmured. 'Come down, Therese.'

Therese felt sick with dread suddenly, not of the man but of Carol's annoyance at his coming.

He was coming up the stairs. When he saw Therese, he slowed, and a faint surprise crossed his face, and then he looked at Carol.

'Harge, this is Miss Belivet,' Carol said. 'Mr Aird.'

'How do you do?' Therese said.

Harge only glanced at Therese, but his nervous blue eyes inspected her from head to toe. He was a heavily built man with a rather pink face. One eyebrow was set higher than the other, rising in an alert peak in the centre, as if it might have been distorted by a scar. 'How do you do?' Then to Carol, 'I'm sorry to disturb you. I only wanted to get one or two things.' He went past her and opened the door to a room Therese had not seen. 'Things for Rindy,' he added.

'Pictures on the wall?' Carol asked.

The man was silent.

Carol and Therese went downstairs. In the living room Carol sat down but Therese did not.

'Play some more, if you like,' Carol said.

Therese shook her head.

'Play some,' Carol said firmly.

Therese was frightened by the sudden white anger in her eyes. 'I can't,' Therese said, stubborn as a mule.

And Carol subsided. Carol even smiled.

They heard Harge's quick steps cross the hall and stop, then descend the stairs slowly. Therese saw his dark-clad figure and then his pinkish-blond head appear.

'I can't find that watercolour set. I thought it was in my room,' he said complainingly.

'I know where it is.' Carol got up and started towards the stairs.

'I suppose you want me to take her something for Christmas,' Harge said.

'Thanks, I'll give the things to her.' Carol went up the stairs.

They are just divorced, Therese thought, or about to be divorced.

Harge looked at Therese. He had an intense expression that curiously mingled anxiety and boredom. The flesh around his mouth was firm and heavy, rounding into the line of his mouth so that he seemed lipless. 'Are you from New York?' he asked.

Therese felt the disdain and incivility in the question, like the sting of a slap in the face. 'Yes, from New York,' she answered.

He was on the brink of another question to her, when Carol came down the stairs. Therese had steeled herself to be alone with him for minutes. Now she shuddered as she relaxed, and she knew that he saw it.

'Thanks,' Harge said as he took the box from Carol. He walked to his overcoat that Therese had noticed on the loveseat, sprawled open with its black arms spread as if it were fighting and would take possession of the house. 'Goodbye,' Harge said to her. He put the overcoat on as he walked to the door. 'Friend of Abby's?' he murmured to Carol.

'A friend of mine,' Carol answered.

'Are you going to take the presents to Rindy? When?'

'What if I gave her nothing, Harge?'

'Carol – ' He stopped on the porch, and Therese barely heard him say something about making things unpleasant. Then, 'I'm going over to see Cynthia now. Can I stop by on the way back? It'll be before eight.'

'Harge, what's the purpose?' Carol said wearily. 'Especially when you're so disagreeable.'

'Because it concerns Rindy.' Then his voice faded unintelligibly.

Then, an instant later, Carol came in alone and closed the door. Carol stood against the door with her hands behind her, and they heard the car outside leaving. Carol must have agreed to see him tonight, Therese thought.

'I'll go,' Therese said. Carol said nothing. There was a deadness in the silence between them now, and Therese grew more uneasy. 'I'd better go, hadn't I?'

'Yes. I'm sorry. I'm sorry about Harge. He's not always so rude. It was a mistake to say I had any guest here at all.'

'It doesn't matter.'

Carol's forehead wrinkled and she said with difficulty, 'Do you mind if I put you on the train tonight, instead of driving you home?'

'No.' She couldn't have borne Carol's driving her home and driving back alone tonight in the darkness.

They were silent also in the car. Therese opened the door as soon as the car stopped at the station.

'There's a train in about four minutes,' Carol said.

Therese blurted suddenly, 'Will I see you again?'

Carol only smiled at her, a little reproachfully, as the window between them rose up. 'Au revoir,' she said.

Of course, of course, she would see her again, Therese thought. An idiotic question.

The car backed fast and turned away into the darkness.

Therese longed for the store again, longed for Monday, because Carol might come in again on Monday. But it wasn't likely. Tuesday was Christmas Eve. Certainly she could telephone Carol by Tuesday, if only to wish her a merry Christmas.

But there was not a moment when she did not see Carol in her mind, and all she saw, she seemed to see through Carol. That evening, the dark flat streets of New York, the tomorrow of work, the milk bottle dropped and broken in her sink, became unimportant. She flung herself on her bed and drew a line with a pencil on a piece of paper. And another line, carefully, and another. A world was born around her, like a bright forest with a million shimmering leaves.

CHAPTER SEVEN

The man looked at it, holding it carelessly between thumb and forefinger. He was bald except for long strands of black hair that grew from a former brow line, plastered sweatily down over the naked scalp. His underlip was thrust out with the contempt and negation that had fixed itself on his face as soon as Therese had come to the counter and spoken her first words.

'No,' he said at last.

'Can't you give me anything for it?' Therese asked.

The lip came out further. 'Maybe fifty cents.' And he tossed it back across the counter.

Therese's fingers crept over it possessively. 'Well, what about this?' From her coat pocket she dragged up the silver chain with the St Christopher medallion.

Again the thumb and forefinger were eloquent of scorn, turning the coin like filth. 'Two fifty.'

But it cost at least twenty dollars, Therese started to say, but she didn't because that was what everybody said. 'Thanks.' She picked up the chain and went out.

Who were all the lucky people, she wondered, who had managed to sell their old pocketknives, broken wrist watches and carpenters' planes that hung in clumps in the front window? She could not resist looking back through the window, finding the man's face again under the row of hanging hunting knives. The man was looking at her, too, smiling at her. She felt he understood every move she made. Therese hurried down the sidewalk.

In ten minutes, Therese was back. She pawned the silver medallion for two dollars and fifty cents.

She hurried westward, ran across Lexington Avenue, then Park, and turned down Madison. She clutched the little box in her pocket until its sharp edges cut her fingers. Sister Beatrice had given it to her. It was inlaid brown wood and mother-of-pearl, in a checked pattern. She didn't know what it was worth in money, but she had assumed it was rather precious. Well, now she knew it wasn't. She went into a leather goods shop.

'I'd like to see the black one in the window – the one with the strap and the gold buckles,' Therese said to the salesgirl.

It was the handbag she had noticed last Saturday morning on the way to meet Carol for lunch. It had looked like Carol, just at a glance. She had thought, even if Carol didn't keep the appointment that day, if she could never see Carol again, she must buy the bag and send it to her anyway.

'I'll take it,' Therese said.

'That's seventy-one eighteen with the tax,' the salesgirl said. 'Do you want that gift-wrapped?'

'Yes, please.' Therese counted six crisp ten-dollar bills across the counter and the rest in singles. 'Can I leave it here till about six-thirty tonight?'

Therese left the shop with the receipt in her billfold. It wouldn't do to risk bringing the handbag into the store. It might be stolen, even if it was Christmas Eve. Therese smiled. It was her last day of work at the store. And in four more days came the job at the Black Cat. Phil was going to bring her a copy of the play the day after Christmas.

She passed Brentano's. Its window was full of satin ribbons, leather-bound books, and pictures of knights in armour. Therese turned back and went into the store, not to buy but to look, just for a moment, to see if there was anything here more beautiful than the handbag.

An illustration in one of the counter displays caught her eye. It was a young knight on a white horse, riding through a bouquet-like forest, followed by a line of page boys, the last bearing a cushion with a gold ring on it. She took the leather-bound book in her hand. The price inside the cover was twenty-five dollars. If she simply went to the bank now and got twenty-five dollars more, she could buy it. What was twenty-five dollars? She hadn't needed to pawn the silver medallion. She knew she had pawned it only because it was from Richard, and she didn't want it any longer. She closed the book and looked at the edges of the pages that were like a concave bar of gold. But would Carol really like it, a book of love poems of the Middle Ages? She didn't know. She couldn't remember the slightest clue as to Carol's taste in books. She put the book down hurriedly and left.

Upstairs in the doll department, Miss Santini was strolling along behind the counter, offering everybody candy from a big box.

'Take two,' she said to Therese. 'Candy department sent 'em up.'

'I don't mind if I do.' Imagine, she thought, biting into a nougat, the Christmas spirit had struck the candy department. There was a strange atmosphere in the store today. It was unusually quiet, first of all. There were plenty of customers, but they didn't seem in a hurry, even though it was Christmas Eve. Therese glanced at the elevators, looking for Carol. If Carol didn't come in, and she probably wouldn't, Therese was going to telephone her at six-thirty, just to wish her a happy Christmas. Therese knew her telephone number. She had seen it on the telephone at the house.

'Miss Belivet!' Mrs Hendrickson's voice called, and Therese jumped to attention. But Mrs Hendrickson only waved her hand for the benefit of the Western Union messenger who laid a telegram in front of Therese.

Therese signed for it in a scribble, and tore it open. It said: 'MEET YOU DOWNSTAIRS AT 5 P.M. CAROL.'

Therese crushed it in her hand. She pressed it hard with her thumb into her palm, and watched the messenger boy who was really an old man walk back towards the elevators. He walked ploddingly, with a stoop that thrust his knees far ahead of him, and his puttees were loose and wobbly.

'You look happy,' Mrs Zabriskie said dismally to her as she went by.

Therese smiled. 'I am.' Mrs Zabriskie had a two-months'-old baby, she had told Therese, and her husband was out of work now. Therese wondered if Mrs Zabriskie and her husband were in love with each other, and really happy. Perhaps they were, but there was nothing in Mrs Zabriskie's blank face and her trudging gait that would suggest it. Perhaps once Mrs Zabriskie had been as happy as she. Perhaps it had gone away. She remembered reading – even Richard once saying – that love usually dies after two years of marriage. That was a cruel thing, a trick. She tried to imagine Carol's face, the smell of her perfume, becoming meaningless. But in the first place could she say she was in love with Carol? She had come to a question she could not answer.

At a quarter to five, Therese went to Mrs Hendrickson and asked permission to leave a half-hour early. Mrs Hendrickson might have thought the telegram had something to do with it, but she let Therese go without even a complaining look, and that was another thing that made the day a strange one.

Carol was waiting for her in the foyer where they had met before.

'Hello!' Therese said. 'I'm through.'

'Through what?'

'Through with working. Here.' But Carol seemed depressed, and it dampened Therese instantly. She said anyway, 'I was awfully happy to get the telegram.'

'I didn't know if you'd be free. Are you free tonight?'

'Of course.'

And they walked on, slowly, amid the jostling crowd, Carol in her delicate-looking suede pumps that made her a couple of inches taller than Therese. It had begun to snow about an hour before, but it was stopping already. The snow was no more than a film underfoot, like thin white wool drawn across the street and sidewalk.

'We might have seen Abby tonight, but she's busy,' Carol said. 'Anyway, we can take a drive, if you'd like. It's good to see you. You're an angel to be free tonight. Do you know that?'

'No,' Therese said, still happy in spite of herself, though Carol's mood was disquieting. Therese felt something had happened.

'Do you suppose there's a place to get a cup of coffee around here?'

'Yes. A little further east.'

Therese was thinking of one of the sandwich shops between Fifth and Madison, but Carol chose a small bar with an awning in front. The waiter was reluctant at first, and said it was the cocktail hour, but when Carol started to leave, he went away and got the coffee. Therese was anxious about picking up the handbag. She didn't want

64

to do it when Carol was with her, even though the package would be wrapped.

'Did something happen?' Therese asked.

'Something too long to explain.' Carol smiled at her but the smile was tired, and a silence followed, an empty silence as if they travelled through space away from each other.

Probably Carol had had to break an engagement she had looked forward to, Therese thought. Carol would of course be busy on Christmas Eve.

'I'm not keeping you from doing anything now?' Carol asked.

Therese felt herself growing tense, helplessly. 'I'm supposed to pick up a package on Madison Avenue. It's not far. I can do it now, if you'll wait for me.'

'All right.'

Therese stood up. 'I can do it in three minutes with a taxi. But I don't think you will wait for me, will you?'

Carol smiled and reached for her hand. Indifferently, Carol squeezed her hand and dropped it. 'Yes, I'll wait.'

The bored tone of Carol's voice was in her ears as she sat on the edge of the taxi seat. On the way back, the traffic was so slow, she got out and ran the last block.

Carol was still there, her coffee only half finished.

'I don't want my coffee.' Therese said, because Carol seemed ready to go.

'My car's downtown. Let's get a taxi down.'

They went down into the business section not far from the Battery. Carol's car was brought up from an underground garage. Carol drove west to the Westside Highway.

'This is better.' Carol shed her coat as she drove. 'Throw it in back, will you?'

And they were silent again. Carol drove faster, changing her lane to pass cars, as if they had a destination. Therese set herself to say something, anything at all, by the time they reached the George Washington Bridge. Suddenly it occurred to her that if Carol and her husband were divorcing, Carol had been downtown to see a lawyer today. The district there was full of law offices. And something had gone wrong. Why were they divorcing? Because Harge was having an affair with the woman called Cynthia? Therese was cold. Carol had lowered the window beside her, and every time the car sped, the wind burst through and wrapped its cold arms around her.

'That's where Abby lives,' Carol said, nodding across the river.

Therese did not even see any special lights. 'Who's Abby?'

'Abby? My best friend.' Then Carol looked at her. 'Aren't you cold with this window open?'

'No.'

'You must be.' They stopped for a red light, and Carol rolled the window up. Carol looked at her, as if really seeing her for the first time that evening, and under her eyes that went from her face to her hands in her lap, Therese felt like a puppy Carol had bought at a roadside kennel, that Carol had just remembered was riding beside her.

'What happened, Carol? Are you getting a divorce now?'

Carol sighed. 'Yes, a divorce,' she said quite calmly, and started the car.

'And he has the child?'

'Just tonight.'

Therese was about to ask another question, when Carol said, 'Let's talk about something else.'

A car went by with the radio playing Christmas carols and everyone singing.

And she and Carol were silent. They drove past Yonkers, and it seemed to Therese she had left every chance of talking further to Carol somewhere behind on the road. Carol insisted suddenly that she should eat something, because it was getting on to eight, so they stopped at a little restaurant by the roadside, a place that sold fried-clam sandwiches. They sat at the counter and ordered sandwiches and coffee, but Carol did not eat. Carol asked her questions about Richard, not in the concerned way she had Sunday afternoon, but rather as if she talked to keep Therese from asking more questions about her. They were personal questions, yet Therese answered them mechanically and impersonally. Carol's quiet voice went on and on, much quieter than the voice of the counter boy talking with someone three yards away.

'Do you sleep with him?' Carol asked.

'I did. Two or three times.' Therese told her about those times, the first time and the three times afterwards. She was not embarrassed, talking about it. It had never seemed so dull and unimportant before. She felt Carol could imagine every minute of those evenings. She felt Carol's objective, appraising glance over her, and she knew Carol was about to say she did not look particularly cold, or, perhaps, emotionally starved. But Carol was silent, and Therese stared uncomfortably at the list of songs on the little music box in front of her. She remembered someone telling her once she had a passionate mouth, she couldn't remember who.

'Sometimes it takes time,' Carol said. 'Don't you believe in giving people another chance?'

'But – why? It isn't pleasant. And I'm not in love with him.'

'Don't you think you might be, if you got this worked out?'

'Is that the way people fall in love?'

Carol looked up at the deer's head on the wall behind the counter. 'No,' she said, smiling. 'What do you like about Richard?'

'Well, he has – ' But she wasn't sure if it really was sincerity. He wasn't sincere, she felt, about his ambition to be a painter. 'I like his attitude – more than most men's. He does treat me like a person instead of just a girl he can go so far with or not. And I like his family – the fact that he has a family.'

'Lots of people have families.'

Therese tried again. 'He's flexible. He changes. He's not like most men that you can label doctor or – or insurance salesman.'

'I think you know him better than I knew Harge after months of marriage. At least you're not going to make the same mistake I did, to marry because it was the thing to do when you were about twenty, among the people I knew.'

'You mean you weren't in love?'

'Yes, I was, very much. And so was Harge. And he was the kind of man who could wrap your life up in a week and put it in his pocket. Were you ever in love, Therese?'

She waited, until the word from nowhere, false, guilty, moved her lips. 'No.'

'But you'd like to be.' Carol was smiling.

'Is Harge still in love with you?'

Carol looked down at her lap, impatiently, and perhaps she was shocked at her bluntness, Therese thought, but when Carol spoke her voice was the same as before. 'Even I don't know. In a way, he's the same emotionally as he's always been. It's just that now I can see how he really is. He said I was the first woman he'd ever been in love with. I think it's true, but I don't think he was in love with me – in the usual sense of the word – for more than a few months. He's never been interested in anyone else, it's true. Maybe he'd be more human if he were. That I could understand and forgive.'

'Does he like Rindy?'

'Dotes on her.' Carol glanced at her, smiling. 'If he's in love with anyone, it's Rindy.'

'What kind of a name is that?'

'Nerinda. Harge named her. He wanted a son, but I think he's even more pleased with a daughter. I wanted a girl. I wanted two or three children.'

'And – Harge didn't?'

'I didn't.' She looked at Therese again. 'Is this the right conversation for Christmas Eve?' Carol reached for a cigarette, and accepted the one Therese offered her, a Philip Morris.

'I like to know all about you,' Therese said.

'I didn't want any more children, because I was afraid our marriage was going on the rocks anyway, even with Rindy. So you want to fall in love? You probably will soon, and if you do, enjoy it, it's harder later on.'

'To love someone?'

'To fall in love. Or even to have the desire to make love. I think sex flows more sluggishly in all of us than we care to believe, especially men care to believe. The first adventures are usually nothing but a satisfying of curiosity, and after that one keeps repeating the same actions, trying to find – what?'

'What?' Therese asked.

'Is there a word? A friend, a companion, or maybe just a sharer. What good are words? I mean, I think people often try to find through sex things that are much easier to find in other ways.'

What Carol said about curiosity, she knew was true. 'What other ways?' she asked.

Carol gave her a glance. 'I think that's for each person to find out. I wonder if I can get a drink here.'

But the restaurant served only beer and wine, so they left. Carol did not stop anywhere for her drink as they drove back towards New

York. Carol asked her if she wanted to go home or come out to her house for a while, and Therese said to Carol's house. She remembered the Kellys had asked her to drop in on the wine and fruitcake party they were having tonight, and she had promised to, but they wouldn't miss her, she thought.

'What a rotten time I give you,' Carol said suddenly. 'Sunday and now this. I'm not the best company this evening. What would you like to do? Would you like to go to a restaurant in Newark where they have lights and Christmas music tonight? It's not a night-club. We could have a decent dinner there, too.'

'I really don't care about going anywhere – for myself.'

'You've been in that rotten store all day, and we haven't done a thing to celebrate your liberation.'

'I just like to be here with you,' Therese said, and hearing the explanatory tone in her voice, she smiled.

Carol shook her head, not looking at her. 'Child, child, where do you wander – all by yourself?'

Then, a moment later, on the New Jersey highway, Carol said, 'I know what.' And she turned the car into a gravelled section off the road and stopped. 'Come out with me.'

They were in front of a lighted stand piled high with Christmas trees. Carol told her to pick a tree, one not too big and not too small. They put the tree in the back of the car, and Therese sat in front beside Carol with her arms full of holly and fir branches. Therese pressed her face into them and inhaled the dark green sharpness of their smell, their clean spice that was like a wild forest and like all the artifices of Christmas – tree baubles, gifts, snow, Christmas music, holidays. It was being through with the store and being beside Carol now. It was the purr of the car's engine, and the needles of the fir branches that she could touch with her fingers. I am happy, I am happy, Therese thought.

'Let's do the tree now,' Carol said as soon as they entered the house.

Carol turned the radio on in the living room, and fixed a drink for both of them. There were Christmas songs on the radio, bells breaking resonantly, as if they were inside a great church. Carol brought a blanket of white cotton for the snow around the tree, and Therese sprinkled it with sugar so it would glisten. Then she cut an elongated angel out of some gold ribbon and fixed it to the top of the tree, and folded tissue paper and cut a string of angels to thread along the branches.

'You're very good at that,' Carol said, surveying the tree from the hearth. 'It's superb. Everything but presents.'

Carol's present was on the sofa beside Therese's coat. The card she had made for it was at home, however, and she didn't want to give it without the card. Therese looked at the tree. 'What else do we need?'

'Nothing. Do you know what time it is?'

The radio had signed off. Therese saw the mantel clock. It was after one. 'It's Christmas,' she said.

'You'd better stay the night.'

'All right.'

'What do you have to do tomorrow.'

'Nothing.'

Carol got her drink from the radio top. 'Don't you have to see Richard?'

She did have to see Richard, at twelve noon. She was to spend the day at his house. But she could make some kind of excuse. 'No. I said I might see him. It's not important.'

'I can drive you in early.'

'Are you busy tomorrow?'

Carol finished the last inch of her drink. 'Yes,' she said.

Therese began to clean up the mess she had made, the scraps of tissue and snippets of ribbon. She hated cleaning up after making something.

'Your friend Richard sounds like the kind of man who needs a woman around him to work for. Whether he marries her or not,' Carol said. 'Isn't he like that?'

Why talk of Richard now, Therese thought irritably. She felt that Carol liked Richard – which could only be her own fault – and a distant jealousy pricked her, sharp as a pin.

'Actually, I admire that more than the men who live alone or think they live alone, and end by making the stupidest blunders with women.'

Therese stared at Carol's pack of cigarettes on the coffee table. She had absolutely nothing to say on the subject. She could find

Carol's perfume like a fine thread in the stronger smell of evergreen, and she wanted to follow it, to put her arms around Carol.

'It has nothing to do with whether people marry, has it.'

'What?' Therese looked at her and saw her smiling a little.

'Harge is the kind of man who doesn't let a woman enter his life. And on the other hand, your friend Richard might never marry. But the pleasure Richard will get out of thinking he wants to marry.' Carol looked at Therese from head to foot. 'The wrong girls,' she added. 'Do you dance, Therese? Do you like to dance?'

Carol seemed suddenly cool and bitter, and Therese could have wept. 'No,' she said. She should never have told her anything about Richard, Therese thought, but now it was done.

'You're tired. Come on to bed.'

Carol took her to the room that Harge had gone into on Sunday, and turned down the covers of one of the twin beds. It might have been Harge's room, Therese thought. There was certainly nothing about it that suggested a child's room. She thought of Rindy's possessions that Harge had taken from this room, and imagined Harge moving first from the bedroom he shared with Carol, then letting Rindy bring her things into this room, keeping them here, closing himself and Rindy away from Carol.

Carol laid some pyjamas on the foot of the bed. 'Good night, then,' she said at the door. 'Merry Christmas. What do you want for Christmas?'

Therese smiled suddenly. 'Nothing.'

That night she dreamed of birds, long, bright red birds like flamingos, zipping through a black forest and making scallopy patterns, arcs of red that curved like their cries. Then her eyes opened and she heard it really, a soft whistle curving, rising and coming down again with an extra note at the end, and behind it the real, feebler twitter of birds. The window was a bright grey. The whistling began again, just below the window, and Therese got out of bed. There was a long open-topped car in the driveway, and a woman standing in it, whistling. It was like a dream she looked out on, a scene without colour, misty at the edges.

Then she heard Carol's whisper, as clearly as if all three of them were in the same room together. 'Are you going to bed or getting up?'

The woman in the car with her foot on the seat said, just as softly, 'Both,' and Therese heard the tremor of repressed laughter in the word and liked her instantly. 'Go for a ride?' the woman asked. She was looking up at Carol's window with a big smile that Therese had just begun to see.

'You nitwit,' Carol whispered.

'You alone?'

'No.'

'Oh-oh.'

'It's all right. Do you want to come in?'

The woman got out of the car.

Therese went to the door of her room and opened it. Carol was just coming into the hall, tying the belt of her robe.

'Sorry I wakened you,' Carol said. 'Go back to bed.'

'I don't mind. Can I come down?'

'Well, of *course*!' Carol smiled suddenly. 'Get a robe out of the closet.'

Therese got a robe, probably a robe of Harge's, she thought, and went downstairs.

'Who made the Christmas tree?' the woman was asking.

They were in the living room.

'She did.' Carol turned to Therese. 'This is Abby. Abby Gerhard, Therese Belivet.'

'Hello,' Abby said.

'How do you do.' Therese had hoped it was Abby. Abby looked at her now with the same bright, rather pop-eyed expression of amusement that Therese had seen when she stood in the car.

'You made a fine tree,' Abby told her.

'Will everybody stop whispering?' Carol asked.

Abby chafed her hands together and followed Carol into the kitchen. 'Got any coffee, Carol?'

Therese stood by the kitchen table, watching them, feeling at ease because Abby paid no further attention to her, only took off her coat and started helping Carol with the coffee. Her waist and hips looked perfectly cylindrical, without any front or back, under her purple knitted suit. Her hands were a little clumsy, Therese noticed, and her feet had none of the grace of Carol's. She looked older than Carol, and there were two wrinkles across her forehead that cut deep

72

when she laughed, and her strong arched eyebrows rose higher. And she and Carol kept laughing now, while they fixed coffee and squeezed orange juice, talking in short phrases about nothing, or nothing that was important enough to be followed.

Except Abby's sudden, 'Well' – fishing a seed out of the last glass of orange juice and wiping her finger carelessly on her own dress – 'how's old Harge?'

'The same,' Carol said. Carol was looking for something in the refrigerator, and, watching, Therese failed to hear all of what Abby said next, or maybe it was another of the fragmentary sentences that Carol alone understood, but it made Carol straighten up and laugh, suddenly and hard, made her whole face change, and Therese thought with sudden envy, she could not make Carol laugh like that, but Abby could.

'I'm going to tell him that,' Carol said. 'I can't resist.'

It was something about a Boy Scout pocket gadget for Harge.

'And tell him where it came from,' Abby said, looking at Therese and smiling broadly, as if she should share in the joke, too. 'Where're you from?' she asked Therese as they sat down in the table alcove at one side of the kitchen.

'She's from New York,' Carol answered for her, and Therese thought Abby was going to say, why, how unusual, or something silly, but Abby said nothing at all, only looked at Therese with the same expectant smile, as if she awaited the next cue from her.

For all their fussing about breakfast, there was only orange juice and coffee and some unbuttered toast that nobody wanted. Abby lighted a cigarette before she touched anything.

'Are you old enough to smoke?' she asked Therese, offering her a red box that said Craven A's.

Carol put her spoon down. 'Abby, what is this?' she asked with an air of embarrassment that Therese had never seen before.

'Thanks, I'd like one,' Therese said, taking a cigarette.

Abby settled her elbows on the table. 'Well, what's what?' she asked Carol.

'I suspect you're a little tight,' Carol said.

'Driving for hours in the open air? I left New Rochelle at two, got home and found your message, and here I am.'

She probably had all the time in the world, Therese thought, probably did nothing all day except what she felt like doing.

'Well?' Abby said.

'Well – I didn't win the first round,' Carol said.

Abby drew on her cigarette, showing no surprise at all. 'For how long?'

'For three months.'

'Starting when?'

'Starting now. Starting last night, in fact.' Carol glanced at Therese, then looked down at her coffee cup, and Therese knew Carol would not say any more with her sitting there.

'That's not set already, is it?' Abby asked.

'I'm afraid it is,' Carol answered casually, with a shrug in her tone. 'Just verbally, but it'll hold. What're you doing tonight? Late.'

'I'm not doing anything early. Dinner's at two today.'

'Call me some time.'

'Sure.'

Carol kept her eyes down, looking down at the orange-juice glass in her hand, and Therese saw a downward slant of sadness in her mouth now, a sadness not of wisdom but of defeat.

'I'd take a trip,' Abby said. 'Take a little trip away somewhere.' Then Abby looked at Therese, another of the bright, irrelevant, friendly glances, as if to include her in something it was impossible she could be included in, and anyway, Therese had gone stiff with the thought that Carol might take a trip away from her.

'I'm not much in the mood,' Carol said, but Therese heard the play of possibility in it nevertheless.

Abby squirmed a little and looked around her. 'This place is gloomy as a coalpit in the mornings, isn't it?'

Therese smiled a little. A coalpit, with the sun beginning to yellow the window-sill, and the evergreen tree beyond it?

Carol was looking at Abby fondly, lighting one of Abby's cigarettes. How well they must know each other, Therese thought, so well that nothing either of them said or did to the other could ever surprise, ever be misunderstood.

'Was it a good party?' Carol asked.

'Mm,' Abby said indifferently. 'Do you know someone called Bob Haversham?'

'No.'

'He was there tonight. I met him somewhere before in New York. Funnily enough, he said he was going to work for Rattner and Aird in the brokerage department.'

'Really.'

'I didn't tell him I knew one of the bosses.'

'What time is it?' Carol asked after a moment.

Abby looked at her wrist watch, a small watch set in a pyramid of gold panels. 'Seven-thirty. About. Do you care?'

'Want to sleep some more, Therese?'

'No. I'm fine.'

'I'll drive you in whenever you have to go,' Carol said.

But it was Abby who drove her finally, around ten o'clock, because she had nothing else to do, she said, and she would enjoy it.

Abby was another one who liked cold air, Therese thought as they picked up speed on the highway. Who rode in an open-topped car in December?

'Where'd you meet Carol?' Abby yelled at her.

Therese felt she might almost, but not quite, have told Abby the truth. 'In a store,' Therese yelled back.

'Oh?' Abby drove erratically, whipping the big car around curves, putting on speed where one didn't expect it. 'Do you like her?'

'Of course!' What a question! Like asking her if she believed in God.

Therese pointed out her house to Abby when they turned into the street. 'Do you mind doing something for me?' Therese asked. 'Could you wait here a minute? I want to give you something to give to Carol.'

'Sure,' Abby said.

Therese ran upstairs and got the card she had made, and stuck it under the ribbon of Carol's present. She took it back down to Abby. 'You're going to see her tonight, aren't you?'

Abby nodded, slowly, and Therese sensed the ghost of a challenge in Abby's curious black eyes, because she was going to see Carol and Therese wasn't, and what could Therese do about it?

'And thanks for the ride in.'

Abby smiled. 'Sure you don't want me to take you anywhere else?'

'No, thanks,' Therese said, smiling, too, because Abby would certainly have been glad to take her even to Brooklyn Heights.

She climbed her front steps and opened her mailbox. There were two or three letters in it, Christmas cards, one from Frankenberg's. When she looked into the street again, the big cream-coloured car was gone, like a thing she had imagined, like one of the birds in the dream.

CHAPTER EIGHT

'And now you make a wish,' Richard said.

Therese wished it. She wished for Carol.

Richard had his hands on her arms. They were standing under a thing that looked like a beaded crescent, or a section of a starfish, that hung from the hall ceiling. It was ugly, but the Semco family attributed almost magical powers to it, and hung it up on special occasions. Richard's grandfather had brought it from Russia.

'What did you wish?' He smiled down at her possessively. This was his house, and he had just kissed her, though the door was open and the living room filled with people.

'You're not supposed to tell,' Therese said.

'You can tell in Russia.'

'Well, I'm not in Russia.'

The radio roared louder suddenly, voices singing a carol. Therese drank the rest of the pink eggnog in her glass.

'I want to go up to your room,' she said.

Richard took her hand, and they started up the stairs.

'Ri—chard?'

The aunt with the cigarette holder was calling him from the living-room door.

Richard said a word Therese didn't understand, and waved a hand at her. Even on the second floor, the house trembled with the crazy dancing below, the dancing that had nothing to do with the music. Therese heard another glass fall, and pictured the pink foamy eggnog rolling across the floor. This was tame compared to the real Russian Christmases they had used to celebrate in the first week in January, Richard said. Richard smiled at her as he closed the door of his room.

'I like my sweater,' he said.

'I'm glad.' Therese swept her full skirt in an arc and sat on the edge of Richard's bed. The heavy Norwegian sweater she had given Richard was on the bed behind her, lying across its tissued box. Richard had given her a skirt from an East India shop, a long skirt with green and gold bands and embroidery. It was lovely, but Therese did not know where she could ever wear it.

'How about a real shot? That stuff downstairs is sickening.' Richard got his bottle of whisky from his closet floor.

Therese shook her head. 'No, thanks.'

'This'd be good for you.'

She shook her head again. She looked around her at the high-ceilinged, almost square room, at the wallpaper with the barely discernible pattern of pink roses, at the two peaceful windows curtained in slightly yellowed white muslin. From the door, there were two pale trails in the green carpet, one to the bureau and one to the desk in the corner. The pot of brushes and the portfolio on the floor by the desk were the only signs of Richard's painting. Just as painting took up only a corner of his brain, she felt, and she wondered how much longer he would go on with it before he dropped it for something else. And she wondered, as she had often wondered before, if Richard liked her only because she was more sympathetic with his ambitions than anyone else he happened to know now, and because he felt her criticism was a help to him. Therese got up restlessly and went to the window. She loved the room – because it stayed the same and stayed in the same place – yet today she felt an impulse to burst from it. She was a different person from the one who had stood here three weeks ago. This morning she had awakened in Carol's house. Carol was like a secret spreading through her, spreading through this house, too, like a light invisible to everyone but her.

'You're different today,' Richard said, so abruptly that a thrill of peril passed down her body.

'Maybe it's the dress,' she said.

She was wearing a blue taffeta dress that was God knows how old, that she hadn't put on since her first months in New York. She sat down on the bed again, and looked at Richard who stood in the middle of the floor with the little glass of straight whisky in his hand, his clear blue eyes moving from her face to her feet in the new high-heeled black shoes, back to her face again.

'Terry.' Richard took her hands, pinned her hands to the bed on either side of her. The smooth, thin lips, descended on hers, firmly, with the flick of his tongue between her lips and the aromatic smell of fresh whisky. 'Terry, you're an angel,' Richard's deep voice said, and she thought of Carol saying the same thing.

She watched him pick up his little glass from the floor and set it with the bottle into the closet. She felt immensely superior to him suddenly, to all the people below stairs. She was happier than any of them. Happiness was a little like flying, she thought, like being a kite. It depended on how much one let the string out –

'Pretty?' Richard said.

Therese sat up. 'It's a beauty!'

'I finished it last night. I thought if it was a good day, we'd go to the park and fly it.' Richard grinned like a boy, proud of his handiwork. 'Look at the back.'

It was a Russian kite, rectangular and bowed like a shield, its slim frame notched and tied at the corners. On the front, Richard had painted a cathedral with whirling domes and a red sky behind it.

'Let's go fly it now,' Therese said.

They carried the kite downstairs. Then everybody saw them and came into the hall, uncles, aunts and cousins, until the hall was a din and Richard had to hold the kite in the air to protect it. The noise irritated Therese, but Richard loved it.

'Stay for the champagne, Richard!' one of the aunts shouted, one of the aunts with a fat midriff straining like a second bosom under a satin dress.

'Can't,' Richard said, and added something in Russian, and Therese had a feeling she often had, seeing Richard with his family, that there must have been a mistake, that Richard might be an orphan himself, a changeling, left on the doorstep and brought up a son of this family. But there was his brother Stephen standing in the doorway, with Richard's blue eyes, though Stephen was even taller and thinner.

'What roof?' Richard's mother asked shrilly. 'This roof?'

Someone had asked if they were going to fly the kite on the roof, and since the house hadn't a roof one could stand on, Richard's mother had gone off into peals of laughter. Then the dog began to bark.

'I'm going to make you that dress!' Richard's mother called to Therese, wagging her finger admonishingly. 'I know your measurements!'

They had measured her with a tape in the living room, in the midst of all the singing and present opening, and a couple of the men had tried to help, too. Mrs Semco put her arm around Therese's waist, and suddenly Therese embraced her and kissed her firmly on the cheek, her lips sinking into the soft powdered cheek, in that one second pouring out in the kiss, and in the convulsive clasp of her arm, the affection Therese really had for her, that Therese knew would hide itself again as if it did not exist, in the instant she released her.

Then she and Richard were free and alone, walking down the front sidewalk. It wouldn't be any different, if they were married, Therese thought, visiting the family on Christmas Day. Richard would fly his kites even when he was an old man, like his grandfather who had flown kites in Prospect Park until the year he died, Richard had told her.

They took the subway to the park, and walked to the treeless hill where they had come a dozen times before. Therese looked around here. There were some boys playing with a football down on the flat field at the edge of the trees, but otherwise the park looked quiet and still. There was not much wind, not really enough, Richard said, and the sky was densely white as if it carried snow.

Richard groaned, failing again. He was trying to get the kite up by running with it.

Therese, sitting on the ground with her arms around her knees, watched him put his head up and turn in all directions, as if he had lost something in the air. 'Here it is!' She got up, pointing.

'Yes, but it's not steady.'

Richard ran the kite into it anyway, and the kite sagged on its long string, then jerked up as if something had sprung it. It made a big arc, then began to climb in another direction.

'It's found its own wind!' Therese said.

'Yes, but it's slow.'

'What a gloomy Gus! Can I hold it?'

'Wait'll I get it higher.'

Richard pumped at it with long swings of his arms, but the kite stayed at the same place in the cold sluggish air. The golden domes of the cathedral wagged from side to side, as if the whole kite were shaking its head saying no, and the long limp tail followed foolishly, repeating the negation.

'Best we can do,' Richard said. 'It can't carry any more string.'

Therese did not take her eyes from it. Then the kite steadied and stopped, like a picture of a cathedral pasted on the thick white sky. Carol wouldn't like kites probably, Therese thought. Kites wouldn't amuse her. She would glance at one, and say it was silly.

'Want to take it?'

Richard poked the string stick into her hands, and she got to her feet. She thought, Richard had worked on the kite last night when she was with Carol, which was why he hadn't called her, and didn't know she had not been home. If he had called, he would have mentioned it. Soon there would come the first lie.

Suddenly the kite broke its mooring in the sky and tugged sharply to get away. Therese let the stick turn fast in her hands, as long as she dared to under Richard's eyes, because the kite was still low. And now it rested again, stubbornly still.

'Jerk it!' Richard said. 'Keep working it up.'

She did. It was like playing with a long elastic band. But the string was so long and slack now, it was all she could do to stir the kite. She pulled and pulled and pulled. Then Richard came and took it, and Therese let her arms hang. Her breath came harder, and little muscles in her arms were quivering. She sat down on the ground. She hadn't won against the kite. It hadn't done what she wanted it to do.

'Maybe the string's too heavy,' she said. It was a new string, soft and white and fat as a worm.

'String's very light. Look now. Now it's going!'

Now it was climbing in short, upward darts, as if it had found its own mind suddenly, and a will to escape.

'Let out more string!' she shouted.

Therese stood up. A bird flew under the kite. She stared at the rectangle that was growing smaller and smaller, jerking back and back like a ship's billowed sail going backward. She felt the kite meant something, this particular kite, at this minute.

'Richard?'

'What?'

She could see him in the corner of her eye, crouched with his hands out in front of him, as if he rode a surfboard. 'How many times were you in love?' she asked.

Richard laughed, a short, hoarse laugh. 'Never till you.'

'Yes, you were. You told me about two times.'

'If I count those, I might count twelve others, too,' Richard said quickly, with the bluntness of preoccupation.

The kite was starting to take arcing steps downward.

Therese kept her voice on the same level. 'Were you ever in love with a boy?'

'A boy?' Richard repeated, surprised.

'Yes.'

Perhaps five seconds passed before he said, 'No,' in a positive and final tone.

At least he troubled to answer, Therese thought. What would you do if you were, she had an impulse to ask, but the question would hardly serve a purpose. She kept her eyes on the kite. They were both looking at the same kite, but with what different thoughts in their minds. 'Did you ever hear of it?' she asked.

'Hear of it? You mean people like that? Of course.' Richard was standing straight now, winding the string in with figure-of-eight movements of the stick.

Therese said carefully, because he was listening, 'I don't mean people like that. I mean two people who fall in love suddenly with each other, out of the blue. Say two men or two girls.'

Richard's face looked the same as it might have if they had been talking about politics. 'Did I ever know any? No.'

Therese waited until he was working with the kite again, trying to pump it higher. Then she remarked, 'I suppose it could happen, though, to almost anyone, couldn't it?'

He went on, winding the kite. 'But those things don't just happen. There's always some reason for it in the background.'

'Yes,' she said agreeably. Therese had thought back into the background. The nearest she could remember to being 'in love' was the way she had felt about a boy she had seen a few times in the town of Montclair, when she rode in the school bus. He had curly black hair and a handsome, serious face, and he had been perhaps twelve years old, older than she then. She remembered a short time when she had thought of him every day. But that was nothing, nothing like what she felt for Carol. Was it love or wasn't it that she felt for Carol? And how absurd it was that she didn't even know. She had heard about girls falling in love, and she knew what kind of people they were and what they looked like. Neither she nor Carol looked like that. Yet the way she felt about Carol passed all the tests for love and fitted all the descriptions. 'Do you think I could?' Therese asked simply, before she could debate whether she dared to ask.

'What!' Richard smiled. 'Fall in love with a girl? Of course not! My God, you haven't, have you?'

'No,' Therese said, in an odd, inconclusive tone, but Richard did not seem to notice the tone.

'It's going again. Look, Terry!'

The kite was wobbling straight up, faster and faster, and the stick was whirling in Richard's hands. At any rate, Therese thought, she was happier than she had ever been before. And why worry about defining everything?

'Hey!' Richard sprinted after the stick that was leaping crazily around the ground, as if it were trying to leave the earth, too. 'Want to hold it?' he asked, capturing it. 'Practically takes you up!'

Therese took the stick. There was not much string left, and the kite was all but invisible now. When she let her arms go all the way up, she could feel it lifting her a little, delicious and buoyant, as if the kite might really take her up if it got all its strength together.

'Let it out!' Richard shouted, waving his arms. His mouth was open, and two spots of red had come in his cheeks. 'Let it out!'

'There's no more string!'

'I'm going to cut it!'

Therese couldn't believe she had heard it, but glancing over at him, she saw him reaching under his overcoat for his knife. 'Don't,' she said.

Richard came running over, laughing.

'Don't!' she said angrily. 'Are you crazy?' Her hands were tired, but she clung all the harder to the stick.

'Let's cut it! It's more fun!' And Richard bumped into her rudely, because he was looking up.

Therese jerked the stick sideways, out of his reach, speechless with anger and amazement. There was an instant of fear, when she felt Richard might really have lost his mind, and then she staggered backward, the pull gone, the empty stick in her hand. 'You're mad!' she yelled at him. 'You're insane!'

'It's only a kite!' Richard laughed, craning up at the nothingness.

Therese looked in vain, even for the dangling string. 'Why did you do it?' Her voice was shrill with tears. 'It was such a beautiful kite!'

'It's only a kite!' Richard repeated. 'I can make another kite!'

CHAPTER NINE

Therese started to get dressed, then changed her mind. She was still in her robe, reading the script of *Small Rain* that Phil had brought over earlier, and that was now spread all over the couch. Carol had said she was at Forty-eighth and Madison. She could be here in ten minutes. Therese glanced around her room, and at her face in the mirror, and decided to let it all go.

She took some ash-trays to the sink and washed them, and stacked the play script neatly on her work table. She wondered if Carol would have her new handbag with her. Carol had called her last night from some place in New Jersey where she was with Abby, had told her she thought the bag was beautiful but much too grand a present. Therese smiled, remembering Carol's suggesting that she take it back. At least Carol liked it.

The doorbell sounded in three quick rings.

Therese looked down the stairwell, and saw Carol was carrying something. She ran down.

'It's empty. It's for you,' Carol said, smiling.

It was a suitcase, wrapped. Carol slipped her fingers from under the handle and let Therese carry it. Therese put it on the couch in her room, and cut the brown paper off carefully. The suitcase was of thick light brown leather, perfectly plain.

'It's terribly good looking!' Therese said.

'Do you like it? I don't even know if you need a suitcase.'

'Of course, I like it.' This was the kind of suitcase for her, this

exactly and no other. Her initials were on it in small gold letters –
T.M.B. She remembered Carol asking her her middle name on
Christmas Eve.

'Work the combination and see if you like the inside.'

Therese did. 'I like the smell, too,' she said.

'Are you busy? If you are, I'll leave.'

'No. Sit down. I'm not doing anything – except reading a play.'

'What play?'

'A play I have to do sets for.' She realized suddenly she had never
mentioned stage designing to Carol.

'Sets for?'

'Yes – I'm a stage designer.' She took Carol's coat.

Carol smiled astonishedly. 'Why the hell didn't you tell me?' she
asked quietly. 'How many other rabbits are you going to pull out of
your hat?'

'It's the first real job. And it's not a Broadway play. It's going to
be done in the Village. A comedy. I haven't got a union membership
yet. I'll have to wait for a Broadway job for that.'

Carol asked her about the union, the junior and senior member-
ships that cost fifteen hundred and two thousand dollars respectively.
Carol asked her if she had all that money saved up.

'No – just a few hundred. But if I get a job, they'll let me pay it
off in instalments.'

Carol was sitting on the straight chair, the chair Richard often sat
in, watching her, and Therese could read in Carol's expression that
she had risen suddenly in Carol's estimation, and she couldn't
imagine why she hadn't mentioned before that she was a stage
designer, and in fact already had a job. 'Well,' Carol said, 'if a
Broadway job comes out of this, would you consider borrowing the
rest of the money from me? Just as a business loan?'

'Thanks. I – '

'I'd like to do it for you. You shouldn't be bothered paying off
two thousand dollars at your age.'

'Thanks. But I won't be ready for one for another couple of years.'

Carol lifted her head and blew her smoke out in a thin stream.
'Oh, they don't really keep track of apprenticeships, do they?'

Therese smiled. 'No. Of course not. Would you like a drink? I've
got a bottle of rye.'

'How nice. I'd love one, Therese.' Carol got up and peered at her kitchenette shelves as Therese fixed the two drinks. 'Are you a good cook?'

'Yes. I'm better when I have someone to cook for. I can make good omelettes. Do you like them?'

'No,' Carol said flatly, and Therese laughed. 'Why don't you show me some of your work?'

Therese got a portfolio down from the closet. Carol sat on the couch and looked at everything carefully, but from her comments and questions, Therese felt she considered them too bizarre to be usable, and perhaps not very good either. Carol said she liked best the *Petrushka* set on the wall.

'But it's the same thing,' Therese said. 'The same thing as the drawings, only in model form.'

'Well, maybe it's your drawings. They're very positive, anyway. I like that about them.' Carol picked up her drink from the floor and leaned back on the couch. 'You see, I didn't make a mistake, did I.'

'About what?'

'About you.'

Therese did not know exactly what she meant. Carol was smiling at her through her cigarette smoke, and it rattled her. 'Did you think you had?'

'No,' Carol said. 'What do you have to pay for an apartment like this?'

'Fifty a month.'

Carol clicked her tongue. 'Doesn't leave you much out of your salary, does it?'

Therese bent over her portfolio, tying it up. 'No. But I'll be making more soon. I won't be living here for ever either.'

'Of course you won't. You'll travel, too, the way you do in imagination. You'll see a house in Italy you'll fall in love with. Or maybe you'll like France. Or California, or Arizona.'

The girl smiled. She probably wouldn't have the money for it, when that happened. 'Do people always fall in love with things they can't have?'

'Always,' Carol said, smiling, too. She pushed her fingers through her hair. 'I think I shall take a trip after all.'

'For how long?'

'Just a month or so.'

Therese set the portfolio in the closet. 'How soon will you be going?'

'Right away. I suppose as soon as I can arrange everything. And there isn't much to arrange.'

Therese turned around. Carol was rolling the end of her cigarette in the ash-tray. It meant nothing to her, Therese thought, that they wouldn't see each other for a month. 'Why don't you go somewhere with Abby?'

Carol looked up at her, and then at the ceiling. 'I don't think she's free in the first place.'

Therese stared at her. She had touched something, mentioning Abby. But Carol's face was unreadable now.

'You're very nice to let me see you so often,' Carol said. 'You know, I don't feel like seeing the people I generally see just now. One can't, really. Everything's supposed to be done in pairs.'

How frail she is, Therese felt suddenly, how different from the day of the first lunch. Then Carol got up, as if she knew her thoughts, and Therese sensed a flaunt of assurance in her lifted head, in her smile as she passed her so close their arms brushed.

'Why don't we do something tonight?' Therese asked. 'You can stay here if you want to, and I'll finish reading the play. We can spend the evening together.'

Carol didn't answer. She was looking at the flower box in the bookshelf. 'What kind of plants are these?'

'I don't know.'

'You don't know?'

They were all different, a cactus with fat leaves that hadn't grown a bit since she bought it a year ago, another plant like a miniature palm tree, and a droopy red-green thing that had to be supported by a stick. 'Just plants.'

Carol turned around, smiling. 'Just plants,' she repeated.

'What about tonight?'

'All right. But I won't stay. It's only three. I'll give you a ring around six.' Carol dropped her lighter in her handbag. It was not the handbag Therese had given her. 'I feel like looking at furniture this afternoon.'

'Furniture? In stores?'

'In stores or at the Parke-Bernet. Furniture does me good.' Carol reached for her coat on the armchair, and again Therese noticed the long line from her shoulder to the wide leather belt, continued in her leg. It was beautiful, like a chord of music or a whole ballet. She was beautiful, and why should her days be so empty now, Therese wondered, when she was made to live with people who loved her, to walk in a beautiful house, in beautiful cities, along blue sea coasts with a long horizon and a blue sky to background her.

'Bye-bye,' Carol said, and in the same movement with which she put on her coat, she put her arm around Therese's waist. It was only an instant, too disconcerting with Carol's arm suddenly about her, to be relief or end or beginning, before the doorbell rang in their ears like the tearing of a brass wall. Carol smiled. 'Who is it?' she asked.

Therese felt the sting of Carol's thumbnail in her wrist as she released her. 'Richard probably.' It could only be Richard, because she knew his long ring.

'Good. I'd like to meet him.'

Therese pressed the bell, then heard Richard's firm, hopping steps on the stairs. She opened the door.

'Hello,' Richard said. 'I decided – '

'Richard, this is Mrs Aird,' Therese said. 'Richard Semco.'

'How do you do?' Carol said.

Richard nodded, with almost a bow. 'How do you do,' he said, his blue eyes stretched wide.

They stared at each other, Richard with a square box in his hands as if he were about to present it to her, and Carol standing, neither staying nor leaving. Richard put the box on an end table.

'I was so near, I thought I'd come up,' he said, and under its note of explanation Therese heard the unconscious assertion of a right, just as she had seen behind his inquisitive stare a spontaneous mistrust of Carol. 'I had to take a present to a friend of Mamma's. This is *lebkuchen*.' He nodded at the box and smiled, disarmingly. 'Anybody want some now?'

Carol and Therese declined. Carol was watching Richard as he opened the box with his pocketknife. She liked his smile, Therese thought. She likes him, the gangling young man with unruly blond hair, the broad lean shoulders, and the big funny feet in moccasins.

'Please sit down,' Therese said to Carol.

'No, I'm going,' she answered.

'I'll give you half, Terry, then I'll be going too,' he said.

Therese looked at Carol, and Carol smiled at her nervousness and sat down on a corner of the couch.

'Anyway, don't let me rush you off,' Richard said, lifting the paper with the cake in it to a kitchen shelf.

'You're not. You're a painter, aren't you, Richard?'

'Yes.' He popped some loose icing into his mouth, and looked at Carol, poised because he was incapable of being unpoised, Therese thought, his eyes frank because he had nothing to hide. 'Are you a painter, too?'

'No,' Carol said with another smile. 'I'm nothing.'

'The hardest thing to be.'

'Is it? Are you a good painter?'

'I will be. I can be,' said Richard, unperturbed. 'Have you got any beer, Terry? I've got an awful thirst.'

Therese went to the refrigerator and got out the two bottles that were there. Richard asked Carol if she would like some, but Carol refused. Then Richard strolled past the couch, looking at the suitcase and the wrappings, and Therese thought he was going to say something about it, but he didn't.

'I thought we might go to a movie tonight, Terry. I'd like to see that thing at the Victoria. Do you want to?'

'I can't tonight. I've got a date with Mrs Aird.'

'Oh.' Richard looked at Carol.

Carol put out her cigarette and stood up. 'I must be going.' She smiled at Therese. 'Call you back around six. If you change your mind it's not important. Goodbye, Richard.'

'Goodbye,' Richard said.

Carol gave her a wink as she went down the stairs. 'Be a good girl,' Carol said.

'Where'd the suitcase come from?' Richard asked when she came back in the room.

'It's a present.'

'What's the matter, Terry?'

'Nothing's the matter.'

'Did I interrupt anything important? Who is she?'

Therese picked up Carol's empty glass. There was a little lipstick at the rim. 'She's a woman I met at the store.'

'Did she give you that suitcase?'

'Yes.'

'It's quite a present. Is she that rich?'

Therese glanced at him. Richard's aversion to the wealthy, to the bourgeois, was automatic. 'Rich? You mean the mink coat? I don't know. I did her a favour. I found something she lost in the store.'

'Oh?' he said. 'What? You didn't say anything about it.'

She washed and dried Carol's glass and set it back on the shelf. 'She left her billfold on the counter and I took it to her, that's all.'

'Oh. Damned nice reward.' He frowned. 'Terry, what is it? You're not still sore about that silly kite, are you?'

'No, of course not,' she said impatiently. She wished he would go. She put her hands in her robe pockets and walked across the room, stood where Carol had stood, looking at the box of plants. 'Phil brought the play over this morning. I started reading it.'

'Is that what you're worried about?'

'What makes you think I'm worried?' She turned around.

'You're in another of those miles-away moods again.'

'I'm not worried and I'm not miles away.' She took a deep breath. 'It's funny – you're so conscious of some moods and so unconscious of others.'

Richard looked at her. 'All right, Terry,' he said with a shrug, as if he conceded it. He sat down in the straight chair and poured the rest of the beer into his glass. 'What's this date you have with that woman tonight?'

Therese's lips widened in a smile as she ran the end of her lipstick over them. For a moment, she stared at the eyebrow tweezers that lay on the little shelf fixed to the inside of the closet door. Then she put the lipstick down on the shelf. 'It's sort of a cocktail party, I think. Sort of a Christmas benefit thing. In some restaurant, she said.'

'Hmm. Do you want to go?'

'I said I would.'

Richard drank his beer, frowning a little over his glass. 'What about afterwards? Maybe I could hang around here and read the play while you're gone, and then we could grab a bite and go to the movie.'

'Afterwards, I thought I'd better finish the play. I'm supposed to start on Saturday, and I ought to have some ideas in my head.'

Richard stood up. 'Yep,' he said casually, with a sigh.

Therese watched him idle over to the couch and stand there, looking down at the manuscript. Then he bent over, studying the title-page, and the cast pages. He looked at his wrist watch, and then at her.

'Why don't I read it now?' he asked.

'Go ahead,' she answered with a brusqueness that Richard either didn't hear or ignored, because he simply lay back on the couch with the manuscript in his hands and began to read. She picked up a book of matches from the shelf. No, he only recognized the 'miles-away' moods, she thought, when he felt himself deprived of her by distance. And she thought suddenly of the times she had gone to bed with him, of her distance then compared to the closeness that was supposed to be, that everyone talked about. It hadn't mattered to Richard then, she supposed, because of the physical fact they were in bed together. And it crossed her mind now, seeing Richard's complete absorption in his reading, seeing the plump, stiff fingers catch a front lock of his hair between them and pull it straight down towards his nose, as she had seen him do a thousand times before, it occurred to her Richard's attitude was that his place in her life was unassailable, her tie with him permanent and beyond question, because he was the first man she had ever slept with. Therese threw the match cover at the shelf, and a bottle of something fell over.

Richard sat up, smiling a little, surprised. ''S matter, Terry?'

'Richard, I feel like being alone – the rest of the afternoon. Would you mind?'

He got up. The surprise did not leave his face. 'No. Of course not.' He dropped the manuscript on the couch again. 'All right, Terry. It's probably better. Maybe you ought to read this now – read it alone,' he said argumentatively, as if he persuaded himself. He looked at his watch again. 'Maybe I'll go down and try to see Sam and Joan for a while.'

She stood there, not moving, not even thinking of anything except of the few seconds of time to pass until he would be gone, while he brushed his hand once, a little clingy with its moisture, over her hair, and bent to kiss her. Then quite suddenly she remembered the Degas book she had bought days ago, the book of reproductions that Richard wanted and hadn't been able to find anywhere. She got it from the bottom drawer of the bureau. 'I found this. The Degas book.'

'Oh, swell. Thanks.' He took it in both hands. It was still wrapped. 'Where'd you find it?'

'Frankenberg's. Of all places.'

'Frankenberg's.' Richard smiled. 'It's six bucks, isn't it?'

'Oh, that's all right.'

Richard had his wallet out. 'But I asked you to get it for me.'

'Never mind, really.'

Richard protested, but she didn't take the money. And a minute later he was gone, with a promise to call her tomorrow at five. They might do something tomorrow night, he said.

Carol called at ten past six. Did she feel like going to Chinatown, Carol asked. Therese said, of course.

'I'm having cocktails with someone in the St Regis,' Carol said. 'Why don't you pick me up here? It's the little room, not the big one. And listen, we're going on to some theatre thing you've asked me to. Get it?'

'Some sort of Christmas benefit cocktail party?'

Carol laughed. 'Hurry up.'

Therese flew.

Carol's friend was a man called Stanley McVeigh, a tall and very attractive man of about forty with a moustache and a boxer dog on a leash. Carol was ready to go when Therese arrived. Stanley walked out with them, put them into a taxi and gave the driver some money through the window.

'Who's he?' Therese asked.

'An old friend. Seeing more of me now that Harge and I are separating.'

Therese looked at her. Carol had a wonderful little smile in her eyes tonight. 'Do you like him?'

'So-so,' Carol said. 'Driver, will you make that Chinatown instead of the other?'

It began to rain while they were having dinner. Carol said it always rained in Chinatown, every time she had been here. But it didn't matter much, because they ducked from one shop to another, looking at things and buying things. Therese saw some sandals with platform heels that she thought were beautiful, rather more Persian-looking than Chinese, and she wanted to buy them for Carol, but Carol said Rindy wouldn't approve. Rindy was a conservative, and didn't like her even to go without stockings in summer, and Carol conformed to her. The same store had Chinese suits of a black shiny material, with plain trousers and a high-collared jacket, and Carol bought one for Rindy. Therese bought the sandals for Carol, anyway, while Carol was arranging for Rindy's suit to be sent. She knew the right size just by looking at the sandals, and it pleased Carol after all that she bought them. Then they spent a weird hour in a Chinese theatre where people in the audience were sleeping through all the clangour. And finally they went uptown for a late supper in a restaurant where a harp played. It was a glorious evening, a really magnificent evening.

CHAPTER TEN

On Tuesday, the fifth day of work, Therese sat in a little bare room with no ceiling at the back of the Black Cat Theatre, waiting for Mr Donohue, the new director, to come and look at her cardboard model. Yesterday morning, Donohue had replaced Cortes as director, had thrown out her first model, and had also thrown out Phil McElroy as the second brother in the play. Phil had walked out yesterday in a huff. It was lucky she hadn't been thrown out along with her model, Therese thought, so she had followed Mr Donohue's instructions to the letter. The new model hadn't the movable section she had put into the first, which would have permitted the living-room scene to be converted into the terrace scene for the last act. Mr Donohue seemed to be adamant against anything unusual or even simple. By setting the whole play in the living room, a lot of the dialogue had to be changed in the last act, and some of the cleverest lines had been lost. Her new model indicated a fireplace, broad french windows giving on to a terrace, two doors, a sofa and a couple of armchairs and a bookcase. It would look, when finished, like a room in a model house at Sloan's, lifelike down to the last ash-tray.

Therese stood up, stretched herself, and reached for the corduroy jacket that was hanging on a nail on the door. The place was cold as a barn. Mr Donohue probably wouldn't come in until afternoon, or not even today if she didn't remind him again. There was no hurry about the scenery. It might have been the least important matter in

95

the whole production, but she had sat up until late last night, enthusiastically working on the model.

She went out to stand in the wings again. The cast was all on stage with scripts in hand. Mr Donohue kept running the cast through the whole play, to get the flow of it, he said, but today it seemed to be only putting them to sleep. All the cast looked lazy except Tom Harding, a tall blond young man who had the male lead, and he was a little too energetic. Georgia Halloran was suffering with sinus headaches, and had to stop every hour to put drops in her nose and lie down for a few minutes. Geoffrey Andrews, a middle-aged man who played the heroine's father, grumbled constantly between his lines because he didn't like Donohue.

'No, no, no, no,' said Mr Donohue for the tenth time that morning, stopping everything and causing everybody to lower his script and turn to him with a puzzled, irritated docility. 'Let's start again from page twenty-eight.'

Therese watched him waving his arms to indicate the speakers, putting up a hand to silence them, following the script with his head down as if he led an orchestra. Tom Harding winked at her, and pulled his hand down his nose. After a moment, Therese went back to the room behind the partition, where she worked, where she felt a little less useless. She knew the play almost by heart now. It had a rather Sheridanesque comedy of errors plot – two brothers who pretend to be valet and master in order to impress an heiress with whom one of the brothers is in love. The dialogue was witty and altogether not bad, but the dreary, matter-of-fact set that Donohue had ordered for it – Therese hoped something could be done with the colour they would use.

Mr Donohue did come in just after twelve o'clock. He looked at her model, lifted it up and looked at it from below and from both sides, without any change in his nervous, harassed expression. 'Yes, this is fine. I like this very much. You see how much better this is than those empty walls you had before, don't you?'

Therese took a deep breath of relief. 'Yes,' she said.

'A set grows out of the needs of the actors. This isn't a ballet set you're designing, Miss Belivet.'

She nodded, looking at the model, too, and trying to see how it possibly was better, possibly more functional.

96

'The carpenter's coming in this afternoon about four. We'll get together and have a talk about this.' Mr Donohue went out.

Therese stared at the cardboard model. At least she would see it used. At least she and the carpenters would make it something real. She went to the window and looked out at the grey but luminous winter sky, at the backs of some five-storey houses garlanded with fire escapes. In the foreground was a small vacant lot with a runted leafless tree in it, all twisted up like a signpost gone wild. She wished she could call Carol and invite her for lunch. But Carol was an hour and a half away by car.

'Is your name Beliver?'

Therese turned to the girl in the doorway. 'Belivet. Telephone?'

'The phone by the lights.'

'Thanks.' Therese hurried, hoping it was Carol, knowing more likely it was Richard. Carol hadn't yet called her here.

'Hello, this is Abby.'

'Abby?' Therese smiled. 'How'd you know I was here?'

'You told me, remember? I'd like to see you. I'm not far away. Have you had lunch yet?'

They agreed to meet at the Palermo, a restaurant a block or two from the Black Cat.

Therese whistled a song as she walked there, happy as if she were meeting Carol. The restaurant had sawdust on the floor, and a couple of black kittens played around under the rail of the bar. Abby was sitting at a table in the back.

'Hi,' Abby said as she came up. 'You're looking very chipper. I almost didn't recognize you. Would you like a drink?'

Therese shook her head. 'No, thanks.'

'You mean, you're so happy without it?' Abby asked, and she chuckled with that secret amusement that in Abby was somehow not offensive.

Therese took the cigarette that Abby offered her. Abby knew, she thought. And perhaps she was in love with Carol, too. It put Therese on guard with her. It created a tacit rivalry that gave her a curious exhilaration, a sense of certain superiority over Abby – emotions that Therese had never known before, never dared to dream of, emotions consequently revolutionary in themselves. So their lunching together in the restaurant became nearly as important as the meeting with Carol.

'How is Carol?' Therese asked. She had not seen Carol in three days.

'She's very fine,' Abby said, watching her.

The waiter came, and Abby asked him if he could recommend the mussels and the scaloppine.

'Excellent, madame!' He beamed at her as if she were a special customer.

It was Abby's manner, the glow in her face, as if today, or every day, were a special holiday for her. Therese liked that. She looked admiringly at Abby's suit of red and blue weave, her cufflinks that were scrolly G's, like filigree buttons in silver. Abby asked her about her job at the Black Cat. It was tedious to Therese, but Abby seemed impressed. Abby was impressed, Therese thought, because she did nothing herself.

'I know some people in the producing end of the theatre,' Abby said. 'I'll be glad to put in a word for you any time.'

'Thanks.' Therese played with the lid of the grated-cheese bowl in front of her. 'Do you know anyone called Andronich? I think he's from Philadelphia.'

'No,' Abby said.

Mr Donohue had told her to go and see Andronich next week in New York. He was producing a show that would open this spring in Philadelphia, and then on Broadway.

'Try the mussels.' Abby was eating hers with gusto. 'Carol likes these, too.'

'Have you known Carol a long time?'

'Um-hm,' Abby nodded, looking at her with the bright eyes that revealed nothing.

'And you know her husband, too, of course.'

Abby nodded again, silently.

Therese smiled a little. Abby was out to question her, she felt, but not to disclose anything about herself or about Carol.

'How about some wine? Do you like Chianti?' Abby summoned a waiter with a snap of her fingers. 'Bring us a bottle of Chianti, please. A good one. Builds up the blood,' she added to Therese.

Then the main course arrived, and two waiters fussed around the table, uncorking the Chianti, pouring more water and bringing fresh butter. The radio in the corner played a tango – a little cheesebox of a radio with a broken front, but the music might have come from a string orchestra behind them, at Abby's request. No wonder Carol likes her, Therese thought. She complemented Carol's solemnity, she could remind Carol to laugh.

'Did you always live by yourself?' Abby asked.

'Yes. Since I got out of school.' Therese sipped her wine. 'Do you? Or do you live with your family?'

'With my family. But I've got my own half of the house.'

'And do you work?' Therese ventured.

'I've had jobs. Two or three of them. Didn't Carol tell you we had a furniture shop once? We had a shop just outside of Elizabeth on the highway. We bought up antiques or plain second-hand stuff and fixed it up. I never worked so hard in my life.' Abby smiled at her gaily, as if every word might be untrue. 'Then my other job. I'm an entomologist. Not a very good one, but good enough to pull bugs out of Italian lemon crates and things like that. Bahama lilies are full of bugs.'

'So I've heard,' Therese smiled.

'I don't think you believe me.'

'Yes, I do. Do you still work at that?'

'I'm on reserve. Just in time of emergency, I work. Like Easter.'

Therese watched Abby's knife cutting the scaloppine into small bites before she picked any up. 'Do you take trips a lot with Carol?'

'A lot? No, why?' Abby asked.

'I should think you'd be good for her. Because Carol's so serious.' Therese wished she could lead the conversation to the heart of things, but just what the heart of things was, she didn't know. The wine ran slow and warm in her veins, down to her fingertips.

'Not all the time,' Abby corrected, with the laughter under the surface of her voice, as it had been in the first word Therese had heard her say.

The wine in her head promised music or poetry or truth, but she was stranded on the brink. Therese could not think of a single question that would be proper to ask, because all her questions were so enormous.

'How'd you meet Carol?' Abby asked.

'Didn't Carol tell you?'

'She just said she met you at Frankenberg's when you had a job there.'

'Well, that's how,' Therese said, feeling a resentment in her against Abby building up, uncontrollably.

'You just started talking?' Abby asked with a smile, lighting a cigarette.

'I waited on her,' Therese said, and stopped.

And Abby waited, for a precise description of that meeting, Therese knew, but she wouldn't give it to Abby or to anyone else. It belonged to her. Surely Carol hadn't told Abby, she thought, told her the silly story of the Christmas card. It wouldn't be important enough to Carol for Carol to have told her.

'Do you mind telling me who started talking first?'

Therese laughed suddenly. She reached for a cigarette and lighted it, still smiling. No, Carol hadn't told her about the Christmas card, and Abby's question struck her as terribly funny. 'I did,' Therese said.

'You like her a lot, don't you?' Abby asked.

Therese explored it for hostility. It was not hostile, but jealous. 'Yes.'

'Why do you?'

'Why do I? Why do you?'

Abby's eyes still laughed. 'I've known Carol since she was four years old.'

Therese said nothing.

'You're awfully young, aren't you? Are you twenty-one?'

'No. Not quite.'

'You know Carol's got a lot of worries right now, don't you?'

'Yes.'

'And she's lonely now,' Abby added, her eyes watching.

'Do you mean that's why she sees me?' Therese asked calmly. 'Do you want to tell me I shouldn't see her?'

Abby's unblinking eyes blinked twice after all. 'No, not a bit. But I don't want you to get hurt. I don't want you to hurt Carol either.'

'I'd never hurt Carol,' Therese said. 'Do you think I would?'

Abby was still watching her alertly, had never taken her eyes from her. 'No, I don't think you would,' Abby replied as if she had just

100

decided it. And she smiled now as if she were especially pleased about something.

But Therese did not like the smile, and realizing her face showed her feelings, she looked down at the table. There was a glass of hot zabaglione standing on a plate in front of her.

'Would you like to come to a cocktail party this afternoon, Therese? It's uptown at about six o'clock. I don't know if there'll be any stage designers there, but one of the girls who's giving it is an actress.'

Therese put her cigarette out. 'Is Carol going to be there?'

'No. She won't be. But they're all easy to get along with. It's a small party.'

'Thanks. I don't think I should go. I may have to work late today, too.'

'Oh. I was going to give you the address anyway, but if you won't come – '

'No,' Therese said.

Abby wanted to walk around the block after they came out of the restaurant. Therese agreed, though she was tired of Abby now. Abby with her cocksureness, her blunt, careless questions, made Therese feel she had gotten an advantage over her. And Abby had not let her pay the bill.

Abby said, 'Carol thinks a lot of you, you know. She says you have a lot of talent.'

'Does she?' Therese said, only half believing it. 'She never told me.' She wanted to walk faster, but Abby held their pace back.

'You must know she thinks a lot of you, if she wants you to take a trip with her.'

Therese glanced and saw Abby smiling at her, guilelessly. 'She didn't say anything to me about that either,' Therese said quietly, though her heart had begun pumping.

'I'm sure she will. You'll go with her, won't you?'

Why should Abby know about it before she did, Therese wondered. She felt a flush of anger in her face. What was it all about? Did Abby hate her? If she did, why wasn't she consistent about it? Then in the next instant, the rise of anger fell and left her weak, left her vulnerable and defenceless. She thought, if Abby pressed her against the wall at that moment and said: Out with it. What do you want from Carol? How much of her do you want to take from me? she would have babbled it all. She would have said: I want to be with her. I love to be with her, and what has it got to do with you?

'Isn't that for Carol to talk about? Why do you ask me these things?' Therese made an effort to sound indifferent. It was hopeless.

Abby stopped walking. 'I'm sorry,' she said, turning to her. 'I think I understand better now.'

'Understand what?'

'Just – that you win.'

'Win what?'

'What,' Abby echoed with her head up, looking up at the corner of a building, at the sky, and Therese suddenly felt furiously impatient.

She wanted Abby to go so she could telephone Carol. Nothing mattered but the sound of Carol's voice. Nothing mattered but Carol, and why did she let herself forget for a moment?

'No wonder Carol thinks such a lot of you,' Abby said, but if it was a kind remark, Therese did not accept it as such. 'So long, Therese. I'll see you again no doubt.' Abby held out her hand.

Therese took it. 'So long,' she said. She watched Abby walking towards Washington Square, her step quicker now, her curly head high.

Therese went into the drugstore at the next corner and called Carol. She got the maid and then Carol.

'What's the matter?' Carol asked. 'You sound low.'

'Nothing. It's dull at work.'

'Are you doing anything tonight? Would you like to come out?'

Therese came out of the drugstore smiling. Carol was going to pick her up at five-thirty. Carol insisted on picking her up, because it was such a rotten trip by train.

Across the street, walking away from her, she saw Dannie Mc-Elroy, striding along without a coat, carrying a naked bottle of milk in his hand.

'Dannie!' she called.

Dannie turned and walked towards her. 'Come by for a few minutes?' he yelled.

Therese started to say no, then, as he came up to her, she took his arm. 'Just for a minute. I've had a long lunch hour already.'

Dannie smiled down at her. 'What time is it? I've been studying till I'm blind.'

'After two.' She felt Dannie's arm tensed hard against the cold. There were goosepimples under the dark hair on his forearm. 'You're mad to go out without a coat,' she said.

'It clears my head.' He held the iron gate for her that led to his door. 'Phil's out somewhere.'

The room smelled of pipe smoke, rather like hot chocolate cooking. The apartment was a semi-basement, generally darkish, and the lamp made a warm pool of light on the desk that was always cluttered. Therese looked down at the opened books on his desk, the pages and pages covered with symbols that she could not understand, but that she liked to look at. Everything the symbols stood for was true and proven. The symbols were stronger and more definite than words. She felt Dannie's mind swung on them, from one fact to another, as if he bore himself on strong chains, hand over hand through space. She watched him assembling a sandwich, standing at the kitchen table. His shoulders looked very broad and rounded with muscle under his white shirt, shifting a little with the motions of laying the salami and cheese slices on to the big piece of rye bread.

'I wish you'd come by more often, Therese. Wednesday's the only day I'm not home at noon. We wouldn't bother Phil, having lunch, even if he's sleeping.'

'I will,' Therese said. She sat down in his desk chair that was half turned around. She had come once for lunch, and once after work. She liked visiting Dannie. One did not have to make small talk with him.

In the corner of the room, Phil's sofa-bed was unmade, a tangle of blankets and sheets. The two times she had come in before, the bed had been unmade, or Phil had still been in it. The long bookcase pulled out at right angles to the sofa made a unit of Phil's corner of the room, and it was always in disorder, in a frustrated and nervous disorder not at all like the working disorder of Dannie's desk.

Dannie's beer can hissed as he opened it. He leaned against the wall with the beer and the sandwich, smiling, delighted to have her here. 'Remember what you said about physics not applying to people?'

'Umm. Vaguely.'

'Well, I'm not sure you're right,' he said as he took a bite. 'Take friendships, for instance. I can think of a lot of cases where the two people have nothing in common. I think there's a definite reason for every friendship just as there's a reason why certain atoms unite and others don't – certain missing factors in one, or certain present factors in the other – what do you think? I think friendships are the result of certain needs that can be completely hidden from both people, sometimes hidden forever.'

'Maybe. I can think of a few cases, too.' Richard and herself, for one. Richard got on with people, elbowed his way through the world in a way she couldn't. She had always been attracted to people with Richard's kind of self-assurance. 'And what's weak about you, Dannie?'

'Me?' he said, smiling. 'Do you want to be my friend?'

'Yes. But you're about the strongest person I know.'

'Really? Shall I enumerate my shortcomings?'

She smiled, looking at him. A young man of twenty-five who had known where he was going since he was fourteen. He had driven all his energy into one channel – just the opposite of what Richard had done.

'I have a secret and very buried need for a cook,' Dannie said, 'and a dancing teacher, and someone to remind me to do little things like take my laundry and get haircuts.'

'I can't remember to take my laundry either.'

'Oh,' he said sadly. 'Then it's out. And I'd had some hope. I'd had a little feeling of destiny. Because, you see, what I mean about affinities is true from friendships down to even the accidental glance at someone on the street – there's always a definite reason somewhere. I think even the poets would agree with me.'

She smiled. '*Even* the poets?' She thought of Carol, and then of Abby, of their conversation at lunch that had been so much more than a glance and so much less, and the sequence of emotions it had evoked in her. It depressed her. 'But you have to make allowances for people's perversities, things that don't make much sense.'

'Perversities? That's only a subterfuge. A word used by the poets.'

'I thought it was used by the psychologists,' Therese said.

'I mean, to make allowances – that's a meaningless term. Life is an exact science on its own terms, it's just a matter of finding them and defining them. What doesn't make any sense to you?'

'Nothing. I was thinking of something that doesn't matter anyway.' She was suddenly angry again, as she had been on the sidewalk after the lunch.

'What?' he persisted, frowning.

'Like the lunch I just had,' she said.

'With whom?'

'It doesn't matter. If it did, I'd go into it. It's just a waste, like losing something, I thought. But maybe something that didn't exist anyway.' She had wanted to like Abby because Carol did.

'Except in your mind? That can still be a loss.'

'Yes – but there are some people or some things people do that you can't salvage anything from finally, because nothing connects with you.' It was of something else she wanted to talk about, though, not this at all. Not Abby or Carol, but before. Something that made perfect connection and perfect sense. She loved Carol. She leaned her forehead against her hand.

Dannie looked at her for a moment, then pushed himself off from the wall. He turned to the stove, and got a match from his shirt pocket, and Therese sensed that the conversation dangled, would always dangle and never be finished, whatever they went on to say. But she felt if she told Dannie every word that she and Abby had exchanged, he could clear away its subterfuges with a phrase, as if he sprinkled a chemical in the air that would dry up the mist instantly. Or was there always something that logic couldn't touch? Something illogical, behind the jealousy, the suspicion and the hostility in Abby's conversation, that was Abby all by herself?

'Everything's not as simple as a lot of combinations,' Therese added.

'Some things don't react. But everything's alive.' He turned around with a broad smile, as if quite another train of thought had entered his head. He was holding up the match, which was still smoking. 'Like this match. And I'm not talking physics, about the indestructibility of smoke. In fact, I feel rather poetic today.'

'About the match?'

'I feel as if it were growing, like a plant, not disappearing. I feel everything in the world must have the texture of a plant sometimes to a poet. Even this table, like my own flesh.' He touched the table edge with his palm. 'It's like a feeling I had once riding up a hill on a horse. It was in Pennsylvania. I didn't know how to ride very well then, and I remember the horse turning his head and seeing the hill, and deciding by himself to run up it, his hind legs sank before we took off, and suddenly we were going like blazes and I wasn't afraid at all. I felt completely in harmony with the horse and the land, as if we were a whole tree simply being stirred by the wind in its branches. I remember being sure that nothing would happen to me then, but some other time, yes, eventually. And it made me very happy. I thought of all the people who are afraid and hoard things, and themselves, and I thought, when everybody in the world comes to realize what I felt going up the hill, then there'll be a kind of right economy of living and of using and using up. Do you know what I mean?' Dannie had clenched his fist, but his eyes were bright as if he still laughed at himself. 'Did you ever wear out a sweater you particularly liked, and throw it away finally?'

She thought of the green woollen gloves of Sister Alicia, which she had neither worn nor thrown away. 'Yes,' she said.

'Well, that's all I mean. And the lambs who didn't realize how much wool they were losing when somebody sheared them to make the sweater, because they could grow more wool. It's very simple.' He turned to the coffeepot he had reheated, which was already boiling.

'Yes.' She knew. And like Richard and the kite, because he could make another kite. She thought of Abby with a sense of vacuity suddenly, as if the luncheon had been eradicated. For an instant, she felt as if her mind had overflowed a brim and was swimming emptily into space. She stood up.

Dannie came towards her, put his hands on her shoulders, and though she felt it was only a gesture, a gesture instead of a word, the spell was broken. She was uneasy at his touch, and the uneasiness was a point of concreteness. 'I should go back,' she said. 'I'm way late.'

His hands came down, pinning her elbows hard against her sides, and he kissed her suddenly, held his lips hard against hers for a moment, and she felt his warm breath on her upper lip before he released her.

'You are,' he said, looking at her.

'Why did you – ' She stopped, because the kiss had so mingled tenderness and roughness, she didn't know how to take it.

'*Why*, Terry?' he said, turning away from her, smiling. 'Did you mind?'

'No,' she said.

'Would Richard mind?'

'I suppose.' She buttoned her coat. 'I must go,' she said, moving towards the door.

Dannie swung the door open for her, smiling his easy smile, as if nothing had happened. 'Come back tomorrow? Come for lunch.'

She shook her head. 'I don't think so. I'm busy this week.'

'All right, come – next Monday, maybe?'

'All right.' She smiled, too, and put her hand out automatically and Dannie shook it once, politely.

She ran the two blocks to the Black Cat. A little like the horse, she thought. But not enough, not enough to be perfect, and what Dannie meant was perfect.

CHAPTER ELEVEN

'The pastimes of idle people,' Carol said, stretching her legs out before her on the swing seat. 'It's time Abby got herself a job again.'

Therese said nothing. She hadn't told Carol all the conversation at lunch, but she didn't want to talk about Abby any more.

'Don't you want to sit in a more comfortable chair?'

'No,' Therese said. She was sitting on a leather stool near the swing seat. They had finished dinner a few moments ago, and then come up to this room that Therese had not seen before, a glass-enclosed porch off the plain green room.

'What else did Abby say that bothers you?' Carol asked, still looking straight before her, down her long legs in the navy blue slacks.

Carol seemed tired. She was worried about other things, Therese thought, more important things than this. 'Nothing. Does it bother you, Carol?'

'Bother me?'

'You're different with me tonight.'

Carol glanced at her. 'You imagine,' she said, and the pleasant vibration of her voice faded into silence again.

The page she had written last night, Therese thought, had nothing to do with this Carol, was not addressed to her. *I feel I am in love with you*, she had written, *and it should be spring. I want the sun throbbing on my head like chords of music. I think of a sun like*

Beethoven, a wind like Debussy, and bird-calls like Stravinsky. But the tempo is all mine.

'I don't think Abby likes me,' Therese remarked. 'I don't think she wants me to see you.'

'That's not true. You're imagining again.'

'I don't mean she said it.' Therese tried to sound as calm as Carol. 'She was very nice. She invited me to a cocktail party.'

'Whose party?'

'I don't know. She said uptown. She said you wouldn't be there, so I didn't particularly want to go.'

'Where uptown?'

'She didn't say. Just that one of the girls giving it was an actress.'

Carol set her lighter down with a click on the glass table, and Therese sensed her displeasure. 'She did,' Carol murmured, half to herself. 'Sit over here, Therese.'

Therese got up, and sat down at the very foot of the swing seat.

'You mustn't think Abby feels that way about you. I know her well enough to know she wouldn't.'

'All right,' Therese said.

'But Abby's incredibly clumsy sometimes in the way she talks.'

Therese wanted to forget the whole thing. Carol was still so distant even when she spoke, even when she looked at her. A bar of light from the green room lay across the top of Carol's head, but she could not see Carol's face now.

Carol poked her with the back of her toe. 'Hop up.'

But Therese was slow to move, and Carol swung her feet over Therese's head and sat up. Then Therese heard the maid's step in the next room, and the plump, Irish-looking maid in the grey and white uniform came in bearing a coffee tray, shaking the porch floor with her quick, eager little steps that sounded so eager to please.

'The cream's in here, ma'am,' she said, pointing to a pitcher that didn't match the demitasse set. Florence glanced at Therese with a friendly smile and round blank eyes. She was about fifty, with a bun at the back of her neck under the starched white band of her cap. Therese could not establish her somehow, could not determine her allegiance. Therese had heard her refer to Mr Aird twice as if she were very devoted to him, and whether it was professional or genuine, Therese did not know.

'Will there be anything else, ma'am?' Florence asked. 'Shall I put out the lights?'

'No, I like the lights. We won't need anything else, thanks. Did Mrs Riordan call?'

'Not yet, ma'am.'

'Will you tell her I'm out when she does?'

'Yes, ma'am.' Florence hesitated. 'I was wondering if you were finished with that new book, ma'am. The one about the Alps.'

'Go in my room and get it, if you'd like it, Florence. I don't think I want to finish it.'

'Thank you, ma'am. Good night, ma'am. Good night, miss.'

'Good night,' Carol said.

While Carol was pouring the coffee, Therese asked, 'Have you decided how soon you're going away?'

'Maybe in about a week.' Carol handed her the demitasse with cream in it. 'Why?'

'Just that I'll miss you. Of course.'

Carol was motionless for a moment, and then she reached for a cigarette, a last one, and crumpled the pack up. 'I was thinking, in fact, you might like to go with me. What do you think, for three weeks or so?'

There it was, Therese thought, as casual as if she suggested their taking a walk together. 'You mentioned it to Abby, didn't you?'

'Yes,' Carol said. 'Why?'

Why? Therese could not put into words why it hurt her that Carol had. 'It just seems strange you'd tell her before you said anything to me.'

'I didn't tell her. I only said I might ask you.' Carol came over to her and put her hands on Therese's shoulders. 'Look, there's no reason for you to feel like this about Abby – unless Abby said a lot else to you at lunch that you didn't tell me.'

'No,' Therese said. No, but it was the undercurrents, it was worse. She felt Carol's hands leave her shoulders.

'Abby's a very old friend of mine,' Carol said. 'I talk over everything with her.'

'Yes,' Therese said.

'Well, do you think you'd like to go?'

Carol had turned away from her, and suddenly it meant nothing, because of the way Carol asked her, as if she didn't really care one way or the other if she went. 'Thanks – I don't think I can afford it just now.'

'You wouldn't need much money. We'd go in the car. But if you have a job offered you right away, that's different.'

As if she wouldn't turn down a job on a ballet set to go away with Carol – to go with her through country she had never seen before, over rivers and mountains, not knowing where they would be when night came. Carol knew that, and knew she would have to refuse if Carol asked her in this way. Therese felt suddenly sure that Carol taunted her, and she resented it with the bitter resentment of a betrayal. And the resentment resolved itself into a decision never to see Carol again. She glanced at Carol, who was waiting for her answer, with that defiance only half masked by an air of indifference, an expression that Therese knew would not change at all if she should give a negative answer. Therese got up and went to the box on the end table for a cigarette. There was nothing in the box but some phonograph needles and a photograph.

'What is it?' Carol asked, watching her.

Therese felt Carol had been reading all her thoughts. 'It's a picture of Rindy,' Therese said.

'Of Rindy? Let's see it.'

Therese watched Carol's face as she looked at the picture of the little girl with the white-blonde hair and the serious face, with the taped white bandage on her knee. In the picture, Harge was standing in a rowing boat, and Rindy was stepping from a dock into his arms.

'It's not a very good picture,' Carol said, but her face had changed, grown softer. 'That's about three years old. Would you like a cigarette? There's some over here. Rindy's going to stay with Harge for the next three months.'

Therese had supposed that from the conversation in the kitchen that morning with Abby. 'Is that in New Jersey, too?'

'Yes. Harge's family lives in New Jersey. They've a big house.' Carol waited. 'The divorce will come through in a month, I think, and after March, I'll have Rindy the rest of the year.'

'Oh. But you'll see her again before March, won't you?'

'A few times. Probably not much.'

Therese looked at Carol's hand holding the photograph, beside her on the swing seat, carelessly. 'Won't she miss you?'

'Yes, but she's very fond of her father, too.'

'Fonder than she is of you?'

'No. Not really. But he's bought her a goat to play with now. He takes her to school on his way to work, and he picks her up at four. Neglects his business for her – and what more can you ask of a man?'

'You didn't see her Christmas, did you?' Therese said.

'No. Because of something that happened in the lawyer's office. That was the afternoon Harge's lawyer wanted to see us both, and Harge had brought Rindy, too. Rindy said she wanted to go to Harge's house for Christmas. Rindy didn't know I wasn't going to be there this year. They have a big tree that grows on the lawn and they always decorate it, so Rindy was set on it. Anyway, it made quite an impression on the lawyer, you know, the child asking to go home for Christmas with her father. And naturally I didn't want to tell Rindy then I wasn't going, or she'd have been disappointed. I couldn't have said it anyway, in front of the lawyer. Harge's machinations are enough.'

Therese stood there, crushing the unlighted cigarette in her fingers. Carol's voice was calm, as it might have been if she talked to Abby, Therese thought. Carol had never said so much to her before. 'But the lawyer understood?'

Carol shrugged. 'It's Harge's lawyer, not mine. So I agreed to the three-month arrangement now, because I don't want her to be tossed back and forth. If I'm to have her nine months and Harge three – it might as well start now.'

'You won't even visit her?'

Carol waited so long to answer, Therese thought she was not going to. 'Not very often. The family isn't too cordial. I talk to Rindy every day on the telephone. Sometimes she calls me.'

'Why isn't the family cordial?'

'They never cared for me. They've been complaining ever since Harge met me at some deb party. They're very good at criticizing. I sometimes wonder just who would pass with them.'

'What do they criticize you for?'

'For having a furniture shop, for instance. But that didn't last a year. Then for not playing bridge, or not liking to. They pick out the funny things, the most superficial things.'

'They sound horrid.'

'They're not horrid. One's just supposed to conform. I know what they'd like, they'd like a blank they could fill in. A person already filled in disturbs them terribly. Shall we play some music? Don't you ever like the radio?'

'Sometimes.'

Carol leaned against the window-sill. 'And now Rindy's got television every day. Hopalong Cassidy. How she'd love to go out West. That's the last doll I'll ever buy for her, Therese. I only got it because she said she wanted one, but she's outgrown them.'

Behind Carol, an airport searchlight made a pale sweep in the night, and disappeared. Carol's voice seemed to linger in the darkness. In its richer, happier tone, Therese could hear the depths within her where she loved Rindy, deeper than she would probably ever love anyone else. 'Harge doesn't make it easy for you to see her, does he?'

'You know that,' Carol said.

'I don't see how he could be so much in love with you.'

'It's not love. It's a compulsion. I think he wants to control me. I suppose if I were a lot wilder but never had an opinion on anything except his opinion – Can you follow all this?'

'Yes.'

'I've never done anything to embarrass him socially, and that's all he cares about really. There's a certain woman at the club I wish he'd married. Her life is entirely filled with giving exquisite little dinner parties and being carried out of the best bars feet first – She's made her husband's advertising business a great success, so he smiles on her little faults. Harge wouldn't smile, but he'd have some definite reason for complaint. I think he picked me out like a rug for his living room, and he made a bad mistake. I doubt if he's capable of loving anyone, really. What he has is a kind of acquisitiveness, which isn't much separate from his ambition. It's getting to be a disease, isn't it, not being able to love?' She looked at Therese. 'Maybe it's the times. If one wanted to, one could make out a case for racial suicide. Man trying to catch up with his own destructive machines.'

Therese said nothing. It reminded her of a thousand conversations with Richard, Richard mingling war and big business and Congressional witch-hunts and finally certain people he knew into one grand enemy, whose only collective label was hate. Now Carol, too. It shook Therese in the profoundest part of her where no words were, no easy words like death or dying or killing. Those words were somehow future, and this was present. An inarticulate anxiety, a desire to *know*, know anything, for certain, had jammed itself in her throat so for a moment she felt she could hardly breathe. Do you think, do you think, it began. Do you think both of us will die violently someday, be suddenly shut off? But even that question wasn't definite enough. Perhaps it was a statement after all: I don't want to die yet without knowing you. Do you feel the same way, Carol? She could have uttered the last question, but she could not have said all that went before it.

'You're the young generation,' Carol said. 'And what have you got to say?' She sat down on the swing seat.

'I suppose the first thing is not to be afraid.' Therese turned and saw Carol's smile. 'You're smiling because you think I am afraid, I suppose.'

'You're about as weak as this match.' Carol held it burning for a moment after she lighted her cigarette. 'But given the right conditions, you could burn a house down, couldn't you?'

'Or a city.'

'But you're even afraid to take a little trip with me. You're afraid because you think you haven't got enough money.'

'That's not it.'

'You've got some very strange values, Therese. I asked you to go with me, because it would give me pleasure to have you. I should think it'd be good for you, too, and good for your work. But you've got to spoil it by a silly pride about money. Like that handbag you gave me. Out of all proportion. Why don't you take it back, if you need the money? I don't need the handbag. It gave you pleasure to give it to me, I suppose. It's the same thing, you see. Only I make sense and you don't.' Carol walked by her and turned to her again, poised with one foot forward and her head up, the short blonde hair as unobtrusive as a statue's hair. 'Well, do you think it's funny?'

Therese was smiling. 'I don't care about the money,' she said quietly

'What do you mean?'

'Just that,' Therese said. 'I've got the money to go. I'll go.'

Carol stared at her. Therese saw the sullenness leave her face, and then Carol began to smile, too, with surprise, a little incredulously.

'Well, all right,' Carol said. 'I'm delighted.'

'I'm delighted.'

'What brought this happy change about?'

Doesn't she really know, Therese thought. 'You do seem to care whether I go or not,' Therese said simply.

'Of course I care. I asked you, didn't I?' Carol said, still smiling, but with a twist of her toe she turned her back on Therese and walked towards the green room.

Therese watched her go, her hands in her pockets and her moccasins making light slow clicks on the floor. Therese looked at the empty doorway. Carol would have walked out exactly the same way, she thought, if she had said no, she wouldn't go. She picked up her half-finished demitasse, then set it down again.

She went out and across the hall, to the door of Carol's room. 'What are you doing?'

Carol was bending over her dressing table, writing. 'What am I doing?' She stood up and slipped a piece of paper into her pocket. She was smiling now, really smiling in her eyes, like the moment in the kitchen with Abby. 'Something,' Carol said. 'Let's have some music.'

'Fine.' A smile spread over her face.

'Why don't you get ready for bed first? It's late, do you know that?'

'It always gets late with you.'

'Is that a compliment?'

'I don't feel like going to bed tonight.'

Carol crossed the hall to the green room. 'You get ready. You've got circles under your eyes.'

Therese undressed quickly in the room with the twin beds. The phonograph in the other room played 'Embraceable You'. Then the telephone rang. Therese opened the top drawer of the bureau. It was empty except for a couple of men's handkerchiefs, an old clothes brush and a key. And a few papers in the corner. Therese picked up a card covered in isinglass. It was an old driver's licence belonging to Harge. Hargess Foster Aird. Age: 37. Height: 5'8½". Weight: 168. Hair: blond. Eyes: blue. She knew all that. A 1950 Oldsmobile. Colour: dark blue. Therese put it back and closed the drawer. She went to the door and listened.

'I am sorry, Tessie, but I did get stuck after all,' Carol was saying regretfully, but her voice was happy. 'Is it a good party? . . . Well, I'm not dressed and I'm tired.'

Therese went to the bed table and got a cigarette from the box there. A Philip Morris. Carol had put them there, not the maid, Therese knew, because Carol remembered that she liked them. Naked now, Therese stood listening to the music. It was a song she didn't know.

Was Carol on the telephone again?

'Well, I don't like it,' she heard Carol say, half angry, half joking, 'one damn bit.'

. . . it's easy to live . . . when you're in love . . .

'How do I know what kind of people they are? . . . Oh-ho! Is that so?'

Abby, Therese knew. She blew her smoke out and snuffled at the slightly sweet-smelling wisps of it, remembering the first cigarette she had ever smoked, a Philip Morris, on the roof of a dormitory at the Home, four of them passing it around.

'Yes, we're going,' Carol said emphatically. 'Well, I am. Don't I sound it?'

. . . For you . . . maybe I'm a fool but it's fun . . . People say you rule me with one . . . wave of your hand . . . darling, it's grand . . . they just don't understand . . .

It was a good song. Therese closed her eyes and leaned on the half-open door, listening. Behind the voice was a slow piano that rippled all over the keyboard. And a lazy trumpet.

Carol said, 'That's nobody's business but mine, is it? . . . Nonsense!' and Therese smiled at her vehemence.

Therese closed the door. The phonograph had dropped another record.

'Why don't you come say hello to Abby?' Carol said.

Therese had ducked behind the bathroom door because she was naked. 'Why?'

'Come along,' Carol said, and Therese put on a robe and went.

'Hello,' Abby said. 'I hear you're going.'

'Is that news to you?'

Abby sounded silly, as if she wanted to talk all night. She wished Therese a pleasant trip, and told her about the roads in the corn belt, how bad they could be in winter.

'Will you forgive me if I was rude today?' Abby said for the second time. 'I like you OK, Therese.'

'Cut it, cut it!' Carol called down.

'She wants to talk to you again,' Therese said.

'Tell Abigail I'm in the tub.'

Therese told her, and got away.

Carol had brought a bottle and two little glasses into the room.

'What's the matter with Abby?' Therese asked.

'What do you mean, what's the matter with her?' Carol poured a brown-coloured liquor into the two glasses. 'I think she's had a couple tonight.'

'I know. But why did she want to have lunch with me?'

'Well – I guess a lot of reasons. Try some of this stuff.'

'It just seems vague,' Therese said.

'What does?'

'The whole lunch.'

Carol gave her a glass. 'Some things are always vague, darling.'

It was the first time Carol had called her darling. 'What things?' Therese asked. She wanted an answer, a definite answer.

Carol sighed. 'A lot of things. The most important things. Taste your drink.'

Therese sipped it, sweet and dark brown, like coffee, with the sting of alcohol. 'Tastes good.'

'You would think so.'

'Why do you drink it if you don't like it?'

'Because it's different. This is to our trip, so it's got to be something different.' Carol grimaced and drank the rest of her glass.

In the light of the lamp, Therese could see all the freckles on half of Carol's face. Carol's white-looking eyebrow bent like a wing around the curve of her forehead. Therese felt ecstatically happy all at once. 'What's that song that was playing before, the one with just the voice and the piano?'

'Hum it.'

She whistled part of it, and Carol smiled.

'"Easy Living",' Carol said. 'That's an old one.'

'I'd like to hear it again.'

'I'd like you to get to bed. I'll play it again.'

Carol went into the green room, and stayed there while it played. Therese stood by the door of her room, listening, smiling.

... I'll never regret ... the years I'm giving ... They're easy to give, when you're in love ... I'm happy to do whatever I do for you ...

That was her song. That was everything she felt about Carol. She went in the bathroom before it was over, and turned the water on in the tub, got in and let the greenish-looking water tumble about her feet.

'Hey!' Carol called. 'Have you ever been to Wyoming?'

'No.'

'It's time you saw America.'

Therese lifted the dripping rag and pressed it against her knee. The water was so high now, her breasts looked like flat things floating on the surface. She studied them, trying to decide what they looked like besides what they were.

'Don't go to sleep in there,' Carol called in a preoccupied voice, and Therese knew she was sitting on the bed, looking at a map.

'I won't.'

'Well, some people do.'

'Tell me more about Harge,' she said as she dried herself. 'What does he do?'

'A lot of things.'

'I mean, what's his business?'

'Real-estate investment.'

'What's he like? Does he like to go to the theatre? Does he like people?'

'He likes a little group of people who play golf,' Carol said with finality. Then in a louder voice, 'And what else? He's very very meticulous about everything. But he forgot his best razor. It's in the medicine cabinet and you can see it if you want to and you probably do. I've got to mail it to him, I suppose.'

Therese opened the medicine cabinet. She saw the razor. The medicine cabinet was still full of men's things, after-shave lotions and lather brushes. 'Was this his room?' she asked as she came out of the bathroom. 'Which bed did he sleep in?'

Carol smiled. 'Not yours.'

'Can I have some more of this?' Therese asked, looking at the liqueur bottle.

'Of course.'

'Can I kiss you goodnight?'

Carol was folding the road map, pursing her lips as if she would whistle, waiting. 'No,' she said.

'Why not?' Anything seemed possible tonight.

'I'll give you this instead.' Carol pulled her hand out of her pocket.

It was a cheque. Therese read the sum, two hundred dollars, made out to her. 'What's this for?'

'For the trip. I don't want you to spend the money you'll need for that union membership thing.' Carol took a cigarette. 'You won't need all of that, I just want you to have it.'

'But I don't need it,' Therese said. 'Thanks. I don't care if I spend the union money.'

'No backtalk,' Carol interrupted her. 'It gives me pleasure, remember?'

'But I won't take it.' She sounded curt, so she smiled a little as she put the cheque down on the table top by the liqueur bottle. But she had thumped the cheque down, too. She wished she could explain it to Carol. It didn't matter at all, the money, but since it did give Carol pleasure, she hated not to take it. 'I don't like the idea,' Therese said. 'Think of something else.' She looked at Carol. Carol was watching her, was not going to argue with her, Therese was glad to see.

'To give me pleasure?' Carol asked.

Therese's smile broadened. 'Yes,' she said, and picked up the little glass.

'All right,' Carol said. 'I'll think. Good night.' Carol had stopped by the door.

It was a funny way of saying good night, Therese thought, on such an important night. 'Good night,' Therese answered.

She turned to the table and saw the cheque again. But it was for Carol to tear up. She slid it under the edge of the dark blue linen table runner, out of sight.

II

CHAPTER TWELVE

January.

It was all things. And it was one thing, like a solid door. Its cold sealed the city in a grey capsule. January was moments, and January was a year. January rained the moments down, and froze them in her memory: the woman she saw peering anxiously by the light of a match at the names in a dark doorway, the man who scribbled a message and handed it to his friend before they parted on the sidewalk, the man who ran a block for a bus and caught it. Every human action seemed to yield a magic. January was a two-faced month, jangling like jester's bells, crackling like snow crust, pure as any beginning, grim as an old man, mysteriously familiar yet unknown, like a word one can almost but not quite define.

A young man named Red Malone and a bald-headed carpenter worked with her on the *Small Rain* set. Mr Donohue was very pleased with it. He said he had asked a Mr Baltin to come in and see her work. Mr Baltin was a graduate of a Russian academy, and had designed a few sets for theatres in New York. Therese had never heard of him. She tried to get Mr Donohue to arrange an appointment for her to see Myron Blanchard or Ivor Harkevy, but Mr Donohue never promised anything. He couldn't, Therese supposed.

Mr Baltin came in one afternoon, a tall, bent man in a black hat and a seedy overcoat, and looked intently at the work she showed him. She had brought only three or four models down to the theatre, her very best ones. Mr Baltin told her of a play that was to start in production in about six weeks. He would be glad to recommend her as an assistant, and Therese said that would work out very well, because she would be out of town until then, anyway. Everything was working out very well in these last days. Mr Andronich had promised her a two-week job in Philadelphia in the middle of February, which would be just about the time she would be back from the trip with Carol. Therese wrote down the name and address of the man Mr Baltin knew.

'He's looking for someone now, so call him the first of the week,' Mr Baltin said. 'It'll just be a helper's job, but his former helper, a pupil of mine, is working with Harkevy now.'

'Oh. Do you suppose you – or he could arrange for me to see Harkevy?'

'Nothing easier. All you have to do is call Harkevy's studio and ask to speak to Charles. Charles Winant. Tell him that you've spoken with me. Let's see – call him Friday. Friday afternoon around three.'

'All right. Thank you.' Friday was a whole week off. Harkevy was not unapproachable, Therese had heard, but he had the reputation of never making appointments, much less keeping them if he did make them, because he was very busy. But maybe Mr Baltin knew.

'And don't forget to call Kettering,' Mr Baltin said as he left.

Therese looked again at the name he had given her: Adolph Kettering, Theatrical Investments, Inc., at a private address. 'I'll call him Monday morning. Thanks a lot.'

That was the day, a Saturday, when she was to meet Richard in the Palermo after work. There were eleven days left before the date she and Carol planned to leave. She saw Phil standing with Richard at the bar.

'Well, how's the old Cat?' Phil asked her, dragging up a stool for her. 'Working Saturdays, too?'

'The cast didn't work. Just my department,' she said.

'When's the opening?'

'The twenty-first.'

'Look,' Richard said. He pointed to a spot of dark green paint on her skirt.

'I know. I did that days ago.'

'What would you like to drink?' Phil asked her.

'I don't know. Maybe I'll have a beer, thanks.' Richard had turned his back on Phil, who stood on the other side of him, and she sensed an ill-feeling between them. 'Did you do any painting today?' she asked Richard.

Richard's mouth was down at both corners. 'Had to pinch hit for some driver who was sick. Ran out of gas in the middle of Long Island.'

'Oh. That's rotten. Maybe you'd rather paint than go anywhere tomorrow.' They had talked of going over to Hoboken tomorrow, just to walk around and eat at the Clam House. But Carol would be in town tomorrow, and had promised to call her.

'I'll paint if you'll sit for me,' Richard said.

Therese hesitated uncomfortably. 'I just don't feel in the mood for sitting these days.'

'All right. It's not important.' He smiled. 'But how can I ever paint you if you'll never sit?'

'Why don't you do it out of the air?'

Phil slid his hand out and held the bottom of her glass. 'Don't drink that. Have something better. I'll drink this.'

'All right. I'll try a rye and water.'

Phil was standing on the other side of her now. He looked cheerful, but a little dark around the eyes. For the past week, in a sullen mood, he had been writing a play. He had read a few scenes of it aloud at his New Year's party. Phil called it an extension of Kafka's *Metamorphosis*. She had drawn a rough sketch for a set New Year's morning, and showed it to Phil when she came down to see him. And suddenly it occurred to her that was what was the matter with Richard.

'Terry, I wish you'd make a model we can photograph from that sketch you showed me. I'd like to have a set to go with the script.' Phil pushed the rye and water towards her, and leaned on the bar close beside her.

'I might,' Therese said. 'Are you really going to try to get it produced?'

'Why not?' Phil's dark eyes challenged her above his smile. He snapped his fingers at the barman. 'Check?'

'I'll pay,' Richard said.

'No, you won't. This is mine.' Phil had his old black wallet in his hand.

125

His play would never be produced, Therese thought, might not even be finished, because Phil's moods were capricious.

'I'll be moving along,' Phil said. 'Drop by soon, Terry. Cheerio, Rich.'

She watched him go off and up the little front stairs, shabbier than she had ever seen him in his sandals and threadbare polo coat, yet with an attractive nonchalance about his shabbiness. Like a man walking through his house in his favourite old bathrobe, Therese thought. She waved back at him through the front window.

'I hear you took Phil sandwiches and beer New Year's Day,' Richard said.

'Yes. He called up and said he had a hangover.'

'Why didn't you mention it?'

'I forgot, I suppose. It wasn't important.'

'Not important. If you – ' Richard's stiff hand gestured slowly, hopelessly. 'If you spend half the day in a guy's apartment, bringing him sandwiches and beer? Didn't it occur to you I might have wanted some sandwiches, too?'

'If you did, you had plenty of people to get them for you. We'd eaten and drunk everything in Phil's house. Remember?'

Richard nodded his long head, still smiling the downward, disgruntled smile. 'And you were alone with him, just the two of you.'

'Oh, Richard – ' She remembered, and it was so unimportant. Dannie hadn't been back from Connecticut that day. He had spent New Year's at the house of one of his professors. She had hoped Dannie would come in that afternoon at Phil's, but Richard would probably never think that, never guess she liked Dannie a lot better than Phil.

'If any other girl did that, I'd suspect something was brewing and I'd be right,' Richard went on.

'I think you're being silly.'

'I think you're being naïve.' Richard was looking at her stonily, resentfully, and Therese thought, it surely couldn't be only this he was so resentful about. He resented the fact that she wasn't and never could be what he wished her to be, a girl who loved him passionately and would love to go to Europe with him. A girl like herself, with her face, her ambitions, but a girl who adored him. 'You're not Phil's type, you know,' he said.

'Whoever said I was? Phil?'

'That twerp, that half-baked dilettante,' Richard murmured. 'And he has the nerve to sound off tonight and say you don't give a damn for me.'

'He hasn't any right to say that. I don't discuss you with him.'

'Oh, that's a fine answer. Meaning if you had, he'd know you didn't give a damn, eh?' Richard said it quietly, but his voice shook with anger.

'What's Phil suddenly got against you?' she asked.

'That's not the point!'

'What is the point?' she said impatiently.

'Oh, Terry, let's stop it.'

'You can't find any point,' she said, but seeing Richard turn away from her and shift his elbows on the bar, almost as if he writhed physically under her words, she felt a sudden compassion for him. It was not now, not last week, that galled him, but the whole past and future futility of his own feelings about her.

Richard plunged his cigarette into the ash-tray on the bar. 'What do you want to do tonight?' he asked.

Tell him about the trip with Carol, she thought. Twice before she had meant to tell him, and put it off. 'Do you want to do anything?' She emphasized the last word.

'Of course,' he said depressedly. 'What do you say we have dinner, then call up Sam and Joan? Maybe we can walk up and see them tonight.'

'All right.' She hated it. Two of the most boring people she had ever met, a shoe clerk and a secretary, happily married on West Twentieth Street, and she knew Richard meant to show her an ideal life in theirs, to remind her that they might live together the same way one day. She hated it, and any other night she might have protested, but the compassion for Richard was still in her, dragging after it an amorphous wake of guilt and a necessity to atone. Suddenly, she remembered a picnic they had had last summer, off the road near Tarrytown, remembered precisely Richard's reclining on the grass, working ever so slowly with his pocketknife at the cork in the wine bottle, while they talked of – what? But she remembered that moment of contentment, that conviction that they shared something wonderfully real and rare together that day, and she wondered now where it had gone to, on what it had been based. For now even his long flat figure standing beside her seemed to oppress her with its weight. She forced down her resentment, but it only grew heavy inside her, like a thing of substance. She looked at the chunky figures of the two Italian workmen standing at the bar, and at the two girls at the end of the bar whom she had noticed before, and now that they were leaving, she saw that they were in slacks. One had hair cut like a boy's. Therese looked away, aware that she avoided them, avoided being seen looking at them.

'Want to eat here? Are you hungry yet?' Richard asked.

'No. Let's go somewhere else.'

So they went out and walked north, in the general direction of where Sam and Joan lived.

Therese rehearsed the first words until all their sense was rubbed out. 'Remember Mrs Aird, the woman you met in my house that day?'

'Sure.'

'She's invited me to go on a trip with her, a trip West in a car for a couple of weeks or so. I'd like to go.'

'West? California?' Richard said, surprised. 'Why?'

'Why?'

'Well – do you know her as well as that?'

'I've seen her a few times.'

'Oh. Well, you didn't mention it.' Richard walked along with his hands swinging at his sides, looking at her. 'Just the two of you?'

'Yes.'

'When would you be leaving?'

'Around the eighteenth.'

'Of this month? – Then you won't get to see your show.'

She shook her head. 'I don't think it's so much to miss.'

'Then it's definite?'

'Yes.'

He was silent a moment. 'What kind of a person is she? She doesn't drink or anything, does she?'

'No.' Therese smiled. 'Does she look like she drinks?'

'No. I think she's very good-looking, in fact. It's just damned surprising, that's all.'

'Why?'

'You so seldom make up your mind about anything. You'll probably change your mind again.'

'I don't think so.'

'Maybe I can see her again some time with you. Why don't you arrange it?'

'She said she'd be in the city tomorrow. I don't know how much time she's got – or really whether she'll call or not.'

Richard didn't continue and neither did Therese. They did not mention Carol again that evening.

Richard spent Sunday morning painting, and came to Therese's apartment around two. He was there when Carol telephoned a little later. Therese told her that Richard was with her, and Carol said, 'Bring him along.' Carol said she was near the Plaza, and they might meet there in the Palm Room.

Half an hour later, Therese saw Carol look up at them from a table near the centre of the room, and almost like the first time, like the echo of an impact that had been tremendous, Therese was jolted by the sight of her. Carol was wearing the same black suit with the green and gold scarf that she had worn the day of the luncheon. But now Carol paid more attention to Richard than to her.

The three of them talked of nothing, and Therese, seeing the calm in Carol's grey eyes that only once turned to her, seeing a quite ordinary expression on Richard's face, felt a kind of disappointment. Richard had gone out of his way to meet her, but Therese thought it was even less from curiosity than because he had nothing else to do. She saw Richard looking at Carol's hands, the nails manicured in a bright red, saw him notice the ring with the clear green sapphire, and the wedding ring on the other hand. Richard could not say they were useless hands, idle hands, despite the longish nails. Carol's hands were strong, and they moved with an economy of motion. Her voice emerged from the flat murmur of other voices around them, talking of nothing at all with Richard, and once she laughed.

Carol looked at her. 'Did you tell Richard we might go on a trip?' she asked.

'Yes. Last night.'

'West?' Richard asked.

'I'd like to go up to the North-west. It depends on the roads.'

And Therese was suddenly impatient. Why did they sit here

129

having a conference about it? Now they were talking about temperatures, and the state of Washington.

'Washington's my home state,' Carol said. 'Practically.'

Then a few moments later, Carol asked if anyone wanted to take a walk in the park. Richard paid for their beer and coffee, pulling a bill from the tangle of bills and change that bulged a pocket of his trousers. How indifferent he was to Carol after all, Therese thought. She felt he didn't see her, as he sometimes hadn't seen figures in rock or cloud formations when she had tried to point them out to him. He was looking down at the table now, the thin, careless line of his mouth half smiling as he straightened up and shoved his hand quickly through his hair.

They walked from the entrance of the park at Fifty-ninth Street towards the zoo, and through the zoo at a strolling pace. They walked on under the first bridge over the path, where the path bent and the real park began. The air was cold and still, a little overcast, and Therese felt a motionlessness about everything, a lifeless stillness even in their slowly moving figures.

'Shall I hunt up some peanuts?' Richard asked.

Carol was stooped at the edge of the path, holding her fingers out to the squirrel. 'I have something,' she said softly, and the squirrel started at her voice but advanced again, seized her fingers in a nervous grip, and fixed its teeth on something, and dashed away. Carol stood up, smiling. 'Had something in my pocket from this morning.'

'Do you feed squirrels out where you live?' Richard asked.

'Squirrels and chipmunks,' Carol replied.

What dull things they talked of, Therese thought.

Then they sat on a bench and smoked a cigarette, and Therese, watching a diminutive sun bring its orange fire down finally into the scraggly black twigs of a tree, wished the night were here already and that she were alone with Carol. They began to walk back. If Carol had to go home now, Therese thought, she would do something violent. Like jump off the Fifty-ninth Street Bridge. Or take the three Benzedrine tablets Richard had given her last week.

'Would you people like to have some tea somewhere?' Carol asked as they neared the zoo again. 'How about that Russian place over by Carnegie Hall?'

'Rumpelmayer's is right here,' Richard said. 'Do you like Rumpelmayer's?'

Therese sighed. And Carol seemed to hesitate. But they went there. Therese had been here once with Angelo, she remembered. She did not care for the place. Its bright lights gave her a feeling of nakedness, and it was annoying not to know if one were looking at a real person or at a reflection in a mirror.

'No, none of that, thanks,' Carol said, shaking her head at the great tray of pastry the waitress was holding.

But Richard chose something, chose two pastries, though Therese had declined.

'What's that for, in case I change my mind?' she asked him, and Richard winked at her. His nails were dirty again, she noticed.

Richard asked Carol what kind of car she had, and they began discussing the merits of various car makes. Therese saw Carol glance about at the tables in front of her. She doesn't like it here either, Therese thought. Therese stared at a man in the mirror that was set obliquely behind Carol. His back was to Therese, and he leaned forward, talking animatedly to a woman, jerking his spread left hand for emphasis. She looked at the thin, middle-aged woman he spoke to, and back at him, wondering if the aura of familiarity about him were real or an illusion like the mirror, until a memory fragile as a bubble swam upward in her consciousness and burst at the surface. It was Harge.

Therese glanced at Carol, but if Carol had noticed him, she thought, Carol would not know that he was in the mirror behind her. A moment later, Therese looked over her shoulder, and saw Harge in profile, much like one of the images she carried in her memory from the house – the short high nose, the full lower face, the receding twist of blond hair above the usual hairline. Carol must have seen him, only three tables away to her left.

Carol looked from Richard to Therese. 'Yes,' she said to her, smiling a little, and turned back to Richard and went on with her conversation. Her manner was just as before, Therese thought, not different at all. Therese looked at the woman with Harge. She was not young, not very attractive. She might have been one of his relatives.

Then Therese saw Carol mash out a long cigarette. Richard had stopped talking. They were ready to leave. Therese was looking at

Harge the moment he saw Carol. After his first glimpse of her, his eyes drew almost shut as if he had to squint to believe her, and then he said something to the woman he was with and stood up and went to her.

'Carol,' Harge said.

'Hello, Harge.' She turned to Therese and Richard. 'Would you excuse me a minute?'

Watching from the doorway where she stood with Richard, Therese tried to see it all, to see beyond the pride and aggressiveness in Harge's anxious, forward-leaning figure that was not quite so tall as the crown of Carol's hat, to see beyond Carol's acquiescent nods as he spoke, to surmise not what they talked of now but what they had said to each other five years ago, three years ago, that day of the picture in the rowing boat. Carol had loved him once, and that was hard to remember.

'Can we get free now, Terry?' Richard asked her.

Therese saw Carol nod goodbye to the woman at Harge's table, then turn away from Harge. Harge looked past Carol, to her and Richard, and without apparently recognizing her, he went back to his table.

'I'm sorry,' Carol said as she rejoined them.

On the sidewalk, Therese drew Richard aside and said, 'I'll say goodnight, Richard. Carol wants me to visit a friend of hers tonight with her.'

'Oh.' Richard frowned. 'I had those concert tickets for tonight, you know.'

Therese remembered suddenly. 'Alex's. I forgot. I'm sorry.'

He said gloomily, 'It's not important.'

It wasn't important. Richard's friend Alex was accompanying somebody in a violin concert, and had given Richard the tickets, she remembered, weeks ago.

'You'd rather see her than me, wouldn't you?' he asked.

Therese saw that Carol was looking for a taxi. Carol would leave them both in a moment. 'You might have mentioned the concert this morning, Richard, reminded me, at least.'

'Was that her husband?' Richard's eyes narrowed under his frown. 'What is this, Terry?'

'What's what?' she said. 'I don't know her husband.'

Richard waited a moment, then the frown left his eyes. He smiled, as if he conceded he had been unreasonable. 'Sorry. I just took it for granted I'd see you tonight.' He walked towards Carol. 'Good night,' he said.

He looked as if he were leaving by himself, and Carol said, 'Are you going downtown? Maybe I can drop you.'

'I'm walking, thanks.'

'I thought you two had a date,' Carol said to Therese.

Therese saw that Richard was lingering, and she walked towards Carol, out of his hearing. 'Not an important one. I'd rather stay with you.'

A taxi had slid up beside Carol. Carol put her hand on the door handle. 'Well, neither is our date so important, so why don't you go on with Richard tonight?'

Therese glanced at Richard, and saw that he had heard her.

'Bye-bye, Therese,' Carol said.

'Good night,' Richard called.

'Good night,' Therese said, and watched Carol pull the taxi door shut after her.

'So,' Richard said.

Therese turned towards him. She wouldn't go to the concert, and neither would she do anything violent, she knew, nothing more violent than walk quickly home and get to work on the set she wanted to finish by Tuesday for Harkevy. She could see the whole evening ahead, with a half dismal, half defiant fatality, in the second it took for Richard to walk to her. 'I still don't want to go to the concert,' she said.

To her surprise, Richard stepped back and said angrily, 'All right, don't!' and turned away.

He walked west on Fifty-ninth Street in his loose, lopsided gait that jutted his right shoulder ahead of the other, hands swinging unrhythmically at his sides, and she might have known from the walk alone that he was angry. And he was out of sight in no time. The rejection from Kettering last Monday flashed across her mind. She stared at the darkness where Richard had disappeared. She did not feel guilty about tonight. It was something else. She envied him. She envied him his faith that there would always be a place, a home, a job, someone else for him. She envied him that attitude. She almost resented his having it.

CHAPTER THIRTEEN

R ichard began it.
'Why do you like her so much?'

It was an evening on which she had broken a date with Richard on the slim chance Carol would come by. Carol hadn't, and Richard had come by instead. Now at five past eleven in the huge pink-walled cafeteria on Lexington Avenue, she had been about to begin, but Richard was ahead of her.

'I like being with her, I like talking with her. I'm fond of anybody I can talk to.' The phrases of some letter she had written to Carol and never mailed drifted across her mind as if to answer Richard. *I feel I stand in a desert with my hands outstretched, and you are raining down upon me.*

'You've got a hell of a crush on her,' Richard announced, explanatorily and resentfully.

Therese took a deep breath. Should she be simple and say yes, or should she try to explain it? What could he ever understand of it, even if she explained it in a million words?

'Does she know it? Of course she knows it.' Richard frowned and drew on his cigarette. 'Don't you think it's pretty silly? It's like a crush that schoolgirls get.'

'You don't understand,' she said. She felt so very sure of herself. *I will comb you like music caught in the heads of all the trees in the forest . . .*

'What's there to understand? But she understands. She shouldn't indulge you. She shouldn't play with you like this. It's not fair to you.'

'Not fair to me?'

'What's she doing, amusing herself with you? And then one day she'll get tired of you and kick you out.'

Kick me out, she thought. What was in or out? How did one kick out an emotion? She was angry, but she did not want to argue. She said nothing.

'You're in a daze!'

'I'm wide awake. I never felt more awake.' She picked up the table knife and rubbed her thumb back and forth on the ridge at the base of the blade. 'Why don't you leave me alone?'

He frowned. 'Leave you alone?'

'Yes.'

'You mean, about Europe, too?'

'Yes,' she said.

'Listen, Terry – ' Richard wriggled in his chair and leaned forward, hesitated, then took another cigarette, lighting it distastefully, throwing the match on the floor. 'You're in some kind of trance! It's worse – '

'Just because I don't want to argue with you?'

'It's worse than being lovesick, because it's so completely unreasonable. Don't you understand that?'

No, she didn't understand a word.

'But you're going to get over it in about a week. I hope. My God!' He squirmed again. 'To say – to say for a minute you practically want to say goodbye to me because of some silly crush!'

'I didn't say that. You said it.' She looked back at him, at his rigid face that was beginning to redden in the centre of the flat cheeks. 'But why should I want to be with you if all you do is argue about this?'

He sat back. 'Wednesday, next Saturday, you won't feel like this at all. You haven't known her three weeks yet.'

She looked over towards the steam tables, where people edged slowly along, choosing this and that, drifting towards the curve in the counter where they dispersed. 'We may as well say goodbye,' she said, 'because neither of us will ever be any different from what we are this minute.'

'Therese, you're like a person gone so crazy, you think you're saner than ever!'

'Oh, let's stop it!'

Richard's hand with its row of knuckles embedded in the white, freckled flesh was clenched on the table motionless, but a picture of a hand that had hammered some ineffectual, inaudible point. 'I'll tell you one thing, I think your friend knows what she's doing. I think she's committing a crime against you. I've half a mind to report her to somebody, but the trouble is you're not a child. You're just acting like one.'

'Why do you make so much out of it?' she asked. 'You're practically in a frenzy.'

'You make enough out of it to want to say goodbye to me! What do you know about her?'

'What do *you* know about her?'

'Did she ever make any passes at you?'

'God!' Therese said. She felt like saying it a dozen times. It summed up everything, her imprisonment now, here, yet. 'You don't understand.' But he did, and that was why he was angry. But did he understand that she would have felt the same way if Carol had never touched her? Yes, and if Carol had never even spoken to her after that brief conversation about a doll's valise in the store. If Carol, in fact, had never spoken to her at all, for it had all happened in that instant she had seen Carol standing in the middle of the floor, watching her. Then the realization that so much had happened after that meeting made her feel incredibly lucky suddenly. It was so easy for a man and woman to find each other, to find someone who would do, but for her to have found Carol – 'I think I understand you better than you understand me. You don't really want to see me again, either, because you said yourself I'm not the same person. If we keep on seeing each other, you'll only get more and more – like this.'

'Terry, forget for a minute I ever said I wanted you to love me, or that I love you. It's you as a person, I mean. I like you. I'd like – '

'I wonder sometimes why you think you like me, or did like me. Because you didn't even know me.'

'You don't know yourself.'

'But I do – and I know you. You'll drop painting some day, and me with it. Just as you've dropped everything else you ever started, as far as I can see. The dry-cleaning thing, or the used-car lot – '

'That's not true,' Richard said sullenly.

'But why do you think you like me? Because I paint a little, too, and we can talk about that? I'm just as impractical as a girlfriend for you as painting is as a business for you.' She hesitated a minute, then said the rest of it. 'You know enough about art anyway to know you'll never make a good painter. You're like a little boy playing truant as long as you can, knowing all the time what you ought to be doing and what you'll finally be doing, working for your father.'

Richard's blue eyes had gone suddenly cold. The line of his mouth was straight and very short now, the thin upper lip faintly curling. 'All that isn't quite the point now, is it?'

'Well – yes. It's part of your hanging on when you know it's hopeless, and when you know you'll finally let go.'

'I will not!'

'Richard, there's no point – '

'You're going to change your mind, you know.'

She understood that. It was like a song he kept singing to her.

A week later, Richard stood in her room with the same expression of sullen anger on his face, talking in the same tone. He had called up at the unusual hour of three in the afternoon, and insisted on seeing her for a moment. She was packing a bag to take to Carol's for the weekend. If she hadn't been packing for Carol's house, Richard might have been in quite another mood, she thought, because she had seen him three times the past week, and he had never been pleasanter, never been more considerate of her.

'You can't just give me marching orders out of your life,' he said, flinging his long arms out, but there was a lonesome tone in it, as if he had already started on that road away from her. 'What really makes me sore is that you act like I'm not worth anything, that I'm completely ineffectual. It isn't fair to me, Terry. I can't compete!'

No, she thought, of course he couldn't. 'I don't have any quarrel with you,' she said. 'It's you who choose to quarrel over Carol. She hasn't taken anything away from you, because you didn't have it in the first place. But if you can't go on seeing me – ' She stopped, knowing he could and probably would go on seeing her.

'What logic,' he said, rubbing the heel of his hand into his eye.

Therese watched him, caught by the idea that had just come to her, that she knew suddenly was a fact. Why hadn't it occurred to her the night of the theatre, days ago? She might have known it from a hundred gestures, words, looks, this past week. But she remembered the night of the theatre especially – he had surprised her with tickets to something she particularly wanted to see – the way he had held her hand that night, and from his voice on the telephone, not just telling her to meet him here or there, but asking her very sweetly if she could. She hadn't liked it. It was not a manifestation of affection, but rather a means of ingratiating himself, of somehow paving the way for the sudden questions he had asked so casually that night: 'What do you mean you're fond of her? Do you want to go to bed with her?' Therese had replied, 'Do you think I would tell you if I did?' while a quick succession of emotions – humiliation, resentment, loathing of him – had made her speechless, had made it almost impossible for her to keep walking beside him. And glancing at him, she had seen him looking at her with that soft, inane smile that in memory now looked cruel, and unhealthy. And its unhealthiness might have escaped her, she thought, if it weren't that Richard was so frankly trying to convince her she was unhealthy.

Therese turned and tossed into the overnight bag her toothbrush and her hairbrush, then remembered she had a toothbrush at Carol's.

'Just what do you want from her, Therese? Where's it going to go from here?'

'Why are you so interested?'

He stared at her, and for a moment beneath the anger she saw the fixed curiosity she had seen before, as if he were watching a spectacle through a keyhole. But she knew he was not so detached as that. On the contrary, she sensed that he was never so bound to her as now, never so determined not to give her up. It frightened her. She could imagine the determination transformed to hatred and to violence.

Richard sighed, and twisted the newspaper in his hands. 'I'm interested in *you*. You can't just say to me, "Find someone else." I've never treated you the way I treated the others, never thought of you that way.'

She didn't answer.

'Damn!' Richard threw the newspaper at the bookshelf, and turned his back on her.

The newspaper flicked the Madonna, and it tipped back against the wall as if astonished, fell over, and rolled off the edge. Richard made a lunge for it and caught it in both hands. He looked at Therese and smiled involuntarily.

'Thanks.' Therese took it from him. She lifted it to set it back, then brought her hands down quickly and smashed the figure to the floor.

'Terry!'

The Madonna lay in three or four pieces.

'Never mind it,' she said. Her heart was beating as if she were angry, or fighting.

'But – '

'To hell with it!' she said, pushing the pieces aside with her shoe.

Richard left a moment later, slamming the door.

What was it, Therese wondered, the Andronich thing or Richard? Mr Andronich's secretary had called about an hour ago and told her that Mr Andronich had decided to hire an assistant from Philadelphia instead of her. So that job would not be there to come back to, after the trip with Carol. Therese looked down at the broken Madonna. The wood was quite beautiful inside. It had cracked cleanly along the grain.

Carol asked her in detail that evening about her talk with Richard. It irked Therese that Carol was so concerned as to whether Richard were hurt or not.

'You're not used to thinking of other people's feelings,' Carol said bluntly to her.

They were in the kitchen fixing a late dinner, because Carol had given the maid the evening off.

'What real reason have you to think he's not in love with you?' Carol asked.

'Maybe I just don't understand how he works. But it doesn't seem like love to me.'

Then in the middle of dinner, in the middle of a conversation about the trip, Carol remarked suddenly, 'You shouldn't have talked to Richard at all.'

It was the first time Therese had told Carol any of it, any of the first conversation in the cafeteria with Richard. 'Why not? Should I have lied to him?'

Carol was not eating. Now she pushed back her chair and stood up. 'You're much too young to know your own mind. Or what you're talking about. Yes, in that case, lie.'

Therese laid her fork down. She watched Carol get a cigarette and light it. 'I had to say goodbye to him and I did. I have. I won't see him again.'

Carol opened a panel in the bottom of the bookcase and took out a bottle. She poured some into an empty glass and slammed the panel shut. 'Why did you do it now? Why not two months ago or two months from now? And why did you mention me?'

'I know – I think it fascinates him.'

'It probably does.'

'But if I simply don't see him again – ' She couldn't finish it, about his not being apt to follow her, spy on her. She didn't want to say such things to Carol. And besides, there was the memory of Richard's eyes. 'I think he'll give it up. He said he couldn't compete.'

Carol struck her forehead with her hand. 'Couldn't compete,' she repeated. She came back to the table and poured some of the water from her glass into the whisky. 'How true. Finish your dinner. I may be making too much of it, I don't know.'

But Therese did not move. She had done the wrong thing. And at best, even doing the right thing, she could not make Carol happy as Carol made her happy, she thought as she had thought a hundred times before. Carol was happy only at moments here and there, moments that Therese caught and kept. One had been in the evening they put away the Christmas decorations, and Carol had refolded the string of angels and put them between the pages of a book. 'I'm going to keep these,' she had said. 'With twenty-two angels to defend me, I can't lose.' Therese looked at Carol now, and though Carol was watching her, it was through that veil of preoccupation that Therese so often saw, that kept them a world apart.

'Lines,' Carol said. 'I can't compete. People talk of classics. These lines are classic. A hundred different people will say the same words.

There are lines for the mother, lines for the daughter, for the husband and the lover. I'd rather see you dead at my feet. It's the same play repeated with different casts. What do they say makes a play a classic, Therese?'

'A classic – ' Her voice sounded tight and stifled. 'A classic is something with a basic human situation.'

When Therese awakened, the sun was in her room. She lay for a moment, watching the watery looking sunspots rippling on the pale green ceiling, listening for any sound of activity in the house. She looked at her blouse, hanging over the edge of the bureau. Why was she so untidy in Carol's house? Carol didn't like it. The dog that lived somewhere beyond the garages was barking intermittently, half-heartedly. There had been one pleasant interval last evening, the telephone call from Rindy. Rindy back from a birthday party at nine-thirty. Could she give a birthday party on her birthday in April. Carol said of course. Carol had been different after that. She had talked about Europe, and summers in Rapallo.

Therese got up and went to the window, raised it higher and leaned on the sill, tensing herself against the cold. There were no mornings anywhere like the mornings from this window. The round bed of grass beyond the driveway had darts of sunlight in it, like scattered gold needles. There were sparks of sun in the moist hedge leaves, and the sky was a fresh solid blue. She looked at the place in the driveway where Abby had been that morning, and at the bit of white fence beyond the hedges that marked the end of the lawn. The ground looked breathing and young, even though the winter had browned the grass. There had been trees and hedges around the school in Montclair, but the green had always ended in part of a red brick wall, or a grey stone building that was part of the school – an infirmary, a woodshed, a toolhouse – and the green each spring had seemed old already, used and handed down by one generation of children to the next, as much a part of school paraphernalia as textbooks and uniforms.

She dressed in the plaid slacks she had brought from home, and one of the shirts she had left from another time, which had been

141

laundered. It was twenty past eight. Carol liked to get up about eight-thirty, liked to be awakened by someone with a cup of coffee, though Therese had noticed she never had Florence do it.

Florence was in the kitchen when she went down, but she had only just started the coffee.

'Good morning,' Therese said. 'Do you mind if I fix the breakfast?' Florence hadn't minded the two other times she had come in and found Therese fixing them.

'Go ahead, miss,' Florence said. 'I'll just make my own fried eggs. You like doing things for Mrs Aird yourself, don't you,' she said like a statement.

Therese was getting two eggs out of the refrigerator. 'Yes,' she said, smiling. She dropped one of the eggs into the water, which was just beginning to heat. Her answer sounded rather flat, but what other answer was there? When she turned around after setting the breakfast tray, she saw Florence had put the second egg in the water. Therese took it out with her fingers. 'She wants only one egg,' Therese said. 'That's for my omelette.'

'Does she? She always used to eat two.'

'Well – she doesn't now,' Therese said.

'Shouldn't you measure that egg anyway, miss?' Florence gave her the pleasant professional smile. 'Here's the egg timer, top of the stove.'

Therese shook her head. 'It comes out better when I guess.' She had never gone wrong yet on Carol's egg. Carol liked it a little better done than the egg timer made it. Therese looked at Florence, who was concentrating now on the two eggs she was frying in the skillet. The coffee was almost all filtered. In silence, Therese prepared the cup to take up to Carol.

Later in the morning, Therese helped Carol take in the white iron chairs and the swing seat from the lawn in back of the house. It would be simpler with Florence there, Carol said, but Carol had sent her away marketing, then had a sudden whim to get the furniture in. It was Harge's idea to leave them out all winter, she said, but she thought they looked bleak. Finally only one chair remained by the round fountain, a prim little chair of white metal with a bulging bottom and four lacy feet. Therese looked at it and wondered who had sat there.

'I wish there were more plays that happened out of doors,' Therese said.

'What do you think of first when you start to make a set?' Carol asked. 'What do you start from?'

'The mood of the play, I suppose. What do you mean?'

'Do you think of the kind of play it is, or of something you want to see?'

One of Mr Donohue's remarks brushed Therese's mind with a vague unpleasantness. Carol was in an argumentative mood this morning. 'I think you're determined to consider me an amateur,' Therese said.

'I think you're rather subjective. That's amateurish, isn't it?'

'Not always.' But she knew what Carol meant.

'You have to know a lot to be absolutely subjective, don't you? In those things you showed me, I think you're too subjective – without knowing enough.'

Therese made fists of her hands in her pockets. She had so hoped Carol would like her work, unqualifiedly. It had hurt her terribly that Carol hadn't liked in the least a certain few sets she had shown her. Carol knew nothing about it, technically, yet she could demolish a set with a phrase.

'I think a look at the West would do you good. When did you say you had to be back? The middle of February?'

'Well, now I don't – I just heard yesterday.'

'What do you mean? It fell through? The Philadelphia job?'

'They called me up. They want somebody from Philadelphia.'

'Oh, baby. I'm sorry.'

'Oh, it's just this business,' Therese said. Carol's hand was on the back of her neck, Carol's thumb rubbing behind her ear as Carol might have fondled a dog.

'You weren't going to tell me.'

'Yes, I was.'

'When?'

'Some time on the trip.'

'Are you very disappointed?'

'No,' Therese said positively.

They heated the last cup of coffee and took it out to the white chair on the lawn and shared it.

'Shall we have lunch out somewhere?' Carol asked her. 'Let's go to the club. Then I ought to do some shopping in Newark. How about a jacket? Would you like a tweed jacket?'

Therese was sitting on the edge of the fountain, one hand pressed against her ear because it was aching from the cold. 'I don't particularly need one,' she said.

'But I'd particularly like to see you in one.'

Therese was upstairs, changing her clothes, when she heard the telephone ring. She heard Florence say, 'Oh, good morning, Mr Aird. Yes, I'll call her right now,' and Therese crossed the room and closed the door. Restlessly, she began to put the room in order, hung her clothes in the closet, and smoothed the bed she had already made. Then Carol knocked on the door and put her head in. 'Harge is coming by in a few minutes. I don't think he'll be long.'

Therese did not want to see him. 'Would you like for me to take a walk?'

Carol smiled. 'No. Stay up here and read a book, if you want to.'

Therese got the book she had bought yesterday, the *Oxford Book of English Verse*, and tried to read it, but the words stayed separate and meaningless. She had a disquieting sense of hiding, so she went to the door and opened it.

Carol was just coming from her room, and for an instant Therese saw the same look of indecision cross her face that Therese remembered from the first moment she had entered the house. Then she said, 'Come down.'

Harge's car drove up as they walked into the living room. Carol went to the door, and Therese heard their greeting, Carol's only cordial, but Harge's very cheerful, and Carol came in with a long flower box in her arms.

'Harge, this is Miss Belivet. I think you met her once,' Carol said.

Harge's eyes narrowed a little, then opened. 'Oh, yes. How do you do?'

'How do you do?'

Florence came in, and Carol handed the flower box to her.

'Would you put these in something?' Carol said.

'Ah, here's that pipe. I thought so.' Harge reached behind the ivy on the mantel, and brought forth a pipe.

'Everything is fine at home?' Carol asked as she sat down at the end of the sofa.

'Yes. Very.' Harge's tense smile did not show his teeth, but his face and the quick turns of his head radiated geniality and self-satisfaction. He watched with proprietary pleasure as Florence brought in the flowers, red roses, in a vase, and set them on the coffee table in front of the sofa.

Therese wished suddenly that she had brought Carol flowers, brought them on any of a half a dozen occasions past, and she remembered the flowers Dannie had brought to her one day when he simply dropped in at the theatre. She looked at Harge, and his eyes glanced away from her, the peaked brow lifting still higher, the eyes darting everywhere, as if he looked for little changes in the room. But it might all be pretence, Therese thought, his air of good cheer. And if he cared enough to pretend, he must also care in some way for Carol.

'May I take one for Rindy?' Harge asked.

'Of course.' Carol got up, and she would have broken a flower, but Harge stepped forward and put a little knife blade against the stem and the flower came off. 'They're very beautiful. Thank you, Harge.'

Harge lifted the flower to his nose. Half to Carol, half to Therese, he said, 'It's a beautiful day. Are you going to take a drive?'

'Yes, we were,' Carol said. 'By the way, I'd like to drive over one afternoon next week. Perhaps Tuesday.'

Harge thought a moment. 'All right. I'll tell her.'

'I'll speak to her on the phone. I meant tell your family.'

Harge nodded once, in acquiescence, then looked at Therese. 'Yes, I remember you. Of course. You were here about three weeks ago. Before Christmas.'

'Yes. One Sunday.' Therese stood up. She wanted to leave them alone. 'I'll go upstairs,' she said to Carol. 'Goodbye, Mr Aird.'

Harge made her a little bow. 'Goodbye.'

As she went up the stairs, she heard Harge say, 'Well, many happy returns, Carol. I'd like to say it. Do you mind?'

Carol's birthday, Therese thought. Of course, Carol wouldn't have told her.

She closed the door and looked around the room, realized she was

145

looking for any sign that she had spent the night. There was none. She stopped at the mirror and looked at herself for a moment, frowningly. She was not so pale as she had been three weeks ago when Harge saw her; she did not feel like the drooping, frightened thing Harge had met then. From the top drawer, she got her handbag and took her lipstick out of it. Then she heard Harge knock on the door, and she closed the drawer.

'Come in.'

'Excuse me. I must get something.' He crossed the room quickly, went into the bathroom, and he was smiling as he came back with the razor in his hand. 'You were in the restaurant with Carol last Sunday, weren't you?'

'Yes,' Therese said.

'Carol said you do stage designing.'

'Yes.'

He glanced from her face to her hands, to the floor, and up again. 'I hope you see that Carol gets out enough,' he said. 'You look young and spry. Make her take some walks.'

Then he went briskly out the door, leaving behind him a faint shaving-soap scent. Therese tossed her lipstick on to the bed, and wiped her palms down the side of her skirt. She wondered why Harge troubled to let her know he took it for granted she spent a great deal of time with Carol.

'Therese!' Carol called suddenly. 'Come down!'

Carol was sitting on the sofa. Harge had gone. She looked at Therese with a little smile. Then Florence came in and Carol said, 'Florence, you can take these somewhere else. Put them in the dining room.'

'Yes, ma'am.'

Carol winked at Therese.

Nobody used the dining room, Therese knew. Carol preferred to eat anywhere else. 'Why didn't you tell me it was your birthday?' Therese asked her.

'Oh!' Carol laughed. 'It's not. It's my wedding anniversary. Get your coat and let's go.'

As they backed out of the driveway, Carol said, 'If there's anything I can't stand, it's a hypocrite.'

'What did he say?'

'Nothing of any importance.' Carol was still smiling.

'But you said he was a hypocrite.'

'Par excellence.'

'Pretending all this good humour?'

'Oh – just partially that.'

'Did he say anything about me?'

'He said you looked like a nice girl. Is that news?' Carol shot the car down the narrow road to the village. 'He said the divorce will take about six weeks longer than we'd thought, due to some more red tape. That's news. He has an idea I still might change my mind in the meantime. That's hypocrisy. I think he likes to fool himself.'

Was life, were human relations like this always, Therese wondered. Never solid ground underfoot. Always like gravel, a little yielding, noisy so the whole world could hear, so one always listened, too, for the loud, harsh step of the intruder's foot.

'Carol, I never took that cheque, you know,' Therese remarked suddenly. 'I stuck it under the cloth on the table by the bed.'

'What made you think of that?'

'I don't know. Do you want me to tear it up? I started to that night.'

'If you insist,' Carol said.

CHAPTER FOURTEEN

Therese looked down at the big cardboard box. 'I don't want to take it.' Her hands were full. 'I can let Mrs Osborne take the food out and the rest can stay here.'

'Bring it,' Carol said, going out the door. She carried down the last dribble of things, the books and the jackets Therese had decided at the last minute that she wanted.

Therese came back upstairs for the box. It had come an hour ago by messenger – a lot of sandwiches in wax paper, a bottle of blackberry wine, a cake, and a box containing the white dress Mrs Semco had promised her. Richard had had nothing to do with the box, she knew, or there would have been a book or an extra note in it.

An unwanted dress still lay out on the couch, a corner of the rug was turned back, but Therese was impatient to be off. She pulled the door shut, and hurried down the steps with the box, past the Kellys' who were both away at work, past Mrs Osborne's door. She had said goodbye to Mrs Osborne an hour ago when she had paid the next month's rent.

Therese was just closing the car door when Mrs Osborne called her from the front steps.

'Telephone call!' Mrs Osborne shouted, and reluctantly Therese got out, thinking it was Richard.

It was Phil McElroy, calling her to ask about the interview with Harkevy yesterday. She had told Dannie about it last night when they had had dinner together. Harkevy hadn't promised her a job, but he had said to keep in touch, and Therese felt he meant it. He had let her come to see him backstage in the theatre where he was supervising the set for *Winter Town*. He had chosen three of her cardboard models and looked very carefully at them, dismissed one as a little dull, pointed out some impracticality in the second, and liked best the hall-like set Therese had started the evening she had come back from the first visit to Carol's house. He was the first person who had ever given her less conventional sets a serious consideration. She had called Carol up immediately and told her about the meeting. She told Phil about the Harkevy interview, but she didn't mention that the Andronich job had fallen through. She knew it was because she didn't want Richard to hear about it. Therese asked Phil to let her know what play Harkevy was doing sets for next, because he said he hadn't decided himself between two plays. There was more of a chance he would take her on as apprentice if he chose the English play he had talked about yesterday.

'I don't know any address to give you yet,' Therese said. 'I know we'll get to Chicago.'

Phil said he might drop her a letter general delivery there.

'Was that Richard?' Carol asked when she came back.

'No. Phil McElroy.'

'So you haven't heard from Richard?'

'I haven't for the last few days. He sent me a telegram this morning.' Therese hesitated, then took it from her pocket and read it. 'I HAVE NOT CHANGED. NEITHER HAVE YOU. WRITE TO ME. I LOVE YOU. RICHARD.'

'I think you should call him,' Carol said. 'Call him from my house.'

They were going to spend the night at Carol's house and leave early tomorrow morning.

'Will you put on that dress tonight?' Carol asked.

'I'll try it on. It looks like a wedding dress.'

Therese put on the dress just before dinner. It hung below her calf, and the waist tied in back with long white bands that in front were stitched down and embroidered. She went down to show it to Carol. Carol was in the living room writing a letter.

'Look,' Therese said, smiling.

Carol looked at her for a long moment, then came over and examined the embroidery at the waist. 'That's a museum piece. You look adorable. Wear it this evening, will you?'

'It's so elaborate.' She didn't want to wear it, because it made her think of Richard.

'What the hell kind of style is it, Russian?'

Therese gave a laugh. She liked the way Carol cursed, always casually, and when no one else could hear her.

'Is it?' Carol repeated.

Therese was going upstairs. 'Is it what?'

'Where did you get this habit of not answering people?' Carol demanded, her voice suddenly harsh with anger.

Carol's eyes had the angry white light she had seen in them the time she refused to play the piano. And what angered her now was just as trifling. 'I'm sorry, Carol. I guess I didn't hear you.'

'Go ahead,' Carol said, turning away. 'Go on up and take it off.'

It was Harge still, Therese thought. Therese hesitated a minute, then went upstairs. She untied the waist and the sleeves, glanced at herself in the mirror, then tied them all back again. If Carol wanted her to keep it on, she would.

They fixed dinner themselves, because Florence had already started her three weeks' leave. They opened some special jars of things that Carol said she had been saving, and they made stingers in the cocktail shaker just before dinner. Therese thought Carol's mood had passed, but when she started to pour a second stinger for herself, Carol said shortly, 'I don't think you should have any more of that.'

And Therese deferred, with a smile. And the mood went on. Nothing Therese said or did could change it, and Therese blamed the inhibiting dress for not being able to think of the right things to say. They took brandied chestnuts and coffee up to the porch after dinner, but they said even less to each other in the semi-darkness, and Therese only felt sleepy and rather depressed.

The next morning, Therese found a paper bag on the back doorstep. Inside it was a toy monkey with grey and white fur. Therese showed it to Carol.

'My God,' Carol said softly, and smiled. 'Jacopo.' She took the monkey and rubbed her forefinger against its slightly dirty white cheek. 'Abby and I used to have him hanging in the back of the car,' Carol said.

'Abby brought it? Last night?'

'I suppose.' Carol went on to the car with the monkey and a suitcase.

Therese remembered wakening from a doze on the swing seat last night, awakening to an absolute silence, and Carol sitting there in the dark, looking straight before her. Carol must have heard Abby's car last night. Therese helped Carol arrange the suitcases and the lap rug in the back of the car.

'Why didn't she come in?' Therese asked.

'Oh, that's Abby,' Carol said with a smile, with the fleeting shyness that always surprised Therese. 'Why don't you go call Richard?'

Therese sighed. 'I can't now, anyway. He's left the house by this time.' It was eight-forty, and his school began at nine.

'Call his family then. Aren't you going to thank them for the box they sent you?'

'I was going to write them a letter.'

'Call them now, and you won't have to write them a letter. It's much nicer to call anyway.'

Mrs Semco answered the telephone. Therese praised the dress and Mrs Semco's needlework, and thanked her for all the food and the wine.

'Richard just left the house,' Mrs Semco said. 'He's going to be awfully lonely. He mopes around already.' But she laughed, her vigorous, high-pitched laugh that filled the kitchen where Therese knew she stood, a laugh that would ring through the house, even to Richard's empty room upstairs. 'Is everything all right with you and Richard?' Mrs Semco asked with the faintest suspicion, though Therese could tell she still smiled.

Therese said yes. And she promised she would write. Afterwards, she felt better because she had called.

Carol asked her if she had closed her window upstairs, and Therese went up again, because she couldn't remember. She hadn't closed the window, and she hadn't made her bed either, but there wasn't time now. Florence could take care of the bed when she came in on Monday to lock the house up.

Carol was on the telephone when Therese came downstairs. She looked up at Therese with a smile and held the telephone towards her. Therese knew from the first tone that it was Rindy.

' . . . at – uh – Mr Byron's. It's a farm. Have you ever been there, Mother?'

'Where is it, sweetheart?' Carol said.

'At Mr Byron's. He has horses. But not the kind you would like.'

'Oh. Why not?'

'Well, these are heavy.'

Therese tried to hear anything in the shrill, rather matter-of-fact voice that resembled Carol's voice, but she couldn't.

'Hello,' Rindy said. 'Mother?'

'I'm still here.'

'I've got to say goodbye now. Daddy's ready to leave.' And she coughed.

'Have you got a cough?' Carol asked.

'No.'

'Then don't cough into the phone.'

'I wish you would take me on the trip.'

'Well, I can't because you're in school. But we'll have trips this summer.'

'Can you still call me?'

'On the trip? Of course I will. Every day.' Carol took the telephone and sat back with it, but she still watched Therese the minute or so more that she talked.

'She sounds so serious,' Therese said.

'She was telling me all about the big day yesterday. Harge let her play hooky.'

Carol had seen Rindy the day before yesterday, Therese remembered. It had evidently been a pleasant visit, from what Carol had told Therese over the telephone, but she hadn't mentioned any details about it, and Therese had not asked her anything.

Just as they were about to leave, Carol decided to make a last call to Abby. Therese wandered back into the kitchen, because the car was too cold to sit in.

'I don't know any small towns in Illinois,' Carol was saying. 'Why Illinois? . . . All right, Rockford . . . I'll remember, I'll think of

Roquefort . . . Of course I'll take good care of him. I wish you'd come in, nitwit . . . Well, you're mistaken, very mistaken.'

Therese took a sip from Carol's half-finished coffee on the kitchen table, drank from the place where the lipstick was.

'Not a word,' Carol said, drawling the phrase. 'No one, so far as I know, not even Florence . . . Well, you do that, darling. Cheerio now.'

Five minutes later, they were leaving Carol's town on the highway marked on the strip map in red, the highway they would use until Chicago. The sky was overcast. Therese looked around her at the country that had grown familiar now, the clump of woods off to the left that the road to New York passed, the tall flagstaff in the distance that marked the club Carol belonged to.

Therese let a crack of air in at her window. It was quite cold, and the heater felt good on her ankles. The clock on the dashboard said quarter to ten, and she thought suddenly of the people working in Frankenberg's, penned in there at a quarter to ten in the morning, this morning and tomorrow morning and the next, the hands of clocks controlling every move they made. But the hands of the clock on the dashboard meant nothing now to her and Carol. They would sleep or not sleep, drive or not drive, whenever it pleased them. She thought of Mrs Robichek, selling sweaters this minute on the third floor, commencing another year there, her fifth year.

'Why so silent?' Carol asked. 'What's the matter?'

'Nothing.' She did not want to talk. Yet she felt there were thousands of words choking her throat, and perhaps only distance, thousands of miles, could straighten them out. Perhaps it was freedom itself that choked her.

Somewhere in Pennsylvania they went through a section of pale sunshine, like a leak in the sky, but around noon it began to rain. Carol cursed, but the sound of the rain was pleasant, drumming irregularly on the windshield and the roof.

'You know what I forgot?' Carol said. 'A raincoat. I'll have to pick one up somewhere.'

And suddenly, Therese remembered she had forgotten the book she was reading. And there was a letter to Carol in it, one sheet that stuck out both ends of the book. Damn. It had been separate from her other books, and that was why she had left it behind, on the table by the bed. She hoped Florence wouldn't decide to look at it. She tried to remember if she had written Carol's name in the letter, and she couldn't. And the cheque. She had forgotten to tear that up, too.

'Carol, did you get that cheque?'

'That cheque I gave you? – You said you were going to tear it up.'

'I didn't. It's still under the cloth.'

'Well, it's not important,' Carol said.

When they stopped for gas, Therese tried to buy some stout, which Carol liked sometimes, at a grocery store next to the gas station, but they had only beer. She bought one can, because Carol didn't care for beer. Then they drove into a little road off the highway and stopped, and opened the box of sandwiches Richard's mother had put up. There was also a dill pickle, a mozzarella cheese, and a couple of hard-boiled eggs. Therese had forgotten to ask for an opener, so she couldn't open the beer, but there was coffee in the thermos. She put the beer can on the floor in the back of the car.

'Caviar. How very, very nice of them,' Carol said, looking inside a sandwich. 'Do you like caviar?'

'No. I wish I did.'

'Why?'

Therese watched Carol take a small bite of the sandwich from which she had removed the top slice of bread, a bite where the most caviar was. 'Because people always like caviar so much when they do like it,' Therese said.

Carol smiled, and went on nibbling, slowly. 'It's an acquired taste. Acquired tastes are always more pleasant – and hard to get rid of.'

Therese poured more coffee into the cup they were sharing. She was acquiring a taste for black coffee. 'How nervous I was the first time I held this cup. You brought me coffee that day. Remember?'

'I remember.'

'How'd you happen to put cream in it that day?'

'I thought you'd like it. Why were you so nervous?'

Therese glanced at her. 'I was so excited about you,' she said, lifting the cup. Then she looked at Carol again and saw a sudden stillness, like a shock, in Carol's face. Therese had seen it two or three times before when she had said something like that to Carol about the way she felt, or paid Carol an extravagant compliment. Therese could not tell if she was pleased or displeased. She watched Carol fold the wax paper around the other half of her sandwich.

There was cake, but Carol didn't want any. It was the brown-coloured spice cake that Therese had often had at Richard's house. They put everything back, into the valise that held the cartons of cigarettes and the bottle of whisky, with a painstaking neatness that would have annoyed Therese in anyone but Carol.

'Did you say Washington was your home state?' Therese asked her.

'I was born there, and my father's there now. I wrote him I might visit him, if we get out that far.'

'Does he look like you?'

'Do I look like him, yes – more than like my mother.'

'It's strange to think of you with a family,' Therese said.

'Why?'

'Because I just think of you as you. *Sui generis*.'

Carol smiled, her head lifted as she drove. 'All right, go ahead.'

'Brothers and sisters?' Therese asked.

'One sister. I suppose you want to know all about her, too? Her name is Elaine, she has three children and she lives in Virginia. She's older than I am, and I don't know if you'd like her. You'd think she was dull.'

Yes. Therese could imagine her, like a shadow of Carol, with all Carol's features weakened and diluted.

Late in the afternoon, they stopped at a roadside restaurant which had a miniature Dutch village in the front window. Therese leaned on the rail beside it and looked at it. There was a little river that came out of a faucet at one end, which flowed in an oval stream and turned a windmill. Little figures in Dutch costume stood about the village, stood on patches of live grass. She thought of the electric train in Frankenberg's toy department, and the fury that drove it on the oval course that was about the same size as the stream.

'I never told you about the train in Frankenberg's,' Therese remarked to Carol. 'Did you notice it when you – '

'An electric train?' Carol interrupted her.

Therese had been smiling, but something constricted her heart suddenly. It was too complicated to go into, and the conversation stopped there.

Carol ordered some soup for both of them. They were stiff and cold from the car.

'I wonder if you'll really enjoy this trip,' Carol said. 'You so prefer things reflected in a glass, don't you? You have your private conception of everything. Like that windmill. It's practically as good as being in Holland to you. I wonder if you'll even like seeing real mountains and real people.'

Therese felt as crushed as if Carol had accused her of lying. She felt Carol meant, too, that she had a private conception of her, and that Carol resented it. Real people? She thought suddenly of Mrs Robichek. And she had fled her because she was hideous.

'How do you ever expect to create anything if you get all your experiences second-hand?' Carol asked her, her voice soft and even, and yet merciless.

Carol made her feel she had done nothing, was nothing at all, like a wisp of smoke. Carol had lived like a human being, had married, and had a child.

The old man from behind the counter was coming towards them. He had a limp. He stood by the table next to them and folded his arms. 'Ever been to Holland?' he asked pleasantly.

Carol answered. 'No, I haven't. I suppose you've been. Did you make the village in the window?'

He nodded. 'Took me five years to make.'

Therese looked at the man's bony fingers, the lean arms with the purple veins twisting just under the thin skin. She knew better than Carol the work that had gone into the little village, but she could not get a word out.

The man said to Carol, 'Got some fine sausages and hams next door, if you like real Pennsylvania made. We raise our own hogs and they're killed and cured right here.'

They went into the whitewashed box of a store beside the restaurant. There was a delicious smell of smoked ham inside it, mingled with the smell of woodsmoke and spice.

'Let's pick something we don't have to cook,' Carol said, looking into the refrigerated counter. 'Let's have some of this,' she said to the young man in the earlapped cap.

Therese remembered standing in the delicatessen with Mrs Robichek, her buying the thin slices of salami and liverwurst. A sign on the wall said they shipped anywhere, and she thought of sending Mrs Robichek one of the big cloth-wrapped sausages, imagined the delight on Mrs Robichek's face when she opened the package with her trembling hands and found a sausage. But should she after all, Therese wondered, make a gesture that was probably motivated by pity, or by guilt, or by some perversity in her? Therese frowned, floundering in a sea without direction or gravity, in which she knew only that she could mistrust her own impulses.

'Therese – '

Therese turned around, and Carol's beauty struck her like a glimpse of the Winged Victory of Samothrace. Carol asked her if she thought they should buy a whole ham.

The young man slid all the bundles across the counter, and took Carol's twenty-dollar bill. And Therese thought of Mrs Robichek tremulously pushing her single dollar bill and a quarter across the counter that evening.

'See anything else?' Carol asked.

'I thought I might send something to somebody. A woman who works in the store. She's poor and she once asked me to dinner.'

Carol picked up her change. 'What woman?'

'I don't really want to send her anything.' Therese wanted suddenly to leave.

Carol frowned at her through her cigarette smoke. 'Do it.'

'I don't want to. Let's go, Carol.' It was like the nightmare again, when she couldn't get away from her.

'Send it,' Carol said. 'Close the door and send her something.'

Therese closed the door and chose one of the six-dollar sausages, and wrote on a gift card: 'This comes from Pennsylvania. I hope it'll last a few Sunday mornings. With love from Therese Belivet.'

Later, in the car, Carol asked her about Mrs Robichek, and Therese answered as she always did, succinctly, and with the involuntary and absolute honesty that always depressed her afterwards. Mrs Robichek and the world she lived in was so different from that of Carol, she might have been describing another species of animal life, some ugly beast that lived on another planet. Carol made no comment on the story, only questioned and questioned her as she drove. She made no comment when there was nothing more to ask, but the taut, thoughtful expression with which she had listened stayed on her face even when they began to talk of other things. Therese gripped her thumbs inside her hands. Why did she let Mrs Robichek haunt her? And now she had spread it into Carol and could never take it back.

'Please don't mention her again, will you, Carol? Promise me.'

CHAPTER FIFTEEN

Carol walked barefoot with little short steps to the shower room in the corner, groaning at the cold. She had red polish on her toenails, and her blue pyjamas were too big for her.

'It's your fault for opening the window so high,' Therese said.

Carol pulled the curtain across, and Therese heard the shower come on with a rush. 'Ah, divinely hot!' Carol said. 'Better than last night.'

It was a luxurious tourist cabin, with a thick carpet and wood-panelled walls and everything from cellophane-sealed shoe rags to television.

Therese sat on her bed in her robe, looking at a road map, spanning it with her hand. A span and a half was about a day's driving, theoretically, though they probably would not do it. 'We might get all the way across Ohio today,' Therese said.

'Ohio. Noted for rivers, rubber, and certain railroads. On our left the famous Chillicothe drawbridge, where twenty-eight Hurons once massacred a hundred – morons.'

Therese laughed.

'And where Lewis and Clark once camped,' Carol added. 'I think I'll wear my slacks today. Want to see if they're in that suitcase? If not, I'll have to get into the car. Not the light ones, the navy blue gaberdines.'

Therese went to Carol's big suitcase at the foot of the bed. It was full of sweaters and underwear and shoes, but no slacks. She saw a nickel-plated tube sticking out of a folded sweater. She lifted the sweater out. It was heavy. She unwrapped it, and started so she almost dropped it. It was a gun with a white handle.

'No?' Carol asked.

'No.' Therese wrapped the gun up again and put it back as she had found it.

'Darling, I forgot my towel. I think it's on a chair.'

Therese got it and took it to her, and in her nervousness as she put the towel into Carol's outstretched hand her eyes dropped from Carol's face to her bare breasts and down, and she saw the quick surprise in Carol's glance as she turned around. Therese closed her eyes tight and walked slowly towards the bed, seeing before her closed lids the image of Carol's naked body.

Therese took a shower, and when she came out, Carol was standing at the mirror, almost dressed.

'What's the matter?' Carol asked.

'Nothing.'

Carol turned to her, combing her hair that was darkened a little by the wet of the shower. Her lips were bright with fresh lipstick, a cigarette between them. 'Do you realize how many times a day you make me ask you that?' she said. 'Don't you think it's a little inconsiderate?'

During breakfast, Therese said, 'Why did you bring that gun along, Carol?'

'Oh. So that's what's bothering you. It's Harge's gun, something else he forgot.' Carol's voice was casual. 'I thought it'd be better to take it than to leave it.'

'Is it loaded?'

'Yes, it's loaded. Harge got a permit, because we had a burglar at the house once.'

'Can you use it?'

Carol smiled at her. 'I'm no Annie Oakley. I can use it. I think it worries you, doesn't it? I don't expect to use it.'

Therese said nothing more about it. But it disturbed her whenever she thought of it. She thought of it the next night, when a bellhop set the suitcase down heavily on the sidewalk. She wondered if a gun could ever go off from a jolt like that.

They had taken some snapshots in Ohio, and because they could

160 .

get them developed early the next morning, they spent a long evening and the night in a town called Defiance. All evening they walked around the streets, looking in store windows, walking through silent residential streets where lights showed in front parlours, and homes looked as comfortable and safe as birds' nests. Therese had been afraid Carol would be bored by aimless walks, but Carol was the one who suggested going one block further, walking all the way up the hill to see what was on the other side. Carol talked about herself and Harge. Therese tried to sum up in one word what had separated Carol and Harge, but she rejected the words almost at once – boredom, resentment, indifference. Carol told her of one time that Harge had taken Rindy away on a fishing trip and not communicated for days. That was a retaliation for Carol's refusing to spend Harge's vacation with him at his family's summer house in Massachusetts. It was a mutual thing. And the incidents were not the start.

Carol put two of the snapshots in her billfold, one of Rindy in jodhpurs and a derby that had been on the first part of the roll, and one of Therese, with a cigarette in her mouth and her hair blowing back in the wind. There was one unflattering picture of Carol standing huddled in her coat that Carol said she was going to send to Abby because it was so bad.

They got to Chicago late one afternoon, crept into its grey, sprawling disorder behind a great truck of a meat-distributing company. Therese sat up close to the windshield. She couldn't remember anything about the city from the trip with her father. Carol seemed to know Chicago as well as she knew Manhattan. Carol showed her the famous Loop, and they stopped for a while to watch the trains and the homeward rush of five-thirty in the afternoon. It couldn't compare to the madhouse of New York at five-thirty.

At the main post office, Therese found a post-card from Dannie, nothing from Phil, and a letter from Richard. Therese glanced at the letter and saw it began and ended affectionately. She had expected just that, Richard's getting the general delivery address from Phil and writing her an affectionate letter. She put the letter in her pocket before she went back to Carol.

'Anything?' Carol said.

'Just a post-card. From Dannie. He's finished his exams.'

Carol drove to the Drake Hotel. It had a black and white checked floor, a fountain in the lobby, and Therese thought it magnificent. In their room, Carol took off her coat and flung herself down on one of the twin beds.

'I know a few people here,' she said sleepily. 'Shall we look somebody up?'

But Carol fell asleep before they quite decided.

Therese looked out the window at the light-bordered lake and at the irregular, unfamiliar line of tall buildings against the still greyish sky. It looked fuzzy and monotonous, like a Pissarro painting. A comparison Carol wouldn't appreciate, she thought. She leaned on the sill, staring at the city, watching a distant car's lights chopped into dots and dashes as it passed behind trees. She was happy.

'Why don't you ring for some cocktails?' Carol's voice said behind her.

'What kind would you like?'

'What kind would you?'

'Martinis.'

Carol whistled. 'Double Gibsons,' Carol interrupted her as she was telephoning. 'And a plate of canapés. Might as well get four Martinis.'

Therese read Richard's letter while Carol was in the shower. The whole letter was affectionate. You are not like any of the other girls, he wrote. He had waited and he would keep on waiting, because he was absolutely confident that they could be happy together. He wanted her to write to him every day, send at least a post-card. He told her how he had sat one evening rereading the three letters she had sent him when he had been in Kingston, New York, last summer. There was a sentimentality in the letter that was not like Richard at all, and Therese's first thought was that he was pretending. Perhaps in order to strike at her later. Her second reaction was aversion. She came back to the old decision, that not to write him, not to say anything more, was the shortest way to end it.

The cocktails arrived, and Therese paid for them instead of signing. She could never pay a bill except behind Carol's back.

'Will you wear your black suit?' Therese asked when Carol came in.

Carol gave her a look. 'Go all the way to the bottom of that suitcase?' she said, going to the suitcase. 'Drag it out, brush it off, steam the wrinkles out of it for half an hour?'

'We'll be a half-hour drinking these.'

'Your powers of persuasion are irresistible.' Carol took the suit into the bathroom and turned the water on in the tub.

It was the suit she had worn the day they had had the first lunch together.

'Do you realize this is the only drink I've had since we left New York?' Carol said. 'Of course you don't. Do you know why? I'm happy.'

'You're beautiful,' Therese said.

And Carol gave her the derogatory smile that Therese loved, and walked to the dressing table. She flung a yellow silk scarf around her neck and tied it loosely, and began to comb her hair. The lamp's light framed her figure like a picture, and Therese had a feeling all this had happened before. She remembered suddenly: the woman in the window brushing up her long hair, remembered the very bricks in the wall, the texture of the misty rain that morning.

'How about some perfume?' Carol asked, moving towards her with the bottle. She touched Therese's forehead with her fingers, at the hairline where she had kissed her that day.

'You remind me of the woman I once saw,' Therese said, 'somewhere off Lexington. Not you but the light. She was combing her hair up.' Therese stopped, but Carol waited for her to go on. Carol always waited, and she could never say exactly what she wanted to say. 'Early one morning when I was on the way to work, and I remember it was starting to rain,' she floundered on. 'I saw her in a window.' She really could not go on, about standing there for perhaps three or four minutes, wishing with an intensity that drained her strength that she knew the woman, that she might be welcome if she went to the house and knocked on the door, wishing she could do that instead of going on to her job at the Pelican Press.

'My little orphan,' Carol said.

Therese smiled. There was nothing dismal, no sting in the word when Carol said it.

'What does your mother look like?'

'She had black hair,' Therese said quickly. 'She didn't look anything like me.' Therese always found herself talking about her mother in the past tense, though she was alive this minute, somewhere in Connecticut.

'You really don't think she'll ever want to see you again?' Carol was standing at the mirror.

'I don't think so.'

'What about your father's family? Didn't you say he had a brother?'

'I never met him. He was a kind of geologist, working for an oil company. I don't know where he is.' It was easier talking about the uncle she had never met.

'What's your mother's name now?'

'Esther – Mrs Nicolas Strully.' The name meant as little to her as one she might see in a telephone book. She looked at Carol, suddenly sorry she had said the name. Carol might some day – A shock of loss, of helplessness, came over her. She knew so little about Carol after all.

Carol glanced at her. 'I'll never mention it,' she said, 'never mention it again. If that second drink's going to make you blue, don't drink it. I don't want you to be blue tonight.'

The restaurant where they dined overlooked the lake, too. They had a banquet of a dinner with champagne and brandy afterwards. It was the first time in her life that Therese had been a little drunk, in fact much drunker than she wanted Carol to see. Her impression of Lakeshore Drive was always to be of a broad avenue studded with mansions all resembling the White House in Washington. In the memory there would be Carol's voice, telling her about a house here and there where she had been before, and the disquieting awareness that for a while this had been Carol's world, as Rapallo, Paris, and other places Therese did not know had for a while been the frame of everything Carol did.

That night, Carol sat on the edge of her bed, smoking a cigarette before they turned the light on. Therese lay in her own bed, sleepily watching her, trying to read the meaning of the restless, puzzled look in Carol's eyes that would stare at something in the room for a moment and then move on. Was it of her she thought, or of Harge, or of Rindy? Carol had asked to be called at seven tomorrow, in order to telephone Rindy before she went to school. Therese remembered their telephone conversation in Defiance. Rindy had had a fight with

164

some other little girl, and Carol had spent fifteen minutes going over it, and trying to persuade Rindy she should take the first step and apologize. Therese still felt the effects of what she had drunk, the tingling of the champagne that drew her painfully close to Carol. If she simply asked, she thought, Carol would let her sleep tonight in the same bed with her. She wanted more than that, to kiss her, to feel their bodies next to each other's. Therese thought of the two girls she had seen in the Palermo bar. They did that, she knew, and more. And would Carol suddenly thrust her away in disgust, if she merely wanted to hold her in her arms? And would whatever affection Carol now had for her vanish in that instant? A vision of Carol's cold rebuff swept her courage clean away. It crept back humbly in the question, couldn't she ask simply to sleep in the same bed with her?

'Carol, would you mind – '

'Tomorrow we'll go to the stockyards,' Carol said at the same time, and Therese burst out laughing. 'What's so damned funny about that?' Carol asked, putting out her cigarette, but she was smiling, too.

'It just is. It's terribly funny,' Therese said, still laughing, laughing away all the longing and the intention of the night.

'You're giggly on champagne,' Carol said as she pulled the light out.

Late the next afternoon they left Chicago and drove in the direction of Rockford. Carol said she might have a letter from Abby there, but probably not, because Abby was a bad correspondent. Therese went to a shoe-repair shop to get a moccasin stitched, and when she came back, Carol was reading the letter in the car.

'What road do we take out?' Carol's face looked happier.

'Twenty, going west.'

Carol turned on the radio and worked the dial until she found some music. 'What's a good town for tonight on the way to Minneapolis?'

'Dubuque,' Therese said, looking at the map. 'Or Waterloo looks fairly big, but it's about two hundred miles away.'

'We might make it.'

They took Highway 20 towards Freeport and Galena, which was starred on the map as the home of Ulysses S. Grant.

'What did Abby say?'

'Nothing much. Just a very nice letter.'

Carol said little to her in the car, or even in the café where they stopped later for coffee. Carol went over and stood in front of a juke box, dropping nickels slowly.

'You wish Abby'd come along, don't you?' Therese said.

'No,' Carol said.

'You're so different since you got the letter from her.'

Carol looked at her across the table. 'Darling, it's just a silly letter. You can even read it if you want to.' Carol reached for her handbag, but she did not get the letter out.

Some time that evening, Therese fell asleep in the car and woke up with the lights of a city on her face. Carol was resting both arms tiredly on the top of the wheel. They had stopped for a red light.

'Here's where we stay the night,' Carol said.

Therese's sleep still clung to her as she walked across the hotel lobby. She rode up in an elevator and she was acutely conscious of Carol beside her, as if she dreamed a dream in which Carol was the subject and the only figure. In the room, she lifted her suitcase from the floor to a chair, unlatched it and left it, and stood by the writing table, watching Carol. As if her emotions had been in abeyance all the past hours, or days, they flooded her now as she watched Carol opening her suitcase, taking out, as she always did first, the leather kit that contained her toilet articles, dropping it on to the bed. She looked at Carol's hands, at the lock of hair that fell over the scarf tied around her head, at the scratch she had gotten days ago across the toe of her moccasin.

'What're you standing there for?' Carol asked. 'Get to bed, sleepy-head.'

'Carol, I love you.'

Carol straightened up. Therese stared at her with intense, sleepy eyes. Then Carol finished taking her pyjamas from the suitcase and pulled the lid down. She came to Therese and put her hands on her shoulders. She squeezed her shoulders hard, as if she were exacting a promise from her, or perhaps searching her to see if what she had said were real. Then she kissed Therese on the lips, as if they had kissed a thousand times before.

'Don't you know I love you?' Carol said.

Carol took her pyjamas into the bathroom, and stood for a moment, looking down at the basin.

'I'm going out,' Carol said. 'But I'll be back right away.'

Therese waited by the table while Carol was gone, while time passed indefinitely or maybe not at all, until the door opened and Carol came in again. She set a paper bag on the table, and Therese knew she had only gone to get a container of milk, as Carol or she herself did very often at night.

'Can I sleep with you?' Therese asked.

'Did you see the bed?'

It was a double bed. They sat up in their pyjamas, drinking milk and sharing an orange that Carol was too sleepy to finish. Then Therese set the container of milk on the floor and looked at Carol who was sleeping already, on her stomach, with one arm flung up as she always went to sleep. Therese pulled out the light. Then Carol slipped her arm under her neck, and all the length of their bodies touched, fitting as if something had prearranged it. Happiness was like a green vine spreading through her, stretching fine tendrils, bearing flowers through her flesh. She had a vision of a pale white flower, shimmering as if seen in darkness, or through water. Why did people talk of heaven, she wondered.

'Go to sleep,' Carol said.

Therese hoped she would not. But when she felt Carol's hand move on her shoulder, she knew she had been asleep. It was dawn now. Carol's fingers tightened in her hair, Carol kissed her on the lips, and pleasure leaped in Therese again as if it were only a continuation of the moment when Carol had slipped her arm under her neck last night. I love you, Therese wanted to say again, and then the words were erased by the tingling and terrifying pleasure that spread in waves from Carol's lips over her neck, her shoulders, that rushed suddenly the length of her body. Her arms were tight around Carol, and she was conscious of Carol and nothing else, of Carol's hand that slid along her ribs, Carol's hair that brushed her bare breasts, and then her body too seemed to vanish in widening circles that leaped further and further, beyond where thought could follow. While a thousand memories and moments, words, the first darling, the second time Carol had met her at the store, a thousand memories of Carol's face, her voice, moments of anger and laughter flashed like the tail of a comet across her brain. And now it was pale blue distance and space, an expanding space in which she took flight suddenly like a long arrow. The arrow seemed to cross an impossibly wide abyss with ease, seemed to arc on and on in space, and not quite to stop. Then she realized that she still clung to Carol, that she trembled violently, and the arrow was herself. She saw Carol's pale hair across her eyes, and now Carol's head was close against hers. And she did not have to ask if this was right, no one had to tell her, because this could not have been more right or perfect. She held Carol tighter against her, and felt Carol's mouth on her own smiling mouth. Therese lay still, looking at her, at Carol's face only inches away from her, the grey eyes calm as she had never seen them, as if they retained some of the space she had just emerged from. And it seemed strange that it was still Carol's face, with the freckles, the bending blonde eyebrow that she knew, the mouth now as calm as her eyes, as Therese had seen it many times before.

'My angel,' Carol said. 'Flung out of space.'

Therese looked up at the corners of the room, that were much brighter now, at the bureau with the bulging front and the shield-shaped drawer pulls, at the frameless mirror with the bevelled edge, at the green-patterned curtains that hung straight at the windows, and the two grey tips of buildings that showed just above the sill. She would remember every detail of this room for ever.

'What town is this?' she asked.

Carol laughed. 'This? This is Waterloo.' She reached for a cigarette. 'Isn't that awful.'

Smiling, Therese raised up on her elbow. Carol put a cigarette between her lips. 'There's a couple of Waterloos in every state,' Therese said.

CHAPTER SIXTEEN

Therese went out to get some newspapers while Carol was dressing. She stepped into the elevator and turned around in the exact centre of it. She felt a little odd, as if everything had shifted and distances were not quite the same, balance was not quite the same. She walked across the lobby to the newspaper stand in the corner.

'The *Courier* and the *Tribune*,' she said to the man, taking them, and even to utter words was as strange as the names of the newspapers she bought.

'Eight cents,' the man said, and Therese looked down at the change he had given her and saw there was still the same difference between eight cents and a quarter.

She wandered across the lobby, looked through the glass into the barber shop where a couple of men were getting shaves. A black man was shining shoes. A tall man with a cigar and a broad-brimmed hat, with Western boots, walked by her. She would remember this lobby, too, for ever, the people, the old-fashioned looking woodwork at the base of the registration desk, and the man in the dark overcoat who looked at her over the top of his newspaper, and slumped in his chair and went on reading beside the black and cream-coloured marble column.

When Therese opened the room door, the sight of Carol went through her like a spear. She stood a moment with her hand on the knob.

Carol looked at her from the bathroom, holding the comb suspended over her head. Carol looked at her from head to foot. 'Don't do that in public,' Carol said.

Therese threw the newspapers on the bed and came to her. Carol seized her suddenly in her arms. They stood holding each other as if they would never separate. Therese shuddered, and there were tears in her eyes. It was hard to find words, locked in Carol's arms, closer than kissing.

'Why did you wait so long?' Therese asked.

'Because – I thought there wouldn't be a second time, that I wouldn't want it. But that's not true.'

Therese thought of Abby, and it was like a slim shaft of bitterness dropping between them. Carol released her.

'And there was something else – to have you around reminding me, knowing you and knowing it would be so easy. I'm sorry. It wasn't fair to you.'

Therese set her teeth hard. She watched Carol walk slowly away across the room, watched the space widen, and remembered the first time she had seen her walk so slowly away in the department store, Therese had thought for ever. Carol had loved Abby, too, and Carol reproached herself for it. As Carol would one day for loving her, Therese wondered. Therese understood now why the December and January weeks had been made up of anger and indecision, reprimands alternating with indulgences. But she understood now that whatever Carol said in words, there were no barriers and no indecisions now. There was no Abby, either, after this morning, whatever had happened between Carol and Abby before.

'Was it?' Carol asked.

'You've made me so happy ever since I've known you,' Therese said.

'I don't think you can judge.'

'I can judge this morning.'

Carol did not answer. Only the rasp of the door lock answered her. Carol had locked the door and they were alone. Therese came towards her, straight into her arms.

'I love you,' Therese said, just to hear the words. 'I love you, I love you.'

But Carol seemed deliberately to pay almost no attention to her that day. There was more arrogance in the tilt of her cigarette, in the way she backed the car away from a kerb, cursing, not quite joking. 'Damned if I'll put a dime in a parking meter with a prairie right in sight,' Carol said. But when Therese did catch her looking at her, Carol's eyes were laughing. Carol teased her, leaning on her shoulder as they stood in front of a cigarette machine, touching her foot under tables. It made Therese limp and tense at the same time. She thought of people she had seen holding hands in movies, and why shouldn't she and Carol? Yet when she simply took Carol's arm as they stood choosing a box of candy in a shop, Carol murmured, 'Don't.'

Therese sent a box of candy to Mrs Robichek from the candy shop in Minneapolis, and a box also to the Kellys. She sent an extravagantly big box to Richard's mother, a double-deck box with wooden compartments that she knew Mrs Semco would use later for sewing articles.

'Did you ever do that with Abby?' Therese asked abruptly that evening in the car.

Carol's eyes understood suddenly and she blinked. 'What questions you ask,' she said. 'Of course.'

Of course. She had known it. 'And now – ?'

'Therese – '

She asked stiffly, 'Was it very much the same as with me?'

Carol smiled. 'No, darling.'

'Don't you think it's more pleasant than sleeping with men?'

Her smile was amused. 'Not necessarily. That depends. Who have you ever known except Richard?'

'No one.'

'Well, don't you think you'd better try some others?'

Therese was speechless for a moment, but she tried to be casual, drumming her fingers on the book in her lap.

'I mean some time, darling. You've got a lot of years ahead.'

Therese said nothing. She could not imagine ever leaving Carol either. That was another terrible question that had sprung into her mind at the start, that hammered at her brain now with a painful insistence to be answered. Would Carol ever want to leave her?

'I mean, whom you sleep with depends so much on habit,' Carol went on. 'And you're too young to make enormous decisions. Or habits.'

'Are you just a habit?' she asked, smiling, but she heard the resentment in her voice. 'You mean it's nothing but that?'

'Therese – of all times to get so melancholic.'

'I'm not melancholic,' she protested, but the thin ice was under her feet again, the uncertainties. Or was it that she always wanted a little more than she had, no matter how much she had? She said impulsively, 'Abby loves you, too, doesn't she?'

Carol started a little, and put her fork down. 'Abby has loved me practically all her life – even as you.'

Therese stared at her.

'I'll tell you about it one day. Whatever happened is past. Months and months ago,' she said, so softly Therese could hardly hear.

'Only months?'

'Yes.'

'Tell me now.'

'This isn't the time or the place.'

'There's never a time,' Therese said. 'Didn't you say there never was a right time?'

'Did I say that? About what?'

But neither of them said anything for a moment, because a fresh barrage of wind hurled the rain like a million bullets against the hood and windshield, and for a moment they could have heard nothing else. There was no thunder, as if the thunder, somewhere up above, modestly refrained from competing with this other god of rain. They waited in the inadequate shelter of a hill at the side of the road.

'I might tell you the middle,' Carol said, 'because it's funny – and ironic. It was last winter when we had the furniture shop together. But I can't begin without telling you the first part – and that was when we were children. Our families lived near each other in New Jersey, so we saw each other during vacations. Abby always had a mild crush on me, I thought, even when we were about six and eight. Then she wrote me a couple of letters when she was about fourteen and away at school. And by that time I'd heard of girls who preferred girls. But the books also tell you it goes away after that age.' There

172

were pauses between her sentences, as if she left out sentences in between.

'Were you in school with her?' Therese asked.

'I never was. My father sent me to a different school, out of town. Then Abby went to Europe when she was sixteen, and I wasn't at home when she came back. I saw her once at some party around the time I got married. Abby looked quite different then, not like a tomboy any more. Then Harge and I lived in another town, and I didn't see her again – really for years, till long after Rindy was born. She came once in a while to the riding stable where Harge and I used to ride. A few times we all rode together. Then Abby and I started playing tennis on Saturday afternoons when Harge usually played golf. Abby and I always had fun together. Abby's former crush on me never crossed my mind – we were both so much older and so much had happened. I had an idea about starting a shop, because I wanted to see less of Harge. I thought we were getting bored with each other and it would help. So I asked Abby if she wanted to be partners in it, and we started the furniture shop. After a few weeks, to my surprise, I felt I was attracted to her,' Carol said in the same quiet voice. 'I couldn't understand it, and I was a little afraid of it – remembering Abby from before, and realizing she might feel the same way, or that both of us could. So I tried not to let Abby see it, and I think I succeeded. But finally – here's the funny part finally – there was the night in Abby's house one night last winter. The roads were snowed in that night, and Abby's mother insisted that we stay together in Abby's room, simply because the room I'd stayed in before hadn't any sheets on the bed then, and it was very late. Abby said she'd fix the sheets, we both protested, but Abby's mother insisted.' Carol smiled a little, and glanced at her, but Therese felt Carol didn't even see her. 'So I stayed with Abby. Nothing would have happened, if not for that night, I'm sure of it. If not for Abby's mother, that's the ironic thing, because she doesn't know anything about it. But it did happen, and I felt very much as you, I suppose, as happy at you.' Carol blurted out the end, though her voice was still level and somehow without emotion of any kind.

Therese stared at her, not knowing if it was jealousy or shock or anger that was suddenly jumbling everything. 'And after that?' she asked.

'After that, I knew I was in love with Abby. I don't know, why not call it love, it had all the earmarks. But it lasted only two months, like a disease that came and went.' Carol said in a different tone, 'Darling, it's got nothing to do with you, and it's finished now. I knew you wanted to know, but I didn't see any reason for telling you before. It's that unimportant.'

'But if you felt the same way about her – '

'For two months?' Carol said. 'When you have a husband and child, you know, it's a little different.'

Different from her, Carol meant, because she hadn't any responsibilities. 'Is it? You can just start and stop?'

'When you haven't got a chance,' Carol answered.

The rain was abating, but only by so much that she could see it as rain now and not solid silver sheets. 'I don't believe it.'

'You're hardly in a state to talk.'

'Why are you so cynical?'

'Cynical? Am I?'

Therese was not sure enough to answer. What was it to love someone, what was love exactly, and why did it end or not end? Those were the real questions, and who could answer them?

'It's letting up,' Carol said. 'How about going on and finding a good brandy somewhere? Or is this a dry state?'

They drove on to the next town and found a deserted bar in the biggest hotel. The brandy was delicious, and they ordered two more.

'It's French brandy,' Carol said. 'Some day we'll go to France.'

Therese turned the little bowl of a glass between her fingers. A clock ticked at the end of the bar. A train whistle blew in the distance. And Carol cleared her throat. Ordinary sounds, yet the moment was not an ordinary one. No moment had been an ordinary once since the morning in Waterloo. Therese stared at the bright brown light in the brandy glass, and suddenly she had no doubt that she and Carol would one day go to France. Then out of the shimmering brown sun in the glass, Harge's face emerged, mouth and nose and eyes.

'Harge knows about Abby, doesn't he?' Therese said.

'Yes. He asked me something about her a few months ago – and I told him the whole truth from start to finish.'

'You did – ' She thought of Richard, imagined how Richard would react. 'Is that why you're getting the divorce?'

'No. It's got nothing to do with the divorce. That's another ironic thing – that I told Harge after it was all over. A mistaken effort at honesty, when Harge and I had nothing left to salvage. We'd already talked about a divorce. Please don't remind me of mistakes!' Carol frowned.

'You mean – he certainly must have been jealous.'

'Yes. Because however I chose to tell it, I suppose it came out that I'd cared more about Abby at one period than I'd ever cared for him. At one point, even with Rindy I'd have left everything behind to go with her. I don't know how it was that I didn't.'

'And taken Rindy with you?'

'I don't know. I know the fact that Rindy existed stopped me from leaving Harge then.'

'Do you regret it?'

Carol shook her head slowly. 'No. It wouldn't have lasted. It didn't last, and maybe I knew it wouldn't. With my marriage failing, I was too afraid and too weak – ' She stopped.

'Are you afraid now?'

Carol was silent.

'Carol – '

'I am not afraid,' she said stubbornly, lifting her head.

Therese looked at her face in profile in the dim light. What about Rindy now, she wanted to ask, what will happen? But she knew Carol was on the brink of growing suddenly impatient, giving her a careless answer, or no answer at all. Another time, Therese thought, not this moment. It might destroy everything, even the solidity of Carol's body beside her, and the bend of Carol's body in the black sweater seemed the only solid thing in the world. Therese ran her thumb down Carol's side, from under the arm to the waist.

'I remember Harge was particularly annoyed about a trip I took with Abby to Connecticut. Abby and I went up to buy some things for the shop. It was only a two-day trip, but he said, "Behind my back. You had to run away."' Carol said it bitterly. There was more self-reproach in her voice than imitation of Harge.

'Does he still talk about it?'

'No. Is it anything to talk about? Is it anything to be proud of?'

'Is it anything to be ashamed of?'

'Yes. You know that, don't you?' Carol asked in her even, distinct voice. 'In the eyes of the world it's an abomination.'

The way she said it, Therese could not quite smile. 'You don't believe that.'

'People like Harge's family.'

'They're not the whole world.'

'They are enough. And you have to live in the world. You, I mean — and I don't mean anything just now about whom you decide to love.' She looked at Therese, and at last Therese saw a smile rising slowly in her eyes, bringing Carol with it. 'I mean responsibilities in the world that other people live in and that might not be yours. Just now it isn't, and that's why in New York I was exactly the wrong person for you to know — because I indulge you and keep you from growing up.'

'Why don't you stop?'

'I'll try. The trouble is, I like to indulge you.'

'You're exactly the right person for me to know,' Therese said.

'Am I?'

On the street, Therese said, 'I don't suppose Harge would like it if he knew we were away on a trip, either, would he?'

'He's not going to know about it.'

'Do you still want to go to Washington?'

'Absolutely, if you've got the time. Can you stay away all of February?'

Therese nodded. 'Unless I hear something in Salt Lake City. I told Phil to write there. It's a pretty slim chance.' Probably Phil wouldn't even write, she thought. But if there was the least chance of a job in New York, she should go back. 'Would you go on to Washington without me?'

Carol glanced at her. 'As a matter of fact, I wouldn't,' she said with a little smile.

Their hotel room was so overheated when they came back that evening, they had to throw open the windows for a while. Carol leaned on the window-sill, cursing the heat for Therese's amusement, calling her a salamander because she could bear it. Then Carol asked abruptly, 'What did Richard have to say yesterday?'

176

Therese had not even known that Carol knew about the last letter. The one he had promised, in the Chicago letter, to send to Minneapolis and to Seattle. 'Nothing much,' Therese said. 'Just a one-page letter. He still wants me to write to him. And I don't intend to.' She had thrown the letter away, but she remembered it:

I haven't heard from you, and it's beginning to dawn on me what an incredible conglomeration of contradictions you are. You are sensitive and yet so insensitive, imaginative and yet so unimaginative . . . If you get stranded by your whimsical friend, let me know and I'll come after you. This won't last, Terry. I know a little about such things. I saw Dannie and he wanted to know what I'd heard from you, what you were doing. How would you like it if I had told him? I didn't say anything, for your sake, because I think one day you'll blush. I still love you, I admit it. I'll come out to you – and show you what America's really like – if you care enough about me to write and say so . . .

It was insulting to Carol, and Therese had torn it up. Therese sat on the bed with her arms around her knees, gripping her wrists inside the sleeves of her robe. Carol had overdone the ventilation, and the room was cold. The Minnesota winds had taken possession of the room, were seizing Carol's cigarette smoke and tearing it to nothing. Therese watched Carol calmly brushing her teeth at the basin.

'Do you mean that about not writing to him? That's your decision?' Carol asked.

'Yes.'

Therese watched Carol knock the water out of her toothbrush, and turn from the basin, blotting her face with a towel. Nothing about Richard mattered so much to her as the way Carol blotted her face with a towel.

'Let's say no more,' Carol said.

She knew Carol would say no more. She knew Carol had been pushing her towards him, until this moment. Now it seemed it might all have been for this moment as Carol turned and walked towards her and her heart took a giant's step forward.

They went on westward, through Sleepy Eye, Tracy and Pipestone, sometimes taking an indirect highway on a whim. The West unfolded like a magic carpet, dotted with the neat, tight units of farmhouse, barn, and silo that they could see for half an hour before they came abreast of them. They stopped once at a farmhouse to ask if they could buy enough gas to get to the next station. The house smelled like fresh cold cheese. Their steps sounded hollow and lonely on the solid brown planks of the floor, and Therese thought in a fervid burst of patriotism – *America*. There was a picture of a rooster on the wall, made of coloured patches of cloth sewn on a black ground, beautiful enough to hang in a museum. The farmer warned them about ice on the road directly west, so they took another highway going south.

They discovered a one-ring circus that night beside a railroad track in a town called Sioux Falls. The performers were not very expert. Therese and Carol sat on a couple of orange crates in the first row. One of the acrobats invited them into the performers' tent after the show, and insisted on giving Carol a dozen of the circus posters, because she had admired them. Carol sent some of them to Abby and some to Rindy, and sent Rindy as well a green chameleon in a pasteboard box. It was an evening Therese would never forget, and unlike most such evenings, this one registered as unforgettable while it still lived. It was a matter of the bag of popcorn they shared, the circus, and the kiss Carol gave her back of some booth in the performers' tent. It was a matter of that particular enchantment that came from Carol – though Carol took their good times so for granted – and seemed to work on all the world around them, a matter of everything going perfectly, without disappointments or hitches, going just as they wished it to.

Therese walked from the circus with her head down, lost in thought. 'I wonder if I'll ever want to create anything again,' she said.

'What brought this on?'

'I mean – what was I ever trying to do but this? I'm happy.'

Carol took her arm and squeezed it, dug her thumb in so hard that Therese yelled. Carol looked up at a street marker and said, 'Fifth and Nebraska. I think we go this way.'

'What's going to happen when we get back to New York? It can't be the same, can it?'

'Yes,' Carol said. 'Till you get tired of me.'

Therese laughed. She heard the soft snap of Carol's scarf end in the wind.

'We might not be living together, but it'll be the same.'

They couldn't live together with Rindy, Therese knew. It was useless to dream of it. But it was more than enough that Carol promised in words it would be the same.

Near the border of Nebraska and Wyoming, they stopped for dinner at a large restaurant built like a lodge in an evergreen forest. They were almost the only people in the big dining room, and they chose a table near the fireplace. They spread out the road map and decided to head straight for Salt Lake City. They might stay there for a few days, Carol said, because it was an interesting place, and she was tired of driving.

'Lusk,' Therese said, looking at the map. 'What a sexy sounding name.'

Carol put her head back and laughed. 'Where is it?'

'On the road.'

Carol picked up her wine glass and said, 'Château Neuf-du-Pape in Nebraska. What'll we drink to?'

'Us.'

It was something like the morning in Waterloo, Therese thought, a time too absolute and flawless to seem real, though it was real, not merely props in a play – their brandy glasses on the mantel, the row of deers' horns above, Carol's cigarette lighter, the fire itself. But at moments she felt like an actor, remembered only now and then her identity with a sense of surprise, as if she had been playing in these last days the part of someone else, someone fabulously and excessively lucky. She looked up at the fir branches fixed in the rafters, at the man and woman talking inaudibly together at a table against the wall, at the man alone at his table, smoking his cigarette slowly. She thought of the man sitting with the newspaper in the hotel in Waterloo. Didn't he have the same colourless eyes and the long creases on either side of his mouth? Or was it only that this moment of consciousness was so much the same as that other moment?

They spent the night in Lusk, ninety miles away.

CHAPTER SEVENTEEN

'Mrs H. F. Aird?' The desk clerk looked at Carol after she had signed the register. 'Are you Mrs Carol Aird?'

'Yes.'

'Message for you.' He turned around and got it from a pigeon hole. 'A telegram.'

'Thank you.' Carol glanced at Therese with a little lift of her brows before she opened it. She read it, frowning, then turned to the clerk. 'Where's the Belvedere Hotel?'

The clerk directed her.

'I've got to pick up another telegram,' Carol said to Therese. 'Want to wait here while I get it?'

'Who from?'

'Abby.'

'All right. Is it bad news?'

The frown was still in her eyes. 'Don't know until I see it. Abby just says there's a telegram for me at the Belvedere.'

'Shall I have the bags taken up?'

'Well – just wait. The car is parked.'

'Why can't I come with you?'

'Of course, if you want to. Let's walk. It's only a couple of blocks away.'

Carol walked quickly. The cold was sharp. Therese glanced around her at the flat, orderly looking town, and remembered Carol's saying that Salt Lake City was the cleanest town in the United States. When

180

the Belvedere was in sight, Carol suddenly looked at her and said, 'Abby's probably had a brainstorm and decided to fly out and join us.'

In the Belvedere, Therese bought a newspaper while Carol went to the desk. When Therese turned to her, Carol was just lowering the telegram after reading it. There was a stunned expression on her face. She came slowly towards Therese, and it flashed through Therese's mind that Abby was dead, that this second message was from Abby's parents.

'What's the matter?' Therese asked.

'Nothing. I don't know yet.' Carol glanced around and slapped the telegram against her fingers. 'I've got to make a phone call. It might take a few minutes.' She looked at her watch.

It was a quarter to two. The hotel clerk said she could probably get New Jersey in about twenty minutes. Meanwhile, Carol wanted a drink. They found a bar in the hotel.

'What is it? Is Abby sick?'

Carol smiled. 'No. I'll tell you later.'

'Is it Rindy?'

'No!' Carol finished her brandy.

Therese walked up and down in the lobby while Carol was in the telephone booth. She saw Carol nod slowly several times, saw her fumble to get a cigarette lighted, but by the time Therese got there to light it for her, Carol had it and motioned her away. Carol talked for three or four minutes, then came out and paid her bill.

'What is it, Carol?'

Carol stood looking out the doorway of the hotel for a moment. 'Now we go to the Temple Square Hotel,' she said.

There they picked up another telegram. Carol opened it and glanced at it, and tore it up as they walked to the door.

'I don't think we'll stay here tonight,' Carol said. 'Let's go back to the car.'

They went back to the hotel where Carol had gotten the first telegram. Therese said nothing to her, but she felt something had happened that meant Carol had to get back East immediately. Carol told the clerk to cancel their room reservation.

'I'd like to leave a forwarding address in case of any other messages,' she said. 'That's the Brown Palace, Denver.'

181

'Right you are.'

'Thank you very much. That's good for the next week at least.'

In the car, Carol said, 'What's the next town west?'

'West?' Therese looked at the map. 'Wendover. This is that stretch. A hundred and twenty-seven miles.'

'Christ!' Carol said suddenly. She stopped the car completely and took the map and looked at it.

'What about Denver?' Therese asked.

'I don't want to go to Denver.' Carol folded the map and started the car. 'Well, we'll do it anyway. Light me a cigarette, will you, darling? And watch out for the next place to get something to eat.'

They hadn't had lunch yet, and it was after three. They had talked about this stretch last night, the straight road road west from Salt Lake City across the Great Salt Lake Desert. They had plenty of gas, Therese noticed, and probably the country wasn't entirely deserted, but Carol was tired. They had been driving since six that morning. Carol drove fast. Now and then she pressed the pedal down to the floor and held it there a long while before letting up. Therese glanced at her apprehensively. She felt they were running away from something.

'Anything behind us?' Carol asked.

'No.' On the seat between them, Therese could see a piece of the telegram sticking out of Carol's handbag. 'GET THIS. JACOPO.' was all she could read. She remembered Jacopo was the name of the little monkey in the back of the car.

They came to a gas-station café standing all by itself like a wart on the flat landscape. They might have been the first people who had stopped there in days. Carol looked at her across the white oilcloth table, and sank back in the straight chair. Before she could speak, an old man in an apron came from the kitchen in back, and told them there was nothing but ham and eggs, so they ordered ham and eggs and coffee. Then Carol lighted a cigarette and leaned forward, looking down at the table.

'Do you know what's up?' she said. 'Harge has had a detective following us since Chicago.'

'A detective? What for?'

'Can't you guess?' Carol said in almost a whisper.

182

Therese bit her tongue. Yes, she could guess. Harge had found out they were travelling together. 'Abby told you?'

'Abby found out.' Carol's fingers slid down her cigarette and the fire burned her. When she got the cigarette out of her mouth, her lips began to bleed.

Therese looked around her. The place was empty. 'Following us?' she asked. '*With* us?'

'He may be in Salt Lake City now. Checking on all the hotels. It's a very dirty business, darling. I'm sorry, sorry, sorry.' Carol sat back restlessly in her chair. 'Maybe I'd better put you on a train and send you home.'

'All right – if you think that's the best idea.'

'You don't have to be mixed up in this. Let them follow me to Alaska, if they want to. I don't know what they've got so far. I don't think much.'

Therese sat rigidly on the edge of her chair. 'What's he doing – making notes about us?'

The old man was coming back, bringing them glasses of water.

Carol nodded. 'Then there's the dictaphone trick,' she said as the man went away. 'I'm not sure if they'll go that far. I'm not sure if Harge would do that.' The corner of her mouth trembled. She stared down at one spot on the worn white oilcloth. 'I wonder if they had time for a dictaphone in Chicago. It's the only place we stayed more than ten hours. I rather hope they did. It's so ironic. Remember Chicago?'

'Of course.' She tried to keep her voice steady, but it was pretence, like pretending self-control when something you loved was dead in front of your eyes. They would have to separate here. 'What about Waterloo?' She thought suddenly of the man in the lobby.

'We got there late. It wouldn't have been easy.'

'Carol, I saw someone – I'm not sure, but I think I saw him twice.'

'Where?'

'In the lobby in Waterloo the first time. In the morning. Then I thought I saw the same man in that restaurant with the fireplace.' It was only last night, the restaurant with the fireplace.

Carol made her tell completely about both times and describe the man completely. He was hard to describe. But now she racked her

183

brain to extract the last detail she could, even to the colour of his shoes. And it was odd and rather terrifying, dragging up what was probably a figment of her imagination and tying it to a situation that was real. She felt she might even be lying to Carol as she watched Carol's eyes grow more and more intense.

'What do you think?' Therese asked.

Carol sighed. 'What can anyone think? Just watch out for him the third time.'

Therese looked down at her plate. It was impossible to eat. 'It's about Rindy, isn't it?'

'Yes.' She put down her fork without taking the first bite, and reached for a cigarette. 'Harge wants her – in toto. Maybe with this, he thinks he can do it.'

'Just because we're travelling together?'

'Yes.'

'I should leave you.'

'Damn him,' Carol said quietly, looking off at a corner of the room.

Therese waited. But what was there to wait for? 'I can get a bus somewhere from here, and then get a train.'

'Do you want to go?' Carol asked.

'Of course I don't. I just think it's best.'

'Are you afraid?'

'Afraid? No.' She felt Carol's eyes appraise her as severely as at that moment in Waterloo, when she had told Carol she loved her.

'Then I'm damned if you'll go. I want you with me.'

'Do you mean that?'

'Yes. Eat your eggs. Stop being silly.' And Carol even smiled a little. 'Shall we go to Reno as we'd planned?'

'Any place.'

'And let's take our time.'

A few moments later, when they were on the road, Therese said again, 'I'm still not sure it was the same man the second time, you know.'

'I think you're sure,' Carol said. Then, suddenly, on the long straight road, she stopped the car. She sat for a moment in silence, looking down the road. Then she glanced at Therese. 'I can't go to

Reno. That's a little too funny. I know a wonderful place just south of Denver.'

'Denver?'

'Denver,' Carol said firmly, and backed the car around.

CHAPTER EIGHTEEN

In the morning, they lay in each other's arms long after the sun had come into the room. The sun warmed them through the window of the hotel in the tiny town whose name they hadn't noticed. There was snow on the ground outside.

'There'll be snow in Estes Park,' Carol said to her.

'What's Estes Park?'

'You'll like it. Not like Yellowstone. It's open all year.'

'Carol, you're not worried, are you?'

Carol pulled her close. 'Do I act like I'm worried?'

Therese was not worried. That first panic had vanished. She was watching, but not as she had watched yesterday afternoon just after Salt Lake City. Carol wanted her with her, and whatever happened they would meet it without running. How was it possible to be afraid and in love, Therese thought. The two things did not go together. How was it possible to be afraid, when the two of them grew stronger together every day? And every night. Every night was different, and every morning. Together they possessed a miracle.

The road into Estes Park slanted downward. The snowdrifts piled higher and higher on either side, and then the lights began, strung along the fir trees, arching over the road. It was a village of brown logged houses and shops and hotels. There was music, and people walked in the bright street with their heads lifted up, as if they were enchanted.

'I do like it,' Therese said.

'It doesn't mean you don't have to watch out for our little man.'

They brought the portable phonograph up to their room, and played some records they had just bought and some old ones from New Jersey. Therese played 'Easy Living' a couple of times, and Carol sat across the room watching her, sitting on the arm of a chair with her arms folded.

'What a rotten time I give you, don't I?'

'Oh, Carol – ' Therese tried to smile. It was only a mood of Carol's, only a moment. But it made Therese feel helpless.

Carol looked around at the window. 'And why didn't we go to Europe in the first place? Switzerland. Or fly out here at least.'

'I wouldn't have liked that at all.' Therese looked at the yellow suède shirt that Carol had bought for her, which hung over the back of a chair. Carol had sent Rindy a green one. She had bought some silver earrings, a couple of books, and a bottle of Triple Sec. Half an hour ago, they had been happy, walking through the streets together. 'It's that last rye you got downstairs,' Therese said. 'Rye depresses you.'

'Does it?'

'Worse than brandy.'

'I'm going to take you to the nicest place I know this side of Sun Valley,' she said.

'What's the matter with Sun Valley?' She knew Carol liked skiing.

'Sun Valley just isn't the place,' Carol said mysteriously. 'This place is near Colorado Springs.'

In Denver, Carol stopped and sold her diamond engagement ring at a jeweller's. Therese felt a little disturbed by it, but Carol said the ring meant nothing to her and she loathed diamonds anyway. And it was quicker than wiring her bank for money. Carol wanted to stop at a hotel a few miles out from Colorado Springs, where she had been before, but she changed her mind almost as soon as they got there. It was too much like a resort, she said, so they went to an hotel that backed on the town and faced the mountains.

Their room was long from the door to the square floor-length windows that overlooked a garden, and beyond, the red and white mountains. There were touches of white in the garden, odd little pyramids of stone, a white bench or a chair, and the garden looked foolish compared to the magnificent land that surrounded it, the flat sweep that rose up into mountains upon mountains, filling the horizon like half a world. The room had blonde furniture about the colour of Carol's hair, and there was a bookcase as smooth as she could want it, with some good books amid the bad ones, and Therese knew she would never read any of them while they were here. A painting of a woman in a large black hat and a red scarf hung above the bookcase, and on the wall near the door was spread a pelt of brown leather, not a real pelt but something someone had cut out of a piece of brown suède. Above it was a tin lantern with a candle. Carol also rented the room next to them, which had a connecting door, though they did not use it even to put their suitcases in. They planned to stay a week, or longer if they liked it.

On the morning of the second day, Therese came back from a tour of inspection of the hotel grounds and found Carol stopped by the bed table. Carol only glanced at her, and went to the dressing table and looked under that, and then to the long built-in closet behind the wall panel.

'That's that,' Carol said. 'Now let's forget it.'

Therese knew what she was looking for. 'I hadn't thought of it,' she said. 'I feel like we've lost him.'

'Except that he's probably gotten to Denver by now,' Carol said calmly. She smiled, but she twisted her mouth a little. 'And he'll probably drop in down here.'

It was so, of course. There was even the remotest chance that the detective had seen them when they drove back through Salt Lake City, and followed them. If he didn't find them in Salt Lake City, he might enquire at the hotels. She knew that was why Carol had left the Denver address, in fact, because they hadn't intended to go to Denver. Therese flung herself in the armchair, and looked at Carol. Carol took the trouble to search for a dictaphone, but her attitude was arrogant. She had even invited trouble by coming here. And the explanation, the resolution of those contradictory facts was nowhere but in Carol herself, unresolved, in her slow, restless step as she walked to the door now and turned, in the nonchalant lift of her head, and in the nervous line of her eyebrows that registered irritation in one second and in the next were serene. Therese looked at the big room, up at the high ceiling, at the large, square, plain bed, the room that for all its modernness had a curiously old-fashioned, ample air about it that she associated with the American West, like the oversized Western saddles she had seen in the riding stable downstairs. A kind of cleanness, as well. Yet Carol looked for a dictaphone. Therese watched her, walking back towards her, still in her pyjamas and robe. She had an impulse to go to Carol, crush her in her arms, pull her down on the bed, and the fact that she didn't now made her tense and alert, filled her with a repressed but reckless exhilaration.

Carol blew her smoke up into the air. 'I don't give a damn. I hope the papers find out about it and rub Harge's nose in his own mess. I hope he wastes fifty thousand dollars. Do you want to take that trip that bankrupts the English language this afternoon? Did you ask Mrs French yet?'

They had met Mrs French last night in the game room of the hotel. She hadn't a car, and Carol had asked her if she would like to take a drive with them today.

'I asked her,' Therese said. 'She said she'd be ready right after lunch.'

'Wear your suède shirt.' Carol took Therese's face in her hands, pressed her cheeks, and kissed her. 'Put it on now.'

It was a six- or seven-hour trip to the Cripple Creek gold mine, over Ute Pass and down a mountain. Mrs French went with them, talking the whole time. She was a woman of about seventy, with a Maryland accent and a hearing aid, ready to get out of the car and climb anywhere, though she had to be helped every foot of the way. Therese felt very anxious about her, though she actually disliked even touching her. She felt if Mrs French fell, she would break in a million pieces. Carol and Mrs French talked about the State of Washington, which Mrs French knew well, since she had lived there for the past few years with one of her sons. Carol asked a few questions, and Mrs French told her all about her ten years of travelling since her husband's death, and about her two sons, the one in Washington and the one in Hawaii who worked for a pineapple company. And obviously Mrs French adored Carol, and they were going to see a lot more of Mrs French. It was nearly eleven when they got back to the hotel. Carol asked Mrs French to have supper in the bar with them, but Mrs French said she was too tired for anything but her shredded wheat and hot milk, which she would have in her room.

'I'm glad,' Therese said when she had gone. 'I'd rather be alone with you.'

'Really, Miss Belivet? Whatever do you mean?' Carol asked as she opened the door into the bar. 'You'd better sit down and tell me all about that.'

But they were not alone in the bar more than five minutes. Two men, one named Dave and the other whose name Therese at least did not know and did not care to, came over and asked to join them. They were the two who had come over last night in the game room and asked Carol and her to play gin rummy. Carol had declined last night. Now she said, 'Of course, sit down.' Carol and Dave began a conversation that sounded very interesting, but Therese was seated so that she couldn't participate very well. And the man next to Therese wanted to talk about something else, a horseback trip he had just made around Steamboat Springs. After supper, Therese waited for a sign from Carol to leave, but Carol was still deep in conversation. Therese had read about that special pleasure people got from the fact that someone they loved was attractive in the eyes of other people, too. She simply didn't have it. Carol looked at her every now and then and gave her a wink. So Therese sat there for an hour and a half, and managed to be polite, because she knew Carol wanted her to be.

The people who joined them in the bar and sometimes in the dining room did not annoy her so much as Mrs French, who went with them somewhere almost every day in the car. Then an angry resentment that Therese was actually ashamed of would rise in her because someone was preventing her from being alone with Carol.

'Darling, did you ever think you'll be seventy-one, too, some day?'

'No,' Therese said.

But there were other days when they drove out into the mountains alone, taking any road they saw. Once they came upon a little town they liked and spent the night there, without pyjamas or toothbrushes, without past or future, and the night became another of those islands in time, suspended somewhere in the heart or in the memory, intact and absolute. Or perhaps it was nothing but happiness, Therese thought, a complete happiness that must be rare enough, so rare that very few people ever knew it. But if it was merely happiness, then it had gone beyond the ordinary bounds and become something else, become a kind of excessive pressure, so that the weight of a coffee cup in her hand, the speed of a cat crossing the garden below, the silent crash of two clouds seemed almost more than she could bear. And just as she had not understood a month ago the phenomenon of sudden happiness, she did not understand her state now, which seemed an aftermath. It was more often painful than pleasant, and consequently she was afraid she had some grave and unique flaw. She was as afraid sometimes as if she were walking about with a broken spine. If she ever had an impulse to tell Carol, the words dissolved before she began, in fear and in her usual mistrust of her own reactions, the anxiety that her reactions were like no one else's, and that therefore not even Carol could understand them.

In the mornings, they generally drove out somewhere in the mountains and left the car so they could climb up a hill. They drove aimlessly over the zigzagging roads that were like white chalk lines connecting mountain point to mountain point. From a distance, one could see clouds lying about the projecting peaks, so it seemed they flew along in space, a little closer to heaven than to earth. Therese's favourite spot was on the highway above Cripple Creek, where the road clung suddenly to the rim of a gigantic depression. Hundreds of feet below lay the tiny disorder of the abandoned mining town. There the eye and the brain played tricks with each other, for it was impossible to keep a steady concept of the proportion below, impossible to compare it on any human scale. Her own hand held up in front of her could look Lilliputian or curiously huge. And the town occupied only a fraction of the great scoop in the earth, like a single experience, a single commonplace event, set in a certain immeasurable territory of the mind. The eye, swimming in space, returned to rest on the spot that looked like a box of matches run over by a car, the man-made confusion of the little town.

Always Therese looked for the man with the creases on either side of his mouth, but Carol never did. Carol had not even mentioned him since their second day at Colorado Springs, and now ten days had passed. Because the restaurant of the hotel was famous, new people came every evening to the big dining room, and Therese always glanced about, not actually expecting to see him, but as a kind of precaution that had become a habit. But Carol paid no attention to anyone except Walter, their waiter, who always came up to ask what kind of cocktail they wanted that evening. Many people looked at Carol, however, because she was generally the most attractive woman in the room. And Therese was so delighted to be with her, so proud of her, she looked at no one else but Carol. Then as she read the menu, Carol would slowly press Therese's foot under the table to make her smile.

'What do you think about Iceland in the summer?' Carol might ask, because they made a point of talking about travel, if there was a silence when they first sat down.

'Must you pick such cold places? When'll I ever work?'

'Don't be dismal. Shall we invite Mrs French? Think she'd mind our holding hands?'

One morning, there were three letters – from Rindy, Abby, and Dannie. It was Carol's second letter from Abby, who had had no further news before, and Therese noticed Carol opened Rindy's letter first. Dannie wrote that he was still waiting to hear the outcome of two interviews about jobs. And reported that Phil said Harkevy was going to do the sets for the English play called *The Faint Heart* in March.

'Listen to this,' Carol said. '"Have you seen any armadillos in Colorado? Can you send me one, because the chameleon got lost. Daddy and I looked everywhere in the house for him. But if you send me the armadillo it will be big enough not to get lost." New paragraph. "I got ninety in spelling but only seventy in arithmetic. I hate it. I hate the teacher. Well I must be closing. Love to you and to Abby. Rindy. XX. P.S. Thank you very much for the leather shirt. Daddy bought me a two-wheel bike regular size that he said I was too small for Christmas. I am not too small. It is a beautiful bike." Period. What's the use? Harge can always top me.' Carol put the letter down and picked up Abby's.

'Why did Rindy say "Love to you and to Abby"?' Therese asked. 'Does she think you're with Abby?'

'No.' Carol's wooden letter opener had stopped halfway through Abby's envelope. 'I suppose she thinks I write to her,' she said, and finished slitting the envelope.

'I mean, Harge wouldn't have told her that, would he?'

'No, darling,' Carol said preoccupiedly, reading Abby's letter.

Therese got up and crossed the room, and stood by the window looking out at the mountains. She should write to Harkevy this afternoon, she thought, and ask him if there was a chance of an assistant's job with his group in March. She began composing the letter in her head. The mountains looked back at her like majestic red lions, staring down their noses. Twice she heard Carol laugh, but she did not read any of the letter aloud to her.

'No news?' Therese asked when she was finished.

'No news.'

Carol taught her to drive on the roads around the foot of the mountains, where a car almost never passed. Therese learned faster than she had ever learned anything before, and after a couple of days, Carol let her drive in Colorado Springs. In Denver, she took a test and got a licence. Carol said she could do half the driving back to New York, if she wanted to.

He was sitting one evening at the dinner hour at a table by himself to the left of Carol and behind her. Therese choked on nothing, and put her fork down. Her heart began to beat as if it would hammer its way out of her chest. How had she gotten halfway through the meal without seeing him? She lifted her eyes to Carol's face and saw Carol watching her, reading her with the grey eyes that were not quite so calm as a moment ago. Carol had stopped in the middle of saying something.

'Have a cigarette,' Carol said, offering her one, lighting it for her. 'He doesn't know that you can recognize him, does he?'

'No.'

'Well, don't let him find out.' Carol smiled at her, lighted her own cigarette, and looked away in the opposite direction from the detective. 'Just take it easy,' Carol added in the same tone.

It was easy to say, easy to have thought she could look at him when she saw him next, but what was the use of trying when it was like being struck in the face with a cannon ball?

'No baked Alaska tonight?' Carol said, looking at the menu. 'That breaks my heart. You know what we're going to have?' She called to the waiter. 'Walter!'

Walter came smiling, ardent to serve them, just as he did every evening. 'Yes, madame.'

'Two Remy Martins, please, Walter,' Carol told him.

The brandy helped very little, if at all. The detective did not once look at them. He was reading a book that he had propped up on the metal napkin holder, and even now Therese felt a doubt as strong as in the café outside Salt Lake City, an uncertainty that was somehow more horrible than the positive knowledge would be that he was the detective.

'Do we have to go past him, Carol?' Therese asked. There was a door in back of her, into the bar.

'Yes. That's the way we go out.' Carol's eyebrows lifted with her smile, exactly as on any other night. 'He can't do anything to us. Do you expect him to pull a gun?'

Therese followed her, passed within twelve inches of the man whose head was lowered towards his book. Ahead of her she saw Carol's figure bend gracefully as she greeted Mrs French, who was sitting alone at a table.

'Why didn't you come and join us?' Carol said, and Therese remembered that the two women Mrs French usually sat with had left today.

Carol even stood there a few moments talking with Mrs French, and Therese marvelled at her but she couldn't stand there herself, and went on, to wait for Carol by the elevators.

Upstairs, Carol found the little instrument fastened up in a corner under the bed table. Carol got the scissors and, using both hands, cut through the wire that disappeared under the carpet.

'Did the hotel people let him in here, do you think?' Therese asked, horrified.

'He probably had a key to fit.' Carol yanked the thing loose from the table and dropped it on the carpet, a little black box with a trail of wire. 'Look at it, like a rat,' she said. 'A portrait of Harge.' Her face had flushed suddenly.

'Where does it go to?'

'To some room where it's recorded. Probably across the hall. *Bless* these fancy wall-to-wall carpets!'

Carol kicked the dictaphone towards the centre of the room.

Therese looked at the little rectangular box, and thought of it drinking up their words last night. 'I wonder how long it's been there?'

'How long do you think he could have been here without your seeing him?'

'Yesterday at the worst.' But even as she said it, she knew she could be wrong. She couldn't have seen every face in the hotel.

And Carol was shaking her head. 'Would it take him nearly two weeks to trace us from Salt Lake City to here? No, he just decided to have dinner with us tonight.' Carol turned from the bookshelf with a glass of brandy in her hand. The flush had left her face. Now she even smiled a little at Therese. 'Clumsy fellow, isn't he?' She sat down on the bed, swung a pillow behind her and leaned back. 'Well, we've been here just about long enough, haven't we?'

'When do you want to go?'

'Maybe tomorrow. We'll get ourselves packed in the morning and take off after lunch. What do you think?'

Later, they went down to the car and took a drive, westward into the darkness. We shall not go farther west, Therese thought. She could not stamp out the panic that danced in the very core of her, that she felt due to something gone before, something that had happened long ago, not now, not this. She was uneasy, but Carol was not. Carol was not merely pretending coolness, she really was not afraid. Carol said, what could he do, after all, but she simply didn't want to be spied upon.

'One other thing,' Carol said. 'Try and find out what kind of car he's in.'

That night, talking over the road map about their route tomorrow, talking as matter of factly as a couple of strangers, Therese thought surely tonight would not be like last night. But when they kissed goodnight in bed, Therese felt their sudden release, that leap of response in both of them, as if their bodies were of some materials which put together ine vitably created desire.

CHAPTER NINETEEN

Therese could not find out what kind of car he had, because the cars were locked in separate garages, and though she had a view of the garages from the sunroom, she did not see him come out that morning. Neither did they see him at lunchtime.

Mrs French insisted that they come into her room for a cordial, when she heard they were leaving. 'You must have a stirrup cup,' Mrs French said to Carol. 'Why, I haven't even got your address yet!'

Therese remembered that they had promised to exchange flower bulbs. She remembered a long conversation in the car one day about bulbs that had cemented their friendship. Carol was incredibly patient to the last. One would never have guessed, seeing Carol sitting on Mrs French's sofa with the little glass Mrs French kept filling, that she was in a hurry to get away. Mrs French kissed them both on the cheek when they said goodbye.

From Denver, they took a highway northward towards Wyoming. They stopped for coffee at the kind of place they always liked, an ordinary restaurant with a counter and a juke box. They put nickels into the juke box, but it was not the same as before. Therese knew it would not be the same for the rest of the trip, though Carol talked of going to Washington even yet, and perhaps up into Canada. Therese could feel that Carol's goal was New York.

They spent the first night in a tourist camp that was built like a circle of tepees. While they were undressing, Carol looked up at the ceiling where the tepee poles came to a point, and said boredly, 'The trouble some idiots go to,' and for some reason it struck Therese as hysterically funny. She laughed until Carol got tired of it and threatened to make her drink a tumbler of brandy, if she didn't stop. And Therese was still smiling, standing by the window with a brandy in her hand, waiting for Carol to come out of the shower, when she saw a car drive up beside the large office tepee and stop. After a moment, the man who had gone into the office came out and looked around in the dark area within the circle of tepees, and it was his prowling step that arrested her attention. She was suddenly sure without seeing his face or even his figure very clearly that he was the detective.

'Carol!' she called.

Carol pushed the shower curtain aside and glanced at her and stopped drying herself. 'Is it – '

'I don't know, but I think so,' she said, and saw the anger spread slowly over Carol's face and stiffen it, and it shocked Therese to sobriety, as if she had just realized an insult, to herself or to Carol.

'Chr-rist!' Carol said, and flung the towel at the floor. She drew on her robe and tied the belt of it. 'Well – what's he doing?'

'I think he's stopping here.' Therese stood back at the edge of the window. 'His car's still in front of the office, anyway. If we turn out the light, I'll be able to see a lot better.'

Carol groaned. 'Oh, don't. I couldn't. It bores me,' she said with the utmost boredom and disgust.

And Therese smiled, twistedly, and checked another insane impulse to laugh, because Carol would have been furious if she had laughed. Then she saw the car roll under the garage door of a tepee across the circle. 'Yes, he's stopping here. It's a black two-door sedan.'

Carol sat down on the bed with a sigh. She smiled at Therese, a quick smile of fatigue and boredom, of resignation and helplessness and anger. 'Take your shower. And then get dressed again.'

'But I don't know if it's him at all.'

'That's just the hell of it, darling.'

Therese took a shower and lay down in her clothes beside Carol. Carol had turned out the light. She was smoking cigarettes in the dark, and said nothing to her until finally she touched her arm and

197

said, 'Let's go.' It was three-thirty when they drove out of the tourist camp. They had paid their bill in advance. There was no light anywhere, and unless the detective was watching them with his light out, no one had observed them.

'What do you want to do, sleep again somewhere?' Carol asked her.

'No. Do you?'

'No. Let's see how much distance we can make.' She pressed the pedal to the floor. The road was clear and smooth as far as the headlights swept.

As dawn was breaking, a highway patrolman stopped them for speeding, and Carol had to pay a twenty-dollar fine in a town called Central City, Nebraska. They lost thirty miles by having to follow the patrolman back to the little town, but Carol went through with it without a word, unlike herself, unlike the time she had argued and cajoled the patrolman out of an arrest for speeding, and a New Jersey speed cop at that.

'Irritating,' Carol said when they got back into the car, and that was all she said, for hours.

Therese offered to drive, but Carol said she wanted to. And the flat Nebraska prairie spread out before them, yellow with wheat stubble, brown-splotched with bare earth and stone, deceptively warm-looking in the white winter sun. Because they went a little slower now, Therese had a panicky sensation of not moving at all, as if the earth drifted under them and they stood still. She watched the road behind them for another patrol car, for the detective's car, and for the nameless, shapeless thing she felt pursuing them from Colorado Springs. She watched the land and the sky for the meaningless events that her mind insisted on attaching significance to, the buzzard that banked slowly in the sky, the direction of a tangle of weeds that bounced over a rutted field before the wind, and whether a chimney had smoke or not. Around eight o'clock, an irresistible sleepiness weighted her eyelids and clouded her head, so she felt scarcely any surprise when she saw a car behind them like the car she watched for, a two-door sedan of dark colour.

'There's a car like that behind us,' she said. 'It's got a yellow licence plate.'

Carol said nothing for a minute, but she glanced in the mirror and blew her breath out through pursed lips. 'I doubt it. If it is, he's a better man than I thought.' She was slowing down. 'If I let him pass, do you think you can recognize him?'

'Yes.' Couldn't she recognize the blurriest glimpse of him by now?

Carol slowed almost to a stop and took the road map and laid it across the wheel and looked at it. The other car approached, and it was him inside, and went by.

'Yes,' Therese said. The man hadn't glanced at her.

Carol pressed the gas pedal down. 'You're sure, are you?'

'Positive.' Therese watched the speedometer go up to sixty-five and over. 'What are you going to do?'

'Speak to him.'

Carol slacked her speed as they closed the distance. They drew alongside of the detective's car, and he turned to look at them, the wide straight mouth unchanging, the eyes like round grey dots, expressionless as the mouth. Carol waved her hand downward. The man's car slowed.

'Roll your window down,' Carol said to Therese.

The detective's car pulled over into the sandy shoulder of the road and stopped.

Carol stopped her car with its rear wheels on the highway, and spoke across Therese. 'Do you like our company or what?' she asked.

The man got out of his car and closed his door. Some three yards of ground separated the cars, and the detective crossed half of it and stood. His dead little eyes had darkish rims around their grey irises, like a doll's blank and steady eyes. He was not young. His face looked worn by the weathers he had driven it through, and the shadows of his beard deepened the bent creases on either side of his mouth.

'I'm doing my job, Mrs Aird,' he said.

'That's pretty obvious. It's nasty work, isn't it?'

The detective tapped a cigarette on his thumbnail and lighted it in the gusty wind with a slowness that suggested a stage performance. 'At least it's nearly over.'

'Then why don't you leave us alone,' Carol said, her voice as tense as the arm that supported her on the steering wheel.

'Because I have orders to follow you on this trip. But if you're going back to New York, I won't have to any more. I advise you to go back, Mrs Aird. Are you going back now?'

'No, I'm not.'

'Because I've got some information – information that I'd say was in your interest to go back and take care of.'

'Thanks,' Carol said cynically. 'Thanks so much for telling me. It's not in my plans to go back just yet. But I can give you my itinerary, so you can leave us alone and catch up on your sleep.'

The detective looked at her with a false and meaningless smile, not like a person at all, but like a machine wound up and set on a course. 'I think you'll go back to New York. I'm giving you sound advice. Your child is at stake. I suppose you know that, don't you?'

'My child is my property!'

A crease twitched in his cheek. 'A human being is not property, Mrs Aird.'

Carol raised her voice. 'Are you going to tag along the rest of the way?'

'Are you going back to New York?'

'No.'

'I think you will,' the detective said, and he turned away slowly towards his car.

Carol stepped on the starter. She reached for Therese's hand and squeezed it for a moment in reassurance, and then the car shot forward. Therese sat up with her elbows on her knees and her hands pressed to her forehead, yielding to a shame and shock she had never known before, that she had repressed before the detective.

'Carol!'

Carol was crying, silently. Therese looked at the downward curve of her lips that was not like Carol at all, but rather like a small girl's twisted grimace of crying. She stared incredulously at the tear that rolled over Carol's cheekbone.

'Get me a cigarette,' Carol said.

When Therese handed it to her, lighted, she had wiped the tear away, and it was over. Carol drove for a minute, slowly, smoking the cigarette.

'Crawl in the back and get the gun,' Carol said.

Therese did not move for a moment.

Carol glanced at her. 'Will you?'

Therese slid agilely in her slacks over the seat back, and dragged the navy blue suitcase on to the seat. She opened the clasps and got out the sweater with the gun.

'Just hand it to me,' Carol said calmly. 'I want it in the side pocket.' She reached her hand over her shoulder, and Therese put the white handle of the gun into it, and crawled back into the front seat.

The detective was still following them, half a mile behind them, back of the horse and farm wagon that had turned into the highway from a dirt road. Carol held Therese's hand and drove with her left hand. Therese looked down at the faintly freckled fingers that dug their strong cool tips into her palm.

'I'm going to talk to him again,' Carol said, and pressed the gas pedal down steadily. 'If you want to get out, I'll put you off at the next gas station or something and come back for you.'

'I don't want to leave you,' Therese said. Carol was going to demand the detective's records, and Therese had a vision of Carol hurt, of his pulling a gun with an expert's oily speed and firing it before Carol could even pull the trigger. But those things didn't happen, wouldn't happen, she thought, and she set her teeth. She kneaded Carol's hand in her fingers.

'All right. And don't worry. I just want to talk to him.' She swung the car suddenly into a smaller road off the highway to the left. The road went up between sloping fields, and turned and went through woods. Carol drove fast, though the road was bad. 'He's coming on, isn't he?'

'Yes.'

There was one farmhouse set in the rolling hills, and then nothing but scrubby, rocky land and the road that kept disappearing around the curves before them. Where the road clung to a sloping hill, Carol went round a curve and stopped the car carelessly, half in the road.

She reached for the side pocket and pulled the gun out. She opened something on it, and Therese saw the bullets inside. Then Carol looked through the windshield, and let her hands with the gun fall in her lap. 'I'd better not, better not,' she said quickly, and dropped the gun back in the side pocket. Then she pulled the car up, and straightened it by the side of the hill. 'Stay in the car,' she said to Therese, and got out.

Therese heard the detective's car. Carol walked slowly towards the sound, and then the detective's car came around the curve, not fast, but his brakes shrieked, and Carol stepped to the side of the road. Therese opened the door slightly, and leaned on the window-sill.

The man got out of his car. 'Now what?' he said, raising his voice in the wind.

'What do you think?' Carol came a little closer to him. 'I'd like everything you've got about me – dictaphone tapes and whatever.'

The detective's brows hardly rose over the pale dots of his eyes. He leaned against the front fender of his car, smirking with his wide thin mouth. He glanced at Therese and back at Carol. 'Everything's sent away. I haven't a thing but a few notes. About times and places.'

'All right, I'd like to have them.'

'You mean, you want to buy them?'

'I didn't say that, I said I'd like to have them. Do you prefer to sell them?'

'I'm not one you can buy off,' he said.

'What're you doing this for anyway, if not money?' Carol asked impatiently. 'Why not make a little more? What'll you take for what you've got?'

He folded his arms. 'I told you everything's sent away. You'd be wasting your money.'

'I don't think you mailed the dictaphone records yet from Colorado Springs,' Carol said.

'No?' he asked sarcastically.

'No. I'll give you whatever you ask for them.'

He looked Carol up and down, glanced at Therese, and again his mouth widened.

'Get them – tapes, records or whatever they are,' Carol said, and the man moved.

He walked around his car to the luggage compartment, and Therese heard his keys jingle as he opened it. Therese got out of the car, unable to sit there any longer. She walked to within a few feet of Carol and stopped. The detective was reaching for something in a big suitcase. When he straightened up, the raised lid of the compartment knocked his hat off. He stepped on the brim to hold it from the wind. He had something in one hand now, too small to see.

202

'There's two,' he said. 'I guess they're worth five hundred. They'd be worth more if there weren't more of them in New York.'

'You're a fine salesman. I don't believe you,' Carol said.

'Why? They're in a hurry for them in New York.' He picked up his hat, and closed the luggage compartment. 'But they've got enough now. I told you you'd better go back to New York, Mrs Aird.' He ground his cigarette out in the dirt, twisting his toe in front of him. 'Are you going back to New York now?'

'I don't change my mind,' Carol said.

The detective shrugged. 'I'm not on any side. The sooner you go back to New York, the sooner we call it quits.'

'We can call it quits right now. After you give me those, you can take off and keep going in the same direction.'

The detective had slowly extended his hand in a fist, like the fist in a guessing game in which there might be nothing. 'Are you willing to give me five hundred for these?' he asked.

Carol looked at his hand, then opened her shoulder-strap bag. She took out her billfold, and then her chequebook.

'I prefer cash,' he said.

'I haven't got it.'

He shrugged again. 'All right, I'll take a cheque.'

Carol wrote it, resting it on the fender of his car.

Now as he bent over, watching Carol, Therese could see the little black object in his hand. Therese came closer. The man was spelling his name. When Carol gave him the cheque, he dropped the two little boxes in her hand.

'How long have you been collecting them?' Carol asked.

'Play them and see.'

'I didn't come out here to joke!' Carol said, and her voice broke.

He smiled, folding the cheque. 'Don't say I didn't warn you. What you've gotten from me isn't all of it. There's plenty in New York.'

Carol fastened her bag, and turned towards her car, not even looking at Therese. Then she stopped and faced the detective again. 'If they've got all they want, you can knock off now, can't you? Have I got your promise to do that?'

He was standing with his hand on his car door, watching her. 'I'm still on the job, Mrs Aird – still working for my office. Unless you want to catch a plane for home now. Or for some other place. Give me the slip. I'll have to tell my office something – not having the last few days at Colorado Springs – something more exciting than this.'

'Oh, let them invent something exciting!'

The detective's smile showed a little of his teeth. He got back into his car. He shoved his gear, put his head out to see behind him, and backed the car in a quick turn. He drove off towards the highway.

The sound of his motor faded fast. Carol walked slowly towards the car, got in and sat staring through the windshield at the dry rise of earth a few yards ahead. Her face was as blank as if she had fainted.

Therese was beside her. She put her arm around Carol's shoulder. She squeezed the cloth shoulder of the coat, and felt as useless as any stranger.

'Oh, I think it's mostly bluff,' Carol said suddenly.

But it made Carol's face grey, had taken the energy out of her voice.

Carol opened her hand and looked at the two little round boxes. 'Here's as good a place as any.' She got out of the car, and Therese followed her. Carol opened a box and took out the coil of tape that looked like celluloid. 'Tiny, isn't it. I suppose it burns. Let's burn it.'

Therese struck the match in the shelter of the car. The tape burned fast, and Therese dropped it on the ground, and then the wind blew it out. Carol said not to bother, they could throw both of them in a river.

'What time is it?' Carol asked.

'Twenty to twelve.' She got back in the car, and Carol started immediately, back down the road towards the highway.

'I'm going to call Abby in Omaha, and then my lawyer.'

Therese looked at the road map. Omaha was the next big town, if they made a slight turn south. Carol looked tired, and Therese felt her anger, still unappeased, in the silence she kept. The car jolted over a rut, and Therese heard the bump and clink of the can of beer that rolled somewhere under the front seat, the beer they had not been able to open that first day. She was hungry, had been sickly hungry for hours.

204

'How about my driving?'

'All right,' Carol said tiredly, relaxing as if she surrendered. She slowed the car quickly.

Therese slid across her, under the wheel. 'And how about stopping for a breakfast?'

'I couldn't eat.'

'Or a drink.'

'Let's get it in Omaha.'

Therese sent the speedometer up to sixty-five, and held it just under seventy. It was Highway 30. Then 275 into Omaha, and the road was not first class. 'You don't believe him about dictaphone records in New York, do you?'

'Don't talk about it! – I'm sick of it!'

Therese squeezed the wheel, then deliberately relaxed. She sensed a tremendous sorrow hanging over them, ahead of them, that was just beginning to reveal the edge of itself, that they were driving into. She remembered the detective's face and the barely legible expression that she realized now was malice. It was malice she had seen in his smile, even as he said he was on no side, and she could feel in him a desire that was actually personal to separate them, because he knew they were together. She had seen just now what she had only sensed before, that the whole world was ready to be their enemy, and suddenly what she and Carol had together seemed no longer love or anything happy but a monster between them, with each of them caught in a fist.

'I'm thinking of that cheque,' Carol said.

It fell like another stone inside her. 'Do you think they're going over the house?' Therese asked.

'Possibly. Just possibly.'

'I don't think they'd find it. It's way under the runner.' But there was the letter in the book. A curious pride lifted her spirit for an instant, and vanished. It was a beautiful letter, and she would rather they found it than the cheque, though as to incrimination they would probably have the same weight, and they would make the one as dirty as the other. The letter she had never given, and the cheque she had never cashed. It was more likely they would find the letter, certainly. Therese could not bring herself to tell Carol of the letter, whether from plain cowardice or a desire to spare Carol any more now, she didn't know. She saw a bridge ahead. 'There's a river,' she said. 'How about here?'

'Good enough.' Carol handed her the little boxes. She had put the half-burned tape back in its box.

Therese got out and flung them over the metal rail, and did not watch. She looked at the young man in overalls walking on to the bridge from the other side, hating the senseless antagonism in herself against him.

Carol telephoned from an hotel in Omaha. Abby was not at home, and Carol left a message that she would call at six o'clock that evening, when Abby was expected. Carol said it was of no use to call her lawyer now, because he would be out to lunch until after two by their time. Carol wanted to wash up, and then have a drink.

They had Old Fashioneds in the bar of the hotel, in complete silence. Therese asked for a second when Carol did, but Carol said she should eat something instead. The waiter told Carol that food was not served in the bar.

'She wants something to eat,' Carol said firmly.

'The dining room is across the lobby, madame, and there's a coffee shop – '

'Carol, I can wait,' Therese said.

'Will you please bring me the menu? She prefers to eat here,' Carol said with a glance at the waiter.

The waiter hesitated, then said, 'Yes, madame,' and went to get the menu.

While Therese ate scrambled eggs and sausage, Carol had her third drink. Finally, Carol said in a tone of hopelessness, 'Darling, can I ask you to forgive me?'

The tone hurt Therese more than the question. 'I love you, Carol.'

'But do you see what it means?'

'Yes.' But that moment of defeat in the car, she thought, that had been only a moment, as this time now was only a situation. 'I don't see why it should mean this for ever. I don't see how this can destroy anything,' she said earnestly.

Carol took her hand down from her face and sat back, and now in spite of the tiredness she looked as Therese always thought of her – the eyes that could be tender and hard at once as they tested her, the intelligent red lips strong and soft, though the upper lip trembled the least bit now.

'Do you?' Therese asked, and she realized suddenly it was a question as big as the one Carol had asked her without words in the room in Waterloo. In fact, the same question.

'No. I think you're right,' Carol said. 'You make me realize it.'

Carol went to telephone. It was three o'clock. Therese got the bill, then sat there waiting, wondering when it was going to be over, whether the reassuring word would come from Carol's lawyer or from Abby, or whether it was going to get worse before it got better. Carol was gone about half an hour.

'My lawyer hasn't heard anything,' she said. 'And I didn't tell him anything. I can't. I'll have to write it.'

'I thought you would.'

'Oh, you did,' Carol said with her first smile that day. 'What do you say we get a room here? I don't feel like travelling any more.'

Carol had her lunch sent up to their room. They both lay down to take a nap, but when Therese awakened at a quarter to five, Carol was gone. Therese glanced around the room, noticing Carol's black gloves on the dressing table, and her moccasins side by side near the armchair. Therese sighed, tremulously, unrefreshed by her sleep. She opened the window and looked down. It was the seventh or eighth floor, she couldn't remember which. A streetcar crawled past the front of the hotel, and people on the sidewalk moved in every direction, with legs on either side of them, and it crossed her mind to jump. She looked off at the drab little skyline of grey buildings and closed her eyes on it. Then she turned around and Carol was in the room, standing by the door, watching her.

'Where have you been?' Therese asked.

'Writing that damned letter.'

Carol crossed the room and caught Therese in her arms. Therese felt Carol's nails through the back of her jacket.

When Carol went to the telephone, Therese left the room and wandered down the hall towards the elevators. She went down to the lobby and sat there reading an article on weevils in the *Corngrower's Gazette*, and wondered if Abby knew all that about corn weevils. She watched the clock, and after twenty-five minutes went upstairs again.

207

Carol was lying on the bed, smoking a cigarette. Therese waited for her to speak.

'Darling, I've got to go to New York,' Carol said.

Therese had been sure of that. She came to the foot of the bed. 'What else did Abby say?'

'She saw the fellow named Bob Haversham again.' Carol raised herself on her elbow. 'But he certainly doesn't know as much as I do at this point. Nobody seems to know anything, except that trouble's brewing. Nothing much can happen until I get there. But I've got to be there.'

'Of course.' Bob Haversham was the friend of Abby's who worked in Harge's firm in Newark, not a close friend either of Abby's or Harge's, just a link, a slim link between the two of them, the one person who might know something of what Harge was doing, if he could recognize a detective, or overhear part of a telephone call, in Harge's office. It was worth almost nothing, Therese felt.

'Abby's going to get the cheque,' Carol said, sitting up on the bed, reaching for her moccasins.

'Has she got a key?'

'I wish she had. She's got to get it from Florence. But that'll be all right. I told her to tell Florence I wanted a couple of things sent to me.'

'Can you tell her to get a letter, too? I left a letter to you in a book in my room. I'm sorry I didn't tell you before. I didn't know you were going to have Abby go there.'

Carol gave her a frowning glance. 'Anything else?'

'No. I'm sorry I didn't tell you before.'

Carol sighed, and stood up. 'Oh, let's not worry any more. I doubt if they'll bother about the house, but I'll tell Abby about the letter anyway. Where is it?'

'In the *Oxford Book of English Verse*. I think I left it on top of the bureau.' She watched Carol glance around the room, looking anywhere but at her.

'I don't want to stay here tonight after all,' Carol said.

Half an hour later, they were in the car going eastward. Carol wanted to reach Des Moines that night. After a silence of more than an hour, Carol suddenly stopped the car at the edge of the road, bent her head, and said, 'Damn!'

She could see the darkish sinks under Carol's eyes in the glare of passing cars. Carol hadn't slept at all last night. 'Let's go back to that last town,' Therese said. 'It's still about seventy-five miles to Des Moines.'

'Do you want to go to Arizona?' Carol asked her, as if all they had to do was turn around.

'Oh, Carol – why talk about it?' A feeling of despair came over her suddenly. Her hands were shaking as she lighted a cigarette. She gave the cigarette to Carol.

'Because I want to talk about it. Can you take another three weeks off?'

'Of course.' Of course, of course. What else mattered except being with Carol, anywhere, anyhow? There was the Harkevy show in March. Harkevy might recommend her for a job somewhere else, but the jobs were uncertain and Carol was not.

'I shouldn't have to stay in New York more than a week at most, because the divorce is all set, Fred, my lawyer, said so today. So why don't we have a few more weeks in Arizona? Or New Mexico? I don't want to hang around New York the rest of the winter.' Carol drove slowly. Her eyes were different now. They had come alive, like her voice.

'Of course I'd like to. Anywhere.'

'All right. Come on. Let's get to Des Moines. How about you driving a while?'

They changed places. It was a little before midnight when they got to Des Moines and found a hotel room.

'Why should you go back to New York at all?' Carol asked her. 'You could keep the car and wait for me somewhere like Tucson or Santa Fe, and I could fly back.'

'And leave you?' Therese turned from the mirror where she was brushing her hair.

Carol smiled. 'What do you mean, leave me?'

It had taken Therese by surprise, and now she saw an expression on Carol's face, even though Carol looked at her intently, that made her feel shut off, as if Carol had thrust her away in a back corner of her mind to make room for something more important. 'Just leave you now, I meant,' Therese said, turning back to the mirror. 'No, it might be a good idea. It's quicker for you.'

'I thought you might prefer staying somewhere in the West. Unless you want to do something in New York those few days.' Carol's voice was casual.

'I don't.' She dreaded the cold days in Manhattan, when Carol would be too busy to see her. And she thought of the detective. If Carol flew, she wouldn't be haunted by his trailing her. She tried to imagine it already, Carol arriving in the East alone, to face something she didn't yet know, something impossible to prepare for. She imagined herself in Santa Fe, waiting for a telephone call, waiting for a letter from Carol. But to be two thousand miles away from Carol, she could not imagine that so easily. 'Only a week, Carol?' she asked, drawing the comb along her parting again, flicking the long, fine hair to one side. She had gained weight, but her face was thinner, she noticed suddenly, and it pleased her. She looked older.

In the mirror, she saw Carol come up behind her, and there was no answer but the pleasure of Carol's arms sliding around her, which made it impossible to think, and Therese twisted away more suddenly than she meant to, and stood by the corner of the dressing table looking at Carol, bewildered for a moment by the elusiveness of what they talked about, time and space, and the four feet that separated them now and the two thousand miles. She gave her hair another stroke. 'Only about a week?'

'That's what I said,' Carol replied with a smile in her eyes, but Therese heard the same hardness in it as in her own question, as if they exchanged challenges. 'If you mind keeping the car, I can have it driven East.'

'I don't mind keeping it.'

'And don't worry about the detective. I'll wire Harge that I'm on my way.'

'I won't worry about that.' How could Carol be so cold about it, Therese wondered, thinking of everything else but their leaving each other? She put the hairbrush down on the dressing table.

'Therese, do you think I'm going to enjoy it?'

And Therese thought of the detectives, the divorce, the hostility, all Carol had to face. Carol touched her cheek, pressed both palms hard against her cheeks so her mouth opened like a fish's, and Therese had to smile. Therese stood by the dressing table and watched her, watching every move of her hands, of her feet as she peeled off her stockings and stepped into her moccasins again. There were no words, she thought, after this point. What else did they need to explain, or ask, or promise in words? They did not even need to see each other's eyes. Therese watched her pick up the telephone, and then she lay face down on the bed, while Carol made her plane reservation for tomorrow, one ticket, one way, tomorrow at eleven a.m.

'Where do you think you'll go?' Carol asked her.

'I don't know. I might go back to Sioux Falls.'

'South Dakota?' Carol smiled at her. 'You wouldn't prefer Santa Fe? It's warmer.'

'I'll wait and see it with you.'

'Not Colorado Springs?'

'No!' Therese laughed, and got up. She took her toothbrush into the bathroom. 'I might even take a job somewhere for a week.'

'What kind of a job?'

'Any kind. Just to keep me from thinking of you, you know.'

'I want you to think of me. Not a job in a department store.'

'No.' Therese stood by the bathroom door, watching Carol take off her slip and put her robe on.

'You're not worrying about money again, are you?'

Therese slid her hands into her robe pockets and crossed her feet. 'If I'm broke, I don't care. I'll start worrying when it's used up.'

'I'm going to give you a couple of hundred tomorrow for the car.' Carol pulled Therese's nose as she passed her. 'And you're not to use that car to pick up any strangers.' Carol went into the bathroom and turned on the shower.

Therese came in after her. 'I thought I was using this john.'

'I'm using it, but I'll let you come in.'

'Oh, thanks.' Therese took off her robe as Carol did.

'Well?' Carol said.

'Well?' Therese stepped under the shower.

'Of all the nerve.' Carol got under it, too, and twisted Therese's arm behind her, but Therese only giggled.

Therese wanted to embrace her, kiss her, but her free arm reached out convulsively and dragged Carol's head against her, under the stream of water, and there was the horrible sound of a foot slipping.

'Stop it, we'll fall!' Carol shouted. 'For Christ's sake, can't two people take a shower in peace?'

CHAPTER TWENTY

I n Sioux Falls, Therese stopped the car in front of the hotel they had stayed in before, the Warrior Hotel. It was nine-thirty in the evening. Carol had got home about an hour ago, Therese thought. She was to call Carol at midnight.

She took a room, had her bags carried up, then went out for a walk through the main street. There was a movie house, and it occurred to her she had never seen a movie with Carol. She went in. But she was in no mood to follow the picture, even though there was a woman in it whose voice was a little like Carol's, not at all like the flat nasal voices she heard all around her. She thought of Carol, over a thousand miles away now, thought of sleeping alone tonight, and she got up and wandered out on the street again. There was the drugstore where Carol had bought paper tissues and toothpaste one morning. And the corner where Carol had looked up and read the street names – Fifth and Nebraska streets. She bought a pack of cigarettes at the same drugstore, walked back to the hotel and sat in the lobby, smoking, savouring the first cigarette since she had left Carol, savouring the forgotten state of being alone. It was only a physical state. She really did not feel at all alone. She read some newspapers for a while, then took the letters from Dannie and Phil that had come in the last days at Colorado Springs out of her handbag and glanced over them:

. . . I saw Richard two nights ago in the Palermo all by himself [Phil's letter said]. I asked about you and he said he wasn't writing to you. I gather there has been a small rupture, but I didn't press for information. He was in no mood for talking. And we are not too chummy lately, as you know . . . Have been talking you up to an angel named Francis Puckett who will put up fifty thousand if a certain play from France comes over in April. Shall keep you posted, as there is not even a producer yet . . . Dannie sends his love, I am sure. He is leaving soon for somewhere probably, he has that look, and I'll have to scout for new winter quarters or find a roommate . . . Did you get the clippings I sent you on *Small Rain*?

Best, Phil

Dannie's short letter was:

Dear Therese,

There is a possibility I may go out to the Coast at the end of the month to take a job in California. I must decide between this (a lab job) and an offer in a commercial chemical place in Maryland. But if I could see you in Colorado or anywhere else for a while, I would leave a little early. Shall probably take the California job, as I think it has better prospects. So would you let me know where you'll be? It doesn't matter. There are a lot of ways of getting to California. If your friend wouldn't mind, it would be nice to spend a few days with you somewhere. I'll be in New York until the 28 of February anyway.

Love,
Dannie

She had not yet answered him. She would send him an address tomorrow, as soon as she found a room somewhere in the town. But as to the next destination, she would have to talk to Carol about that. And when would Carol be able to say? She wondered what Carol might already have found tonight in New Jersey, and Therese's courage sank dismally. She reached for a newspaper and looked at the date. February fifteenth. Twenty-nine days since she had left New York with Carol. Could it be so few days?

Upstairs in her room, she put the call through to Carol, and bathed and got into pyjamas. Then the telephone rang.

'Hel-*lo*,' Carol said, as if she had been waiting a long while. 'What's the name of that hotel?'

'The Warrior. But I'm not going to stay here.'

'You didn't pick up any strangers on the road, did you?'

Therese laughed. Carol's slow voice went through her as if she touched her. 'What's the news?' Therese asked.

'Tonight? Nothing. The house is freezing and Florence can't get here till day after tomorrow. Abby's here. Do you want to say hello to her?'

'Not right there with you.'

'No-o. Upstairs in the green room with the door shut.'

'I *don't* really want to talk to her now.'

Carol wanted to know everything she had done, how the roads were, and whether she had on the yellow pyjamas or the blue ones. 'I'll have a hard time getting to sleep tonight without you.'

'Yes.' Immediately, out of nowhere, Therese felt tears pressing behind her eyes.

'Can't you say anything but yes?'

'I love you.'

Carol whistled. Then silence. 'Abby got the cheque, darling, but no letter. She missed my wire, but there isn't any letter anyway.'

'Did you find the book?'

'We found the book, but there's nothing in it.'

Therese wondered if the letter could be in her own apartment after all. But she had a picture of the letter in the book, marking a place. 'Do you think anybody's been through the house?'

'No, I can tell by various things. Don't worry about that. Will you?'

A moment later, Therese slid down into bed and pulled her light out. Carol had asked her to call tomorrow night, too. For a while the sound of Carol's voice was in her ears. Then a melancholy began to seep into her. She lay on her back with her arms straight at her sides, with a sense of empty space all around her, as if she were laid out ready for the grave, and then she fell asleep.

215

The next morning, Therese found a room she liked in a house on one of the streets that ran uphill, a large front room with a bay window full of plants and white curtains. There was a four-poster bed and an oval hooked rug on the floor. The woman said it was seven dollars a week, but Therese said she was not sure if she would be here a week, so she had better take it by the day.

'That'll be the same thing,' the woman said. 'Where're you from?'

'New York.'

'Are you going to live here?'

'No. I'm just waiting for a friend to join me.'

'Man or a woman?'

Therese smiled. 'A woman,' she said. 'Is there any space in those garages in back? I've got a car with me.'

The woman said there were two garages empty, and that she didn't charge for the garages, if people lived here. She was not old, but she stooped a little and her figure was frail. Her name was Mrs Elizabeth Cooper. She had been keeping roomers for fifteen years, she said, and two of the three she had started with were still here.

The same day, she made the acquaintance of Dutch Huber and his wife who ran the diner near the public library. He was a skinny man of about fifty with small curious blue eyes. His wife Edna was fat and did the cooking, and talked a great deal less than he. Dutch had worked in New York for a while years ago. He asked her questions about sections of the city she happened not to know at all, while she mentioned places Dutch had never heard of or had forgotten, and somehow the slow, dragging conversation made them both laugh. Dutch asked her if she would like to go with him and his wife to the motorcycle races that were to be held a few miles out of town on Saturday, and Therese said yes.

She bought cardboard and glue and worked on the first of the models she meant to show Harkevy when she got back to New York. She had it nearly done when she went out at eleven-thirty to call Carol from the Warrior.

Carol was not in and no one answered. Therese tried until one o'clock, then went back to Mrs Cooper's house.

Therese reached her the next morning around ten-thirty. Carol said she had talked over everything with her lawyer the day before, but there was nothing she or her lawyer could do until they knew

Harge's next move. Carol was a little short with her, because she had a luncheon appointment in New York and a letter to write first. She seemed anxious for the first time about what Harge was doing. She had tried to call him twice without being able to reach him. But it was her brusqueness that disturbed Therese most of all.

'You haven't changed your mind about anything,' Therese said.

'Of course not, darling. I'm giving a party tomorrow night. I'll miss you.'

Therese tripped on the hotel threshold as she went out, and she felt the first hollow wave of loneliness break over her. What would she be doing tomorrow night? Reading in the library until it closed at nine? Working on another set? She went over the names of the people Carol had said were coming to the party – Max and Clara Tibbett, the couple who had a greenhouse on some highway near Carol's house and whom Therese had met once, Carol's friend Tessie she had never met, and Stanley McVeigh, the man Carol had been with the evening they went to Chinatown. Carol hadn't mentioned Abby.

And Carol hadn't said to call tomorrow.

She walked on, and the last moment she had seen Carol came back as if it were happening in front of her eyes again. Carol waving from the door of the plane at the Des Moines airport, Carol already small and far away, because Therese had had to stand back of the wire fence across the field. The ramp had been moved away, but Therese had thought, there were still a few seconds of time before they closed the door, and then Carol had appeared again, just long enough to stand still in the doorway for a second, to find her again, and make the gesture of blowing her a kiss. But it meant an absurd lot that she had come back.

Therese drove out to the motorcycle races on Saturday, and took Dutch and Edna with her, because Carol's car was bigger. Afterwards, they invited her to supper at their house, but she did not accept. There hadn't been a letter from Carol that day, and she had expected a note at least. Sunday depressed her, and even the drive she took up the Big Sioux River to Dell Rapids in the afternoon did not change the scene inside her mind.

Monday morning, she sat in the library reading plays. Then

around two, when the noonday rush was slacking off in Dutch's diner, she went in and had some tea, and talked with Dutch while she played the songs on the juke box that she and Carol had used to play. She had told Dutch that the car belonged to the friend for whom she was waiting. And gradually, Dutch's intermittent questions led her to tell him that Carol lived in New Jersey, that she would probably fly out, that Carol wanted to go to New Mexico.

'Carol does?' Dutch said, turning to her as he polished a glass.

Then a strange resentment rose in Therese because he had said her name, and she made a resolution not to speak of Carol again at all, not to anyone in the city.

Tuesday the letter came from Carol, nothing but a short note, but it said Fred was more optimistic about everything, and it looked as if there would be nothing but the divorce to worry about and she could probably leave the twenty-fourth of February. Therese began to smile as she read it. She wanted to go out and celebrate with someone, but there was no one, so there was nothing to do but take a walk, have a lonely drink at the bar of the Warrior, and think of Carol five days away. There was no one she would have wanted to be with, except perhaps Dannie. Or Stella Overton. Stella was jolly, and though she couldn't have told Stella anything about Carol — whom could she tell? — it would have been good to see her now. She had meant to write Stella a card days ago, but she hadn't yet.

She wrote to Carol late that night.

The news is wonderful. I celebrated with a single daiquiri at the Warrior. Not that I am conservative, but did you know that one drink has the kick of three when you are alone? . . . I love this town because it all reminds me of you. I know you don't like it any more than any other town, but that isn't the point. I mean you are here as much as I can bear you to be, not being here . . .

Carol wrote:

I never liked Florence. I say this as a prelude. It seems Florence found the note you wrote to me and sold it to Harge — at a price. She is also responsible for Harge's knowing where we (or at least I) were going, I've no doubt. I don't know what I left around the house or what she might have overheard, I thought I was pretty silent, but if Harge took the trouble to bribe her, and I'm sure he did, there's no telling. They picked us up in Chicago, anyway. Darling, I had no idea how far this thing had gone. To give you the atmosphere – nobody tells me anything, things are just suddenly discovered. If anyone is in possession of the facts, it is Harge. I spoke with him on the phone, and he refuses to tell me anything, which of course is calculated to terrorize me into giving all my ground before the fight has even begun. They don't know me, any of them, if they think I will. The fight of course is over Rindy, and yes, darling, I'm afraid there will be one, and I can't leave the 24th. That much Harge did tell me when he sprang the letter this morning on the phone. I think the letter may be his strongest weapon (the dictaphone business only went on in Colorado S. so far as I can possibly imagine) hence his letting me know about it. But I can imagine the kind of letter it is, written even before we took off, and there'll be a limit to what even Harge can read into it. Harge is merely threatening – in the peculiar form of silence – hoping I will back out completely as far as Rindy is concerned. I won't, so there will come some kind of a showdown, I hope not in court. Fred is prepared for anything however. He is wonderful, the only person who talks straight to me, but unfortunately he knows least of all too.

You ask if I miss you. I think of your voice, your hands, and your eyes when you look straight into mine. I remember your courage that I hadn't suspected, and it gives me courage. Will you call me, darling? I don't want to call you if your phone is in the hall. Call me collect around 7 p.m. preferably, which is 6 your time.

And Therese was about to call her that day when a telegram came:

DON'T TELEPHONE FOR A WHILE. EXPLAIN LATER. ALL MY LOVE, DARLING. CAROL.

Mrs Cooper watched her reading it in the hall. 'That from your friend?' she asked.

'Yes.'

'Hope nothing's the matter.' Mrs Cooper had a way of peering at people, and Therese lifted her head deliberately.

'No, she's coming,' Therese said. 'She's been delayed.'

CHAPTER TWENTY-ONE

Albert Kennedy, Bert to people he liked, lived in a room at the back of the house, and was one of Mrs Cooper's original lodgers. He was forty-five, a native of San Francisco, and more like a New Yorker than anyone Therese had met in the town, and this fact alone inclined her to avoid him. Often he asked Therese to go to the movies with him, but she had gone only once. She was restless and she preferred to wander about by herself, mostly just looking and thinking, because the days were too cold and windy for any outdoor sketching. And the scenes she had liked at first had grown too stale to sketch, from too much looking, too much waiting. Therese went to the library almost every evening, sat at one of the long tables looking over half a dozen books, and then took a meandering course homeward.

She came back to the house only to wander out again after a while, stiffening herself against the erratic wind, or letting it turn her down streets she would not otherwise have followed. In the lighted windows she would see a girl seated at a piano, in another a man laughing, in another a woman sewing. Then she remembered she could not even call Carol, admitted to herself she did not even know what Carol was doing at this moment, and she felt emptier than the wind. Carol did not tell her everything in her letters, she felt, did not tell her the worst.

In the library, she looked at books with photographs of Europe in them, marble fountains in Sicily, ruins of Greece in sunlight, and she wondered if she and Carol would really ever go there. There was still so much they had not done. There was the first voyage across the Atlantic. There was simply the mornings, mornings anywhere, when she could lift her head from a pillow and see Carol's face, and know that the day was theirs and that nothing would separate them.

And there was the beautiful thing, transfixing the heart and the eyes at once, in the dark window of an antique shop in a street where she had never been. Therese stared at it, feeling it quench some forgotten and nameless thirst inside her. Most of its porcelain surface was painted with small bright lozenges of coloured enamel, royal blue and deep red and green, outlined with coin gold as shiny as silk embroidery, even under its film of dust. There was a gold ring at the rim for the finger. It was a tiny candlestick holder. Who had made it, she wondered, and for whom?

She came back the next morning and bought it to give to Carol.

A letter from Richard had come that morning, forwarded from Colorado Springs. Therese sat down on one of the stone benches in the street where the library was, and opened it. It was on business stationery: The Semco Bottled Gas Company. Cooks – Heats – Makes Ice. Richard's name was at the top as General Manager of the Port Jefferson Branch.

Dear Therese,

I have Dannie to thank for telling me where you are. You may think this letter unnecessary and perhaps it is to you. Perhaps you are still in that fog you were when we talked that evening in the cafeteria. But I feel it is necessary to make one thing clear, and that is that I no longer feel the way I did even two weeks ago, and the letter I wrote you last was nothing but a last spasmodic effort, and I knew it was hopeless when I wrote it, and I knew you wouldn't answer and I didn't want you to. I know I had stopped loving you then, and now the uppermost emotion I feel towards you is one that was present from the first – disgust. It is your hanging on to this woman to the exclusion of everyone else, this relationship which I am sure has become sordid and pathological by now, that disgusts me. I know that it will not last, as I said from the first. It is only regrettable that you will be disgusted later yourself, in proportion to how much of your life you waste now with it. It is rootless and infantile, like living on lotus blossoms or some sickening candy instead of the bread and meat of life. I have often thought of those questions you asked me the day we were flying the kite. I wish I had acted then before it was too late, because I loved you enough then to try to rescue you. Now I don't.

People still ask me about you. What do you expect me to tell them? I intend to tell them the truth. Only that way can I get it out of myself – and I can no longer bear to carry it around with me. I have sent a few things you had at the house back to your apartment. The slightest memory or contact with you depresses me, makes me not want to touch you or anything concerned with you. But I am talking sense and very likely you are not understanding a word of it. Except maybe this: I want nothing to do with you.

Richard

She saw Richard's thin soft lips tensed in a straight line as they must have looked when he wrote the letter, a line that still did not keep the tiny, taut curl in the upper lip from showing – she saw his face clearly for a moment, and then it vanished with a little jolt that seemed as muffled and remote from her as the clamour of Richard's letter. She stood up, put the letter back in the envelope, and walked on. She hoped he succeeded in purging himself of her. But she could only imagine him telling other people about her with that curious attitude of passionate participation she had seen in New York before she left. She imagined Richard telling Phil as they stood some evening at the Palermo bar, imagined him telling the Kellys. She wouldn't care at all, whatever he said.

She wondered what Carol was doing now, at ten o'clock, at eleven in New Jersey. Listening to some stranger's accusations? Thinking of her, or was there time for that?

It was a fine day, cold and almost windless, bright with sun. She could take the car and drive somewhere. She had not used the car for three days. Suddenly she realized she did not want to use it. The day she had taken it out and driven it up to ninety on the straight road to Dell Rapids, exultant after a letter from Carol, seemed very long ago.

Mr Bowen, another of the roomers, was on the front porch when she came back to Mrs Cooper's house. He was sitting in the sun with his legs wrapped in a blanket and his cap pulled down over his eyes as if he were asleep, but he called out, 'Hi, there! How's my girl?'

She stopped and chatted with him for a while, asked him about his arthritis, trying to be as courteous as Carol had always been with Mrs French. They found something to laugh at, and she was still smiling when she went to her room. Then the sight of the geranium ended it.

She watered the geranium and set it at the end of the window-sill, where it would get the sun for the longest time. There was even brown at the tips of the smallest leaves at the top. Carol had bought it for her in Des Moines just before she took the plane. The pot of ivy had died already – the man in the shop had warned them it was delicate, but Carol had wanted it anyway – and Therese doubted that the geranium would live. But Mrs Cooper's motley collection of plants flourished in the bay window.

'I walk and walk around the town,' she wrote to Carol, 'but I wish I could keep walking in one direction – east – and finally come to you. When can you come, Carol? Or shall I come to you? I really cannot stand being away from you so long . . . '

She had her answer the next morning. A cheque fluttered out of Carol's letter on to Mrs Cooper's hall floor. The cheque was for two hundred and fifty dollars. Carol's letter – the long loops looser and lighter, the t-bars stretching the length of the word – said that it was impossible for her to come out within the next two weeks, if then. The cheque was for her to fly back to New York and have the car driven East.

'I'd feel better if you took the plane. Come now and don't wait,' was the last paragraph.

Carol had written the letter in haste, had probably snatched a moment to write it, but there was a coldness in it, too, that shocked Therese. She went out and walked dazedly to the corner and dropped the letter she had written the night before into the mailbox anyway, a heavy letter with three airmail stamps on it. She might see Carol within twelve hours. The thought did not bring any reassurance.

Should she leave this morning? This afternoon? What had they done to Carol? She wondered if Carol would be furious if she telephoned her, if it would precipitate some crisis into a total defeat if she did?

She was sitting at a table somewhere with coffee and orange juice in front of her, before she looked at the other letter in her hand. In the upper left corner she could just make out the scrawly handwriting. It was from Mrs R. Robichek.

Dear Therese,

Thank you very much for the delicious sausage that came last month. You are a nice sweet girl and I am glad to have the opportunity to thank you many times. It was nice of you to think of me making such a long trip. I enjoy the pretty post-cards, specially the big one from Sioux Falls. How is in South Dakota? Are mountains and cowboys? I have never had chance to travel except Pennsylvania. You are a lucky girl, so young and pretty and kind. Myself I still work. The store is just the same. Everything is the same but it is colder. Please visit me when you come back. I cook a nice dinner for you not from delicatessen. Thank you for the sausage again. I lived from it for many days, really something special and nice. With best regards and yours truly.

Ruby Robichek

Therese slid off the stool, left some money on the counter and ran out. She ran all the way to the Warrior Hotel, put the call in and waited with the receiver against her ear until she heard the telephone ringing in Carol's house. No one answered. It rang twenty times and no one answered. She thought of calling Carol's lawyer, Fred Haymes. She decided she shouldn't. Neither did she want to call Abby.

That day it rained, and Therese lay on her bed in her room, staring up at the ceiling, waiting for three o'clock, when she intended to telephone again. Mrs Cooper brought her a tray of lunch around midday. Mrs Cooper thought she was sick. Therese could not eat the food, however, and she did not know what to do with it.

She was still trying to reach Carol at five o'clock. Finally the ringing stopped and there was confusion on the wire, a couple of operators questioning each other about the call, and the first words Therese heard from Carol were 'Yes, damn it!' Therese smiled and the ache went out of her arms.

'Hello?' Carol said brusquely.

'Hello?' The connection was bad. 'I got the letter – the one with the cheque. What happened, Carol? . . . What?'

Carol's harassed sounding voice repeated through the crackling interference, '*This wire I think is tapped, Therese* . . . Are you all right? Are you coming home? I can't talk very long now.'

Therese frowned, wordless. 'Yes, I suppose I can leave today.' Then she blurted, 'What is it, Carol? I really can't stand this, not knowing anything!'

'*Therese!*' Carol drew the word all across Therese's words, like a deletion. 'Will you come home so I can talk to you?'

Therese thought she heard Carol sigh impatiently. 'But I've got to know now. Can you see me at all when I come back?'

'Hang on to yourself, Therese.'

Was this the way they talked together? Were these the words they used? 'But can you?'

'I don't know,' Carol said.

A chill ran up her arm, into the fingers that held the telephone. She felt Carol hated her. Because it was her fault, her stupid blunder about the letter Florence had found. Something had happened and perhaps Carol couldn't and wouldn't even want to see her again. 'Has the court thing started yet?'

'It's finished. I wrote you about that. I can't talk any longer. Goodbye, Therese.' Carol waited for her to reply. 'I've got to say goodbye.'

Therese put the receiver slowly back on the hook.

She stood in the hotel lobby, staring at the blurred figures around the front desk. She pulled Carol's letter out of her pocket and read it again, but Carol's voice was closer, saying impatiently, 'Will you come home so I can talk to you?' She pulled the cheque out and looked at it again, upside down, and slowly tore it up. She dropped the pieces into a brass spittoon.

But the tears did not come until she got back to the house and saw her room again, the double bed that sagged in the middle, the stack of letters from Carol on the desk. She couldn't stay here another night.

She would go to a hotel for the night, and if the letter Carol had mentioned wasn't here tomorrow morning, she would leave anyway.

Therese dragged her suitcase down from the closet and opened it on the bed. The folded corner of a white handkerchief stuck out of one of the pockets. Therese took it out and lifted it to her nose, remembering the morning in Des Moines when Carol had put it there, with the dash of perfume on it, and the derisive remark Carol had made about putting it there, which she had laughed at. Therese stood with her hand on the back of a chair and the other hand clenched in a fist that rose and fell aimlessly, and what she felt was as blurred as the desk and the letters that she frowned at in front of her. Then her hand reached out suddenly for the letter propped against the books at the back of the desk. She hadn't seen the letter before, though it was in plain view. Therese tore it open. This was the letter Carol had meant. It was a long letter, and the ink was pale blue on some pages and dark on others, and there were words crossed out. She read the first page, then went back and read it again.

Monday

My darling,

I am not even going into court. This morning I was given a private showing of what Harge intended to bring against me. Yes, they have a few conversations recorded — namely Waterloo, and it would be useless to try to face a court with this. I should be ashamed, not for myself oddly enough, but for my own child, to say nothing of not wanting you to have to appear. Everything was very simple this morning – I simply surrendered. The important thing now is what I intend to do in the future, the lawyers said. On this depends whether I would ever see my child again, because Harge has with ease now complete custody of her. The question was would I stop seeing you (and others like you, they said!). It was not so clearly put. There were a dozen faces that opened their mouths and spoke like the judges of doomsday – reminding me of my duties, my position, and my future. (What future have they fixed up for me? Are they going to look in on it in six months?) – I said I would stop seeing you. I wonder if you will understand,

Therese, since you are so young and never even knew a mother who cared desperately for you. For this promise, they present me with their wonderful reward, the privilege of seeing my child a few weeks of the year.

Hours later —

Abby is here. We talk of you – she sends you her love as I send mine. Abby reminds me of the things I know already – that you are very young and you adore me. Abby does not think I should send this to you, but tell you when you come. We have just had quite an argument about it. I tell her she does not know you as well as I, and I think now she does not know me as well as you in some ways, and those ways are the emotions. I am not very happy today, my sweet. I am drinking my ryes and you would tell me they depress me, I know. But I wasn't prepared for these days after those weeks with you. They were happy weeks – you knew it more than I did. Though all we have known is only a beginning. I meant to try to tell you in this letter that you don't even know the rest and perhaps you never will and are not supposed to – meaning destined to. We never fought, never came back knowing there was nothing else we wanted in heaven or hell but to be together. Did you ever care for me that much, I don't know. But that is all part of it and all we have known is only a beginning. And it has been such a short time. For that reason it will have shorter roots in you. You say you love me however I am and when I curse. I say I love you always, the person you are and the person you will become. I would say it in a court if it would mean anything to those people or possibly change anything, because those are not the words I am afraid of. I mean, darling, I shall send you this letter and I think you will understand why I do, why I told the lawyers yesterday I would not see you again and why I had to tell them that, and I would be underestimating you to think you could not and to think you would prefer delay.

She stopped reading and stood up, and walked slowly to her writing table. Yes, she understood why Carol had sent the letter. Because Carol loved her child more than her. And because of that, the lawyers had been able to break her, to force her to do exactly what they wanted her to do. Therese could not imagine Carol forced. Yet here it was in Carol's writing. It was a surrender, Therese knew, no situation in which she was the stake could have wrested from Carol. For an instant there came the fantastic realization that Carol had devoted only a fraction of herself to her, Therese, and suddenly the whole world of the last month, like a tremendous lie, cracked and almost toppled. In the next instant, Therese did not believe that. Yet the fact remained, she had chosen her child. She stared at Richard's envelope on her table, and felt all the words she wanted to say to him, that she had never said to him, rising in a torrent inside her. What right had he to talk about whom she loved or how? What did he know about her? What had he ever known?

. . . exaggerated and at the same time minimized [she read on another page of Carol's letter]. But between the pleasure of a kiss and of what a man and woman do in bed seems to me only a gradation. A kiss, for instance, is not to be minimized, or its value judged by anyone else. I wonder do these men grade their pleasure in terms of whether their actions produce a child or not, and do they consider them more pleasant if they do. It is a question of pleasure after all, and what's the use debating the pleasure of an ice-cream cone versus a football game – or a Beethoven quartet versus the *Mona Lisa*. I'll leave that to the philosophers. But their attitude was that I must be somehow demented or blind (plus a kind of regret, I thought, at the fact a fairly attractive woman is presumably unavailable to men). Someone brought 'aesthetics' into the argument, I mean against me of course. I said did they really want to debate that – it brought the only laugh in the whole show. But the most important point I did not mention and was not thought of by anyone – that the rapport between two men or two women can be absolute and perfect, as it can never be between man and woman, and perhaps some people want just this, as others want that more shifting and uncertain thing that happens between men and women. It was said or at least implied yesterday that my present course would bring me to the depths of human vice and degeneration. Yes, I have sunk a good deal since they took you from me. It is true, if I were to go on like this and be spied upon, attacked, never possessing one person long enough so that knowledge of a person is a superficial thing – that is degeneration.

Or to live against one's grain, that is degeneration by definition.

Darling, I pour all this out to you [the next lines were crossed out]. You will undoubtedly handle your future better than I. Let me be a bad example to you. If you are hurt now beyond what you think you can bear and if it makes you – either now or one day – hate me, and this is what I told Abby, then I shan't be sorry. I may have been that one person you were fated to meet, as you say, and the only one, and you can put it all behind you. Yet if you don't, for all this failure and the dismalness now, I know what you said that afternoon is right – it needn't be like this. I do want to talk with you once when you come back, if you're willing, unless you think you can't.

Your plants are still thriving on the back porch. I water them every day . . .

Therese could not read any more. Beyond her door she heard footsteps slowly descending the stairs, walking more confidently across the hall. When the footsteps were gone, she opened her door and stood there a moment, struggling against an impulse to walk straight out of the house and leave everything behind her. Then she went down the hall to Mrs Cooper's door in the rear.

Mrs Cooper answered her knock, and Therese said the words she had prepared, about leaving that night. She watched Mrs Cooper's face that didn't listen to her but only reacted to the sight of her own face, and Mrs Cooper seemed suddenly her own reflection, which she could not turn away from.

'Well, I'm sorry, Miss Belivet. I'm sorry if your plans have gone wrong,' she said, while her face registered only shock and curiosity.

Then Therese went back to her room and began to pack, laying in the bottom of her suitcase the cardboard models she had folded flat, and then her books. After a moment, she heard Mrs Cooper approaching her door slowly, as if she carried something, and Therese thought, if she was bringing her another tray, she would scream. Mrs Cooper knocked.

'Where shall I forward your mail to, honey, in case there's any more letters?' Mrs Cooper asked.

'I don't know yet. I'll have to write and let you know.' Therese felt lightheaded and sickish when she straightened up.

'You're not starting back for New York this late at night, are you?' Mrs Cooper called anything after six 'night'.

'No,' Therese said. 'I'll just go a little ways.' She was impatient to be alone. She looked at Mrs Cooper's hand bulging the grey checked apron under the waistband, at the cracked soft house shoes worn paper thin on these floors, which had walked these floors years before she came here and would go on in the same foot-tracks years after she was gone.

'Well, you be sure and let me hear how you make out,' Mrs Cooper said.

'Yes.'

She drove to an hotel, a different hotel from the one where she had always called Carol. Then she went out for a walk, restlessly, avoiding all the streets she had been in with Carol. She might have driven to another town, she thought, and stopped, half decided to go back to the car. Then she walked on, not caring, actually, where she was. She walked until she was cold, and the library was the closest place to go and get warm. She passed the diner and glanced in. Dutch saw her, and with the familiar dip of his head, as if he had to look under something to see her through the window, he smiled and waved to her. Automatically, her hand waved back, goodbye, and suddenly she thought of her room in New York, with the dress still on the studio couch, and the corner of the carpet turned back. If she could only reach out now and pull the carpet flat, she thought. She stood staring down the narrowish, solid-looking avenue with its round street-lights. A single figure walked along the sidewalk towards her. Therese went up the library steps.

Miss Graham, the librarian, greeted her as usual, but Therese did not go into the main reading room. There were two or three people there tonight, the bald-headed man with the black-rimmed glasses who was often at the middle table, and how often had she sat in that room with a letter from Carol in her pocket? With Carol beside her. She climbed the stairs, passed the history and art room on the second floor, up to the third floor where she had never been before. There was a single large dusty-looking room with glass-front bookcases around the walls, a few oil paintings and marble busts on pedestals.

Therese sat down at one of the tables, and her body relaxed with an ache. She put her head down on her arms on the table, suddenly

231

limp and sleepy, but in the next second, she slid the chair back and stood up. She felt prickles of terror in the roots of her hair. She had been somehow pretending until this moment that Carol was not gone, that when she went back to New York she would see Carol and everything would be, would have to be, as it had been before. She glanced nervously around the room, as if looking for some contradiction, some redress. For a moment, she felt her body might shatter apart of itself, or might hurl itself through the glass of the long windows across the room. She stared at a pallid bust of Homer, the inquisitively lifted eyebrows delineated faintly by dust. She turned to the door, and for the first time noticed the picture over the lintel.

It was only similar, she thought, not quite the same, not the same, but the recognition had shaken her at the core, was growing as she looked at it, and she knew the picture was exactly the same, only much larger, and she had seen it many times in the hall that led to the music room before they had taken it down when she was still small – the smiling woman in the ornate dress of some court, the hand poised just below the throat, the arrogant head half turned, as if the painter had somehow caught her in motion so that even the pearls that hung from each ear seemed to move. She knew the short, firmly modelled cheeks, the full coral lips that smiled at one corner, the mockingly narrowed lids, the strong, not very high forehead that even in the picture seemed to project a little over the living eyes that knew everything beforehand, and sympathized and laughed at once. It was Carol. Now in the long moment while she could not look away from it, the mouth smiled and the eyes regarded her with nothing but mockery, the last veil lifted and revealing nothing but mockery and gloating, the splendid satisfaction of the betrayal accomplished.

With a shuddering gasp, Therese ran under the picture and down the stairs. In the downstairs hall, Miss Graham said something to her, an anxious question, and Therese heard her own reply like an idiot's babble, because she was still gasping, fighting for breath, and she passed Miss Graham and rushed out of the building.

CHAPTER TWENTY-TWO

In the middle of the block, she opened the door of a coffee shop, but they were playing one of the songs she had heard with Carol everywhere, and she let the door close and walked on. The music lived, but the world was dead. And the song would die one day, she thought, but how would the world come back to life? How would its salt come back?

She walked to the hotel. In her room, she wet a face towel with cold water to put over her eyes. The room was chilly, so she took off her dress and shoes and got into bed.

From outside, a shrill voice, muted in empty space, cried: 'Hey, *Chicago Sun-Times!*'

Then silence, and she debated trying to fall asleep, while fatigue already began to rock her unpleasantly, like drunkenness. Now there were voices in the hall, talking of a misplaced piece of luggage, and a sense of futility overwhelmed her as she lay there with the wet, medicinally smelling face towel over her swollen eyes. The voices wrangled, and she felt her courage running out, and then her will, and in panic she tried to think of the world outside, of Dannie and Mrs Robichek, of Frances Cotter at the Pelican Press, of Mrs Osborne, and of her own apartment still in New York, but her mind refused to survey or to renounce, and her mind was the same as her heart now and refused to renounce Carol. The faces swam together like the voices outside. There was also the face of Sister Alicia, and of her mother. There was the last room she had slept in at school. There

233

was the morning she had sneaked out of the dormitory very early and run across the lawn like a young animal crazy with spring, and had seen Sister Alicia running crazily through a field herself, white shoes flashing like ducks through the high grass, and it had been minutes before she realized that Sister Alicia was chasing an escaped chicken. There was the moment, in the house of some friend of her mother's, when she had reached for a piece of cake and had upset the plate on the floor, and her mother had slapped her in the face. She saw the picture in the hall at school, it breathed and moved now like Carol, mocking and cruel and finished with her, as if some evil and long-destined purpose had been accomplished. Therese's body tensed in terror, and the conversation went on and on in the hall obliviously, falling on her ear with the sharp, alarming sound of ice cracking somewhere out on a pond.

'What do you mean you did?'

'No . . .'

'If you did, the suitcase would be downstairs in the check-room . . .'

'Oh, I told you . . .'

'But you want me to lose a suitcase so you won't lose your job!'

Her mind attached meaning to the phrases one by one, like some slow translator that lagged behind, and at last got lost.

She sat up in bed with the end of a bad dream in her head. The room was nearly dark, its shadows deep and solid in the corners. She reached for the lamp switch and half closed her eyes against the light. She dropped a quarter into the radio on the wall, and turned the volume quite loud at the first sound she got. It was a man's voice, and then music began, a lilting, oriental-sounding piece that had been among the selections in music-appreciation class at school. 'In a Persian Market', she remembered automatically, and now its undulant rhythm that had always made her think of a camel walking took her back to the rather small room at the Home, with the illustrations from Verdi operas around the walls above the high wainscoting. She had heard the piece occasionally in New York, but she had never heard it with Carol, had not heard it or thought of it since she had known Carol, and now the music was like a bridge soaring across time without touching anything. She picked up Carol's letter opener from the bed table, the wooden knife that had somehow

234

gotten into her suitcase when they packed, and she squeezed the handle and rubbed her thumb along its edge, but its reality seemed to deny Carol instead of affirm her, did not evoke her so much as the music they had never heard together. She thought of Carol with a twist of resentment, Carol like a distant spot of silence and stillness.

Therese went to the basin to wash her face in cold water. She should get a job, tomorrow if she could. That had been her idea in stopping here, to work for two weeks or so, not to weep in hotel rooms. She should send Mrs Cooper the hotel name as an address, simply for courtesy's sake. It was another of the things she must do, although she did not want to. And was it worth while to write to Harkevy again, she wondered, after his polite but inexplicit note in Sioux Falls. ' . . . I should be glad to see you again when you come to New York, but it is impossible for me to promise anything this spring. It would be a good idea for you to see Mr Ned Bernstein, the co-producer, when you get back. He can tell you more of what is happening in designing studios than I can . . . ' No, she wouldn't write again about that.

Downstairs, she bought a picture post-card of Lake Michigan, and deliberately wrote a cheerful message on it to Mrs Robichek. It seemed false as she wrote it, but walking away from the box where she had dropped it, she was conscious suddenly of the energy in her body, the spring in her toes, the youth in her blood that warmed her cheeks as she walked faster, and she knew she was free and blessed compared to Mrs Robichek, and what she had written was not false, because she could so well afford it. She was not crumpled or half blind, not in pain. She stood by a store window and quickly put on some more lipstick. A gust of wind made her stop to catch her balance. But she could feel in the wind's coldness its core of spring, like a heart warm and young inside it. Tomorrow morning, she would start to look for a job. She should be able to live on the money she had left, and save whatever she earned to get back to New York on. She could wire her bank for the rest of her money, of course, but that was not what she wanted. She wanted two weeks of working among people she didn't know, doing the kind of work a million other people did. She wanted to step into someone else's shoes.

She answered an advertisement for a receptionist-filing clerk that said little typing required and call in person. They seemed to think she would do, and she spent all morning learning the files. Then one of the bosses came in after lunch and said he wanted a girl who knew some shorthand. Therese didn't. The school had taught her typing, but not shorthand, so she was out.

She looked through the help-wanted columns again that afternoon. Then she remembered the sign on the fence of the lumberyard not far from the hotel. 'Girl wanted for general office work and stock. $40 weekly.' If they didn't demand shorthand, she might qualify. It was around three when she turned into the windy street where the lumberyard lay. She lifted her head and let the wind blow her hair back from her face. And she remembered Carol saying, I like to see you walking. When I see you from a distance, I feel you're walking on the palm of my hand and you're about five inches high. She could hear Carol's soft voice under the babble of the wind, and she grew tense, with bitterness and fear. She walked faster, ran a few steps, as if she could run out of that morass of love and hate and resentment in which her mind suddenly floundered.

There was a wooden shack of an office at the side of the lumberyard. She went in and spoke with a Mr Zambrowski, a slow-moving bald-headed man with a gold watch chain that barely stretched across his front. Before Therese asked him about shorthand, he volunteered that he didn't need it. He said he would try her out the rest of the afternoon and tomorrow. Two other girls came in for the job the next morning, and Mr Zambrowski took their names, but before noon, he said the job was hers.

'If you don't mind getting here at eight in the morning,' Mr Zambrowski said.

'I don't mind.' She had come in at nine that morning. But she would have gotten there at four in the morning if he had asked her to.

Her hours were from eight to four-thirty, and her duties consisted simply in checking the mill shipments to the yard against the orders received, and in writing letters of confirmation. She did not see much lumber from her desk in the office, but the smell of it was in the air, fresh as if the saws had just exposed the surface of the white pine boards, and she could hear it bouncing and rattling as the trucks pulled into the centre of the yard. She liked the work, liked Mr Zambrowski, and liked the lumberjacks and truck drivers who came into the office to warm their hands at the fire. One of the lumberjacks named Steve, an attractive young man with a golden stubble of beard, invited her a couple of times to have lunch with him in the cafeteria down the street. He asked her for a date on Saturday night, but Therese did not want to spend a whole evening with him or with anyone yet.

One night, Abby telephoned her.

'Do you know I had to call South Dakota twice to find you?' Abby said irritably. 'What're you doing out there? When're you coming back?'

Abby's voice brought Carol as close as if it were Carol she heard. It brought the hollow tightness in her throat again, and for a moment she couldn't answer anything.

'Therese?'

'Is Carol there with you?'

'She's in Vermont. She's been sick,' Abby's hoarse voice said, and there was no smile in it now. 'She's taking a rest.'

'She's too sick to call me? Why don't you tell me, Abby? Is she getting better or worse?'

'Better. Why didn't you try to call to find out?'

Therese squeezed the telephone. Yes, why hadn't she? Because she had been thinking of a picture instead of Carol. 'What's the matter with her? Is she – '

'That's a fine question. Carol wrote you what happened, didn't she?'

'Yes.'

'Well, do you expect her to bounce up like a rubber ball? Or chase you all over America? What do you think this is, a game of hide and seek?'

All the conversation of that lunch with Abby crashed down on Therese. As Abby saw it, the whole thing was her fault. The letter Florence had found was only the final blunder.

'When're you coming back?' Abby asked.

'In about ten days. Unless Carol wants the car sooner.'

'She doesn't. She won't be home in ten days.'

Therese forced herself to say, 'About that letter – the one I wrote – do you know if they found it before or after?'

'Before or after what?'

'After the detectives started following us.'

'They found it afterwards,' Abby said, sighing.

Therese set her teeth. But it didn't matter what Abby thought of her, only what Carol thought. 'Where is she in Vermont?'

'I wouldn't call her if I were you.'

'But you're not me and I want to call her.'

'Don't. That much I can tell you. I can give her any message — that's important.' And there was a cold silence. 'Carol wants to know if you need any money and what about the car.'

'I don't need any money. The car's all right.' She had to ask one more question. 'What does Rindy know about this?'

'She knows what the word divorce means. And she wanted to stay with Carol. That doesn't make it easier for Carol, either.'

Very well, very well, Therese wanted to say. She wouldn't trouble Carol by telephoning, by writing, by any messages, unless it was a message about the car. She was shaking when she put the telephone down. And she immediately picked it up again. 'This is room six eleven,' she said. 'I don't want to take any more long-distance calls — none at all.'

She looked at Carol's letter opener on the bed table, and now it meant Carol, the person of flesh and blood, the Carol with freckles and the corner nicked off one tooth. Did she owe Carol anything, Carol the person? Hadn't Carol been playing with her, as Richard had said? She remembered Carol's words, 'When you have a husband and child it's a little different.' She frowned at the letter opener, not understanding why it had become only a letter opener suddenly, why it was a matter of indifference to her whether she kept it or threw it away.

Two days later, a letter arrived from Abby enclosing a personal cheque for a hundred and fifty dollars, which Abby told her to 'forget about'. Abby said she had spoken with Carol, and that Carol would like to hear from her, and she gave Carol's address. It was a rather cold letter, but the gesture of the cheque was not cold. It hadn't been prompted by Carol, Therese knew.

'Thank you for the cheque,' Therese wrote back to her. 'It's terribly nice of you, but I won't use it and I don't need it. You ask me to write to Carol. I don't think I can or that I should.'

238

Dannie was sitting in the hotel lobby one afternoon when she came home from work. She could not quite believe it was he, the dark-eyed young man who got up from the chair smiling and came slowly towards her. Then the sight of his loose black hair, mussed a little more by the upturned coat collar, the symmetrical broad smile, was as familiar as if she had seen him only the day before.

'Hello, Therese,' he said. 'Surprised?'

'Well, terrifically! I'd given you up. No word from you in – two weeks.' She remembered the twenty-eighth was the day he said he would leave New York, and it was the day she had come to Chicago.

'I'd just about given you up,' Dannie said, laughing. 'I got delayed in New York. I guess it's lucky I did, because I tried to telephone you and your landlady gave me your address.' Dannie's fingers kept a firm grip on her elbow. They were walking slowly towards the elevators. 'You look wonderful, Therese.'

'Do I? I'm awfully glad to see you.' There was an open elevator in front of them. 'Do you want to come up?'

'Let's go have something to eat. Or is it too early? I didn't have any lunch today.'

'It's certainly not too early, then.'

They went to a place Therese knew about, which specialized in steaks. Dannie even ordered cocktails, though he usually never drank.

'You're here by yourself?' he said. 'Your landlady in Sioux Falls told me you left by yourself.'

'Carol couldn't come out finally.'

'Oh. And you decided to stay out longer?'

'Yes.'

'Until when?'

'Until just about now. I'm going back next week.'

Dannie listened with his warm dark eyes fixed on her face, without any surprise. 'Why don't you just go west instead of east and spend a little time in California? I've got a job in Oakland. I have to be there day after tomorrow.'

'What kind of a job?'

'Researching – just what I asked for. I came out better than I thought I would on my exams.'

'Were you first in the class?'

'I don't know. I doubt it. They weren't graded like that. You didn't answer my question.'

'I want to get back to New York, Dannie.'

'Oh.' He smiled, looking at her hair, her lips, and it occurred to her Dannie had never seen her with this much make-up on. 'You look grown up all of a sudden,' he said. 'You changed your hair, didn't you?'

'A little.'

'You don't look frightened any more. Or even so serious.'

'That pleases me.' She felt shy with him, yet somehow close, a closeness charged with something she had never felt with Richard. Something suspenseful, that she enjoyed. A little salt, she thought. She looked at Dannie's hand on the table, at the strong muscle that bulged below the thumb. She remembered his hands on her shoulders that day in his room. The memory was a pleasant one.

'You did miss me a little, didn't you, Terry?'

'Of course.'

'Did you ever think you might care something about me? As much as you did for Richard, for instance?' he asked, with a note of surprise in his own voice, as if it were a fantastic question.

'I don't know,' she said quickly.

'But you're not still thinking about Richard, are you?'

'You must know I'm not.'

'Who is it then? Carol?'

She felt suddenly naked, sitting there opposite him. 'Yes. It was.'

'But not now?'

Therese was amazed that he could say the words without any surprise, any attitude at all. 'No. It's — I can't talk to anyone about it, Dannie,' she finished, and her voice sounded deep and quiet in her ears, like the voice of another person.

'Don't you want to forget it, if it's past?'

'I don't know. I don't know just how you mean that.'

'I mean, are you sorry?'

'No. Would I do the same thing again? Yes.'

'Do you mean with somebody else, or with her?'

'With her,' Therese said. The corner of her mouth went up in a smile.

'But the end was a fiasco.'

'Yes. I mean I'd go through the end, too.'

'And you're still going through it.'

Therese didn't say anything.

'Are you going to see her again? Do you mind if I ask you all these questions?'

'I don't mind,' she said. 'No, I'm not going to see her again. I don't want to.'

'But somebody else?'

'Another woman?' Therese shook her head. 'No.'

Dannie looked at her and smiled, slowly. 'That's what matters. Or rather, that's what makes it not matter.'

'What do you mean?'

'I mean, you're so young, Therese. You'll change. You'll forget.'

She did not feel young. 'Did Richard talk to you?' she asked.

'No. I think he wanted to one night, but I cut it off before he got started.'

She felt the bitter smile on her mouth, and she took a last pull on her short cigarette and put it out. 'I hope he finds somebody to listen to him. He needs an audience.'

'He feels jilted. His ego's suffering. Don't ever think I'm like Richard. I think people's lives are their own.'

Something Carol had said once came suddenly to her mind: every adult has secrets. Said as casually as Carol said everything, stamped as indelibly in her brain as the address she had written on the sales slip in Frankenberg's. She had an impulse to tell Dannie the rest, about the picture in the library, the picture in the school. And about the Carol who was not a picture, but a woman with a child and a husband, with freckles on her hands and a habit of cursing, of growing melancholy at unexpected moments, with a bad habit of indulging her will. A woman who had endured much more in New York than she had in South Dakota. She looked at Dannie's eyes, at his chin with the faint cleft. She knew that up to now she had been under a spell that prevented her from seeing anyone in the world but Carol.

'Now what are you thinking?' he asked.

'Of what you said once in New York, about using things and throwing them away.'

'Did she do that to you?'

241

Therese smiled. 'I shall do it.'

'Then find someone you'll never want to throw away.'

'Who won't wear out,' Therese said.

'Will you write to me?'

'Of course.'

'Write me in three months.'

'Three months?' But suddenly she knew what he meant. 'And not before?'

'No.' He was looking at her steadily. 'That's a fair time, isn't it?'

'Yes. All right. It's a promise.'

'Promise me something else – take tomorrow off so you can be with me. I've got till nine tomorrow night.'

'I can't, Dannie. There's work to do – and I've got to tell him anyway that I'm leaving in another week.' Those weren't quite the reasons, she knew. And perhaps Dannie knew, looking at her. She didn't want to spend tomorrow with him; it would be too intense, he would remind her too much of herself, and she still was not ready.

Dannie came round to the lumberyard the next day at noon. They had intended to have lunch together, but they walked and talked on Lake Shore Drive for the whole hour instead. That evening at nine, Dannie took a plane westward.

Eight days later, she started for New York. She meant to move away from Mrs Osborne's as soon as possible. She wanted to look up some of the people she had run away from last fall. And there would be other people, new people. She would go to night school this spring. And she wanted to change her wardrobe completely. Everything she had now, the clothes she remembered in her closet in New York, seemed juvenile, like clothes that had belonged to her years ago. In Chicago she had looked around in the stores and hungered for the clothes she couldn't buy yet. All she could afford now was a new haircut.

CHAPTER TWENTY-THREE

Therese went into her old room, and the first thing she noticed was that the carpet corner lay flat. And how small and tragic the room looked. And yet hers, the tiny radio on the bookshelf, and the pillows on the studio couch, as personal as a signature she had written long ago and forgotten. Like the two or three set models hanging on the walls that she deliberately avoided looking at.

She went to the bank and took out a hundred of her last two hundred dollars, and bought a black dress and a pair of shoes.

Tomorrow, she thought, she would call Abby and arrange something about Carol's car, but not today.

That same afternoon, she made an appointment with Ned Bernstein, the co-producer of the English show for which Harkevy was to do the sets. She took three of the models she had made in the West and also the *Small Rain* photographs to show him. An apprentice job with Harkevy, if she got it, wouldn't pay enough to live on, but there were other sources, other than department stores, anyway. There was television, for instance.

Mr Bernstein looked at her work indifferently. Therese said she hadn't spoken to Mr Harkevy yet, and asked Mr Bernstein if he knew anything about his taking on helpers. Mr Bernstein said that was up to Harkevy, but as far as he knew, he didn't need any more assistants. Neither did Mr Bernstein know of any other set studio that needed anyone at the moment. And Therese thought of the sixty-dollar dress. And of the hundred dollars left in the bank. And she had told Mrs Osborne she might show the apartment any time she wished, because she was moving. Therese hadn't yet any idea where. She got up to leave, and thanked Mr Bernstein anyway for looking at her work. She did it with a smile.

'How about television?' Mr Bernstein asked. 'Have you tried to start that way? It's easier to break into.'

'I'm going over to see someone at Dumont later this afternoon.' Mr Donohue had given her a couple of names last January. Mr Bernstein gave her some more names.

Then she telephoned Harkevy's studio. Harkevy said he was just going out, but she could drop her models by his studio today and he could look at them tomorrow morning.

'By the way, there'll be a cocktail party at the St Regis for Genevieve Cranell tomorrow at about five o'clock. If you care to drop in,' Harkevy said, with his staccato accent that made his soft voice as precise as mathematics, 'at least we'll be sure to see each other tomorrow. Can you come?'

'Yes. I'd love to come. Where in the St Regis?'

He read from the invitation. Suite D. Five to seven o'clock. 'I shall be there by six.'

She left the telephone booth feeling as happy as if Harkevy had just taken her into partnership. She walked the twelve blocks to his studio, and left the models with a young man there, a different young man from the one she had seen in January. Harkevy changed his assistants often. She looked around his workroom reverently before she closed the door. Perhaps he would let her come soon. Perhaps she would know tomorrow.

She went into a drugstore on Broadway and called Abby in New Jersey. Abby's voice was entirely different from the way it had sounded in Chicago. Carol must be much better, Therese thought. But she did not ask about Carol. She was calling to arrange about the car.

'I can come and get it if you want me to,' Abby said. 'But why don't you call Carol about it? I know she'd like to hear from you.' Abby was actually bending over backwards.

'Well – ' Therese didn't want to call her. But what was she afraid of? Carol's voice? Carol herself? 'All right. I'll take the car to her, unless she doesn't want me to. In that case, I'll call you back.'

'When? This afternoon?'

'Yes. In a few minutes.'

Therese went to the door of the drugstore and stood there for a few moments, looking out at the Camel advertisement with the giant face puffing smoke rings like gigantic doughnuts, at the low-slung, sullen-looking taxis manoeuvring like sharks in the after-matinée rush, at the familiar hodgepodge of restaurant and bar signs, awnings, front steps and windows, that reddish-brown confusion of the side street that was like hundreds of streets in New York. She remembered walking in a certain street in the West Eighties once, the brownstone fronts, overlaid and overlaid with humanity, human lives, some beginning and some ending there, and she remembered the sense of oppression it had given her, and how she had hurried through it to get to the avenue. Only two or three months ago. Now the same kind of street filled her with a tense excitement, made her want to plunge headlong into it, down the sidewalk with all the signs and theatre marquees and rushing, bumping people. She turned and walked back to the telephone booths.

A moment later, she heard Carol's voice.

'When did you get in, Therese?'

There was a brief, fluttering shock at the first sound of her voice, and then nothing. 'Yesterday.'

'How are you? Do you still look the same?' Carol sounded repressed, as if someone might be with her, but Therese was sure there was no one else.

'Not exactly. Do you?'

Carol waited. 'You sound different.'

'I am.'

'Am I going to see you? Or don't you want to? Once.' It was Carol's voice, but the words were not hers. The words were cautious and uncertain. 'What about this afternoon? Have you got the car?'

'I've got to see a couple of people this afternoon. There won't be time.' When had she ever refused Carol when Carol wanted to see her? 'Would you like me to drive the car out tomorrow?'

'No, I can come in for it. I'm not an invalid. Did the car behave itself?'

'It's in good shape,' Therese said. 'No scratches anywhere.'

'And you?' Carol asked, but Therese didn't answer anything.

'Shall I see you tomorrow? Do you have any time in the afternoon?'

They arranged to meet in the bar of the Ritz Tower on Fifty-seventh Street at four-thirty, and then they hung up.

Carol was a quarter of an hour late. Therese sat waiting for her at a table where she could see the glass doors that led into the bar, and finally she saw Carol push open one of the doors, and the tension broke in her with a small dull ache. Carol wore the same fur coat, the same black suède pumps she had worn the day Therese first saw her, but now a red scarf set off the blonde lifted head. She saw Carol's face, thinner now, alter with surprise, with a little smile, as Carol caught sight of her.

'Hello,' Therese said.

'I didn't even know you at first.' And Carol stood by the table a moment, looking at her, before she sat down. 'It's nice of you to see me.'

'Don't say that.'

The waiter came, and Carol ordered tea. So did Therese, mechanically.

'Do you hate me, Therese?' Carol asked her.

'No.' Therese could smell Carol's perfume faintly, that familiar sweetness that was strangely unfamiliar now, because it did not evoke what it had once evoked. She put down the match cover she had been crushing in her hand. 'How can I hate you, Carol?'

'I suppose you could. You did for a while, didn't you?' Carol said, as if she told her a fact.

'Hate you? No.' Not quite, she might have said. But she knew that Carol's eyes were reading it in her face.

'And now – you're all grown up – with grown-up hair and grown-up clothes.'

Therese looked into her grey eyes that were more serious now, somehow wistful, too, despite the assurance of the proud head, and she looked down again, unable to fathom them. She was still beautiful, Therese thought with a sudden pang of loss. 'I've learned a few things,' Therese said.

'What?'

'That I – ' Therese stopped, her thoughts obstructed suddenly by the memory of the portrait in Sioux Falls.

'You know, you look very fine,' Carol said. 'You've come out all of a sudden. Is that what comes of getting away from me?'

'No,' Therese said quickly. She frowned down at the tea she didn't want. Carol's phrase 'come out' had made her think of being born, and it embarrassed her. Yes, she had been born since she left Carol. She had been born the instant she saw the picture in the library, and her stifled cry then was like the first yell of an infant, being dragged into the world against its will. She looked at Carol. 'There was a picture in the library at Sioux Falls,' she said. Then she told Carol about it, simply and without emotion, like a story that had happened to somebody else.

And Carol listened, never taking her eyes from her. Carol watched her as she might have watched from a distance someone she could not help. 'Strange,' Carol said quietly. 'And horrifying.'

'It was.' Therese knew Carol understood. She saw the sympathy in Carol's eyes, too, and she smiled, but Carol did not smile back. Carol was still staring at her. 'What are you thinking?' Therese asked.

Carol took a cigarette. 'What do you think? Of that day in the store.'

Therese smiled again. 'It was so wonderful when you came over to me. Why did you come to me?'

Carol waited. 'For such a dull reason. Because you were the only girl not busy as hell. You didn't have a smock, either, I remember.'

Therese burst out laughing. Carol only smiled, but she looked suddenly like herself, as she had been in Colorado Springs, before anything had happened. All at once, Therese remembered the candlestick in her handbag. 'I bought you this,' she said, handing it to her. 'I found it in Sioux Falls.'

Therese had only twisted some white tissue around it. Carol opened it on the table.

'I think it's charming,' Carol said. 'It looks just like you.'

'Thank you. I thought it looked like you.' Therese looked at Carol's hand, the thumb and the tip of the middle finger resting on the thin rim of the candlestick, as she had seen Carol's fingers on the saucers of coffee cups in Colorado, in Chicago, and places forgotten. Therese closed her eyes.

'I love you,' Carol said.

247

Therese opened her eyes, but she did not look up.

'I know you don't feel the same about me. Do you?'

Therese had an impulse to deny it, but could she? She didn't feel the same. 'I don't know, Carol.'

'That's the same thing.' Carol's voice was soft, expectant, expecting affirmation or denial.

Therese stared at the triangles of toast on the plate between them. She thought of Rindy. She had put off asking about her. 'Have you seen Rindy?'

Carol sighed. Therese saw her hand draw back from the candlestick. 'Yes, last Sunday for an hour or so. I suppose she can come and visit me a couple of afternoons a year. Once in a blue moon. I've lost completely.'

'I thought you said a few weeks of the year.'

'Well, a little more happened – privately between Harge and me. I refused to make a lot of promises he asked me to make. And the family came into it, too. I refused to live by a list of silly promises they'd made up like a list of misdemeanours – even if it did mean that they'd lock Rindy away from me as if I were an ogre. And it did mean that. Harge told the lawyers everything – whatever they didn't know already.'

'God,' Therese whispered. She could imagine what it meant, Rindy visiting one afternoon, accompanied by a staring governess who had been forewarned against Carol, told not to let the child out of her sight, probably, and Rindy would soon understand all that. What would be the pleasure in a visit at all? Harge – Therese did not want to say his name. 'Even the court was kinder,' she said.

'As a matter of fact, I didn't promise very much in court, I refused there, too.'

Therese smiled a little in spite of herself, because she was glad Carol had refused, that Carol had still been that proud.

'But it wasn't a court, you know, just a round-table discussion. Do you know how they made that recording in Waterloo? They drove a spike into the wall, probably just about as soon as we got there.'

'A *spike*?'

'I remember hearing somebody hammering something. I think it was when we'd just finished in the shower. Do you remember?'

'No.'

Carol smiled. 'A spike that picks up sound like a dictaphone. He had the room next to us.'

Therese didn't remember the hammering, but the violence of all of it came back, shattering, destroying –

'It's all over,' Carol said. 'You know, I'd almost prefer not to see Rindy at all any more. I'm never going to demand to see her, if she stops wanting to see me. I'll just leave that up to her.'

'I can't imagine her ever not wanting to see you.'

Carol's eyebrows lifted. 'Is there any way of predicting what Harge can do to her?'

Therese was silent. She looked away from Carol, and saw a clock. It was five thirty-five. She should be at the cocktail party before six, she thought, if she went at all. She had dressed for it, in the new black dress with a white scarf, in her new shoes, with her new black gloves. And how unimportant the clothes seemed now. She thought suddenly of the green woollen gloves that Sister Alicia had given her. Were they still in the ancient tissue at the bottom of her trunk? She wanted to throw them away.

'One gets over things,' Carol said.

'Yes.'

'Harge and I are selling the house, and I've taken an apartment up on Madison Avenue. And a job, believe it or not. I'm going to work for a furniture house on Fourth Avenue as a buyer. Some of my ancestors must have been carpenters.' She looked at Therese. 'Anyway, it's a living and I'll like it. The apartment's a nice big one – big enough for two. I was hoping you might like to come and live with me, but I guess you won't.'

Therese's heart took a jump, exactly as it had when Carol had telephoned her that day in the store. Something responded in her against her will, made her feel happy all at once, and proud. She was proud that Carol had the courage to do such things, to say such things, that Carol always would have the courage. She remembered Carol's courage, facing the detective on the country road. Therese swallowed, trying to swallow the beating of her heart. Carol had not even looked at her. Carol was rubbing her cigarette-end back and forth in the ash-tray. To live with Carol? Once that had been impossible, and had been what she wanted most in the world. To

249

live with her and share everything with her, summer and winter, to walk and read together, to travel together. And she remembered the days of resenting Carol, when she had imagined Carol asking her this, and herself answering no.

'Would you?' Carol looked at her.

Therese felt she balanced on a thin edge. The resentment was gone now. Nothing but the decision remained now, a thin line suspended in the air, with nothing on either side to push her or pull her. But on the one side, Carol, and on the other an empty question mark. On the one side, Carol, and it would be different now, because they were both different. It would be a world as unknown as the world just past had been when she first entered it. Only now, there were no obstacles. Therese thought of Carol's perfume that today meant nothing. A blank to be filled in, Carol would say.

'Well,' Carol said smiling, impatient.

'No,' Therese said. 'No, I don't think so.' Because you would betray me again. That was what she had thought in Sioux Falls, what she had intended to write or say. But Carol had not betrayed her. Carol loved her more than she loved her child. That was part of the reason why she had not promised. She was gambling now as she had gambled on getting everything from the detective that day on the road, and she lost then, too. And now she saw Carol's face changing, saw the little signs of astonishment and shock so subtle that perhaps only she in the world could have noticed them, and Therese could not think for a moment.

'That's your decision,' Carol said.

'Yes.'

Carol stared at her cigarette lighter on the table. 'That's that.'

Therese looked at her, wanting still to put out her hands, to touch Carol's hair and to hold it tight in all her fingers. Hadn't Carol heard the indecision in her voice? Therese wanted suddenly to run away, to rush quickly out the door and down the sidewalk. It was a quarter to six. 'I've got to go to a cocktail party this afternoon. It's important because of a possible job. Harkevy's going to be there.' Harkevy would give her some kind of a job, she was sure. She had called him at noon today about the models she had left at his studio. Harkevy had liked them all. 'I got a television assignment yesterday, too.'

Carol lifted her head, smiling. 'My little big shot. Now you look like you might do something good. Do you know, even your voice is different?'

'Is it?' Therese hesitated, finding it harder and harder to sit there. 'Carol, you could come to the party if you want to. It's a big party in a couple of rooms at an hotel – welcoming the woman who's going to do the lead in Harkevy's play. I know they wouldn't mind if I brought someone.' And she didn't know quite why she was asking her, why Carol would possibly want to go to a cocktail party now any more than she did.

Carol shook her head. 'No, thanks, darling. You'd better run along by yourself. I've got a date at the Elysée in a minute as a matter of fact.'

Therese gathered her gloves and her handbag in her lap. She looked at Carol's hands, the pale freckles sprinkled on their backs – the wedding ring was gone now – and at Carol's eyes. She felt she would never see Carol again. In two minutes, less, they would part on the sidewalk. 'The car's outside. Out in front to the left. And here's the keys.'

'I know, I saw it.'

'Are you going to stay on?' Therese asked her. 'I'll take care of the check.'

'I'll take care of the check,' Carol said. 'Go on, if you have to.'

Therese stood up. She couldn't leave Carol sitting here at the table where their two teacups were, with the ashes of their cigarettes in front of her. 'Don't stay. Come out with me.'

Carol glanced up with a kind of questioning surprise in her face. 'All right,' she said. 'There are a couple of things of yours out at the house. Shall I – '

'It doesn't matter,' Therese interrupted her.

'And your flowers. Your plants.' Carol was paying the check the waiter had brought over. 'What happened to the flowers I gave you?'

'The flowers you gave me – they died.'

Carol's eyes met hers for a second, and Therese looked away.

They parted on the sidewalk, at the corner of Park Avenue and Fifty-seventh Street. Therese ran across the avenue, just making it ahead of the green lights that released a pack of cars behind her, that blurred her view of Carol when she turned on the other sidewalk. Carol was walking slowly away, past the Ritz Tower doorway, and on. And that was the way it should be, Therese thought, not with a lingering handclasp, not with backward glances. Then as she saw Carol touch the handle of the car door, she remembered the beer can still under the front seat, remembered its clink as she had driven up the ramp from the Lincoln Tunnel coming into New York. She had thought then, she must get it out before she gave the car back to Carol, but she had forgotten. Therese hurried on to the hotel.

People were already spilling out of the two doorways into the hall, and a waiter was having difficulty pushing his rolling table of ice buckets into the room. The rooms were noisy, and Therese did not see Bernstein or Harkevy anywhere. She didn't know anyone, not a soul. Except one face, a man she had talked to months ago, somewhere, about a job that didn't materialize. Therese turned around. A man poked a tall glass into her hand.

'Mademoiselle,' he said with a flourish. 'Are you looking for one of these?'

'Thank you.' She didn't stay with him. She thought she saw Mr Bernstein over in the corner. There were several women with big hats in the way.

'Are you an actress?' the same man asked her, thrusting with her through the crowd.

'No. A set designer.'

It was Mr Bernstein, and Therese sidled between a couple of groups of people and reached him. Mr Bernstein held out a plump, cordial hand to her, and got up from his radiator seat.

'Miss Belivet!' he shouted. 'Mrs Crawford, the make-up consultant – '

'Let's not talk business!' Mrs Crawford shrieked.

'Mr Stevens, Mr Fenelon,' Mr Bernstein went on, and on and on, until she was nodding to a dozen people and saying 'How do you do?' to about half of them. 'And Ivor – Ivor!' Mr Bernstein called.

There was Harkevy, a slim figure with a slim face and a small moustache, smiling at her, reaching a hand over for her to shake. 'Hello,' he said. 'I'm glad to see you again. Yes, I liked your work. I see your anxiety.' He laughed a little.

'Enough to let me squeeze in?' she asked.

'You want to know,' he said, smiling. 'Yes, you can squeeze in.

252

Come up to my studio tomorrow at about eleven. Can you make that?'

'Yes.'

'Come and join me later. I must say goodbye to these people who are leaving.' And he went away.

Therese set her drink down on the edge of a table, and reached for a cigarette in her handbag. It was done. She glanced at the door. A woman with upswept blonde hair, with bright, intense blue eyes had just come into the room and was causing a small furore of excitement around her. She had quick, positive movements as she turned to greet people, to shake hands, and suddenly Therese realized she was Genevieve Cranell, the English actress who was to play the lead. She looked different from the few stills Therese had seen of her. She had the kind of face that must be seen in action to be attractive.

'Hello, hello!' she called to everyone finally as she glanced around the room, and Therese saw the glance linger on her for an instant, while in Therese there took place a shock a little like that she had known when she had seen Carol for the first time, and there was the same flash of interest in the woman's blue eyes that had been in her own, she knew, when she saw Carol. And now it was Therese who continued to look, and the other woman who glanced away, and turned around.

Therese looked down at the glass in her hand, and felt a sudden heat in her face and her fingertips, the rush inside her that was neither quite her blood nor her thoughts alone. She knew before they were introduced that this woman was like Carol. And she was beautiful. And she did not look like the picture in the library. Therese smiled as she sipped her drink. She took a long pull at the drink to steady herself.

'A flower, madame?' A waiter was extending a tray full of white orchids.

'Thank you very much.' Therese took one. She had trouble with the pin, and someone – Mr Fenelon or Mr Stevens it was – came up and helped. 'Thanks,' she said.

Genevieve Cranell was coming towards her, with Mr Bernstein behind her. The actress greeted the man with Therese as if she knew him very well.

'Did you meet Miss Cranell?' Mr Bernstein asked Therese.

Therese looked at the woman. 'My name is Therese Belivet.' She took the hand the woman extended.

'How do you do? So you're the set department?'

'No. Only part of it.' She could still feel the handclasp when the woman released her hand. She felt excited, wildly and stupidly excited.

'Isn't anybody going to bring me a drink?' Miss Cranell asked anybody.

Mr Bernstein obliged. Mr Bernstein finished introducing Miss Cranell to the people around him who hadn't met her. Therese heard her tell someone that she had just gotten off a plane and that her luggage was piled in the lobby, and while she spoke, Therese saw her glance at her a couple of times past the men's shoulders. Therese felt an exciting attraction in the neat back of her head, in the funny, careless lift of her nose at the end, the only careless feature of her narrow, classic face. Her lips were rather thin. She looked extremely alert, and imperturbably poised. Yet Therese sensed that Genevieve Cranell might not talk to her again at the party for the simple reason that she probably wanted to.

Therese made her way to a wall mirror, and glanced to see if her hair and her lipstick were still all right.

'Therese,' said a voice near her. 'Do you like champagne?'

Therese turned and saw Genevieve Cranell. 'Of course.'

'Of course. Well, toddle up to six-nineteen in a few minutes. That's my suite. We're having an inner circle party later.'

'I feel very honoured,' Therese said.

'So don't waste your thirst on highballs. Where did you get that lovely dress?'

'Bonwit's – it's a wild extravagance.'

Genevieve Cranell laughed. She wore a blue woollen suit that actually looked like a wild extravagance. 'You look so young, I don't suppose you'll mind if I ask how old you are.'

'I'm twenty-one.'

She rolled her eyes. 'Incredible. Can anyone still be only twenty-one?'

People were watching the actress. Therese was flattered, terribly flattered, and the flattery got in the way of what she felt, or might feel, about Genevieve Cranell.

Miss Cranell offered her cigarette case. 'For a while, I thought you might be a minor.'

'Is that a crime?'

The actress only looked at her, her blue eyes smiling, over the flame of her lighter. Then as the woman turned her head to light her own cigarette, Therese knew suddenly that Genevieve Cranell would never mean anything to her, nothing apart from this half-hour at the cocktail party, that the excitement she felt now would not continue, and not be evoked again at any other time or place. What was it that told her? Therese stared at the taut line of her blonde eyebrow as the first smoke rose from the cigarette, but the answer was not there. And suddenly a feeling of tragedy, almost of regret, filled Therese.

'Are you a New Yorker?' Miss Cranell asked her.

'*Vivy!*'

The new people who had just come in the door surrounded Genevieve Cranell and bore her away. Therese smiled again, and finished her drink, felt the first soothing warmth of the Scotch spreading through her. She talked with a man she had met briefly in Mr Bernstein's office yesterday, and with another man she didn't know at all, and she looked at the doorway across the room, the doorway that was an empty rectangle at that moment, and she thought of Carol. It would be like Carol to come after all, to ask her once more. Or rather, like the old Carol, but not like this one. Carol would be keeping her appointment now at the Elysée bar. With Abby? With Stanley McVeigh? Therese looked away from the door, as if she were afraid Carol might appear, and she would have to say again, 'No.' Therese accepted another highball, and felt the emptiness inside her slowly filling with the realization she might see Genevieve Cranell very often, if she chose, and though she would never become entangled, might be loved herself.

One of the men beside her asked, 'Who did the sets for *The Lost Messiah*, Therese? Do you remember?'

'Blanchard?' she answered out of nowhere, because she was still thinking of Genevieve Cranell, with a feeling of revulsion, of shame, for what had just occurred to her, and she knew it would never be. She listened to the conversation about Blanchard and someone else, even joined in, but her consciousness had stopped in a tangle where a dozen threads crossed and knotted. One was Dannie. One was Carol. One was Genevieve Cranell. One went on and on out of it, but her mind was caught at the intersection. She bent to take a light for her cigarette, and felt herself fall a little deeper into the network, and she clutched at Dannie. But the strong black thread did not lead anywhere. She knew as if some prognostic voice were speaking now that she would not go further with Dannie. And loneliness swept over her again like a rushing wind, mysterious as the thin tears that covered her eyes suddenly, too thin to be noticed, she knew, as she lifted her head and glanced at the doorway again.

'Don't forget.' Genevieve Cranell was beside her, patting her arm, saying quickly, 'Six-nineteen. We're adjourning.' She started to turn away and came back. 'You are coming up? Harkevy's coming up, too.'

Therese shook her head. 'Thanks, I – I thought I could, but I remember I've got to be somewhere else.'

The woman looked at her quizzically. 'What's the matter, Therese? Did anything go wrong?'

'No.' She smiled, moving towards the door. 'Thanks for asking me. No doubt I'll see you again.'

'No doubt,' the actress said.

Therese went into the room beside the big one and got her coat from the pile on the bed. She hurried down the corridor towards the stairs, past the people who were waiting for the elevator, among them Genevieve Cranell, and Therese didn't care if she saw her or not as she plunged down the wide stairs as if she were running away from something. Therese smiled to herself. The air was cool and sweet on her forehead, made a feathery sound like wings past her ears, and she felt she flew across the streets and up the kerbs. Towards Carol. And perhaps Carol knew at this moment, because Carol had known such things before. She crossed another street, and there was the Elysée awning.

The headwaiter said something to her in the foyer, and she told him, 'I'm looking for somebody,' and went on to the doorway.

She stood in the doorway, looking over the people at the tables in the room where a piano played. The lights were not bright, and she did not see her at first, half hidden in the shadow against the far wall, facing her. Nor did Carol see her. A man sat opposite her,

Therese did not know who. Carol raised her hand slowly and brushed her hair back, once on either side, and Therese smiled because the gesture was Carol, and it was Carol she loved and would always love. Oh, in a different way now, because she was a different person, and it was like meeting Carol all over again, but it was still Carol and no one else. It would be Carol, in a thousand cities, a thousand houses, in foreign lands where they would go together, in heaven and in hell. Therese waited. Then as she was about to go to her, Carol saw her, seemed to stare at her incredulously a moment while Therese watched the slow smile growing, before her arm lifted suddenly, her hand waved a quick, eager greeting that Therese had never seen before. Therese walked towards her.

AFTERWORD

M y inspiration for this book came in late 1948, when I was living in New York. I had just finished *Strangers on a Train*, but it wasn't to be published until 1949. Christmas was approaching, I was vaguely depressed and also short of money, and to earn some I took a job as salesgirl in a big department store in Manhattan during the period known as the Christmas rush, which lasts about a month. I think I lasted two and a half weeks.

The store assigned me to the toy section, in my case the doll counter. There were many types of doll, expensive and not so expensive, real hair or artificial, and size and clothing were of utmost importance. Children, some whose noses barely reached the glass showcase top, pressed forward with their mother or father or both, dazzled by the display of brand-new dolls that cried, opened and closed their eyes, stood on their two feet sometimes, and, of course, loved changes of clothing. A rush it was, and I and the four or five young women I worked with behind the long counter could not sit down from eight-thirty in the morning until the lunch-break. And even then? The afternoon was the same.

One morning, into this chaos of noise and commerce, there walked a blondish woman in a fur coat. She drifted towards the doll counter with a look of uncertainty – should she buy a doll or something else? – and I think she was slapping a pair of gloves absently into one hand. Perhaps I noticed her because she was alone, or because a mink coat was a rarity, and because she was blondish and seemed to give

259

off light. With the same thoughtful air, she purchased a doll, one of two or three I had shown her, and I wrote her name and address on the receipt, because the doll was to be delivered to an adjacent state. It was a routine transaction, the woman paid and departed. But I felt odd and swimmy in the head, near to fainting, yet at the same time uplifted, as if I had seen a vision.

As usual, I went home after work to my apartment, where I lived alone. That evening I wrote out an idea, a plot, a story about the blondish and elegant woman in the fur coat. I wrote some eight pages in longhand in my then current notebook or cahier. This was the entire story of *The Price of Salt*, as *Carol* was originally called. It flowed from my pen as if from nowhere – beginning, middle and end. It took me about two hours, perhaps less.

The following morning I felt even odder, and was aware that I had a fever. It must have been a Sunday, because I remember taking the subway (underground) in the morning, and in those days people had to work Saturday mornings, and all of Saturday in the Christmas rush. I recall nearly fainting while hanging on to a strap in the train. The friend I had an appointment with had some medical knowledge, and I said that I felt sickish, and had noticed a little blister on the skin of my abdomen, when I had taken a shower that morning. My friend took one look at the blister and said, 'Chickenpox.' Unfortunately, I had never had this childhood ailment, though I'd had just about everything else. The disease is not pleasant for adults, as the fever goes up to 104° Fahrenheit for a couple of days, and, worse, the face, torso, upper arms, even ears and nostrils are covered or lined with pustules that itch and burst. One must not scratch them in one's sleep, otherwise scars and pits result. For a month one goes about with bleeding spots, visible to the public on the face, looking as if one has been hit by a volley of air-gun pellets.

I had to give notice to the department store on Monday that I could not return to work. One of the small runny-nosed children there must have passed on the germ, but in a way the germ of a book too: fever is stimulating to the imagination. I did not immediately start writing the book. I prefer to let ideas simmer for weeks. And, too, when *Strangers on a Train* was published and shortly afterwards sold to Alfred Hitchcock, who wished to make a film of it, my publishers and also my agent were saying, 'Write another

book of the same type, so you'll strengthen your reputation as . . . '
As what? *Strangers on a Train* had been published as 'A Harper
Novel of Suspense' by Harper & Bros, as the house was then called,
so overnight I had become a 'suspense' writer, though *Strangers* in
my mind was not categorized, and was simply a novel with an
interesting story. If I were to write a novel about a lesbian relationship, would I then be labelled a lesbian-book writer? That was a
possibility, even though I might never be inspired to write another
such book in my life. So I decided to offer the book under another
name. By 1951, I had written it. I could not push it into the
background for ten months and write something else, simply because
for commercial reasons it might have been wise to write another
'suspense' book.

Harper & Bros rejected *The Price of Salt*, so I was obliged to find
another American publisher – to my regret, as I much dislike
changing publishers. *The Price of Salt* had some serious and respect-
able reviews when it appeared in hardcover in 1952. But the real
success came a year later with the paperback edition, which sold
nearly a million copies and was certainly read by more. The fan
letters came in addressed to Claire Morgan, care of the paperback
house. I remember receiving envelopes of ten and fifteen letters a
couple of times a week and for months on end. A lot of them I
answered, but I could not answer them all without a form letter,
which I never arranged.

My young protagonist Therese may appear a shrinking violet in
my book, but those were the days when gay bars were a dark door
somewhere in Manhattan, where people wanting to go to a certain
bar got off the subway a station before or after the convenient one,
lest they be suspected of being homosexual. The appeal of *The Price
of Salt* was that it had a happy ending for its two main characters,
or at least they were going to try to have a future together. Prior to
this book, homosexuals male and female in American novels had had
to pay for their deviation by cutting their wrists, drowning themselves in a swimming pool, or by switching to heterosexuality (so it
was stated), or by collapsing – alone and miserable and shunned –
into a depression equal to hell. Many of the letters that came to me
carried such messages as 'Yours is the first book like this with a
happy ending! We don't all commit suicide and lots of us are doing

fine.' Others said, 'Thank you for writing such a story. It is a little like my own story . . . ' And, 'I am eighteen and I live in a small town. I feel lonely because I can't talk to anyone . . . ' Sometimes I wrote a letter suggesting that the writer go to a larger town where there would be a chance to meet more people. As I remember, there were as many letters from men as from women, which I considered a good omen for my book. This turned out to be true. The letters trickled in for years, and even now a letter comes once or twice a year from a reader. I never wrote another book like this. My next book was *The Blunderer*. I like to avoid labels. It is American publishers who love them.

24 May 1989

A NOTE ON THE AUTHOR

Patricia Highsmith was born in Fort Worth, Texas, in 1921. Her parents moved to New York when she was six, and she attended Julia Richmond High School and Barnard College. In her senior year she edited the college magazine, having decided at the age of sixteen to become a writer. Her first novel, *Strangers On A Train*, was made into a film by Alfred Hitchcock in 1951. *The Talented Mr Ripley*, published in 1955, was awarded the Edgar Allan Poe Scroll by the Mystery Writers of America and introduced the fascinating anti-hero Tom Ripley, who was to appear in many of her later crime novels. Patricia Highsmith died in Locarno, Switzerland, in February 1995. Her last novel, *Small g: A Summer Idyll*, was published posthumously just over a month later.